WHERE THE DEMONS LIE

A NOVEL

SEAN CONNORS

ISBN: 979-8-9865624-1-4

Editorial service by Inventing Reality

Book cover, layout design & eBook conversion by manuscript2ebook.com

"In your darkest hour, when the demons come,
call on me brother, and we will fight them together."

– Unknown

"It comes to you as to us all,
we're just waiting for the hammer to fall."

– Queen

"Please save our children."

– The Voices

Part 1

Rock Hits Bottom

CHAPTER 1

CANTER'S COFFEE SHOP, ON the first-floor corner of a red brick apartment building in Jamaica Heights, was suffering through its hump-day rush hour of breakfast clients.

Hovering over a hot grill, Joe Canter - a burly, tattooed man who could wrestle alligators as a side hustle - flipped French toast, eggs over-easy, and sizzling bacon. Isabella, a Sicilian immigrant and Joe's wife of forty years, hummed a tune, wiping the chipped and faded lime-green counter clean. Meaningless chatter filled the crowded cafe. Mail carriers. Amazon delivery drivers. A man in a cheap brown suit giving investment advice to a grizzled retired factory worker.

Detective Sergeant Ronan Quinn hunched over a table, running his finger along the rim of a cup of coffee, unsure what day of the week he was living. Wednesday? Tuesday? Let's just forget Tuesday ever happened. How about that?

Ding, ding! Creak, rattle, hiss. Ding, ding! Snap.

Signaling Detective Jack Carter's arrival, those sounds pierced Quinn's brain like a warrior's spear. Carter searched for his partner, his head twisting around like an arctic explorer searching for the North Pole.

Quinn rolled his eyes and shook his head. Brash yet not bright, blonde hair slicked into a ducktail, eyes hidden behind dark aviator glasses, a crisp black suit with sharp creases, and patent leather shoes glistening with high polish, Carter wanted everyone to witness his hoity-toity arrival. He slid back the bottom of his jacket, exposing his sidearm and his glistening gold NYPD detective badge.

For Christ's sake - he raised his hand, beckoning the detective with two fingers. "Carter, I'm literally right in front of you."

Carter spun his head around. "There you are," he said with a smug grin, holding his luminous white teeth hostage.

Why a New York cop was so intent on announcing his presence to the world escaped Quinn. But that was Carter. The brash blonde millennial who whistles as he walks through the precinct. The detective with-an-asterisk who fancies himself as a James Bond, or a Jason Bourne, or an Ethan Hunt. He once told Quinn he didn't join the force to investigate boring burglaries and muggings, but joined to bag terrorists instead. He would've been a Navy Seal, he claimed, but sprained his knee rappelling from a rock face. Quinn, the former Marine, gritted his teeth and ignored Carter's fantasy fiction. He suggested Carter join the military and go bag all the terrorists he wants. They even provide meals and free travel.

Their supervisor, Lieutenant Miá Perez, often paired Carter with Quinn. Her thinking was maybe Carter would grow up a little if he were around someone as seasoned as him. Carter was no sun dazzling with brilliance, but he was no idiot. He survived Miá's threats to send him back to patrol by becoming buddy-buddy with Miá's supervisor. To Quinn, this was pathetic, even by Carter's standards. To Miá, this was treason.

Carter dragged the chair away from the table, the table's legs squealing and scraping the floor in resistance.

"Mornin' Ronan." He said, whisking off his glasses and pulling the laminated menu toward him. Glancing over his shoulder, he yelled above the chatter for a black coffee.

"Yeah, sure, I'll get right on that, buddy," bellowed Joe. Isabella poured the cup, annoyed, narrowed eyes glowering from beneath long, curly gray locks.

Enjoying a schadenfreude moment, Carter turned and rubbed his palms together. "Wow, Ronan, you look like shit."

Quinn drew in a deep breath, running his finger around the rim of the cooling coffee. In the dark recesses of a hangover, he reassessed his life. Most people, in theory, see their life pass before them when they approach the eternal gates. But he had a full-on life-flashing-before-his-eyes experience when he sat down at the coffee shop and exhaled a bile-laced blow of Johnny Walker Blue Label. Last night's drunken debacle cost him more than a headache. It'd cost him his marriage.

Quinn could be an ugly drunk. And for a bear-sized man like him, an ugly drunk was a dangerous drunk. When Quinn drank, he was in Helmand Province. When Quinn drank, he was at Maya Angelou Elementary School. When Quinn drank, he was in Central Park as dawn broke over a slumbering city. Why am I here? He thought as he stared into the black void in a cup. Had he found a new vaccine? Discovered a star nebula? Developed some new renewable energy source that would unite the world?

No. He'd done none of that.

He prevented no crimes. He saved no lives. Nothing in his life, nothing he'd "accomplished," meant anything, because nothing he did mattered. Being a detective was a life living after the fact. Detectives solved crimes. They rarely prevented them. It just all seemed so futile.

The nightly fighting with Alexx would begin as soon as he stepped through the door. This was their routine. The routine of living with an addict. He'd strut through the doorway, averting all eye contact with his wife, and make a beeline for the kitchen. Alexx would tow Beatrice off to her room and tell her it was time for bed. As her mother dragged her down the hallway, Beet would stare at the kitchen as if it were the yawning entrance to a mysterious cavern. Her dad had become as much a mystery to her as a ghost, only ever seeing him for just the briefest of moments. An hour later, the whiskey would take hold, and the screaming would begin.

Which led to last night.

Quinn was screaming at walls, and Alexx was screaming at him. The bedroom became the Battle of the Bulge - both entrenched in a vicious stalemate of pointless rage. Ronan Quinn, looming over Alexx's small frame like a giant, yelled that name again. The name that spilled out of him during every drunken escapade.

"Carlos!" Quinn snatched up the brass lamp with the beige shades from the nightstand. Tossing it in his hand like a pitcher feeling out a baseball, Quinn growled through flexing jaws. "Carlos, you murdering piece of shit!"

"No!" she screamed, her ice-blue eyes bulging open in terror. "Not again!"

He heaved the lamp at Alexx as she scrambled off the bed in a panic. Unbalanced and tumbling bulb-over-base, the wedding-gift lamp glanced off Alexx's forehead just as she ducked out of the way. Her eyes clenched shut as the lamp cut deep into her brow, smashing into the wall behind her. Alexx slapped her hand over the gash, pivoted on her feet, and dashed into the bathroom. The door slammed shut just as he reached it.

He continued bellowing *Carlos* over and over on an endless loop. He pounded on the door, twisting the knob so hard it nearly broke off. The longer she locked him out, the more enraged he became.

"Go away! You're fucking crazy!" Alexx screamed.

There was silence, and he froze. The click of the latch moving away from the door shattered the hush in the room.

Shouting and cursing, he burst into the bathroom. A wide-eyed Alexx sat on the edge of the tub, hiding something behind the curtain. When he reached her, Alexx yanked the hose and showerhead from behind the curtain, spraying a jet of ice-cold water directly into his face. Spraying water into his open mouth and eyes like a firefighter dousing flames, she pushed her way toward him. Dropping to his knees, he buried his face in his palms and sobbed.

Alexx stood over her husband, dousing him with cold shower water until she was positive that Helmand Province, Maya Angelou Elementary, and Central Park all scurried back into Quinn's cave of nightmares. Kneeling beside him, she dropped the shower head to the floor, sweeping water from his jet-black hair with long, elegant fingers.

"Honey, you called me Carlos again." Eyes wistful, Alexx spoke to him softly and assuredly. "I don't know who Carlos is, but I'm not him."

"I'm sorry, Alexx," he slurred, wiping tears from his eyes. "I'm so sorry. It won't happen again." He gazed at Alexx's angelic features. Crisp blue eyes resting on high cheekbones. Subtle creases just beyond the edges of her lips. Long blonde hair secured into a ponytail with a pink ribbon. Streaming past her right eye, blood mixed with her tears, turning it a light pink. He could have killed her.

Standing and placing the shower head back in the tub, she sighed. "It will happen again. It'll keep happening until you get help." She glanced at the open bathroom door. "Oh, no. Beet. Honey."

Quinn looked over his shoulder.

Clutching a stuffed build-a-bear, Beatrice stood at the door in her bright yellow Sponge Bob pajamas. Staring wild-eyed at her father, her lips trembled and her hands shook. He hadn't seen such terror in a very long time.

That was last night.

Now he sat in Canter's Coffee Shop, running his finger around the rim of the cup, Carter speaking at him. And he hadn't just been reliving last night. He'd been describing it to Carter.

"Jesus, dude," Carter said.

"Here ya go, squire," Joe grumbled, placing a black coffee on the table in front of Carter. "Let me know if his lordship wants a donut." He stomped back behind the counter, muttering discontent to Isabella.

Quinn snapped back to reality. He knew someday he'd regret confiding in Carter, one of the gossip queens of the precinct. But the previous night poured out of him like amber whiskey into a bottomless glass. He needed to unload on someone. He felt ashamed. Embarrassed. Afraid of his own strength and uncontrollable rage. Seeing Alexx with the butterfly clip over her eyebrow broke his heart on the spot. But now his life was just a moment in time. Followed by another moment, and another, and another. Living in the moment, this was called, *or some bullshit like that.*

Carter's eyes left the grumbling Joe, turning back to Quinn. "You threw a lamp at her? That's messed up, dude. Is she okay? Did she need stitches?"

Quinn shook his head and said they used a butterfly clip. When he woke up this morning, she and Beet were in the kitchen, both fully dressed, a pair of suitcases by the front door. Alexx was taking Beatrice to her sister's home in New Jersey and she was going to be filing for divorce.

How did I arrive here? What wrong choices did I make? How did I not see the consequences of the path I took? His inner voice echoing in a hagridden brain, he admitted his father may have been right. You'll never be the same, he said. You could've gone to Yale.

"So," Carter said, his eyes shifting every which way. "Can we talk about work now? Because I'd hate to rain on your pity parade, but I've got something to tell you."

Gazing through a window cluttered with aging posters and ads, Quinn watched as rain fell in fat drops, hitting the pavement, erupting at people's feet, everyone scurrying for cover beneath newspapers and coats. "Screw you, Carter," he muttered absentmindedly.

"Yeah, okay. So, the lieutenant got a call from someone at *The Times*. Did you…" Carter stopped and waited for him to guess where he was going with this.

"Did I what?" He grumbled.

"Did you leak something to a reporter? Like a name or something? Because…" he pulled out his phone, tapped the screen, muttered something, held up a finger, told him to *hang on for a second*, and otherwise became annoying.

"Did I what?"

Carter slid the phone across the table. Sweeping it up in his hand, a suspicious Quinn studied Carter. On the website of *The Times*, a headline jumped out at him - *New York's Little Crime Boss is Waging War on Colombia.* The article was short, but it packed a punch - the journalist receiving a tip from someone "with direct knowledge of Panolini's operations."

Heroin and cocaine were moving on the streets.

The Colombians were being forced out of Queens and Brooklyn.

The New York police were powerless to stop the mayhem that was coming.

There was going to be a war on the streets.

The source was a man who went by the name of Stan Cooper. Two detectives at the precinct verified this source, but refused to divulge their own names because of an ongoing investigation and yada yada yada. Quinn put the phone down, sliding it back across the table toward Carter. "I know nothing about that."

"Huh," Carter said as he sat back and crossed his arms. "I don't either. But La Diabla is looking for you. So…"

Quinn gritted his teeth. "Stop calling her La Diabla. It's childish. She's your lieutenant."

Carter saluted him. "Yes sir, sergeant major sir!"

"Go to hell, Carter. Do you have anything else? Something, you know, case related?"

"As a matter of fact, I do," Carter sang in a self-assertive tone. "Flamingo gave us a tip. He says that the Panolinis and the Colombians are having a meet and greet at the docks. He says they're going to talk about dividing up the city. Sounds like a drug lord town council meeting."

Quinn sat up like this new revelation had lashed him to a flagpole. "You're kidding me. They're meeting up? All of them? Pudge Panolini going to be there too?"

"All the rotten eggs in a basket, Ronan. According to Flamingo, this *Times* article got them spooked. Flamingo thinks this Cooper guy in the article is a Panolini snitch. Seriously. Stan Cooper? Can you believe that? What a dumbass. Stan Cooper's an Easter Bunny. They're getting together to 'work things out.'"

This sparked Quinn with fresh enthusiasm, like someone heaved a weight off his shoulders and tossed it onto the worn linoleum floor. This was perfect. "I bet it got them spooked. And New York's 'little' crime boss? Oh, I bet that's got ol' Pudge spinning. When're they meeting?"

"Tomorrow night."

"Because of this article?"

Carter shrugged.

Quinn again gazed out the window. The rain ceased, bright rays of sunlight breaking through charcoal gray clouds. Glimmering rivulets of rainwater rushed through street gutters like tumbling mirrors. He tapped his fingers as he thought through everything that needed to be done. He needed to move fast. He needed approval from the lieutenant. She'll, of course, ask him about the *Times* article. There's no way she could know it was him who leaked the story. No way would she think Ronan Quinn, who she trusted more than anyone else on her team – or in her life for that matter – would leak a fake name to a legitimate newspaper to bait two massive crime mobs into meeting each other for chitchat. No way she'd find out *he was actually both detectives* who verified the story. But now they were meeting. He'd deal with any fallout from *The Times* later. He was living in the moment. Whatever that even meant.

This operation could result in a surveillance gold mine. The team will collect names. Operations. Maybe shipments. Or they'll shoot each other dead, and that would bring a year of Operation Scorpion to a dead stop. It was a risk he would take. He shook off the hangover. His tapping on the table reaching a drum slap crescendo. "Bah-bah, bah-bah!"

Carter jerked.

"We can break this goddammed thing open, Carter. Jesus. They're meeting. Can you believe that?" At this moment, a puffy, shaky, hungover

Ronan Quinn forgot he was losing his marriage and forgot he was losing his mind. The world, once again, had clarity and vision. The leak to *The Times*, a coup de maître. He slapped his hands together. "Call in the team. We plan this at 1100 hours. You're on point. I'll get the subpoena in front of the judge."

Detective Ronan Quinn would finally be ahead of the game.

"I have one question, Ronan," Carter asked.

"What?"

"Who the hell is Carlos?"

Quinn sighed, his eyes growing dark, staring at the faded brown swirling pattern on the pale blue table.

"Honestly, Jack, I don't have the slightest clue."

Raising an eyebrow, Carter smiled. "Oh, okay then." Slurping down coffee, Carter concluded Ronan Quinn had gone completely bonkers.

Chapter 2

Reflecting upon the dark swirling eddies of the East River, the city lights of a distant New York skyline glimmered through a misty night. Lit up in pie slices by streetlamps, dilapidated warehouses and abandoned industrial buildings squatted in a muffled wet silence.

Quinn slouched in a chugging dark Suburban, wiping the booze-inspired perspiration migrating from his armpits. Leaning awkwardly past Carter in the driver's seat, his shoulder pushed into Carter's chest. Carter winced and twisted his head. The gorilla-sized Quinn was no sweet petunia after another night of swilling liquor.

Quinn scanned the steel door entranceway to the graffitied brick warehouse, illuminated in an eerie green through his night vision scope. Sweeping the scope to his left, a black van sat in silence under the streetlights where a sole FBI agent attached to his team listened and recorded everything through his high-tech eavesdropping gear. But until now, they'd heard, and recorded, precisely nothing. Zero, zippo, and nada.

Quinn moved back to his seat and handed the scope to Carter. His phone buzzed and Alexx's beautiful smile lit up the screen. He canceled the call, shoving the phone back into his pocket.

Pudge Panolini and his crew arrived hours earlier. In true form to his arrogance, Pudge arrived in a stretch limo. In some regards, Pudge was just like Carter. Pretentious. Entitled. Narcissistic. He wanted everyone to see him, and all the time. Quinn expected Pudge to be in prison by Christmas – if not entirely dead.

"Real discreet, Pudge," Carter miffed. "If they held the meeting at a Hyatt, yeah, I wouldn't give a thought about a limo showing up. But here? On the East River? A limo and two black sedans? Why not have a marching band meet you at the door?"

Quinn managed a slight smile. Now they just had to wait for the Colombians. He expected seasoned Colombian cartel members to be a little more under the radar. They could arrive by boat from the river, or even on foot. They were pros. Pudge was an amateur disguised as a pro.

But a long, silence-filled two hours had now passed them by. Since Pudge had stepped out of his limo, struck up a smoke, and sauntered through the steel door with his crew, there'd been complete silence.

"Are you sure we can trust Flamingo on this one?" Quinn asked, fidgeting with the handle on the Suburban's door.

"He's done us right before," Carter muttered, studying the entrance to the run-down brick and mortar warehouse. Carter wondered to himself if Flamingo had just been pulling his chain, or if the Panolini's had been pulling Flamingo's.

A brash, up-and-coming member of the Panolini crime family, Pudge's nickname couldn't have been further from the actual truth. Wire thin, he wore his oily black hair in a bun, and his arms, legs, and back, tattooed with flames and skulls and puzzling Latin phrases. And those eyes. Pudge had shifty, unblinking eyes. Staring through people as if they were transparent. One look at Pudge, mouth locked in a perpetual sideways grin, it became immediately clear the man had buried enough bodies to put him away in prison for life - ten times over. Now an upstart Pudge wanted war with the Colombians. The Colombians didn't want a war any more than the Panolinis did. Business was too good. Americans were getting higher than ever.

The Colombians, and even his very own family, saw Pudge as an annoying problem impeding a proposed partnership of crime.

Now they were all meeting and Quinn hoped beyond hope the arrogant, psychotic Pudge would spill names and receiving docks and shipments and product. All to an eavesdropping FBI asset in a van.

---

3 DAYS PRIOR TO THIS night on the East River docks, a Panolini lieutenant approached a jonesing, dime-bag hunting Flamingo. Wearing a blue, double-vested, pinstriped suit and ivory tie – a rather odd ensemble for a day's outing in Harlem - Frank Manzo strode up to a twitchy Flamingo. Manzo was aware Flamingo was a snitch, and he knew about Operation Scorpion and that the NYPD was cooperating with the FBI. Manzo had his own sources in the department. The NYPD couldn't keep a secret any more than a boy getting laid for the first time.

Manzo had an odd preposition for the edgy Flamingo. The Panolini family wanted an inglorious end to Operation Scorpion, and they wanted that flaming drunk detective, Ronan Quinn, humiliated and embarrassed. Frank Manzo was going to accomplish this by having his own cousin, Pudge Panolini, killed. All he asked from Flamingo was to tell that idiot Jack Carter the Cartel and the Panolini crime family were meeting to sort things out. A traitor was amongst them and the *Times* article proved that. But Manzo knew full well this Stan Cooper character was straight out of Alice's Wonderland.

What Manzo didn't tell Flamingo, was that the Panolini family had already made peace with the Gutiérrez Cartel out of Medellín. Pudge was an annoyance alright, and no one wanted to deal with his brainless impulsivity any longer. Not his family, his crew, or the Cartel. Eliminate Pudge along with the NYPD Op, and the Cartel would stay out of Brooklyn and the Bronx. That was the Cartel's offer. The Panolinis didn't hesitate in agreeing. But the Cartel had to do the dirty work. The Panolinis had all the desire to kill that annoying slug, but they lacked the will to kill their own flesh and blood. Something about loyalty.

This all took place in a litter-strewn, breezy alleyway that reeked of urine and rotting trash, three days before Flamingo met with Carter. This gave the Cartel two days to set up a Pudge rat-trap.

On Monday morning, a sanitation truck rumbled up to the west side of an old, graffiti-littered brick warehouse near the docks on the East River. The truck, its hydraulic arms hissing and grinding, dropped off an empty garbage dumpster and carried the old dumpster off. This new dumpster, however, wasn't actually empty.

Sweating throughout the day and surrounded by the stench of rotting food and stale damp cardboard, two assassins waited inside this suffocatingly hot steel prison with a dozen plain cardboard boxes. When night arrived, the dumpster lid creaked open, and the two assassins shot a rope with a grappling hook through a window, shimmying up two floors and through the opening.

They went to work, hauling box after box in through the window after them, busily setting their trap. Job complete, they patiently waited for two days, living off energy bars and tap water from rusty, mold-covered faucets.

"Calypso, this is Cobra," an impatient Quinn asked over the radio. "Are you guys getting anything?"

"Negative, Cobra," crackled the response.

Completely riled, folding his hands into perspiration-soaked armpits, his face puffy like it was made of marshmallows, he turned to Carter. "What the fuck, Jack? Is Flamingo using again? Did he lie to us?"

Carter shrugged.

Frustrated, Quinn shook his head. He told Carter to roll down his window, then shoved his way past him. Carter rolled his eyes, let out a deep sigh, and turned his head. Quinn raised the scope, craning his neck around as he scanned the street. Maybe *The Times* story had been a bad idea, he thought. Maybe the Colombians left town. Maybe they were just seeing what Pudge would do. What moves he would make. After all, the capricious Pudge was a bull in a China shop. Figuring his moves was like placing your entire bet on red. You won big or left broke.

A loud pop came from the warehouse, followed by mist-dampened silence. Then came two more rapid *pops*.

"Cobra! Calypso! Shots fired! Shots fired!"

"You've got to be kidding me." Quinn tightened up. "Are you sure?" he asked over the radio.

"I've got an unsub running out of the warehouse, east side. I see one victim at the entrance. We're proceeding on foot."

"Wait!" Quinn shouted. "Damn it!" He pounded his fist on the glove box.

Carter turned to him with eyebrows raised. "Well, the cat's out of the bag now. Should I call in the SWAT?"

"This is Calypso, we've got a victim alright. East entrance. We've lost the unsub."

A special tactics team composed of a dozen heavily armed, and up to that point, bored officers, blew past Quinn and Carter in their van so fast the Suburban shook.

"They're coming out guns a blazin'!" yelled Carter, as he leaped out of the SUV.

Oh, what the hell, Quinn thought.

The teams assembled at the west entrance to the warehouse, and Quinn told the tactics commander to proceed inside with probable cause. Tremors rippled through his hands as he pulled his service weapon. Barely able to focus, all he could think of was that a year's worth of Operation Scorpion was now swirling around the toilet bowl.

Methodically and in silence, the team cleared the warehouse. Making their way to a row of offices at the rear of the abandoned warehouse, rats scurrying for cover, automatic weapons and narrow beams of light cut through the darkness. Quinn, uneasy and unsure, glanced at Carter. Carter shrugged, proceeding toward the rusted metal stairway leading to the offices on the second floor.

Moving up the grated metal staircase in two-by-two cover formation, they arrived at the grungy, peeling-paint, wooden office door with the words, *Floor Boss,* stenciled on smudgy glass. The commander announced the NYPD's arrival, and then a tactics officer kicked in the door, slamming it into the wall in splinters and broken glass. The team scrambled inside.

Moments later, the "clear!" signal was sounded.

Quinn and Carter moved in.

The two detectives glanced around the room in astonishment. Hundreds of 12-inch x 12-inch squares of soundproofing foam were stuck to the ceiling and walls with adhesive glue. And the office itself displayed carnage. Pinwheel patterns of dark, dried blood, coated peeling brown wallpaper like the works of some raving mad impressionist. Two men lay dead on the floor, curled up like napping children, puddles of a maroon blood settling beneath their swelling heads. Members of Pudge's crew. Shot execution style.

"Oh, Ronan. Man, I think I'm going to puke. Look at that." Carter's finger wagged toward the old oak office desk at the far end of the room.

His crimson blood dripping onto the floor in staccato taps, Pudge's dismembered torso lay on the desk's surface. The assassins had severed Pudge's tattooed arms, legs, and head, tossing them into a corner like a carpenter chucking excess wood. Pudge's once psychotic eyes were wide, opaque, and frozen for eternity with terror. The last thing he'd seen were two faceless men in black garb and hoods rushing toward him brandishing saws.

"Jesus, Ronan. They went full-on Scarface and chopped up Pudge. Gross," Carter said in disbelief.

Below the team, at the east entrance, the third member of Pudge's crew lay dead at the bottom of the stairwell. Shot in the head, he'd miraculously survived long enough to chase one assassin down, and squeezing off a single shot, struck Pudge's killer with a bullet. Then, adrenaline drained, he'd collapsed and died on the damp street.

Carter remarked how impressed he was with Pudge's guy getting off a shot. "That's conviction, bro," he muttered under his breath.

Dragging his hands down his face and groaning, Quinn wondered what he'd just done. He'd just killed Operation Scorpion, that's what.

CHAPTER 3

QUINN REMAINED AT THE East River crime scene until 3 a.m., directing forensics and scribbling notes for his report.

At 3 a.m., he raced home, took a long steaming shower, and slammed back a shot of bourbon to steady his nerves and hands. At 6 a.m., he was back at the precinct as the graveyard shift packed up and headed for the doors. By 8 a.m., he'd dotted the final I and crossed the final T on his preliminary report and submitted it to the lieutenant.

10 a.m. arrived, the effects of alcohol withdrawal gripping his body. The damp perspiration on his forehead, and wetness spreading across his back, grew annoying. His face felt like expanding yeast in an oven. His fingers struggled to manipulate even a pen.

One Colombian assassin now ran loose in New York, while another lay handcuffed to a gurney in New York Hospital Med Center in Queens. Pudge and his dismembered parts, along with his dead crew, were now refrigerated in the morgue. Yup, he thought. This Op was a cluster. Pushing his chair back and shaking the cobwebs out of his head, he stood and strode into Lt. Miá Perez's office, also known as *the shark tank*.

Quinn took a seat, watching trance-like as Miá's long black ponytail whipped from side to side while she swayed in her chair. Moving his hands under his armpits, he dampened the perspiration soaking his shirt sleeves.

Forming a bond of friendship that began when they both became NYPD detectives, he knew her all too well. Miá, raised on the tough streets of The Bronx, was one of five children of Dominican immigrants. Quinn, an only child, grew up in a posh neighborhood on the outskirts of Boston. Despite their dissimilar childhood upbringings, they developed a kindred friendship, having both served as Marines and experienced multiple deployments to combat zones. But Miá soon passed him in rank, receiving a promotion to lieutenant and becoming his supervisor. So, the two kept their professional and personal lives distinctly secret and separate. There were to be no grumblings of perceived professional preference amongst the detectives on the floor.

"Sure, you bet, okay, buh-bye." Miá spun around in her chair, slammed the phone onto the receiver, and faced Quinn. Their eyes met, he squirmed, and the shark tank descended into a stifling silence. As the detectives' floor went about its tasks, Quinn's colleagues snuck glances into the office. He sensed eyes burning into him like laser beams, as if he were the sole actor on a stage with a spotlight beaming down on him.

Miá parted her lips. "Soooo...."

Quinn sat up straight and drew in a deep breath. "Well, Pudge is deceased. So, there's that. We were surveilling the warehouse with four units, including a tactical team if things went south. I got a 'shots fired' call, so we moved in with probable cause. When we got in, we closed off the scene and..."

Miá opened her hand and shook her head. "Okay, let me stop you right there. I've read the report. Ronan, this is a colossal shit-show."

He nodded. "Well, yes, but..."

Miá drew in a deep breath and clenched her jaws. "Okay, I signed off on this Op. I'm going to answer to the chief, and I have no problem with that. It was a good Op that went sideways. It happens. The FBI guys also signed off on this and they're getting some heat from the DOJ, but whatever." Leaning back in her chair, she swung her ponytail off her shoulder. "You know, Ronan, we have to be extra careful with this stuff. We're all working under a microscope these days."

He casually crossed his legs and arms and nodded. "I get it."

Miá's gaze transcended to that of a scorching glare. "Do you get it? Do you really get it, Ronan? I got a call from Alexx this morning. The good news just keeps on coming. You guys are splitting up?"

Quinn stiffened and adjusted his neck. "Yes, well, I kind of..."

"Kind of threw a lamp at her? And this isn't the first time, either. Jesus, Ronan. And who's Carlos?"

Blood rushed to his head, and his mind retreated for shelter. A six-foot-three, two-hundred-and-thirty-pound crab scuttling away from a predator, claws up and snapping defensively. "I don't know who..."

"You assaulted Alexx, Ronan. She's not pressing charges, of course, because that woman adores you, and I don't know why she still does. She's worried about you. She wants you to start treatment and see a therapist. She thinks you may have PTSD."

Quinn rolled his eyes. "C'mon, Miá, I don't need to see a-"

"Detective Quinn, you're not in any position right now to tell anyone what you need or don't need."

The muscles in his neck clenched. What is she getting at? Where is she going with this?

"Ronan, you've lost your focus. You're burned out and understandably so. Operation Scorpion has been dragging on for a year. Before that, Angelou Elementary. Ronan, that would mess any of us up. Then the Central Park murders." Miá leaned forward in her chair, her walnut brown eyes wide and reassuring. "You didn't get those assignments because I was picking on you. You were free. It was just line-of-sight. You were who I had. I also know Helmand Province is still rattling around in that brain. That alone would do anyone in and I know, because I was over there as well."

Where...is...this...going...

Miá leaned back in her chair, folding her arms across her chest. Making an odd clicking sound with her tongue, she gazed at nothing in particular on her desk. Quinn could see her thoughts spinning like the paddlewheel on a riverboat.

"I had a conference this morning with the captain, chief, commissioner, and deputy mayor. Someone here, I have a guess who, talked to someone at *The Times* about the case. Someone gave a reporter a name. A name belonging to someone who, as far as we can tell, doesn't even exist."

Shoulders drooping, Quinn slouched in his seat. Glancing behind him and through the clear glass walls of the shark tank, he searched for Carter. That prick, he was acting all suspicious at the coffee shop, he thought. He snitched.

Miá continued. "So, to make a long story painfully short, legal counsel for *The Times* is threatening us with a lawsuit because someone here leaked a fake name to a journalist, who I might add is now on unpaid leave, and it found its way into the paper, which clearly got Pudge and his Colombian friends to meet up and try to kill each other over. Pudge sure got the raw-end of that deal, didn't he?"

"Did you speak to Carter about it?" He asked, his words strained and cracking.

"Ha!" Miá shouted.

Quinn flinched.

"Carter, that ditz. He's like a child. Don't mistake this. You and I both know who the leaker is." Her eyes narrowed, and he squirmed like a mouse in a trap.

"But, well, okay, I did, but," Quinn stammered incoherently.

"Look," Miá said. "Here's the deal. Are you listening to me?"

He nodded.

"We're Devil Dogs, you and me. We bleed Marine." She thrust her chin at the department floor as curious detectives snuck peeks into the shark tank. "We're not like those pansies out there. So, do the words honor, commitment, and integrity mean anything to you still? Semper Fi? What in God's name were you thinking?"

Quinn, soundly beaten, pleaded. "Look, Miá-"

"It's Lieutenant," she responded in a barbed tone.

"Lieutenant - look, we were going nowhere!" He thrust his arms into the air. "The Bureau guys were providing next to nothing in support, and nada tactical! You know this! Sure, they provided some help, but Carter and I were doing all the heavy lifting. I needed a break. I didn't know the Colombians were going to take it this far. This was strictly an intel Op. We thought-"

Miá cut him off. "You thought, Ronan? You thought!? You should have come to me if you needed support!" *Whap!* Miá's hand smacked her desk. "Now we have a Panolini family member dead, Ronan, along with his crew. And we have a Colombian assassin in the hospital who's already lawyered-up, and another one who's probably on his way back to Colombia by now. You got no intel from this Op. You made exactly," Miá formed a zero with her blue nail-gloss painted index finger and thumb. "These many arrests. But what we got instead, Ronan, is a raging mad newspaper who wants to sue our asses because the NYPD used them as an unwitting accomplice to what is now an international crime involving a cartel and the mob!" Leaning across her desk, Miá pushed her hands toward him, her voice dropping into a deep, menacing tone. "I need a head. I need a head to give to the captain, I need a head to give to the chief, I need a head to give to the commissioner, and I need a head to give to *The Times*, who now needs to print a retraction."

Quinn felt as if he were sinking into a dark abyss filled with menacing creatures.

Miá shook her head. "Boy, oh boy, you really fucked this up. Now, pay attention. Blink twice if you can hear me because you look like you're going to pass out."

He nodded.

With a baleful growl, Miá delivered Quinn's sentence. "I'm putting you on paid administrative leave effective right now. You'll remain on paid administrative leave for fourteen days. Are you following me?"

Quinn nodded, and his chin fell to his chest in defeat.

"During this time, you're going to check into AA. You're going to set up an appointment with the police union therapist. You're going to get your personal affairs in order. You're going to apologize to Alexx."

Ronan nodded, "Thanks, Mi-lieutenant."

Miá scowled. "Oh, don't thank me yet, Detective Sergeant Quinn. I'm not finished. On the fifteenth day, you will be here, at 9 a.m., sharp, at which time you will hand me your resignation from the force."

He shot up. "What!?"

Miá nodded. "Yup. You failed my trust, Ronan. You failed the department's trust. You failed the trust of the people of New York."

His mind spun in circles. *What am I going to do? Where will I go? What have I done?*

Miá sat back in her chair, studying Quinn's reaction. He looked as if he were going to just melt into a puddle of human goo.

"You're my friend, and always will be. I love you with all my heart." Miá wiped away a tear, then pushed back her chair and stood. "But I'm also your boss. And I need a head. And that head is yours." Seeing him shrink before her, she attempted reassurance. "Don't overthink this, Ronan. You just screwed up. Think of this as a do-over, a fresh start, a new beginning."

He grimaced. "Yeah, okay, Miá - whatever." Standing, he pressed his slacks and adjusted his tie.

Miá's expression returned to a sharp glare, her fingernails tapping on the desk. "Fifteenth day. Here! My office! Resignation!" She shouted in a sharp, angular voice for all on the department floor to hear.

Quinn turned to walk out the door.

Miá stopped him. "Hey, and one more thing."

Sighing deeply, his face contorted in anger and humiliation, he turned. "Yes, Miá?"

"Where in the hell did you get this Cooper guy from?"

He shrugged.

"Christ. Carlos and Cooper. Well, you're racking up quite a collection of imaginary friends, aren't you? Stay in touch. I want you to check in with me, okay?"

A dejected Quinn shuffled out of Miá's office and into a deathly quiet department, where everyone tried to avoid eye contact with him and pretended to be busy.

Ripped apart by La Diabla, they muttered amongst themselves like gossipy hairdressers. C*hewed to pieces in the shark tank. He's lucky he's got an ass left to sit on. That poor bastard.*

As he walked through a room of stares and whispers, he only had one thought. I'm screwed.

ALEXX QUINN STOOD ON the wooden stoop at her sister's split-level home in Hackensack, sucking in one last drag of cool smoke from the Camel pinched between her fingers.

Ronan didn't know that she'd begun smoking again. A brief hip habit she'd eventually kicked in college. But Ronan Quinn didn't seem to know about anything outside of Ronan Quinn these days. Anyhow, it was just two smokes a day. What was the harm? One Camel in the morning after he left for work to steady her nerves, and one Camel after Ronan passed out, also to steady her nerves. Dropping the cigarette to the ground, she squashed it under her foot.

Alexx always knew the deal. The deal that came with marrying a Marine. The quiet sacrifices and the silent suffering that come with being a military spouse. The deployments. The war. The horror that deployed military men and women faced.

After the incident in Helmand Province, and the long investigation that followed, Ronan Quinn received the Silver Star for courage under fire. When he told her he was leaving the Marine Corps to join law enforcement, Alexx wept in her car for an hour.

Alexx learned she was pregnant with Beatrice two weeks after Quinn received his honorable discharge. After being hired by the local police department, the couple purchased a modest home in the small town of Haddonfield, New Jersey. When Ronan joined the NYPD, they moved again to East Rutherford. But Helmand Province kept following him like a tailing car, no matter where he landed a job. Then the school happened. Then Central Park. Then the suicides, the robberies, the murders… death flowing into Quinn's life from an open faucet of gloom.

Alexx stepped into her sister's home, the metal screen door clanging behind her. Beatrice worked on her math at the tall kitchen table by the window, her small feet dangling in the air and kicking back and forth as if pedaling an invisible bicycle. Beatrice stopped what she was doing, staring at Alexx with the blank face and searching eyes of a child.

"Are you and dad getting divorced?" Beatrice asked.

Alexx smiled. "Now, sweetie, finish your sums."

"Because Jewels said that all parents get divorced. She says it's like when your fish dies, your mom goes and gets a new fish from the fish store and puts it in the fishbowl, so you always have a pet fish."

A bemused Alexx cocked her head. "What? Jewels said that? No one is dying Beet, and mommy isn't getting a new fish. Finish your homework."

"I know dad isn't dying, mom. It's an aneurism."

"Wait, what?"

"An aneurism. When something isn't true, it helps you understand bad things in a better way."

Alexx bent over, placing a gentle kiss on her curly brown hair. "Euphemism honey. A euphemism. And Jewels was actually using an expression. You'll learn all that in grammar."

Standing straight, she cleared her throat. "In any case, your daddy isn't dying. Daddy just isn't going to live with us anymore."

"Why?"

"Because, Beet, daddy needs to find himself again, and we can no longer help him do that. Finish your math."

Alexx's sister walked into the kitchen and patted Beatrice on the head. She handed her cell phone to Alexx. "It's Ronan. He's been trying to reach you. He's really upset and needs to talk to you."

Alexx glanced at Beatrice, while Beatrice curiously waited for her mom's next move. "Tell him I'll call him back." Then Alexx Quinn hurried from the kitchen and threw herself down on the living room couch. Heartbroken and anguished, she buried her face in her arms and wept.

Chapter 4

Alternating rows of shade and dusky light, filtered through venetian blinds, lent to the sullen atmosphere of the room. Except for a melancholic, recently fired former detective, the Quinn family home sat silent and empty.

After leaving the precinct under a cloud of shame, he spent hours driving aimlessly around Long Island. Arriving at *Dottie's Liquor and Smoke Shop*, he searched for his night companion. Yanking a bottle of scotch whiskey from the shelf, he threw a fifty-dollar bill on the counter, trudged through the twin glass doors, and out of the store.

Now perched on the coffee table like a spiritual shaman, the bottle of amber liquid returned Quinn's thirsty glare.

Outside the vaunted walls of gloom castle, signs of life flowed into his ears. Kids playing a pickup game of street hockey. A trimmer alternating mechanical whines and chugs. Tree branches crashing to the ground in snaps and cracks and whooshes. A world forging ahead, leaving him stuck in this miserable sludge of booze and professional failure. Isn't this the bottom? Isn't this the time for self-reflection? What was I thinking? Making up a name? Using a journalist? Pretending to be two different detective verifications? The Op was a flop and Pudge was dead. And now so was Operation Scorpion. The NYPD would have to start from scratch. Another year of hard, frustrating work down the drain and all because of him. What was I thinking? I was thinking of putting that murderous Pudge away - and at any cost.

Sinking further into the sofa, the amber liquid beckoning him from the coffee table, he imagined the mess that Miá now had to fix. Fending off a lawsuit. Fending off the chief and the captain. Stranded and alone, he was just waiting for hungry sharks to take their pound of flesh. He gazed mindlessly at the sheet of light blue paper lying on the table. Maybe Miá was right. Maybe I have PTSD.

Helmand Province. A smiling man clutching an IR strobe. The LT calling out coordinates.

Maya Angelou Elementary. Children playing, reading, and learning their colors. Children like Beet.

Central Park. Two friends taking a late evening run. Encouraging each other to pick up the pace.

Quinn poured a drink, the fluid glugging and splashing as the bittersweet odor stung his nostrils. Like a goddess summoning him to another universe, the fluid beckoned him in the ebbing twilight.

Taking a solid gulp, his cell phone buzzed on the coffee table like a metallic mouse shocked by an electric prod. Alexx's face filled the screen, and he whisked the phone from the table.

"Hello? Alexx?" He gasped.

"Oh my god, Ronan," Alexx gushed. "You sound horrible. What's happening? Are you okay?"

Quinn dragged his hand down his face, pushing his eyeballs in and squishing his nose. "I fucked up, babe. I don't know what to do." He let out a deep-throated moan. "Miá asked for my resignation..."

"I know. I spoke with her this morning. She said she wouldn't fire you. She gave you an out. To resign from the force looks much better than being fired from the force." Alexx spoke with a calmness, as if this entire scene had played out before her long before it had for her husband. After all, she'd spent years watching him unravel right in front of her.

"Babe, please come home," he pleaded.

"Ronan, honey," Alexx replied in a soft, yet firm, tone. "Beet is, and should be, our number one priority. She needs to feel safe. I need to feel safe. And we don't feel safe around you any longer. We can't watch your Jekyll and Hyde act every single night. It's exhausting."

They don't feel safe? Jekyll and Hyde? I'm a monster? He was supposed to keep his wife and daughter safe, not terrify them.

"Beet and I are going to be fine. We'll stay at my sister's. I'm sure I can get a teaching job somewhere. It's nice here. Really open and peaceful."

The monstrous hand gripping his heart began squeezing the life from him.

"Ronan, we love you. But you've seen things I can't explain. Things I don't even want to explain. Horrible things. Just seeing the pain in your eyes told me everything. But since Afghanistan, you've never been able to move past whatever happened over there. You joined the NYPD and for what? To solve horrible crimes? And I don't believe for one moment this 'line of sight' bullshit Miá says. She chose you. I mean, kids? Really? And those poor women in Central Park? You can't fix everything. You can't make the world a better place and you certainly can't save it one crime at a time. The world is what it is. Are you listening?"

He nodded. "Yeah, I'm listening."

"Sweetie, get help. Stop drinking. See a therapist. Miá can help you with all that. She'll make sure you get the best help. She cares about you. Let her help."

"And us? What about us? What about Beet?"

"I can't allow you to see Beet, not until I know it's her father seeing her, and not some monster. I have to keep her safe."

"But us? You and I?" Silence smothered him. Was she going to tell him everything was going to be okay? Marriage counseling? Happily ever after? Like in those substance-abuse commercials? The ones where the couple in matching white cotton outfits are running along a sunny beach hand in hand? Like that?

"I have to go, Ronan. I'm sorry." The phone went silent. Those final soft-spoken words floated through space like feathers, and landed on Quinn like a 747.

Swallowed by cushions, he slid deeper into the sofa, an otherworldly force pulling him deeper and deeper into the underworld. He tossed back the whiskey and poured another one until the fluid was sloshing over the edge of the glass.

Carter called. Quinn couldn't believe it.

"Hey, bro, what's up? How you doing?" Carter's voice may as well have been an IED going off in Quinn's face - fragments and shrapnel piercing his brain.

"What the hell do you want, Jack?" Quinn grumbled.

"Just wanted to see how you were doing."

"I'm doing fine." Quinn wanted to ask Carter if he went to Miá about *The Times* journalist, but that would just cement his guilt.

"Diabla made us all sign NDAs over the Pudge thing. Keep a lid on it, you know, until Public Affairs can kind of draft some sort of statement. Wow, man, you sure got chewed out in the shark tank."

"What, you were watching? And stop calling her La Diabla!"

"Yeah, okay." Carter continued, ignoring Quinn's growing frustration. "You know, the captain came by and there was a huge yelling match between Diabla and the captain in the shark tank. She stormed out after and didn't come back for hours. Dude, she looked like she was crying. The woman actually has tear ducts."

Oh great, he thought. I've screwed her over as well.

"We're surprised she tore into you like that," Carter continued with an adolescent-like enthusiasm. "Everyone knows you guys are kind of, well, close. There's a pool here. So, whoever proves you're banging the She Devil gets the pot. Five hundred bucks. I sure could use five hundred bucks, man. Now that you're, you know, leaving and all."

Quinn gripped the phone so tightly it nearly flew from his hand. "Don't you guys ever stop? For Christ's sake. You're all a bunch of goddamned gossip queens. She's happily married, Jack, and has been for years."

Carter laughed. "To who? Charles Manson?"

Why am I even talking to him? He ended the call.

10:15 p.m. arrived. Suffering through an alcohol-induced centrifuge, Quinn sat in complete silence. His phone buzzed away on the coffee table, and he gazed down at the device like it might spontaneously combust. Miá's face appeared on the screen. He let it go to voicemail. After a few minutes of staring vacuously into the darkness, he picked up his phone and listened to her message.

Miá cleared her throat several times, then her voice came through the phone. Subdued. Sad. Soft. She'd settled things with the captain, and the captain accepted Quinn's resignation as the final course of action. There would be no legal jeopardy from *The Times.* He was in the clear. She hoped he was making calls like she asked him to, apologized over his situation with Alexx, and asked him, again, to please check in with her on his progress.

"Semper Fi, okay? Love ya," she said with a quivering voice.

The recording ended.

AT 10:45 P.M., THE FLICKERING, wavering light from the television filled the room as Quinn's empty gaze remained fixated on the screen.

For reasons only known to his subconscious, he'd removed his clothes and tossed them into a heap on the floor. Mindlessly holding the television remote control, a zombie-like Quinn scrolled through channel after channel. Voices reached his ears, none saying anything of discernable interest. No voice from the future whispered into his diluted mind and soothed his angst. No voice told him everything was going to work out just fine. Just voices of people he did not know. Would never know. Didn't want to know. His channel surfing ended on NOVA. Not because he was interested or curious or anything like that, but because he was simply tired of holding the remote control in his outreached hand.

In a drunken haze, he sat on the sofa in boxer briefs, his socked feet raised up on the coffee table, staring into the TV, watching as an aerial camera zoomed over a desolate, parched countryside. Riverbeds coursed through the earth, carving deep ravines. Black rocky bluffs reached skyward. Long expanses of dry prairie spread out before him. Soft, budding tips of switchgrass swayed with the breeze of the Great Plains.

God that looks great, he thought, his logy mind managing at least the feeblest thoughts. Wide open. Small towns. Clean people. Good ol' simple folk.

The NOVA documentary was on episode two of four of American history. More precisely, it documented historical sites for those still interested in these sorts of things, and ghost towns in particular. Crumbling away in the vast emptiness of the most remote regions of America, these long-forgotten urban uprisings sat in eerie silence, as if time had ceased to exist one day and everyone had just evaporated. Towns abandoned for this, that, and the other reason.

Gliding through one of these long-abandoned ghost towns, a camera meandered through old crumbling buildings and shattered windows. There were failing houses, what appeared to be a commissary, post exchange, a library, two churches, and a schoolhouse. Moving with deliberation, the camera dropped and passed the rusted hulk of a pickup truck, a green sapling poking its way through the driver's side window.

The narrator, some formerly famous Hollywood actor, described how this dilapidated old town had once been a thriving government community full of civilian workers, military personnel, and their families. Then, in an instant, the military shut down the nearby airfield, packed up, and left. The military reassigned the soldiers and airmen elsewhere, and flew the airplanes off to a boneyard to bake under a scorching Arizona sun. The disenfranchised civilian workers from the base, who now had no jobs and no place to go, moved south of the abandoned base to start up their own town.

Quinn had trouble focusing, but in the distance, beyond the weathered ghost town buildings with peeling white paint and collapsing roofs, he could just make out high barbed-wire fences and very modern-looking buildings. He couldn't rationalize these two things. *I thought it'd been abandoned?*

As his consciousness slipped away, interviews with people from the old base echoed from the TV. Talking to cameras from their living rooms in the town they'd created from scratch, they spoke of their grandmas and grandpas who'd lived and worked at the airfield until the government pulled out. These castaways of the government began new lives as farmers and ranchers, retailers and store owners, creating a whole new civilian town named Woodrock. Now, decades later, there were retail stores, chain restaurants, and even an outdoor mall and a golf course. To Quinn, this seemed like a paradise.

Woodrock, South Dakota. A place as far away from New York as possible without fleeing the country.

He googled the town on his phone, his thumbs and blurred vision betraying him every step of the way. Landing on a web page for the Woodrock Chamber of Commerce, he found an advertisement for the police department.

"Anyone with military or law enforcement experience can apply. Tap on the link for more information."

"Huh," he muttered. "Okay, I'll do this. What do you think of that, Carlos? You son of a bitch. Whoever you are."

Oxygen starved and alcohol-soaked, Quinn's brain surrendered at 11:15 p.m. His eyelids snapped shut, and he fell over onto the sofa where he lay unconscious until 10 a.m. the following morning.

Bright sunlight now streaming through blinds, birds chirping and singing, cars rumbling up and down the street, a slumbering Quinn finally stirred. Coughing and hacking, he swept the inside of his cheeks with his tongue, trying to find saliva to moisten his bone-dry mouth. He rolled onto the floor, stumbled to the bathroom, showered, drank a pot of black coffee, shoved some dry toast down his throat, and took four Tylenol.

Then he began placing calls to the Woodrock Chamber of Commerce.

Part 2

A Death on the Kurtz Curve

Four Years Later.

Woodrock, South Dakota

CHAPTER 5

SIX O'CLOCK ALREADY, I was just in the middle of a dream.

I was kissin' Valentino...

In a monophonic shrill, The Bangles hit *Manic Monday,* blared from Pippa's alarm clock. Through her bedroom window, rolling prairie hills materialized from the darkness like serpent's humps against a hazy mandarin horizon.

Grumbling and moaning, Pippa struck the snooze button and yanked the comforter back over her head. Sensing the puffy blanket being tugged in the opposite direction, she groaned. "Oscar? Is that you?"

A cold wet dab on her cheek followed, then a soft tickle of whiskers, then the full force of Oscar's furry orange head thrusting into her back. The time was 5:30 a.m., and three and a half years had passed since Pippa Simpson left Silicon Valley, arriving in this odd windswept landscape with a U-Haul, a cat, and a promising new career.

"Fine," Pippa grumbled. "I'm up...brat."

Rolling out of bed, Pippa stretched and gazed into the morning light. The white framed bedroom window clattered with a modest gust of prairie wind as her eyes moved beyond the redwood fence enclosing her yard. A long, empty expanse of nothingness lay before her. No backyard neighbors, the agent told her. You'll have a great view, he said. View of what? I may as well live on Mars.

Shuffling half-asleep into the kitchen, she poured kibbles into Oscar's dish - the fluffy orange tabby squatting and diving in. Rubbing crusty sleep from her eyes, she replayed last evening's call with her mother as she fixed a pot of coffee.

"Sweetie, you work with some very successful, smart people," her mother stated, trying to convince Pippa that she was lonely, when in fact she wasn't.

"Mom, please. I'm not going to date work colleagues," Pippa shuddered. "Gross."

"Well, maybe a cowboy wouldn't be so bad. He'd probably treat you like the queen you are, and it's better than listening to your podblasts all night and living alone with that silly cat."

Pippa laughed. "Podcasts, mom. Not pod-blasts...pod-casts."

Often hanging out with a group of women referring to themselves as *the posse*, Pippa was not totally alone. The posse enjoyed an occasional backpacking trip, scenic drive, a holiday on California's north coast, and weekend trips to Las Vegas. But the group was breaking up. Emma was dating the real estate agent who'd told Pippa how much she'd enjoy staring at a barren landscape every morning. Kim was getting married. Only three of the posse remaining were still flying solo and yes, on occasion, Pippa had loneliness creep into her life, resulting in a few flings. So, she figured she'd take dating up again someday, *but not with some South Dakota yahoo who smells like horses. Jeez mom.* But Pippa had a craving for masculine attention. A guy just noticing her, perhaps peeking at her plump breasts, or glancing at her tush. It's the little things in life.

Pippa showered, decided to go one more day without leg-shaving, toweled off, and stood in front of the mirror. She pulled on her blue-framed oversized eyeglasses, lifted her breasts up, and looked them over. "You'd think these things would grab someone's attention," she muttered.

"What else are they good for?" She looked at her waist and legs. I have soft lines, mom says to me. Sheesh, I don't look that bad. A little plump. Maybe I could switch to dairy free ice cream…then again, maybe not. And what does 'soft lines' even mean?

After dressing, she held Oscar while gulping down one last cup of coffee. "See ya, brat," she said to the purring tabby, placing a reluctant cat onto the floor.

BACKING OUT OF THE driveway in her orange Subaru, she waved to Bill Hendrickson, the manager of Plant Five. As she drove down the street, he waved back - no smile as usual - and she wondered why he seemed so tense all the time.

Speeding along the highway, and around the bend of the Kurtz Curve, Pippa glanced at the dilapidated, crumbling buildings of The Old Ghost Town. Enclosed by miles of failing cyclone fencing, the old wooden buildings stood in cemetery silence, their roofs buckling as beams and timber succumbed to hostile South Dakota seasons. She tried to visualize the town in its heyday. Freshly painted homes. Green lawns. People walking around holding hands. Children riding bicycles in the streets. Turning onto the drive that led to the facility, she stopped at the first security gate, pressing her badge against the card reader. *Screech.* The grinding of metal as the first gate chattered open caused her to wince. *Could use some oil, cheapos.*

Stopping at the second gate, two security guards in dockers and black company polos approached her car. Rocky, the bald, goateed, emotion-free guard, held up his hand, gesturing for her to slow down and stop. He looked over her badge and then checked his clipboard - stone faced as usual and always taking his job too seriously.

Chris, the young, blonde, and muscular guard, stepped up to Pippa with a broad, charming grin. “Mornin’, Ms. Simpson,” he said as he tipped his cap, his deep blue eyes burrowing into hers.

The thing about Chris, the action that made her giggle and blush, was he always removed his hat and tipped it toward her when he said good morning. Chivalry is still alive and kicking in the Dakotas, Pippa always thought. And she spoke of Chris to the posse often, referring to Chris as her *guard crush.*

“I have this weird fantasy,” Pippa confessed to Emma one evening over wine and a plate of cheese. “A bunch of zombies are trying to eat my brains, and my guard-crush-Chris zooms up in a big macho truck, and he slays all the zombies, and he lifts me up and carries me to his truck, and I give him a blow job as we drive off into the sunset.”

“Seek help, Pip,” Emma responded flatly as she lathered a cracker with brie. “And we don’t need any zombies eating your brains. Imagine a world full of zombie scientists. Jeez, what a yawn.”

PAT, PAT, PAT. PIPPA’S pointy-toed flats smacked the sterile white floor as she hustled through the complex of halls to her office.

Dropping her backpack onto the chair, she slid out her laptop and snapped it onto the workstation. Then she hurried her way to the break-room and poured some coffee, overhearing Karen Johnson and Gene Smith frantically whispering behind her. Training one ear to eavesdrop on this juicy bit of office gossip, she stirred cream into her coffee.

“I don’t know, Gene. They took him to the police station, and then...”

“Then what, Karen?”

"Then? I don't know, Gene, you tell me. Pangea sent guys to get him out and now no one can get a hold of him. No one has seen him. I hear they can't even reach his wife. I'm thinking of leaving. This place really gives me the creeps."

Well, that's different, Pippa thought. Someone vanished? Not for the first time, though. When someone here ends up in the courthouse, the company bails them out, picks them up, and off they go. You're fired. Sign this NDA. Don't talk or we'll sue your pants off. Then back to where you came from. But vanished? Probably drunk somewhere.

Pippa scampered back to her office and plopped down into her chair, slurping coffee from the MIT Alumni mug as her monitor came to life. She opened her mailbox, scanning through e-mails, spotting a group e-mail from her team - a string of questions and thoughts over how to proceed with repairing the new radioscope. Tapping away at the keyboard, she gave directions to her frustrated team.

Re: Stupid radioscope is down...AGAIN!!!

From: Pippa A. Simpson

To: G.I. Team

Guys,

Call the company in Peoria and ask them if they can send a team to repair it. And get legal to review the contract to see if they can apply any warranties.

Kisha, please set up a team call for 2pm to discuss.

Thanks!

Pippa Simpson – Manager, Global Innovation, Dept. 12

Safety is not a choice, it's a lifestyle!

Scrolling further through her inbox, an odd e-mail grabbed her attention. The subject line simply read, "Iron hand."

Iron hand? Iron man? What is this? Pippa tilted her head. This was curious. When she clicked the subject line to open the e-mail, a message popped up on her screen.

Enter Secure PIN

This is a secure e-mail? she thought. That's a rarity, must be important. It could be from Human Resources, they do this. She typed her pin number, and the message opened. The e-mail itself comprised a long chain of comments. In that chain was a message from her tense neighbor, the manager for Plant Five:

> Re: Iron Hand
>
> From: William K. Hendrickson
>
> To:
>
> Bcc:
>
> Rich,
>
> Specimens are now in final development. I expect all specimens will be ready for deployment in two weeks. The specimen batch A322 has successfully completed testing GLNV and is eager to go.
>
> – Bill
>
> Attch.1 Attch.2 Attch.3

Embedded in the e-mail were three attachments. Pippa slid the band off her ponytail, rearranging her strawberry-blonde hair into a bun, then drew in a deep breath and opened the attachments.

The first attachment was an image - a photo - taken in some dry, mountainous, empty place. A leathery-faced older man wearing creased blue jeans, a plaid shirt, and a white straw cowboy hat stood in an enclosure. An animal pen, it looked like. Appearing rather distressed, he was pointing out toward something in the open desert. Surrounding the weathered old cowboy guy were large beige lumps. Pippa looked closer and adjusted her glasses. Sheep? Are those dead sheep? How odd.

Gripped by a scientist's curiosity, she clicked open the second attachment. Another photo of a stark, flat desert plain with large peaks in the distance. Inside a red photoshopped circle, someone had highlighted an odd creature. Something black or gray, like a large insect, hovering just a few feet off the ground and roughly fifty yards from the photographer. The thing seemed to be glaring at the photographer from behind two narrow, glowing orange eyes, sending a chill down Pippa's spine. Whatever it was, it didn't look very happy or friendly. She closed the attachment and opened the third. The file was large, and it took a few seconds for it to open. When it did open, she read pages and pages of what seemed to be latitudes and longitudes.

Pippa sat back in her chair. What in the high holy hell is this stuff?

She scrolled further down the e-mail chain until she came across a name that she normally didn't see in an e-mail. Samir "Sam" Singh, the CEO of her company, Pangea Dynamic Solutions. She leaned forward, running her finger down the screen.

Re: Iron Hand

From: Samir Singh (CEO)

To:

Bcc:

Rich, ct al,

> JT and GLNV specimens performed beyond all expectations. Well done! Gentlemen, specimens must stay contained, out of sight, at all costs. There is still work to be done at JT. I shouldn't need to remind you that after the NV incident, security is 1000% of our focus. Red Lancer will handle any compromises. Iron Hand must go in Q4. Jupiter is dictating this time, so we must all do our best.
>
> Regards, Sam

With subconscious intuition, Pippa swept her cell phone off the desk, pointed the camera at the screen, waited for the lens to focus, and snapped a picture of the e-mail. Then she closed it as anxiety swept over her.

What in the actual fuck did I just read? What is Iron Hand? What specimens? That thing in the picture? Dead Sheep? Plant 5? Who, or what, is Jupiter? The Planet? Who is Red Lancer? How super creepy!

Switching off her monitor, she inhaled a sizeable volume of air, then turned the monitor back on. The screen flickered to life. "What in the fresh hell?" She muttered, seeing the e-mail had simply vanished. Pushing her eyeglasses up the bridge of her nose, she exhaled a long, deliberate breath and let her shoulders sag. Just as well, she thought to herself. I don't want any part of freaky looking specimens, dead sheep, or planets. She placed her phone back on the desk and scrolled through more e-mails.

AFTER THE 2 P.M. TEAM call, Pippa made her way over to the lab to observe Kisha run diagnostics. She thought at length about even mentioning the e-mail. Those messages, those documents, and *that thing*, were clearly not for Pippa to read and see, but curiosity overcame her. "Hey, Kish, ever hear of anything called Iron Hand?"

Kisha ran her finger up and down the computer screen, her face inches from the complex matrix of numbers and codes. "Nope, never heard of it, Pip." She turned and looked up at Pippa. "Should I have?"

Pippa shook her head. "Forget it, it's nothing." She thought back to the breakroom conversation between Karen and Gene. "Hey, you know anything about anyone, like, vanishing? Getting escorted out of the Woodrock jail? Disappearing?"

"Nope," Kisha replied, typing frenetically and lost in her work. "I really don't pay much attention to that stuff, Pip." Then she stopped, looking up at her manager. "Is there something I should know?"

Pippa shook her head. "No, Kish, forget I mentioned it. Let me know when you're all wrapped up in here."

Kisha raised her thumb and told her she would call when she completed her work.

PIPPA CLOSED UP AT 6:45 P.M., and left for home.

Deciding to just forget the entire weird e-mail incident from earlier in the morning, Pippa headed for the parking garage. She'd received no calls from anyone asking about it. Preet, her boss, didn't call her into his office to discuss Pippa prying into company secrets, if they were even that at all. Plus, the e-mail disappeared from the server, so someone must have added her to the e-mail chain by mistake. Pippa had done it. No harm, no foul.

Driving out toward the main security gate, she could see Rocky and Chris still dutifully standing guard. Rocky, with no warning, stepped in front of the Subaru and held up his hand. Pippa slammed on her brakes, skidding to a stop.

"Jesus! What the hell, Rocky!" She yelled as he strode nonchalantly to the passenger door. Chris stepped up to her window and wound his hand around and around. "Put your window down, please, Ms. Simpson."

Smiling, Pippa followed his instructions. "Working the late shift, Chris?"

"Yes ma'am. Overtime. Could always use the extra pay." He thrust his chin at an impatient Rocky on the passenger side. "Hey, Rocky wants to look at your car."

Pippa tilted her head with a puzzled expression. "Didn't you guys just check me out last week?"

Chris stepped back. "You know these things are random. Your plate came up on the monitor in the shack. We just do what we're told." He paused, awkwardly clearing his throat. "So, Ms. Simpson, you think we could grab a coffee sometime?"

Pippa's jaw dropped, her face turning hot. "What, here? Like, in the cafeteria?" she stuttered. The more she blushed, the more aware of her blushing she became.

Chris laughed, showing a crown of perfect ivory teeth. "No, ma'am, in town."

Pippa smiled, nervously adjusting her hair. "Okay, I'll think about it. But only on the condition you call me Pip, and not Ms. Simpson."

Chris tipped his hat. "Yes, ma'am."

"And not that either."

Rocky opened the Subaru's rear doors, shining his flashlight into the back seat of her car. On the ceiling. Under the seats. Into the passenger seat. He opened the front passenger door, pulling Pippa's backpack from the seat, his thick, clumsy fingers moving her things around. He asked her to pop the rear hatch in an indignant tone, striding to the rear with stormtrooper impertinence.

Hearing rustling and shuffling behind her, Pippa looked over her shoulder at Rocky, who still seemed oddly fascinated with her backpack. He glared at her, and she snapped her head back and stared ahead. Rocky slammed the rear hatch so hard the Subaru shook. Then he made his way back around the side of the car, tossing Pippa's backpack onto the passenger seat.

"Good to go, Ma'am," he grumbled, shining his flashlight directly into Pippa's face.

Shielding her eyes and blinking to regain her eyesight, odd-shaped blobs floated around in her vision. "Yeah, okay," she grumbled testily. "Thanks for the light show, Rocky."

Chris leaned into the window once more. "Think about it? At least?"

Pippa, annoyed, blinking away floating globs in her vision, compliments of Rocky's enormous D-Cell flashlight, responded she would.

She drove past the creaky steel gates, down the long entrance road and onto the highway. Glancing at the Old Ghost Town in the distance, the crumbling buildings casting long shadows, Pippa shuddered. No wonder they're called ghost towns. Jeepers creepers.

Pippa sped toward home. What a really weird day. Specimens and planets and my guard crush just asked me out on a date. I'll take that weirdness! Alone on the highway, Pippa excitedly honked her horn at no one. She rounded the bend of the questionably deemed Kurtz Peak and sped on to Woodrock. The city lights twinkling in the distance as darkness approached.

Chapter 6

After pulling the police SUV into a spot in front of the Woodrock Police Station, Chief of Police Ronan Quinn stepped out and into a fragrant, mild spring day.

Leaning back in a stretch, he gazed toward the adjacent courthouse, dwarfing his single level police station. Tall, grooved pillars. A cypress lined balcony. Indecipherable Latin phrases supporting justice scribed into an overhanging roof. A building inspired by ancient Roman architects, built by contemporary tobacco-spitting American Midwest contractors. Squatting next to the courthouse was an equally tall, cinder-block county jail, whose pragmatic inspiration had apparently been a shoebox.

Ronan Quinn's journey to this moment in time had been a long, tedious trip.

Two days after the Pudge Panolini and *Times* disaster in New York, Quinn brought his silver Chevy Tahoe to an abrupt stop in front of Miá's upscale brownstone in Crown Heights. Pepe, Miá's husband of nearly eight years, met him at the door.

Miá and Pepe had always struck Quinn as an odd pairing. A classically trained baker, Pepe Perez owned a successful chain of boutique bakeries, *The Pink Pamelia,* named after his mother, including a highly profitable store on Fifth Avenue. And Miá, the Bronx raised former

Marine officer and New York homicide detective, had a secret passion for baking. After attending a class instructed by Pepe, the two fell for each other and were married a year later. Pepe worshipped his sculpted, bronze skinned, walnut-eyed wife, and Miá admitted to Quinn once that the pudgy, soft-featured baker she married was hopelessly romantic.

"The guy's a stallion in the sack," she told him with wide, gleaming eyes.

Quinn laughed and thanked her for telling him that which he'd not asked for. When Alexx met this odd couple for the first time at a dinner, she turned to him after Miá and Pepe walked back to the kitchen.

"I don't get it," she whispered from behind a cupped hand.

"He's a stallion in the sack," he whispered back with a wink.

"Oh," Alexx whispered. Then, wearing the curious expression of someone deciphering a Salvador Dali painting, she blurted out. "Really?"

From their oak furnished living room, Miá and Pepe now listened intently to Quinn's plan.

His eyes moving along dozens of framed portraits of Pepe receiving awards, greeting Presidents, Prime Ministers, Queens, and Michelin Star chefs, he picked up a framed photo of Miá, taken at her graduation from the Naval Academy at Annapolis. Sharp black coat. Gleaming gold buttons down the breast. Marine cap tossed into the air. Jubilatory cadets cheering their success. With a smile, he placed the photo back on the table.

"Guys, I'm starting over," he told the couple as they sat on the sofa clutching hands. "I'm taking this job in South Dakota. Finding lost dogs. Saving cats in trees. Writing parking tickets. Maybe breaking up a redneck brawl or two." Reconciling with Alexx, he explained, was a ship that had long sailed, and neither of them wanted to go through the pointless pain of marriage counseling. The inebriated nightly tussles with this internal foe of his, Carlos, could have hurt or even killed Alexx. This was a line in the sand he'd crossed. A line from which there was no return. So, South Dakota it was. Once he had himself straightened out, he would be free to talk to and see Beatrice any time he wished.

As for Carlos, Quinn told them, that puzzle remained unsolved. The police union therapist Miá lined up gave him a rough diagnosis. Post Traumatic Stress Disorder. This Carlos he battled represented all the loss he'd felt and repressed after Afghanistan, Maya Angelou Elementary, and Central Park.

"What bullshit," he said through grinding teeth. "She said that Carlos is my PTSD. I don't have PTSD, and for all she knows, Carlos plays shortstop for the Mets." Miá didn't say a word. Her eyes moistened, and she gave a slight nod of approval.

The Woodrock police chief at the time, coasting to retirement, allowed Ronan Quinn a month to get his affairs straight in New York. Speaking in a thick midwestern drawl and with all the enthusiasm of a bored librarian, the chief told him to take the time he needed. The Woodrock police department wasn't exactly having their doors knocked down by applicants, and Quinn was almost overqualified for the job of a simple police deputy. The chief, spending most of the interview surfing the internet for RVs and griping about having to hire women, never questioned Ronan Quinn's reasons for leaving New York.

He and Alexx put the house on the market, and then he had one final alcohol-soaked evening. The following day, he packed up his truck, hitched a trailer to the bumper, and headed for the new frontier. Unexpectedly, the trip took him five days. Detoxification from endless booze filled nights caused his face and stomach to balloon, made him cramp in the worst kind of way, soaked him in perspiration, and he couldn't stop defecating. He ran into gas station convenience stores, pleading for bathroom keys multiple times a day, managing just five to six hours of driving before collapsing onto stiff beds of sketchy highway motels.

Bearded, sweat soaked and smelling like a salt pond, he arrived at Woodrock on a cold, gray, windy afternoon. But amongst the shakes and sweats and fever dreams, Quinn found something he'd missed for years. Clarity. His brain was free. Free from the iron shackles of drunkenness.

Four years after his arrival on that cold windy day, he stood in front of the police station he now commanded. A journey to redemption, inspired by a dumb NOVA documentary on abandoned ghost towns.

Quinn strode inside the department and said his good mornings. He complimented Rose Remington's appearance. His deputies approached, asked about his night, then went back to working, talking, or pulling on their gear and clipping in their weapons. Stepping into his office, he noticed a FedEx package resting on his desk. Rose followed him inside with her notebook.

"Happy birthday, chief. Oh, that came for you this morning. Overnight delivery. I thought I would just put it on your desk." Quinn weighed the package in his hand. "Hmmm," he hummed thoughtfully. Pulling the package open, he uncovered a pink box. "Oh, boy," he exclaimed excitedly, rubbing his hands in glee. Upon opening the box, he found an organic carrot cake from Pepe's bakery.

"Oh my god, Miá," he muttered. "You're a goddess." He looked at Rose, eyes lit with glee. "Dig in, Rose."

Rose smirked. "Maybe you should've married her."

"Rose, we'd end up killing each other." He opened a small pink greeting card. *Happy Birthday Devil Dog, xxxooo - Miá and Pepe.* Enthusiastically cutting a healthy slice and placing it on his desk, he then closed the box, pushing it toward Rose. "Rose, take this out onto the floor. Tell everyone to enjoy."

Squeezing past Rose as she gathered up the cake for the deputies and staff on the floor, Deputy Callen McClure plopped down into the chair across from Quinn and opened up a small notebook. McClure, a tall lanky deputy with short cropped red hair and an ingenuous face of fading freckles, crossed his legs, pulled a pen from his pocket, and flipped through notes. For reasons as mysterious as black holes and oceanic trenches, McClure had earned the nickname Fig. It was just one of those names that left a set of lips one day, grew in size, and stuck.

Fig ran through the night's activities. Two DUIs, domestic disturbance, drunk and disorderly, four speeding tickets, and a bonfire party at the Old Ghost Town.

"Bonfire party?" Quinn asked, frustrated. "That's federal property. Don't they know that?"

Fig shrugged. "Dumb high schoolers, chief. Probably not."

"Fig, those buildings are falling down. It's dangerous out there."

Fig continued. "Yes, boss, it is. Also, a missing person's report was called in."

Quinn sat back. "Don't tell me. The ghost town?"

"No, someone from Pangea. A couple of his coworkers called it in. But what's weird, boss, is we incarcerated this guy last week. The company posted bail and you know, those Pangea assholes showed up in their black Suburban and took custody of the guy."

Studying his deputy, he folded his hands behind his head. "Well, I don't see how that's a missing person, Fig. I mean, the company always does that, and two days later the moving van shows up and they're sent somewhere else."

"Want me to follow-up with the Pangea folks?"

Quinn thought for a moment, then told Fig to make a few calls. See if they can locate the guy and move on. Waste little time on it. What happened at the Pangea complex was none of their business and, much like the Old Ghost Town, the Pangea complex sat on federal property. Not their jurisdiction. Besides that, Pangea employees pumped a lot of dollars into Woodrock's economy. He didn't want to rock the boat. What happened at that facility stayed at that facility as far as he was concerned.

Fig finished jotting notes and looked at Quinn. "You know, boss, most of these infractions are Pangea employees."

"What're you getting at?"

Fig shrugged. "I dunno," he said, glancing past Quinn and out to the Main Street in front of the station. "They seem super-stressed all the time. I'm glad I don't work for a big corporation like that. Seems like it'd suck big time."

"It probably does," Quinn replied, smacking keys on the keyboard. "Don't spend a lot of time on the missing person, okay?"

Quinn departed the station in the afternoon, driving out to the Old Ghost Town. Rolling down the window of the police SUV, he let warm spring air splash his face, and the sweet aroma of fresh prairie grass dazzled his senses. Rounding the Kurtz Curve, he descended toward the vast plain below where lay upon it the crumbling collection of abandoned buildings. The sprawling Pangea complex, built on a broad plateau, overlooked the Ghost Town below like a guardian sentry, its tall manufacturing buildings and multistoried office structures glistening in the late afternoon sun with waves of shimmering light.

Quinn pulled off the highway, driving down the pothole-peppered road to the security gate that cordoned off the ghost town. He stepped out of the SUV and walked along a rusted fence line struggling to remain upright. Stepping up to the tall cyclone gate, still safely padlocked, he gave it a tug and a push, and the old gate complained in groans and creaks as the hinged section bowed outward. A gap appeared. A gap that any high schooler could easily slip through.

If the federal government didn't want trespassers, he thought, they should spend a little more money on security. And since they consider the ghost town to be a historic landmark, maybe they should fix the place up and let tourists in.

He took a step back, placing his hands on his hips. Falling into a moment of reflection, he recalled how four years earlier he'd seen this wretched town on a NOVA special through a drunken haze in some faraway place in a faraway time.

Stepping back into the SUV, he backed out and left for the station in a cloud of gray dust.

QUINN WORKED WELL INTO the evening, signing paychecks, sorting police reports, and organizing his paperwork for the following day. Leaning back in his chair, he dragged his hands down his face and exhaled a long breath. A framed photo of Alexx and Beatrice sat on the corner of his desk, Beet holding up her *student of the year* certificate with a beaming smile crossing her sweet face. He missed them both dearly. The hollow emptiness of losing Alexx had not yet fully faded from his thoughts.

His mind wandered back to the Old Ghost Town and the bonfire parties. Those kids are morons, he thought. One misplaced match and that whole town would go up in flames and take everyone inside with it.

Quinn bid his deputies a good night. Stepping out into the cool night air, he felt an urge to pay another visit to the Old Ghost Town.

Completely fatigued, this urge confused him, and a brief mental debate took place. Finally relenting to instinct, he sighed. “Whatever,” he grumbled, climbing back into the SUV. He backed out of his spot, beginning the 35-minute drive back along the dark highway to the old abandoned town.

CHAPTER 7

WAVE GOODBYE TO MA' and pa' cause, with the birds I'll share

With the birds, I'll share this lonely viewin'

Stroking her legs daintily with a Lady-Bic razor, Pippa hummed a Red Hot Chili Peppers verse from the hot, steamy shower.

A small dribble of soap wound its way into her eye. "Ouch!" The razor dug into her flesh. "Double ouch!" Raspberry blood swirled around the drain as she rinsed stinging soap from her eye. "Goddammit," she grumbled.

She dabbed the two small Lady-Bic incisions with the bath cloth, relieved they were high up on her inner thigh. A short skirt and pumps were on the fashion menu for this wonderful Friday. She didn't need her business-sexy fashion parade marred by two SpongeBob Band-Aids.

As she toweled herself dry, Pippa fantasized about gate-crush-Chris asking her to step out of her car. Of being frisked by those rough hands and thick forearms. Of brain-thirsty zombies marching the long winding drive to the gate, seeking Pippa's brain-flesh. Of Chris mowing them all down with his fancy rifle, throwing her into his truck like a pillow, and driving her to safety as she leaned over and undid his belt and fly.

A casual fling with Chris would be fun, she thought, wrapping the towel around her head. The sex? Oh, my god. Spectacular! Intellectually?

Suffocating boredom. He probably watches NASCAR at Dave and Busters, and drinks domestic beer from a plastic cup. But boy oh boy, she sure would like to run her hands up and down those arms of his.

Pippa applied blush and mascara, then shuffled into her bedroom, opening her closet, pulling out a gray, figure-hugging knee-length skirt, and selecting a black silk turtleneck as an accompaniment. Stepping in front of the mirror, she ran her hands down her body. Nice hips. Buoyant breasts. Hair falling along her shoulders like a waterfall of strawberry-blonde silk threads. She moved her head left and right, inspecting her face. Full lips. Slightly plump cheeks. Large emerald eyes. I'm no sex goddess, but I'm pretty goddammed cute, she thought. Today, I'm going to be smokin' business hot.

As she dressed, Oscar meowed and clawed the bed. The orange tabby seemed anxious - chirping and clawing and clinging to Pippa all morning long. She tried her best to soothe him as she pulled a pair of red lacy panties from the dresser along with a matching red lacy bra.

"Go big or go home."

She pulled black stockings up her legs, stepped into a pair of black pumps, and admired herself in the mirror. "Oh yeah, business sexy. You go, girl. Feel the power." Then she put the finishing touches of blush on her cheeks. I'd better turn heads today, she thought. I'd better turn Chris's head. If I don't, this all goes in the trash. She placed her oversize eyeglasses on and examined her new style.

World, get ready for a hot nerd!

PIPPA ARRIVED AT THE security gate at 6:50 a.m., only to find Rocky and a guard she hadn't seen before. Rocky approached the Subaru, twirling his hand in the *slowdown and stop and wind down your window and show me your badge* machinations.

"Where's Chris today?" she asked Rocky, trying to suppress the disappointment boiling up inside her.

Rocky checked his sheet and handed her badge back. "He's off today. You're good. Have a nice day." He waved the next car forward. Pippa's heart sank to her stomach. Of course, the one day Chris has off. Jesus Christ.

Shoving down hard on the accelerator, she sped toward the multi-storied parking garage. In the rearview mirror, she glimpsed Rocky watching her hastily leave the gate. Holding his dumb clipboard. Surprise on his dumb face.

Chris's MIA status aside, her style choice for this Friday wasn't a complete loss. Compliments abounded as colleagues mentioned her rarely seen business-power outfit. Striding through the corporate offices in building D, she sensed men's eyes roving up and down her body like TEA agents scanning for explosives.

After lunch, she attended the Friday *look-back look-ahead* strategy session. All the managers had to attend, and just for kicks and company, Pippa brought Kisha along as well. The two women sat at the far end of a long conference room table as Kim Cho, the soon-to-be married member of the posse, dispassionately read off one boring PowerPoint slide after another. Her red laser pointer moved from point to point. Chart to chart. Metric to metric.

Pippa had a brief thought. Kim was the lead MBA in corporate. Maybe she would know what this Iron Hand thing might be? She pushed that thought out of her mind. Iron Hand was none of her business. Being the manager of Global Innovation, she would have known about it if it was. New projects, especially cutting-edge technology projects, came to her team. Pulling her eyeglasses from her face, she wiped the lenses and did her best to show interest in Kim's lecture. For God's sake, Kim, Pippa thought. End it already. Everyone in this room is dying on the inside. Her mind wandered off while Kim droned on.

She imagined herself strutting through Dollie's Tavern in her hot fashion power ensemble. Stomping crushed peanut shells beneath her leather pumps and trolling for rednecks, she'd stride up to some tall cowboy at the pool table.

"Hey, Tex, wanna bang a hot nerd?" She'd say to him with a wink and a smile.

Pippa snorted, slapping her hand over her mouth, trying not to spit out the coffee she'd just swigged all over the conference table. *Wanna bang a hot nerd? Tex? Ha!* Trying to suppress the laughter while averting eye contact, she steadied herself, glancing at the faces around the room. Preet, her boss, stared at the slides projected on the wall with an odd, beguiling grin filling his face. Kisha, puzzled, stared at her. The other dozen attendees studied Pippa with blank expressions, waiting for her to share this hilarious revelation. Kim stood at the head of the table, glaring at Pippa and visibly annoyed.

Oh, lighten up Kim, Pippa thought. It's Friday...geez.

At 5 p.m., Pippa told her team to finish up any critical work, go home, and enjoy the weekend. Remaining in her office well after everyone left, the occasional janitorial staff emptying bins being the only sounds in a silent building, Pippa finished up a few emails and called it a night at 7:45 p.m. Massaging her sore stocking feet, the pumps had grown uncomfortable and her sexy, lacy underwear had bunched up in all the wrong places. She wondered to herself what the point of this Vanity Fair modeling session even was. But, she thought, everyone's entitled to a moment of vanity now and then. This was still fun. She'd caught some colleagues spying her legs and tush in the hallway. Mission accomplished.

Now to dive into some damned pajamas.

The guards waved Pippa on through the gate without inspection, and she drove down the long asphalt drive, merging onto the highway with a sliver of brilliant indigo on the horizon being all that remained of the day. Pippa admired the scene, shifting her vision from the road to the sky and back to the road. Chardonnay, Rachel Maddow's podcasts, and an impatient Oscar waited to greet her. This had been a long, long, strange week, and that mysterious Iron Hand e-mail, whatever it was, still bothered her.

As Pippa reached midway through the Kurtz Curve, the beckoning lights of Woodrock twinkling in the distance, she glanced at her rearview mirror. A pair of headlights suddenly appeared mere feet behind the Subaru. Startled, she sat straight, gripping the steering wheel.

"Where the heck did you come from?" She muttered. The headlights were now close enough to become hidden from view. She guessed the vehicle was a mid-sized pickup truck, driven by a numbskull. Agitated, Pippa toed the brake pedal. The Kurtz Curve was no place for macho driving games. She reached up, massaging her tense, stiffening neck. God, she thought, this idiot is really stressing me out.

In a matter of seconds, Pippa fought to just breathe. Something was wrapping itself around her throat.

Gasping for air, she tried to scream, barely managing a high-pitched whistle. Clawing at her skin and flesh, trying to free herself from a squeezing tentacle, her face grew hot, her skin turned a deep shade of purple, and her head felt as though it would burst like a melon. Lungs screaming in agony and pleading for oxygen, she moved her foot off the accelerator and pushed hard on the brake. Nothing happened. The Subaru did not slow.

A cyclone of panic whirled in Pippa's brain as she fought both her attacker and the Subaru, weaving and swerving and facing a deadly tumble down the steep slope of Kurtz Peak. Through her blurred vision, the headlights of oncoming cars appeared like glowing, evil eyes - their horns blaring as drivers tried to avoid the out-of-control Subaru.

Light. Sound. Confusion.

The truck tailing her backing off, its driver switched on their high-beam headlights; Pippa's rearview mirror exploding with bright white light. The tentacle tightened even more. No longer sensing up from down or right from left, like a spacecraft with no references tumbling off into a black void, a disoriented Pippa lost control.

Lacking a fully conscious driver controlling it, the Subaru shot across the highway shoulder and over the embankment. Weightless, and with a dark black void filling the windshield, Pippa sensed something was wrong. In the few seconds she remained airborne, her barely conscious brain arrived at a grim conclusion.

I think I've just been murdered.

Her car struck the steep, shrub-covered embankment with jarring force. Flipping over three times and smashing into a flat rocky outcropping, the wagon came to rest upside down, wobbling precariously on a ledge with 500-feet of steep, rocky hillside below it. One headlight of Pippa's crumpled Subaru still beamed upward and toward the heavens, fading as it rose into a deep black sky of twinkling stars and quiet, prairie night.

MAKING HIS WAY BACK to the Old Ghost Town, rounding the bend of the Kurtz Curve, something peculiar caught Quinn's eye. A single beam of light, to the left of him, shining upward and outward across the plain. Estimating the source of the light to be 50-yards from the shoulder of the highway, he slowed the SUV, passing through a fog of sandy dust settling onto the highway. A light gray Toyota pickup truck idled on the shoulder. The driver's side door opened, and a shadowy figure stepped out. Swinging the SUV into a U-turn, Quinn switched on the blue pulsing police lights. To his surprise, the figure dashed back into the truck, slamming the door shut and speeding away and out of sight.

Okay, that's not right, he thought.

Parking the SUV on the shoulder, he stepped out and jogged toward the source of the light. Shining his flashlight down the hillside, the beam illuminated large chunks of freshly churned soil and the twisted bumper of a car. He pulled his radio up.

"Dispatch, this is Unit One. I may have a vehicle accident on the highway, southbound, backside of Kurtz Curve, about twelve miles north of town. Over."

A voice crackled back. "You need assistance Unit One? Over?"

Quinn moved his flashlight further down the hillside, following a trail of debris into the darkness below. "Roger, send paramedics and fire. Over." As he slid down the steep slope, digging his heels into the hardened rock and soil, he overheard the dispatcher radioing out his requests.

Following the debris, and using Pippa's headlight beam as a guide, he came to a ledge where a crumpled Subaru rested upside down, creaking and groaning and hissing. Sprawled out on the rock below the open driver's door, lay Pippa. Her glazed eyes wide like saucers, her waxy skin alabaster, she could've passed for a store mannequin.

He stumbled forward, kneeling next to her body. "Ma'am, ma'am!"

Shaking Pippa's limp body, he got no response. He quickly assessed her condition. A gash above her eyebrow. Blueish lips. No pulse. He placed his ear to her mouth, and hearing nothing, ran his hands down her body from neck to feet. He felt a nub of bone pushing through the skin on her right thigh. Leaning over Pippa, he shined the light up inside her car. Finding no other victims, he radioed dispatch.

"Dispatch. I have a single victim with severe trauma. Request Life-Flight out here ASAP. Tell them to look for a spotlight. That's my position. Going off comms. Beginning emergency aid."

Leaning his light against a rock and fumbling with his switchblade, he cut Pippa's silk turtleneck down the middle, tore it open, cut her bra strap, and began chest compressions. One...two...three...four. One... two...three...four.

ah, ah, ah, ah, stayin' alive, stayin' alive,

ah, ah, ah, ah, stayin' alive, stayin' alive...

He stopped and checked for a pulse. Nothing.

Ah, ah, ah, ah, stayin' alive, stayin' alive...c'mon honey, come back, come back to me.

Pippa's eyes fluttered open. Quinn shot up in wide-eyed shock.

"Oh my god," he muttered. He placed his ear to her lips, a soft gurgling sound emanating from deep within her. Suddenly Pippa's pupils constricted, their eyes met, and he froze.

Terror. Desperation. Panic. Words silently spoken through the eyes of a young woman lying on a cold slab of rock in the black of night fighting for her life. A wheezing sound squeezed through her clenched blue lips as if she were breathing through a straw. Her lips quivered and parted. She was trying to tell him something. He leaned over her, his muscles rigid and tense like steel beams.

"Envy," she whispered.

"Don't talk sweetie, just breathe," he replied encouragingly.

A final surge of adrenaline coursed through Pippa's veins, and in a swift move that caught him off guard, she reached up and grasped his collar with clenched fingers. Stunned by her incredible strength, he instinctively tried to pull himself away. Her desperate eyes searched his.

"Envy," she gasped. "Envy. They're all...dead."

Pippa's eyes drifted away, empty, staring off into the universe. Their grip on him now released, her arms flopped lifelessly to the ground.

"No!" He shouted. A searing pain shot through his heart. He was not losing this girl. Not tonight.

He began compressions again. Furious. Desperate. Grunts and frantic pace-keeping carrying through the still, dark night. Sirens wailed as paramedics and fire units approached from the highway above. Far off into the distance, the thwapping of helicopter blades sliced through the night air. Growing ever so closer as the crew searched for Quinn's position. Anxiety overpowered him. A memory. A pain. A familiarity that he never wanted to experience ever again. He wasn't just trying to save a woman from a rocky hillside in South Dakota. He was trying to save her from a desolate peak in the rugged mountains of Afghanistan. With diminishing hope, he continued chest compressions on a lifeless Pippa Simpson.

Paramedics and firefighters soon scrambled down the embankment. Opening their giant tackle boxes of medical equipment, they went to work. Muttering medical lingo. Checking for a pulse. Attaching wires to her chest. Feeding her oxygen. Triaging her shattered body. A paramedic secured a brace on Pippa's neck. Quinn sensed from the young paramedic's body language that the brace, by this point, was merely ceremonial. Shaking his head, the medic pulled the radio up to his mouth.

"Dispatch, this is Medic One."

"*Go ahead, Medic One...*"

"Cancel the Life-Flight."

Quinn knew at that moment, on that steep barren hillside, on that black moonless night, he'd lost her.

Quinn returned to his home, a modest single story near the edge of the Woodrock city limits, at 2 a.m.

He showered, collapsed onto the sofa, and switched on the television. CNN flickered on. A panel of five discussed climate change, heatedly arguing back and forth over who was ultimately responsible for the disaster of the millennium. The arguing panel cut to a clip of the Vice President speaking to an audience in Paris.

He sighed deeply. Pulling himself off the sofa, he stepped into the kitchen, opened the cabinet next to the sink, yanked out a glass, rinsed it under the faucet, then opened the cabinet to his right. Reaching inside, he pushed some sauces and seasonings around, and slid out a bottle of scotch. He unscrewed the cap and tipped the bottle, watching the amber fluid flow into the glass. Then he turned the glass over, dumping the scotch into the sink. He would repeat this act three more times before screwing the cap back on the bottle and placing it back in the cabinet.

An odd ceremony indeed.

He fixed a pot of coffee, shaved as he waited for it to brew, pulled on a fresh uniform, then drove back to the station.

A peace. A serenity. A quiet.

Not a harsh quiet, where one would expect sound, but a wondrous, peaceful silence, as if submerged in a pool of cotton. Weightless and floating through space, a deep velvet blackness surrounded her.

Where was she? What happened? Memories zipped through her consciousness like pulsing lasers. Memories of her parents. Of a playground. Of Kisha. Of Emma. Of Oscar. Visions and memories passing through her like a bullet train.

Her only physical sensation was a bitter cold. A cold from within, and not a cold on her skin. In fact, she couldn't feel any skin at all. Or legs. Or arms. Or even a physical body.

This was all so peculiar.

A light appeared ahead of her, growing in brightness. Then an opening appeared, bordered by the purest gold light she'd ever seen. She felt as if something or someone was pushing her toward it. Then she was floating above a hillside. A woman lay sprawled on the rocky ground. This woman seemed familiar to her. Then she realized she was the woman, her eyes wide and lifeless and staring into nothingness.

A man came into view. A man in a uniform. Like a police officer. He touched her, spoke to her, began pushing on her chest with his hands. Weightless and free, she floated above this odd scene.

Am I dead? Pippa wondered to herself. Is that what this is?

The officer pushed her chest over and over. Frantic. Panicked. Then she flew toward this scene at incredible speed.

Pippa's vision returned. The man hovered over her, eyes in transfixed amazement, and she felt her body once more. Fighting to breathe, the tentacle gripping and crushing her throat, her brain released a torrent of adrenaline. Reaching up, she clutched onto the officer's shirt collar with all her strength.

I'm not done. Don't let me go. Keep me here with you. Please.

Filled with elation, the officer's eyes were as wide as full moons. She sensed his heart tugging at her own. An emotion that she'd never felt before. Pleading to stay on this earth with him, a tether bound them together. She had to tell him what she thought had happened.

Someone bad did this to me.

Someone terrible.

Sensing a world fading, she uttered the only words she could think of as random memories bombarded her subconscious.

Envy. They're all dead.

Once more, she felt herself floating above the scene. The officer pushed and pushed and pushed on her chest, and she sensed his pain and his fear and his desperation.

More men arrived, and the opening vanished. Once again, the ice-cold sensation filled her.

Moving at tremendous speed, Pippa flew through a strange, endless corridor. On one side was the most beautiful fluorescent blue - warm, soft, and tender. On the other side of her, the purest darkness she'd ever seen. Gold-tinged doors opened and closed, and she saw her mom and dad asleep in their bed, Oscar curled up on the couch, and the police officer with his head buried in his hands. Oddly, she felt his pain and sorrow.

Where am I? What is this place? Is this heaven?

Pippa zoomed through an infinite space of alternating light and darkness, of love and hate, of compassion and apathy. Fleeting memories passed through her like bolts of lightning, and a billion voices chattered at once - strange, crying voices, all emanating from a place she could not see.

Chapter 8

Many decades before Pippa Simpson's mysterious death, Colonel William "Bulldog" Kurtz straddled a worn buffalo hide saddle and scanned the horizon. Muscles twitching away flies, his Appaloosa steed nibbled blanched tendrils of switchgrass. A southerly wind blustered in alternating crackles and dull rumbles.

Beneath cotton puff clouds drifting across an azure sky, Kurtz raised his binoculars, surveying the vista from the crest of a steep hill strewn with shattered shale and clumps of drab foliage. Saddled next to the Colonel, on his bronzed Arabian Stallion, Lieutenant Andy Bishop wondered to himself why in the hell he was even in this godforsaken land.

Traveling eastward by train from The Presidio, in San Francisco, the two men had arrived in Rapid City a week earlier, where Kurtz took command of a contingent of soldiers. Tasked with a reconnaissance mission into South Dakota, the Army supplied Kurtz's small expedition with trucks, trailers, horses, and two weeks' worth of provisions.

On the morning of their departure for the great frontier, Kurtz, 5-foot-8 inches tall and stoutly built like an oak cask, paced back and forth in front of his men. His Army Bolling hat pulled down to brow level, barking orders in an expletive-filled speech through clenched bulldog jowls, he strutted before his soldiers as if he were preparing to storm the Bastille.

The object of this expedition was nowhere near as daunting as this performance art made it out to be. Army brass had sent the expedition to find a flat area in a remote location, with sustained prevailing winds that would be suitable for an airfield. The intended use of this airfield would be to train pilots and mechanics in relative secrecy, and away from prying eyes.

He told his men this was an opportunity to "rough it a bit." To become "real frontier men instead of rifle-toting daisy-pullers." But what Bulldog Kurtz privately thought about this mission, and muttered under his breath within earshot of Lt. Bishop, was that this search was a complete waste of time and resources.

Never passing up an opportunity to complain about the Army's growing arsenal of warplanes, someone had once quoted Kurtz as saying aircraft were "flimsy death-traps dropping little bombs and never where you need them." On another occasion, he claimed that "the only good they do is shoot each other down. Nothing will ever replace a finely trained soldier and a well-placed artillery shell." The Imperial Japanese Army was torching its way through China, and the U.S. Army needed more men with rifles and more artillery. Not fragile, temperamental airplanes.

So, on this blustery, parched afternoon in the late spring of 1937, Bulldog Kurtz gazed through his binoculars at a windswept plateau northeast of the Black Hills in South Dakota. With the dry breeze at his back, he surveyed ample space for a runway, airplane hangars, and support buildings. And below this broad plateau, he made out a level area for housing the men and their families. Twisting around in his saddle, he searched south. If a rail spur from the main rail line a hundred miles to the south were established, men and equipment would be transported back and forth by train.

"What do you see, Andy?" Kurtz asked Bishop as he handed his binoculars to the Lieutenant. Bishop, swayed the glasses from west to east. "Honestly, sir, I see little of anything."

Kurtz grabbed the glasses back and scowled. "You've got no imagination, Andy."

A year later, government troops and rail workers laid down a rail spur, and in 1939 construction of the airfield began. Completed in 1940, P-40 Warhawks and Curtiss Bi-planes throbbed around the once peaceful South Dakota skies like circling hawks.

Kurtz visited the new airfield, bustling with men and equipment and shiny new airplanes, on the year of its completion. Pleased with what he'd helped create, Kurtz still growled to everyone within earshot that airplanes were nothing more than a fleeting fancy. He became visibly distraught when he learned they'd named the airfield after General John J. Pershing, a true-blue American Doughboy.

"The day airplanes win wars is the day war has become stupid," he exclaimed one evening, stumbling drunk at the base officers' club. As if anyone had ever thought war was anything but that.

On December 7th of the following year, war broke out with the United States after the Japanese Navy launched a surprise airborne assault on the U.S. naval base at Pearl Harbor. Just two months later, in Bataan, a Japanese Nakajima Kate dive bomber dropped a bomb on Colonel Kurtz's position, killing him and a dozen soldiers, proving irony can sometimes be a very dark mistress.

In 1950, just ten years after the Army had completed Pershing Army Airfield, a relatively new military branch, the United States Air Force, shut the airfield down. They cited airbase consolidation, poor strategic location, and impractical logistics support as their reasoning.

In six months, the base housing complex at the base of the plateau - homes, a library, a school, a post-exchange, a commissary, two clubs, and two churches - sat in a wind hollowed silence. Window shutters banging the sides of deserted homes with every unpredictable gust, only the gophers, coyotes, and antelope paid any attention to the sounds remaining in this abandoned town.

NEARLY EIGHTY YEARS AFTER the Air Force shuttered Pershing Army Airfield, Samir Singh stood upon that same shale-littered hill and trained his own binoculars on that same plateau Kurtz had so many years before. Honoring Bulldog Kurtz's own hubris, and under the protest of many cartographers, the geographical label of "*peak*" was generously applied to this steep, but otherwise insignificant hill bearing his name.

So, from the crest of Kurtz Peak, Singh panned along the crumbling concrete runway, now vanishing beneath the vegetation, and then to the crumbling hangars. Madison Sheppard, Singh's Executive Vice President of Operations, heroically keeping her silk headscarf from blowing off to Nebraska, cotton blouse and black slacks billowing and flapping in the wind like a schooner's sails, stood beside him.

Singh lowered his binoculars and turned to her, his eyes wide with childlike enthusiasm and grinning like an explorer who'd just uncovered long-lost ancient ruins. "What do you see, my dear!?" He shouted to Madison over the gusting wind. "Out there, on that bluff?"

"I see a lot of nothing, Sam!"

"That's because you lack imagination!"

A swift gust blasted them. Madison instinctively snatched her headscarf. Lips curled up in annoyance, she stared at Singh through large, bees-eyes sunglasses. "You do realize, Sam," she shouted over the wind, sweeping her hand along the horizon. "That all of this is federal land?!"

Singh pulled the binoculars back up, admiring the stunning vista. "You let me handle the federal government!"

Madison threw her hands up. "Well, it's your money!" She turned and trudged her way down the hillside to the waiting Land Rover, parked on the highway shoulder below them.

Singh stood on the crest of Kurtz Peak for another hour, using this time for self-reflection. He opened his arms, holding them outward as if they were going to catch a gust and carry him aloft. As he enjoyed the panorama circling him, he thought to himself. Kurtz Peak? Peak? This shale covered excuse for a hill? A tall hill, sure, considering the surrounding geography, but a hill by any other name. Samir Singh had seen *actual* mountain peaks. Massive, ice-cloaked mountains shooting skyward like shark's teeth, ripping open the sky. Summits reaching as high as the cruising altitude of a passenger jet.

An astonishingly fit man in his late thirties, Samir Singh had reached the crests of the Seven Summits - the tallest mountain peaks on each continent. He conquered Everest twice. Scaled the deadly, chiseled North Face of the Eiger. Free-climbed the rock face of El Capitan. Ascended the colossal Annapurna. Summitted the rock and ice juggernaut of Kanchenjunga. He'd stood atop K2. A pure brute of a mountain that nearly took his life in a massive avalanche.

Facing south, a patchwork of streets and buildings making up the small town of Woodrock appeared through a light haze. Well, it's still a pleasant view, he thought. He was just happy to be out in the elements again.

IN THE AFTERNOON, SINGH and Madison drove into Woodrock to have a look around. Having lunch at Old Dave's Cafe on Main Street, they enjoyed fresh sandwiches and sodas and chitchat with the owners, Old Dave and Gretchen, whose grandparents had been employees at the abandoned army airfield when it was abruptly closed.

"What if the airfield became active again?" Singh asked Old Dave. "What would you think of freshly paved town roads, more people, more business, new homes, and more money in your pockets?"

Gretchen, her stringy gray hair tied up in a grandma-bun, interjected with a bear-halting scowl. "We like our lives the way they are, friend. That damned government already screwed us once."

Singh matched her scowl with his broad, charming grin. "I see."

Madison shrugged and bit into her sandwich.

Deeply etched lines cutting through Old Dave's weathered skin like a highway map, he swept gnarled, calloused hands up and down his blue bib coveralls. "You one of them billionaires?" Old Dave bellowed. "Comin' here to buy up the land? You think yer gonna change Woodrock? Put a damned Starbucks on every corner? Give us supermarkets? Damned shopping malls?"

Singh tossed a potato chip into his mouth. "That is precisely what I'm going to do, Dave."

Old Dave and Gretchen asked if the two needed anything else, then stomped their way behind the counter.

After their late afternoon lunch, Singh and Madison strode into *Dollie's Tavern* for a quick drink before making the drive back to the airport in Rapid City. Dark-skinned Singh, in beige cargo pants and Patagonia jacket, and golden-haired Madison, dressed like she'd just left Bloomingdales, strutted through the tavern. Empty peanut shells crunching under their shoes, an odor of sawdust and beer wafting into their nostrils, gawking eyes followed them every step of the way. Singh found a small table and ordered two beers.

He leaned across the table. "What do you think?" He asked Madison.

Madison craned her head around. Everywhere she looked, men leered like predatory cats at a Damnatio ad bestias. "I think I'm in the Colosseum surrounded by lions on a forced diet." She shuddered. "For fuck's sake, Sam. They're undressing me with their eyes."

Singh ignored her concerns. "In five years, a new Pangea complex could be up and running. This town will have paved streets, new homes, and a Starbucks on every corner."

Tim McGraw's *Refried Dreams* suddenly blared through the tavern.

This picture ain't pretty. I'm ragged and dirty.

And wonderin' what I'm doin' here.

Leaving the jukebox for the bar, his gait rocking left to right, a rather large man in bib coveralls, a *Caterpillar* hat tilted back on his head, scowled at Singh. Then he grinned at Madison. Madison sneered back.

The man ambled past them and to the bar. She cupped her hands, shouting over the music. "You're totally nuts! We're in the middle of nowhere!" She glanced around the room. "And these people will hate you forever! Look at them! They think you're an alien! And not the illegal kind either!"

Bobbing his head to the beat of Tim McGraw, Singh looked around the tavern at farm hands, ranchers, and store owners. He held up his beer in a toast to everyone inside the bar. "They'll come around!"

He leaned over and clinked Madison's beer bottle. "Cheers!"

SINGH APPROACHED THE FEDERAL government the following month after he and Madison's small fact-finding expedition to Woodrock. Floating a proposal to lease the 89,000-acre run-down army airfield with the pot-holed, grass-riddled, concrete runway, he was nearly laughed off the call.

The following morning, he took his private jet and flew to Washington D.C., where he set up a person-to-person meeting with the head of the Department of the Interior. Sam Singh knew a thing or two about charm. And he certainly knew how to charm politicians. Especially those wanting to remain as politicians after the next election cycle.

A lease for the desolate land the old army airfield sat on was prepared and signed within a month. Samir Singh could do with the land as he pleased, no questions asked. No one cared about this no-man's-land in the heart of the good ol' USA. The region was nothing more than a rag-tag collection of farms and ranches and a redneck town named Woodrock, the most thriving businesses at the time being an old barn converted into a tavern, *Dollie's*, and *Jerry's Grain and Feed.*

Lying in wait underneath all that charm, good looks, and positivity, a malevolent monster lurked inside Samir Singh. Privately, he despised this world he lived in, envisioning a dark, dystopian future for humanity. The fate of human civilization looming ahead like a dark, sinister monster, something needed to change.

This world is stunningly, abhorrently cruel, a much younger Singh concluded one gloom-filled rainy evening. And human beings are singularly obsessed with themselves, wallowing in greed, apathy and hate. Suffering from an emotional breakdown on that dark, wet evening, everything rational about him flew off like doves fleeing a hunter's rifle.

That evening, just one day removed from a heart-wrenching tragedy, a distraught Samir Singh received an oddly well-timed call. On this call, a strange man spoke to him through what Singh figured was some sort of voice scrambler. He listened intently to this odd metallic voice as it spoke about world events, Singh's recent tragedy, and a vision he'd had that would change the world. The strange voice asked for a meeting the following day. No time to waste, the voice said. Time is not on our side.

An angry and cynical Samir Singh agreed, and they arranged a meeting between himself and this strange man for the following day. A man who referred to himself by just a single name.

Jupiter.

CHAPTER 9

IN THE FOUR YEARS Quinn had been in Woodrock, neither Rose nor Fig nor any of the deputies had seen their chief so distraught.

Gnawing his fingernails, Fig stood next to a fretting Rose. The two leaned against Rose's desk, observing Quinn, each debating internally whether to disturb their chief on what should've been a quiet Saturday morning, sleeping in, or sipping a dark roast.

Quinn looked like a serrated iron snare pulled taut against its springs, ready to snap shut on anyone venturing too close. Fig and Rose studied him in silence, neither uttering even a whisper. He massaged his temples in wide, eccentric circles. Folded his hands behind his head. Leaned toward his monitor. Leaned back in his chair. Spun around and faced the window, gazing out onto Main Street like a shell-shocked soldier.

"You're going to chew those things off," Rose muttered, nodding at Fig's fingers while absentmindedly biting her own lip.

"You going in there?" Fig asked. He'd rather rock-paper-scissors than volunteer to be the first in Quinn's office.

"I'll give him a few minutes," came the soft response from Rose. Ronan Quinn, her chief, seemed consumed by Pippa Simpson's tragic accident on the Kurtz Curve. After all, these things rarely happen here.

When Pangea Dynamic Solutions arrived and built their enormous facility where the abandoned army airfield had once stood, the population of the small farming community of Woodrock exploded. In a matter of just a few years, the town grew from eleven-hundred to *twelve-thousand.* With more people came more accidents, crime, and casualties. Until Samir Singh appeared at Dave's Cafe years earlier, with plans to turn Woodrock into a Silicon Valley wannabe, accidents, crime, and casualties had been as common as hundred-year floods.

In 1964, sixteen-year-old Mary Glover went missing while walking to her rural home after school. She just vanished from the earth, never to be seen again. For decades, journalists, authors, documentary filmmakers, and amateur sleuths from around the world traveled to Woodrock to crack this cold case. Theories of her disappearance ranged from kidnapping, to murder, to alien abduction.

In 1982, the Knudson boys set fire to the Poulsen's barn after a night of binge drinking. The raging inferno burned two horses and a dog alive. Found guilty of arson, Kik Knudson served five years in the penitentiary and Kik's two younger brothers, Cam and J.R. each served probation. After his release, Kik returned to Woodrock, where he still lived to this day, working as a ranch boss for those very Poulsen's whose barn he'd burned to the ground.

In 1998, a freak tornado roared through the region, obliterating five homes. Four townspeople died in that storm, with twelve injured. A grim reminder of nature's relentless strength and fury.

In 2004, a tanker truck carrying chlorine gas overturned on the highway. Authorities evacuated Woodrock for nearly a week.

Indeed, incidents, accidents, and crime mysteries were once as rare as prairie bison, with each incident becoming a sort of legend. Tales passed down from generation to generation over cold beers at Dollie's Tavern, modestly enhanced at each telling. Even to this day, a random sleuth would appear in town, trying to crack the case of Mary Glover's shocking disappearance.

When Samir Singh and Pangea Dynamic Solutions completed construction of their new state-of-the-art facility just three years after Singh had stood atop a blustery Kurtz Peak, the Woodrock Old Timers witnessed a sea change.

Bib coveralls and John Deere baseball caps vanished in an ocean of North Face jackets and slim-fit jeans. At Dave's Café, where once farmers and ranchers chatted about crop reports and farmers' almanacs, suburbanites now hunched over their lunches, gazing at their iPhones. They held Zoom Meetings, speaking in loud voices to unseen people in places like New York, Menlo Park, Singapore, and London. The Old Timers now cohabitated with scientists, engineers, and MBAs, whose rush-rush hectic lives were as familiar to them as the far side of the moon.

Dragged to this vast empty land by their employer, Pangea employees changed Woodrock into a metropolis more suited to their own needs; overhauling the entire landscape. A golf course. A public pool. An outdoor mall. A brand-new subdivision with new modern homes. Pangea viewed this makeover as progress. The Old Timers viewed it as urban colonization.

Yet the mishaps, petty crimes, and casualties Quinn had handled in this budding new metropolis were still a far cry from New York. And an even further cry from Afghanistan. But an elementary school, Central Park, and a night in Helmand Province had all staked claims in his consciousness. These tragic episodes in his life refused to set him free. They represented all that was cruel and vile and wrong with the world. Now a fresh new nightmare had arrived. Pippa's dying words. Her desperate eyes. Her broken body.

To Fig and Rose, and practically everyone in town, Ronan Quinn was a hardened combat veteran and seasoned big city homicide detective. He'd seen death and destruction his entire adult life. How could a car crash possibly affect him in this way? What triggered him? Had Fig and Rose shared in those vivid recollections stored away in Quinn's brain, they'd have better understood his odd behavior after a simple car accident on the Kurtz Curve.

Quinn spun his chair back to his desk and glared at the two watching him from the relative safety of Rose's desk outside the door. He called for Fig to step into his office. Fig's shoulders drooped as he traipsed inside, quietly closing the door behind him. No loud noises, Fig thought. No sudden moves. Avoid eye contact. But Fig's attempts to keep the hornet's nest from stirring fell flat. The tempestuous police chief erupted like a volcano.

"Why has the state not put road reflectors up on their damned highway, Fig?!"

Fig's freckled face blushed a shade of crimson. He tried to shrug, and not shrug, at the same time.

"People at the Pangea complex work late hours, Fig," Quinn growled through clenched teeth. "They're tired, or texting, or just not paying attention. Then they roll their cars down that goddamned hill." His eyes narrowed with anger and frustration. He leaned forward, smacking the desk. "Now a young woman is dead!" He shouted. His booming voice carrying through the office walls, the deputies on the floor froze in place. "All because of red tape and fucking bureaucracy! How hard is it to stick a goddamned reflective stick into the ground?"

Fig swallowed. Frozen in place like a Greek statue, he waited for the storm to abate and after a couple of minutes, Quinn went from boiling to simmer.

Glaring at the computer monitor, Quinn seemed distant. He spoke of the gray Toyota that sped away from Pippa's accident. He didn't have time to get the plate number, but he sure remembered the model, make, and color. So, he asked Fig to look into all the gray Toyota pickup trucks registered in town and then for the entire state. He figured the model was recent, and that should narrow his search.

"That could still result in hundreds of hits," a nervous Fig reminded Quinn. "I mean, Toyota pickup trucks are about as popular as they get."

"I don't care," Quinn responded grittily. "The son of a bitch left the scene of an accident. Go find him."

Fig fled Quinn's office like a startled gazelle. "Don't go in there," he warned Rose. "He looks homicidal." Fig's face had shifted from crimson to a pale freckled cream.

Rose tilted her head at Fig and winked. "I'll be fine, dear," she said confidently. "I've seen worse." She swept her notepad off her desk and strode into Quinn's office, softly closing the door behind her.

Quinn grumbled, smacking keys on the keyboard. "DOT is out at the crash site," he told her, frenetically pecking at keys. "They're starting their investigation. Send a message out on the broadcast system that the highway is closed and post it on the website."

Rose quietly studied Quinn; his jaws clenched so tight they could crack concrete. "Want to talk about it?"

"Talk about what?" Quinn muttered. He didn't seem to process what Rose was asking of him.

"Last night? Do you want to talk about the accident?"

Quinn shook his head. "There's nothing to talk about, Rose."

Rose knew better. She'd been his confidant since the day he showed up, towing a trailer and looking like a worn bath rug. This accident triggered something inside of him.

"Sure, sweetie. I'll be outside if you need anything." Rose waited for him to respond. He kept tapping and reading and tapping.

She stepped out and closed the door.

Quinn and Fig drove out to the accident scene at 8:30 a.m., cruising along the shoulder in the police SUV, and past a traffic jam of highway travelers stretching for two miles.

They arrived at where Pippa's Subaru had departed the highway. Digging their shoes into the hard rock and soil of the hillside, they steadied themselves with the safety ropes firefighters had secured during the night. Just prior to Quinn and Fig's arrival, the tow company had pulled Pippa's crumpled orange Subaru wagon back onto its wheels. Now the small wagon peered up the face of the hillside, awaiting rescue from the rock ledge.

The impact with the side of the hill, and resulting flips, contorted the Subaru's frame and forced the wheels into weird, obtuse angles. The sheer force and energy of the impact amazed even Quinn. Amazing further yet, was that Pippa freed herself from the wreck. A testament to a Subaru's durability, he surmised. Quinn stepped to the edge of the rock platform where the Subaru came to rest and peered down the hillside. If she hadn't hit that ledge, the Subaru would've continued down the hill for hundreds of more feet. It may've been days before anyone even located Pippa.

Fig went about snapping pictures of the scene. He stepped over to a small heap of Pippa's personal effects retrieved from the car. "Do we know who she is yet?"

Quinn nodded, solemnly. "Yeah. Pippa Simpson. I recovered her driver's license before I left last night."

"Oh," Fig responded.

CLAMBERING BACK UP THE hillside, the Subaru was soon hauled up after them. The steel cable grating against rock, the Subaru's frame making squeals and grinds, the winch whining, the truck's diesel engine rumbling, a disorientating mechanical cacophony caused Quinn's head to throb. He turned to the highway, watching the team from the DOT wheel their measuring devices along the road. Orange safety-vested asphalt detectives traced a pair of rubber tire marks as they vanished off the shoulder and into the great expanse. With his fists clenched, he stormed toward an investigator.

"Hey!" he shouted over the din of the winching operation. "Hey you!" he shouted again. Anxious and tense, Fig watched his chief stomp toward the DOT team, trying to grab the attention of the investigators.

"We need reflectors on this curve! When are you people going to get it through your thick skulls?!" A younger man wearing black-rimmed rectangular glasses, attempted to ignore the belligerent chief. "This curve is dangerous," Quinn continued. "Jesus, the sun is right in your fucking face at sunset," he growled, waving his hand along the horizon.

"Look, we get it. Okay?" The investigator replied, stepping away, and trying in vain to avoid Quinn. "We don't enjoy doing this either. But you have the wrong department."

"Well, when you get back, file your report, find the right department, and light a fire under their ass. This has happened too many times."

The investigator nodded agreement. "Understood. Look, there's something we've seen that's interesting."

Quinn placed his hands on his hips. "Well, what is it?"

"There're signs the vehicle may have been out of control for some time, starting well over a mile back." The investigator pointed back to where the Kurtz Curve vanished behind the hill.

Fig, listening in, added his thoughts. "Maybe she was on her cell phone? Maybe she fell asleep. Her phone is probably with her stuff."

Quinn told Fig to dig through Pippa's personal effects and locate her phone. After that, pull records from the local cell tower. The Subaru was pulled onto the shoulder with loud crunches and clangs, the screaming winch and revving engine of the truck relenting.

He looked on as the tow company pulled Pippa's car onto a flatbed trailer. Out of control for an entire mile? This new information perplexed him. Maybe she lost steering, or her brakes. Maybe the mystery Toyota knows something?

SIX ADVIL'S AND TWO coffees later, at 2:30 p.m., Quinn's temper abated into exhaustion. Rose stepped through the door, her lips quivering as she dabbed each cheek with a Kleenex. Her blue sullen eyes and high bony cheeks glistened with tears.

"I've notified the woman's parents in San Jose," she said, her tone subdued and sullen.

He looked up at Rose, and seeing her pain, his heart dropped. A pain he knew all too well.

"Sorry, Rose," he said in an assuring voice. "I know that's tough stuff. I've made those calls myself. Thank you. I'll follow up with them before I go home."

At 5 p.m., Quinn called Pippa's parents back in California. Warbling and every third word indiscernible, her father's voice was barely audible. Pippa's beleaguered mother lay catatonic in her bed, having taken a heavy dose of sedatives. He explained to Pippa's father that the Woodrock Police Department stood by to assist. Rose would make all the arrangements to have Pippa's remains and personal effects sent back home to San Jose.

"I really appreciate that, Chief Quinn," Pippa's father replied. "But her company has already called us. They told us they are taking Pippa to

Chicago. They've made all the arrangements for us to pick her up there and bring her back home. They also said they would mail us all her personal effects."

For a moment, Quinn sat frozen, trying to process this statement from Pippa's father. Leaning back in his chair, he scratched his head. No one from Pangea had called him laying out this plan of theirs. Pippa's remains, being an employee of Pangea aside, were still in *his* custody. And who even notified Pangea of the accident?

He gave his condolences to Pippa's father and ended the call. He dialed Rose's desk. Confusion filling his head, he asked her to come see him.

"Has Pangea called you? Have they said anything about picking up Ms. Simpson's remains and taking them to Chicago?"

Rose shook her head. "No. But that seems odd. They assigned her here, so maybe they cover expenses and make arraignments."

"But why Chicago? Why not just send her back to California? Why the extra stop? Can you or Fig reach out to Pangea, and then tell them to call me, please?" He thought for a moment. "And when you speak with them, just say her remains are still at the coroner's office. I won't be releasing her until Bob McConnell has completed his report. At least 24 hours."

Rose's head tilted, her eyes narrow and gleaming. "What're you thinking, Ronan?" she asked. "I can see that you're thinking about something. Do you have questions about this accident?"

He leaned back in his chair. "Maybe, maybe not, Rose. I just don't like being kept in the dark."

Rose smiled. "I'll make the call."

SHORTLY AFTER ROSE LEFT his office, Bob McConnell, the county coroner, called.

"Hey, Ronan," Bob asked. "Can you, um, can you come over to my office? I need to show you something."

"This sounds mysterious, is this about the accident victim from last night?"

McConnell repeated for him to come over to his office, and to hurry. "I got a call from someone at Pangea. They're on their way to collect the victim."

Quinn slammed the phone down, grabbed his jacket, and dashed out of the office. "If anyone needs me, I'm at Bob McConnell's office," he told Rose, flashing past her desk.

Jesus, he thought. These Pangea guys move fast. And they still haven't called me!

CHAPTER 10

HURRYING DOUBLE-TIME DOWN Main Street, Quinn passed by the Roman-inspired courthouse and the shoebox-inspired county jail. Ditching the sidewalk entirely and jogging across freshly cut grass, he approached the Woodrock Civic building as startled pigeons, squawking and cooing, fluttered into the air.

He ran up the steps, pushing his way through the double glass doors. Shoes echoing in the large, empty, forum, he passed the darkened Chamber of Commerce office and the security desk and on to the coroner's office. He burst through the doors. Bob McConnell's young assistant shot up from his chair.

"Oh, hi chief. Dr. Mc...."

Quinn brushed past the startled assistant, bursting into a cluttered office smelling of aging books, burned coffee, and Febreze tropical orchid scent. From behind an emerald-oxidized framed photo of McConnell posing with an 800-pound marlin strung from a crane, sat McConnell himself. Quinn, huffing and puffing, loomed over the coroner.

McConnell leaned back in his chair. "You need a minute to recover?"

Quinn yanked a chair back and sat down. "I ran here, Bob. Why do you ask? Because you told me to hurry. What've you got?"

"I'm fine, thanks for asking." McConnell pushed a folder across the desk to Quinn. "Here's my preliminary report on last night's fatality."

Quinn placed his reading glasses on, eyeing McConnell suspiciously from over the frames. Opening the folder, he skimmed through the report.

Wait. What? Confused, he looked up from the report and tapped at the top of the page. "I thought this was for the accident victim from last night? What is this, Bob?"

"It is from the accident, Ronan."

Quinn stared at McConnell with an expression of still lingering confusion. He slapped the report down, tapping at Box 5: *Cause of Death.*

"Asphyxiation *and* blunt force trauma? What does that mean?" Quinn, wired on caffeine, sedated by Advil, and sleep deprived, displayed red-faced annoyance. "Asphyxiation from what?"

"All things being equal, I would rule this a homicide by strangulation."

A perplexed Quinn slumped back in his chair. Has Bob lost his ever-loving mind? Was it time for the old coroner to retire to Costa Rica? This was insane. He'd been to the accident scene, not McConnell. He saw Pippa's injuries. He saw her destroyed car. There was no "strangler" in the car with her. If there had been, they'd have been in the morgue along with Pippa.

"Well, Bob," Quinn said beneath raised eyebrows. "Far be it from me to question your skill in these matters, but no one else was at the accident scene. If someone strangled her in her car, there would've been a second victim. No one was walking away from that."

"Precisely."

Quinn shook his head. "Precisely? What do you mean, precisely? The woman was in an accident. Now you're saying homicide." Placing his finger on the desk, he made a long arch to another point on the desk. "Accident.... homicide. That's a big leap, Bob."

Of course, there was a car accident, McConnell explained. But what led to the accident? What caused Pippa to leave the road? Was she distracted? Possibly. The infamous Kurtz Curve has claimed its fair share of distracted drivers and automobiles over the years. But McConnell, during his examination of Pippa's body, found things. Odd things. Things that made no sense. She displayed signs of oxygen deprivation, and an unusual amount of blood was in her eyes, signaling trauma prior to the accident. He found no bruises around her neck, the typical signs of strangulation, but he found something else.

"There are lacerations on her throat and neck. She had tissue and blood under her fingernails. Her own tissue and blood."

A puzzled Quinn sank into his chair. "Defensive wounds," he muttered. "She was fighting off an attacker." He thought back to his visit at the scene that morning with Fig. "Now it makes sense."

McConnell removed his glasses and wiped the lenses. "What makes sense?"

"The guys from DOT told me the victim had lost control of her vehicle a mile before she left the road. But if she was being assaulted, and resisting, that means someone else would've been in the car. And we know there wasn't a perp in the car with her." He leaned toward the balding coroner. "Are you sure, Bob? Are you positive about this? This changes the entire picture. Could there've been anything else that could've done this?"

McConnell placed his eyeglasses back on his face and took the report back. "Sure, a peanut or a bee allergy. Swelling of her airways would cause something like oxygen deprivation. Ronan, I need more time for an examination. That's why I wanted you to hurry. Pangea-"

The office door flew open, smacking against the wall. Startled, Quinn twisted around in his chair. McConnell shot up from his desk.

Followed by the wide-eyed assistant, two men in black suits stormed into the office.

Quinn's first instinct was that these guys were from an agency. After all, who walks the streets of Woodrock in a suit and tie? Unless they're headed to a wedding or a funeral, no one does. Not even the heads at Pangea dressed in suits here. They all dressed like ads for REI.

"Can I help you?" McConnell stuttered.

Grabbing the elbow of a short, dumpy-looking man, the assistant repeated apologies while trying in vain to pull him back through the door. The man yanked his arm away and shot a burning glare at the assistant.

"Take your fucking hands off me," he grumbled threateningly.

Quinn's veins bulged in his temples. Through instinct, he closed his fists and stood.

With a patronizing smirk, the short, dumpy man stared up at Quinn. A squat 5-foot 10-inches tall, belly spilling over an optimistically tightened belt, cheap product greasing his hair to each side, the man looked as though he'd never worn a suit at any point in his life. His deep-set dark eyes shifted between Quinn and McConnell.

Towering beside him stood a shocking specimen of a human. The edges of a dark tattoo peeking over the man's shirt collar, his jacket's arms were at least 3 inches short of where they should be, and his black rayon tie was clearly a cheap clip-on. Thick rolls of flesh formed rungs from his collar to the base of his waxed, cue-ball head. Quinn got the impression this man had seen his fair share of time inside a jail cell, and he worked out his chances in a fight. About fifty-fifty, he thought. Momentarily thinking of taking the first swing, he decided instead to let this play out.

"We're here to pick up Pippa Simpson. You have her at the morgue."

Quinn glanced at McConnell. The coroner shrugged.

"Fella's, how about some ID's?" Quinn calmly asked.

The dumpy man pulled a wallet from his back pocket, displaying a Pangea security badge. Quinn looked over the ID and handed it back to him. "Thanks, Walter." Then he turned to the freakishly large human towering in the room. "How 'bout you, Zed. ID?"

"My name's not Zed, dickhead," he growled, and his sociopathic grin evaporated. Clenching his fists, he stepped up to Quinn.

"Are you threatening a peace officer?" Quinn glanced back at McConnell. "Bob, is he threatening me?"

"Looks to me he is, chief."

Zed's lips split into a grin. "Hmph, chief. Yeah, okay." He stepped back.

"Look guys," Quinn placed his hands on his hips, inching his right hand toward his holster. "We need something more than just company IDs. You're trying to collect a body, not your laundry."

Walter reached into his jacket pocket and Quinn unclipped the holster. Noticing Quinn's action, Walter shook his head, pulled out a folded piece of paper, stepped past Quinn, and thrust it at McConnell.

"A release authorization, Ronan." McConnell handed it to Quinn. The authorization was legit. Signed by Pippa's parents, someone at Pangea, and a court judge in Chicago. The raised seal at the bottom seemed authentic.

“I need a copy of this,” Quinn grumbled. The assistant, still frozen in the doorway, gladly grabbed the authorization and scampered off to make a copy.

“You know I still haven’t completed the full autopsy, right?” McConnell told Walter and Zed.

“We have our own coroner. Pangea will finish it.”

Quinn again glanced at McConnell, then back to Walter. “You guys have your own coroner?”

“Not ours, a contractor,” a smug Walter replied. Then, clearing his throat, Walter’s eyes drifted to the ceiling. “We at Pangea believe our employees are our greatest assets. Pangea is always ready to assist our employees and their families under all circumstances. We have employees across the globe, and it is our duty to assist in any way possible after this unfortunate accident.” Walter looked as if he were reciting a well-rehearsed poem. Quinn cringed.

“Don’t make this harder than it already is,” Zed grunted in a deep, raspy tone. “A family is grieving, so stop playing your little chief power game, bro.”

Quinn ground his teeth. “Well, we still have to run a tox report, Zed. Blood, tissue samples, hair - all that, you know, accident investigation stuff.” A dynamite keg with a fuse getting shorter, he felt McConnell’s hand grab his elbow. *Let it go.*

The bookish assistant rushed into the room, pushing his way between Walter and Zed, handing the photocopy to Quinn.

Walter thanked them for their time. Once more, he gazed thoughtfully at the ceiling. “We thank you for your cooperation, and your care and diligence with Ms. Simpson after this terrible accident.”

Seriously? Quinn thought. Accident? He keeps repeating that word. Had greasy Walter rehearsed this from a notecard in the car? He looked as if he could barely scrape together a meaningful thought on his own.

"We just popped by your station and grabbed her personal effects. Here's the court order. Maybe you should make a copy of that too." Walter handed the order over to Quinn.

What the hell, Quinn thought, sensing his authority as chief of police was being superseded by anyone with a pen on their desk. He looked the order over. Again, signed by Pippa's parents, a judge and someone at Pangea. It hadn't even been 24 hours and they had court orders from Chicago and signed releases from Pippa's parents all the way back in San Jose. Quinn thrust the order at the assistant, and he dashed off to make another photocopy. The repeated emphasis on Pippa's death being an accident still clung to Quinn's thoughts. He told Walter and Zed he expected Pangea's coroner's report ASAP. Then he could close the file on Pippa's death.

Walter and Zed agreed, but neither cared what Quinn did, nor did not, get. They were just there to do a job.

WALTER AND ZED LEFT in a black Dodge van to collect Pippa from the morgue for her trip to Chicago. Quinn watched the van U-turn and speed off down Main Street.

"You know I already collected blood and tissue, right?" McConnell muttered.

Quinn nodded. "Yep, Bob, I do. I was just trying to buy some more time."

"Okay," McConnell said. "Just so we're on the same page."

"When do you get the toxicology results?"

"I sent them to Dallas this afternoon. Today is Saturday, so we won't get them back until midweek."

Quinn shook his head. "It doesn't seem like soon enough. You know what I mean?"

McConnell turned to head back to his office. "I certainly do."

"Hey," Quinn stopped him. "You talk of this to no one but me. Okay? Not even Rose. Just me."

McConnell raised his hand and nodded as he walked up the path and back to his office.

WATCHING TWO TECHNICIANS SLIDE the polyethylene body bag into the back of the Dodge van, Walter cupped his hands and lit a cigarette. He had instructions to carry Pippa's body back to the Pangea complex, where Pippa was to be loaded into a private jet and flown to Chicago. Zed, towering over squat Walter, asked for a cigarette.

"Can't you buy your own?" Walter asked gruffly. He pulled a Marlboro from the pack, thrusting it at Zed.

"You believe this B.S. about the tox report not being done?" Zed asked.

Walter shook his head. "No way. First thing the M.E. does when he gets a body is pull hair, blood, and tissue."

"Oh, yeah," Zed said, sucking in a deep drag of smoke.

The two white-jacketed technicians slammed the van's doors closed, handing Walter a release waiver to sign. Walter scribbled his signature, thanked the technicians, and he and Zed climbed into the van.

Starting the engine, he checked the mirrors and pulled out of the parking lot.

"Toxicology report will come back clean. That chief is just being a dickhead. Lost his power." Walter took in one last deep pull of smoke and tossed the cigarette out the window. "They sent us to retrieve, and we did. Let's finish this and go grab some beers."

Chapter 11

From inside the drawer of a goldenrod nightstand next to the bed, a muffled buzzing penetrated his mind. Samir Singh opened his eyes, regaining focus as he emerged from his meditation.

A soft-green wall bordered with fancy red and gold trim.

A 40-inch wide 4K television.

A stack of folders piled on a desk.

A laptop.

A coffee maker.

A pair of pink panties and bra draped over the back of a leather chair.

A Pieter Bruegel 16th century oil canvas. Enchanted, Singh studied the painting. A pale blue sky speckled with puffy white clouds set the scene. Women and children lay lazily under an apple tree. Nearby, farmers scythed wheat in a field. In the distance, at the end of a winding dirt road, sat a windmill. He felt transported to that very place and time. The rich perfume of orchards. The aroma of freshly cut wheat. Millions of birds chirping. Insects buzzing. No cars. No planes. No phones. Personal connections. Dependency on one another for survival.

The buzzing came from the desk drawer again. Screw it, he thought. The painting's a cheap knockoff.

Unfolding his legs, Singh leaned up against the headboard. Seizing the opportunity as Madison Sheppard washed and hummed a tune from the shower, he opened the drawer, pulling the slender, black, secure communication device from beneath the hotel's complimentary King James Bible. Turning on the back-lit screen, a message appeared.

Red Lancer:

The job is not complete.

What? Singh thought, perplexed. He tapped his response on the device.

Kilimanjaro:

I thought it was done? I saw it on the news. Very unfortunate. Can you handle it? This time correctly?

Red Lancer:

We eliminated the problem, but a cop showed up. Sparrow didn't retrieve the package. I've sent two cleanup teams for retrieval. Probably have to eliminate Sparrow now. He's compromised. Dude was my best asset. We can't have these kinds of slipups. Jupiter is not pleased with this lack of attention to detail. You're the reason we have this problem. WTF.

Kilimanjaro:

You take care of Sparrow. I'll retrieve the package myself.

Red Lancer:

Don't bother. We can't have any more slipups. We can't have any more rogue e-mails sent through company servers. Can we now?

Kilimanjaro:

Fuck off. Freak.

Red Lancer:

Have a nice night. Asshole.

A flood of hot blood rushed to Singh's head. Teeth grinding teeth, he considered heaving the $6,000, specialty manufactured secure comm device at the knockoff Pieter Bruegel.

Waterproof to a thousand feet and resistant to extreme temperatures, his secure comm device was triple encrypted and indestructible. The NSA couldn't hack into it, and a submarine engulfed in flames a thousand feet underwater couldn't destroy it - as if such an implausible thing would ever happen. So, heaving the device at the wall in anger, trying to smash it into oblivion, would be fruitless. And only fifty of the gadgets even existed, distributed to Jupiter's most trusted council - The Five Horsemen, The Apostles, the Disciples, Red Lancer, and the chief designer and architect of their little project, Sam Singh himself.

Placing the device on the bed, Singh exhaled, dragging his hands through his hair. No more messages. No more thoughts. Just breathe. The shower in the bathroom slowed from a torrent to an echoing drip. He swept up the device, ensured it was off, and hid it under the bible in the desk drawer. The door to the bathroom swung open, and Madison emerged from the roiling steam in a flowered robe with a hotel towel wrapped on her head. The strain on Singh's face did not go unnoticed.

"What's wrong?" she asked.

"Nothing's wrong, my dear. Nothing at all," Singh responded, distant and subdued.

"I have this super-duper Captain America shield that's impervious to your bullshit." Madison sat on the bed, running her long fingers down his chest. "Seriously, what's wrong with you, sweetie?"

Singh sighed. "I'm tired of us only being together," he paused and thought about his words. "You know… 'together-together'… in hotel rooms. It's unbecoming."

"Hey, tiger," she said softly. "Discretion is your desire, not mine. You're the one that doesn't want his employees knowing he's banging the company's Veep."

Singh reached up and caressed Madison's silky cheeks. "I suppose you're right."

She stood, striding elegantly back into the bathroom, rustling through her overnight bag, and humming Journey's' *Don't Stop Believin'.'*

Madison, or their physical relationship, was not bothering Singh - this cock-up at Woodrock was. Another error. Another security snafu. Red Lancer was right in his assessment. Jupiter has a low tolerance for mistakes, and with what was riding on this Iron Hand project of theirs, mistakes could lead to disaster.

Chin dropping to his chest, Singh groaned.

What an absolute fucking mess. That stupid e-mail wound up where it shouldn't have wound up. On the wrong company server. Worse than even that, no one on that e-mail chain seemed to notice - everyone just merrily typing out Iron Hand secrets for all the world to see. Pippa Simpson had the unfortunate luck of being added to that e-mail in error. Singh knew this wasn't intentional. No one on the team was trying to leak Iron Hand out to the world. But people were getting sloppy. Rushing to get specimens ready. And about those damned specimens. They could be so frustrating. So temperamental. Just training them was like trying to teach Chinese Checkers to fruit bats.

Singh shut his eyes. That e-mail wound up in that poor, dear girl's hands. She read something she wasn't supposed to read, and though she may not have understood it, she'd still read it. Why did she open it? Why didn't she just stop when the e-mail asked for her pin number?

As much as Singh tried to blame Pippa's death on her irresponsibility, he couldn't. All roads led back to the Iron Hand team's carelessness. An e-mail was routed to the wrong server. If they'd paid attention, and done it the right way, no one could've added her to the e-mail to begin with.

This isn't good. People are making mistakes.

Singh had tried in vain to keep Pippa from participating in Red Lancer's favorite hobby. Assassination. But what was one woman's life? What was one human's life? Singh struggled with this reconciliation. He struggled because he couldn't reconcile anything. He wasn't even sure why. Pippa's death, her murder, her whatever it was - struck him as singularly heartless and cruel. After Rich, their top programmer, realized the e-mail had fallen into her hands, there was a debate about how to handle it. Security breaches were nothing new. And Red Lancer always dealt with them in some horrible fashion.

But in this case, Singh wanted to learn more about Pippa. He read her profile. Studied her CV. Gazed at the grinning woman with long strawberry-blonde hair and oversized blue-rimmed glasses. Graduate of Cal Poly. Master's degree from MIT. Promoted to manager, heading up the Global Innovation Department. Singh became lost in her profile picture. She looked sweet. Innocent. Intelligent. Even witty. Someone he'd like to have known. But Jupiter ignored Singh's pleas during this so-called debate, and gave the go ahead to Red Lancer to proceed, and as it turned out, Red Lancer was going to proceed, regardless. He'd already set everything in motion.

"As of tomorrow night," Jupiter chimed, his metallic voice ringing in Singh's ears. "Ms. Simpson will no longer be a threat. Move on, Sam. We've waited too long."

Seriously, that's what Jupiter referred to her as. A threat.

Gliding out of the bathroom, golden hair flowing like the tail of a comet, Madison stood at the edge of the bed. Her tantalizingly open bathrobe revealed large firm breasts, and perfectly groomed and endless legs.

She stood over Singh as he stared trance-like at the oil painting on the wall. Sitting down on the edge of the bed, she caressed his hair with long, slender fingers, snapping him from his trance. His sheepish eyes moved along her perfect, athletic figure.

"Are you even going to be able to sleep tonight, Sam?"

Singh returned his gaze to the painting, wishing he could just transport himself back to the 16th century with nights so quiet, sleep would be nearly impossible. So clean. So peaceful. So serene. Sure, back then, you could die from a rat's bite or a paper cut. Genocide was a popular pastime. But here you can die from a bullet just picking up your groceries, and genocide still enjoys an occasional appearance.

Things change. Things don't. The world tumbles onward.

Madison let her robe fall to the floor, climbed onto the bed, and straddled him. She reached down to his crotch and began massaging it.

"Forget about that stupid painting, Sam," she whispered. "Let me give you something to help you sleep." She pushed him inside her, rolled her eyes, and moaned.

But Singh just couldn't stop thinking about that painting.

AN IMPATIENT RED LANCER sat on a cheap, pale blue plastic chair inside a musty, windowless, soundproofed room. *Jesus, what a claustrophobic nightmare.*

"I've sent two teams to fix Sam's hot mess at the Woodrock plant," Red Lancer groused, staring into the darkened far end of the room, trying to get a glimpse of the mysterious Jupiter. "You'd think someone who went to Princeton would know better than to send classified e-mails over the regular company server. Encrypted or not."

"Be patient with him," Jupiter's deep, menacing, metallic voice responded. "He has little experience in these matters."

Red Lancer sensed Jupiter was carefully choosing his words.

"He knows the most about the specimens," Jupiter added. "He's trying to rush them into delivery. He's trying to meet our aim. We have to let him do his work."

Red Lancer leaned forward. "Well, with all due respect, our 'aim', as you call it, will not mean jack shit if the feds get a whiff of Iron Hand before we're ready. I don't fancy myself in an orange jumpsuit strapped to an electric chair. So, are you sure he's up to this? How do you know he's not reconsidering? How do you know that this e-mail snafu wasn't intentional?"

"I don't believe that," the voice replied. "I know him. He's been like a son to me."

"Son? Really? You're gonna go there? Look, the guy is way too intellectual. He thinks way too much. He over analyzes everything. And he's always running off to the fucking mountains, getting all introspective or whatever you want to call it. He could reconsider the operation."

"Isn't your team keeping tabs on him? Has he spoken to anyone about reservations? Sam would come to me if he had second thoughts."

"Keeping tabs on him?" An incredulous Red Lancer replied. "Sorry if I don't suit up and climb the Matterhorn. We can't always watch him."

"Look, Sam hates what this world has become," Jupiter replied. "Perhaps more so than you and I. He sees it from a more personal level. He has more of a singular motive for change than you or I. You have to trust me on this."

"What the world has become? Seriously? It's the same as it's always been. There's just a hell of a lot more of us screwing it up now. And I do trust you. But I don't trust him. If he changes his mind? Then what?"

A long silence followed, Red Lancer impatiently tapping fingers on the table.

"Well, if that time comes, I expect I'll let you handle it."

Red Lancer leaned back on the creaking plastic chair. "Well, okay then, Mr. Jupiter. That's just what I wanted to hear."

After the short meeting with Jupiter, Red Lancer rode the elevator down to the first floor. The hidden elevator at the rear of the building. The elevator with just two buttons for changing floors – Up, and Down. When the elevator stopped, and the doors chattered and whooshed open, Red Lancer made a beeline for the rear exit and the trash littered alley behind it, pulling out a secure comm device.

Red Lancer:

I need a big gun. Are you available?

+22 7776 677:

Yep. Can be there in 24 hrs.

Red Lancer:

Good. How much?

+22 7776 6771:

Five million. Wired. Six accounts. I'll send details.

"Ooh. Five mil. Yikes." Red Lancer tapped at the phone.

Red Lancer:

Done. Your code name is Talon.

+22 7776 6771:

Like it. See you soon.

CHAPTER 12

SUNDAY MORNING DAWNED UNSEASONABLY warm and muggy.

Weather forecasters predicted heat for the region rising into the triple digits, and to help misery just be misery, the heat would bring insufferable humidity. Woodrock churchgoers fanned themselves outside the Baptist Church on 4th and Elm. Runners dashed out for early morning runs to beat the heat. Farmers and ranchers placed buckets of extra water in their fields for livestock.

By 2:00 p.m., the Great Plains were sweltering.

The evening hours provided little relief. Roiling cumulonimbus, tinted by a late afternoon sun, rose into the sky like massive mandarin cauliflowers, their dark sinister anvils spreading out across a violet sky. Bursting with energy, the massive storms readied to unleash torrents of rain, blistering winds, hot streaks of lightning, and terrifying booms of thunder.

The storm began rather unfeignedly, with warm fat drops of rain splattering on windshields, smacking into sidewalks, and brushing their way through leaves. In just minutes, a deluge hammered Woodrock. Bone-dry ravines became raging rivers, uprooting trees and drowning wildlife. Relentless wind howling unmercifully, white-hot lightning and ear-splitting cracks of thunder terrified every living thing.

Alone in his small suburban home, Oscar trembled beneath a blanket on Pippa's bed. The windows shook. Walls groaned. The roof roared under a constant pounding of rain.

Oscar's stomach growled in painful hunger. Pippa had been absent for two days now, and his food had long since run out. And with every loud clap of super-heated air, wall hangings, glasses, plates, and bowls, rattled and clanged. In this horror of a night, Oscar longed for Pippa's return and reassurance.

Unburdened with a high-functioning brain like his human companion, the poor cat couldn't make sense of his situation. Like most animals, Oscar couldn't process, analyze, or comprehend the emotions flooding his thoughts. Fear. Anxiety. Longing. Sadness. Mysterious emotions filling his brain like jumbled pieces of a puzzle. For all Oscar knew, this was his new world. An interminable world of chaos and loneliness. Oscar was no meteorologist. He was certainly no existentialist. The future, to no fault of Oscar, is incomprehensible to a cat.

At the crescendo of the storm, a soft sound, like a voice, reached his perked ears. *Hello, brat.*

He crawled to the edge of the bed, peering out from underneath the blanket. Eyes wide, ears flattening against his head, he darted off the bed with great speed and to the front door. Despite the fury that existed outside, he anxiously waited for it to open.

Oscar waited. And waited. And waited.

The fierce storm subsided as fast as it began. Soon, all that remained was a strong breeze rattling the windows and water falling from flooded gutters in a loud gurgling hiss. He rolled onto his side and continued waiting for Pippa - his hopes and desires waning with every moment.

Pippa would never come, but someone else would.

Someone unexpected.

AS THE HARSH STORM raged, and a tormented Oscar struggled with his internal conflict, a man in a long black raincoat dashed into the reception area of *The Woodrock Inn*. Sweeping rain from his jacket and onto the floor, he hurried to the front desk.

Thick, heavyset, born with a permanent scowl, Bald-Man dabbed his shiny scalp and face with a cloth and enquired about a room for the night. Two people, twin beds. He asked about Wi-Fi and made some off-handed joke about needing a life preserver. He complained about the storm forcing him and his friend off the highway for the night. Scribbling his information on the guest card, he explained they were on their way to Minneapolis. Grumbling to Katrina, the young girl behind the desk, he complained this extra stop was going to put a dent in their schedule.

Smiling warmly, Katrina told Bald-Man that Woodrock was happy to have him, and so was she. The sole person on duty, she enjoyed companionship during this frightening storm.

Bald-Man paid for the deposit and the room with cash, and as she printed his receipt, Katrina mentioned that he and his companion were taking an unusual route to Minneapolis. Bald-Man grabbed the receipt for the room, stuffed it in his pocket, hurrying back through the doors without saying a word.

Around 10 p.m., the rain stopped, and a warm damp breeze was the only remnant of the storm. Faces hidden, Bald-Man and his companion dashed out of their room and stepped into a white compact car. Fifteen minutes late for their appointment, they raced out of the lot and onto the road leading to town. Following a route displayed on their GPS, the two men arrived in an older, tree-lined Woodrock neighborhood. Bald-Man quietly rolled the car alongside a drab single-story home and stopped.

"At least he had the sense to park in the garage," grumbled his partner.

Bald-Man's accomplice was an odd-looking man. Face and jaw angular and long, skin pasty like dough, a scar stretched from his right eye to his lips like a jagged fault-line. Dark hair shot outward from his scalp, capacious eyes forming near perfect circles. At first glance, one would think he'd just been electrocuted in the shower.

Bald-Man switched off the headlights and backed into the driveway. Then the two exited the car, stepping up to the front of the house. After some gentle tapping, a man appeared at the door. A brief conversation ensued, then they were let inside.

After their fifteen-minute meeting, Bald-Man and Eye-Scar left the home, headlights off to avoid detection, heading back from where they'd come.

Inside the darkened home, a man codenamed Sparrow sat in silence on a black leather recliner, his opaque eyes drooping toward the floor. A pistol, muzzle still warm, lay on the floor just beyond his lifeless fingers.

Twenty minutes after Bald-Man and Eye-Scar met with Sparrow, they arrived at the caul-de-sac that led to Pippa's quaint modern home. Moving at a crawl past the young saplings, under the dim light of streetlamps, the white compact coasted into Pippa's driveway and went quiet. The two stepped out of the car, and hunched over to avoid detection, hurried to the front door. Bald-Man stuck a penlight between his teeth and fiddled with the lock.

"Hurry," whispered Eye-Scar. "C'mon, man."

Pippa's front door creaked open. "Ha, still got it." Bald-Man swung the lock-pick around his finger, shoving it inside his pocket. But as the door swung open with a creak, a growl, followed by a frightening hiss, came from the dark entranceway. Then, to his horror, a blur of orange fur shot between Eye-Scar's legs.

"A fucking cat!"

"Keep your voice down, moron," grumbled Bald-Man.

After swaying their penlights around the interior of Pippa's home for ten minutes, they emerged, got back into their car, and headed back to the motel. Surfing the web from their phones, discussing the NFL draft and baseball spring training, they relaxed in their beds until sunrise. Then they loaded up their car, heading south toward Rapid City.

With a hundred miles now between them and Woodrock, Bald-Man had a sudden revelation. He hadn't locked the front door behind him when they left Pippa's.

"Don't worry about it." Eye-Scar said, reaching into his pocket and pulling out a phone. "They'll just think the woman forgot to lock her door." He typed a message.

Kestrel:

Sparrow gone. House is clean. On our way back.

Red Lancer:

Good work. Fly safe.

Bald-man and Eye-Scar arrived at a small, primitive airstrip twenty miles east of Rapid City at 1:30 p.m.

The two parked the car, tucking the keys into the visor, and heaving their bags from the trunk. Another man would pick the car up later in the day, where it would be driven to a shop to receive a coat of blue paint and new license plates. Red Lancer liked to recycle cars. Something about efficiency.

Eye-Scar stretched, looking up at a crisp blue sky. "Wow, the weather in this part of the country is crazy. Rain one day and sun the next."

"Beats Detroit."

They scanned the small airfield. A red hay tractor sat next to a wooden shack. Two small planes, one covered with a blue tarp, sat parked on the opposite side. A limp, orange windsock dangled from a tall white pole. At the end of a rough, paved runway sat a twin-turboprop Saab 340, preparing to leave. They ambled toward the slender white plane.

"Hey!" Yelled the Saab's copilot, pointing to their bags. "Give me those. I'll load them in the back." Glancing at their waists, the copilot extended his hand. "No weapons on the plane."

"Why not?" Eye-Scar looked mortified, as if the pilot asked him to hand over his only child.

"C'mon," the pilot replied. "I think it's obvious why we don't let guns inside an airplane. There's a locker in the baggage compartment. It's just us, guys. We do this all the time."

Bald-Man and Eye-Scar handed over their gear, begrudgingly surrendered their pistols, and climbed into a plush executive's cabin replete with cushy, wide leather seats.

"This whole plane, just for us," Bald-Man exclaimed, his eyes moving up and down the aisle.

"Wake me up when we get there," mumbled Eye-Scar. Exhausted, he plopped down on a seat, rolled to his side, tucked in his legs, and nodded off.

The copilot climbed into the plane, raising the ladder from the control panel near the door. He stopped, waving to someone outside, and lowered the ladder back down again.

Bald-Man sat up. "What's wrong?"

A man hurried up the ladder and stumbled into the cabin. "Whew! Nearly missed you guys!"

Bald-Man had never seen this man before. Dressed more for a pickup game of soccer than a flight to Chicago, the stranger wore a blue track-suit and gray Nike running shoes. And he had a way about him. A real confidence. A certain charm. Middle-eastern, but speaking in a British accent, he seemed cheery, articulate, and highly educated. The man held his phone up to the copilot. The copilot nodded and closed the cabin door.

The stranger strode through the narrow cabin. "Hey, what's up?" He said to Bald-Man with a nod, trying to catch his breath and searching for a place to put down his bag. To Bald-Man, this imposter seemed thrilled and excited just to be on the plane, like an adolescent boy embarking on his first adventure.

Wiping his brow, the man fell onto a seat. "Nearly missed the flight." He glanced at a snoring, mumbling, Eye-Scar. "Asleep already?"

"Who are you?" Bald-Man asked.

The man extended his hand. "Yousef, nice to meet you."

Glaring at Yousef with cautious and distrustful eyes, Bald-Man leaned back and kicked Eye-Scar's feet.

"What the fuck, man? What is it?" Eye-Scar groaned, shuffling his manic hair around.

"You know this guy?" Bald-Man asked.

"Never seen him."

"Text Red Lancer. Ask him about some Arab looking guy named Yousef."

Eye-Scar tapped out a message. Seconds later, the phone dinged, and he held it up to Yousef. "Red Lancer says he's glad you made it." Then Eye-Scar rolled back over in his seat and went to sleep.

THE SAAB ROARED DOWN the gravel strip at 2 p.m., leaving a cloud of gray dust to settle back on the runway, droning upward into the sky, and then turning east. Yousef leaned in his seat, peering out the window with a sheepish grin, observing the landscape below with fascination.

Bald-Man leaned over, trying to attract Yousef's attention. "Hey." He stomped his foot on the floor. "Hey!"

Annoyed, Yousef left the panorama outside the plane, turning to Bald-Man. "Yes?"

"Why're you here? I mean, why this plane? I thought it came for us."

"I'm on assignment from our mutual employer."

"Red Lancer sent you to that Woodrock dump?"

"It's best neither of us knows why either of us is here. Red Lancer is very explicit about these things."

"Yeah, well, I don't trust him."

"Yet he signs your checks," Yousef replied with a raised brow. "Interesting."

"So? I don't trust no one. Especially people I work for."

Yousef turned back to the window. "What a sad, exhausting life you must lead," he said, resuming his sightseeing.

AN ABRUPT CHANGE IN the pitch of the props woke Eye-Scar from his peaceful slumber. Rubbing mucus from his eyes, he looked out the window.

Despite Eye-Scar's lack of formal education of nearly any kind, he had enough knowledge to understand that the plane was flying in the wrong direction. Expecting flat open spaces of farms and pasture, mountains blanketed in pines and granite knobs spread out below him instead. Shoving his head into the Plexiglas oval, he thought he could make out Mt. Rushmore. It was clear the plane was not heading toward Chicago.

Eye-Scar turned to wake up Bald-Man, but something about his partner struck him. He lay curled into a fetal position, fingers clutched, eyes clenched, lips a light shade of blue. Eye-Scar shot up from his seat, stumbling across the narrow aisle. Kneeling, he shook his partner. "Dude, wake up! Wake up!"

"Heart attack."

Eye-Scar turned to Yousef standing over him. "What? Heart attack??"

Yousef pointed to a plastic bottle of mountain spring water rolling on the cabin floor, its contents leaking out onto the thin carpeting.

"You poisoned him?"

"Let's just say I encouraged a cardiac arrest." Yousef held up a small syringe, admiring it. "Oleander. Such a beautiful flower. Who'd ever have thought?"

Eye-Scar gaped wide-eyed at Yousef's cold, emotionless face. His charm and dashing smile vanishing, Yousef now had the intense focus of someone completing a task. Lunging for Yousef's legs, Eye-Scar's move was indecisive and half-hearted. One part of his brain telling him to flee, the other commanding him to attack. So, Eye-Scar ended up doing neither. Getting struck on the skull instead with a baton, tucked away in Yousef's tracksuit.

Regaining consciousness after a few minutes, his vision blurred and head throbbing with pain, Eye-Scar's ears were now filled with a deafening sound.

Dragging his limp corpse to the front of the plane, Yousef and the copilot ingloriously shoved Bald-Man through the cabin door. Eye-Scar had trouble processing this event. What's happening? Are we back on the ground? He tried getting to his feet. The cabin spun, and the props screamed through an open cabin door. This was all so confusing.

Hurrying back through the cabin, Yousef helped a dazed Eye-Scar to his feet, assisting him to the cabin door where an expanse of blue sky and bright pearl clouds opened up before him. Like a frightened steer fleeing the slaughterhouse, Eye-Scar screamed, trying to push his way past the copilot and Yousef. His effort was hopeless. Spun around, and with a combined shove in the back, they tossed him from the plane.

Soon after his assisted exit, Eye-Scar's cheeks were being pushed past his gums, his eyes watering so badly the world became a blur of green and blue. At near terminal velocity, the icy air stabbed at him like a million picks.

These two men, the bald man and the man with the long scar, were what Red Lancer referred to as throwaway assets. They were not bright, kind, thoughtful, or compassionate. Loners. Losers. Criminals. Red Lancer's *Tier 3 assassins*. The lowest on the rung. They had all the worth of a nuisance mosquito. Tell them to kill and they did. Pay them. Use them. If they become inconvenient, toss them from a Saab 340 at 14,000 feet. Red Lancer knew that when a disposable asset needed to vanish, no one would come looking for them.

Plummeting toward the pine carpeted Black Hills like space debris entering the atmosphere, the disposable Eye-Scar watched in horror as the world below him grew closer. If this was Eye-Scar's time to repent for his sins, that time never came. Petrified with fear, he slammed into the forest, pine branches tearing flesh from his bones, smashing his face, and crushing his skull. He was dead when he hit the needle carpeted forest floor.

Ripped apart and devoured by opportunistic predators and insects, the bodies of the two men vanished within a week. A wide scattering of indiscernible bones on the forest floor remaining as the only evidence that Bald-Man and Eye-Scar had ever existed in this world.

BRUSHING HIS HANDS ON his tracksuit, Yousef pulled his black secure device from his pocket as the copilot got the reluctant cabin door to close.

Talon:

Two birds with one stone. What's next? The crew?

Red Lancer:

No. I have an expert who will take care of them and the plane. Just wait for further instructions.

Yousef grinned a dimpled smile at the copilot and flashed a quick salute. The copilot returned this gesture with a nod, stepping back into the cockpit. The device buzzed in his hand.

Red Lancer:

We're getting close to go-time. Things are becoming very fluid.

Chapter 13

A smell of impending rain. A pungent odor of warm asphalt. The sun dimmed behind a thickening gray overcast.

On this ordinary muggy June afternoon in the suburban outskirts of Boston, Paul Quinn leaned up against his Audi in a strip-mall parking lot, waving a letter at his son. "Ronan, you have a whole future ahead of you."

Ronan Quinn kicked at the asphalt with his toes.

"Yale, Ronan. This is Yale. A choice of law firms. Anything you want."

Ronan Quinn, shredded by guilt, averted his father's eyes. He thought back to his mother, sweeping away tears at the kitchen table, telling him to go.

"Your grandfather served in Vietnam, Ronan," his father told him. "He still wakes up in the middle of the night screaming orders to no one in the room."

Ronan Quinn continued kicking at the asphalt.

"Ronan, you walk through those doors and you're throwing everything away."

"Dad, they attacked us. Here, in America. They killed thousands. They're killing people all over the world. I have to do this."

"Ronan, your grandfather doesn't want you fighting in another war."

"Vietnam didn't attack America, dad. There's a difference."

"No, there's not, Ronan. There's no difference at all. When the bullets come, will it matter?"

"Dad, I have to do this."

"I won't stop you. Choose your path. But think of what this will do to your mother."

"I have dad. But I can't stop thinking about what they did to us."

His dad embraced him. "I love you, Ronan. Just think about what I've said."

"Yale will be here when I come back, dad."

"No, it won't. Don't kid yourself."

Paul Quinn released his son and nodded toward the office sandwiched between a laundry and a private accountant's. "Just do it. Before I handcuff you to the car."

Ronan Quinn turned away from his father, moping across the lot and disappearing inside a recruiting office for the United States Marine Corps.

OVER TWO DECADES LATER, a sentimental Ronan Quinn gazed at a framed photo on his bedroom dresser. A photo of his team in Afghanistan - loaded down with gear, M-4 rifles slung across their chests, long wooly beards - posing before a fluttering American flag. He and the lieutenant were kneeling in front of their men, the LT's arm slung over Quinn's shoulder.

He could've gone to Yale and been a partner at some firm by now. Living the cosmopolitan life in an apartment on the top floor of some high-rise in Manhattan. He chose country over self. He chose the Marine Corps.

Many years behind him, and many roads traveled, he sat at the end of his bed in a rather plain home, on a rather plain street, in a rather plain town, in a rather plain slice of America.

His thoughts moved to Pippa Simpson and the accident on Kurtz Curve. The speed at which Pangea arrived to claim Pippa's body had been awfully fast.

Rose called Pippa's parents at 2:30 p.m. to inform them their daughter had perished in an awful car accident. He followed up with Pippa's father at 5:00 p.m. Mr. Simpson told him that Pangea had already spoken with him to arrange Pippa's transportation back home.

But Rose never called Pangea to notify them of Pippa's death. So how'd they know Pippa was dead? How could they possibly get a signed release from a judge in Chicago and then from Pippa's parents all the way in California and in less than 20 hours? And courthouses aren't even open on weekends. Pangea would've had to have someone with release forms prepared and a judge ready to go. Pretty amazing stuff, since no one knew the identity of the victim but he, Fig, Rose, and the coroner.

Could the paramedics have notified someone? Why would they have? That's the police department's job.

The Highway Patrol?

The Highway Patrol didn't arrive on the scene until the paramedics were hauling Pippa up the hill, and Quinn didn't pass on her identity until the following morning. The Highway Patrol allowed Quinn's department to notify Pippa's parents, she being a Woodrock citizen and all.

So, who told Pangea? And why did they take her away so fast? They had their own coroner in Chicago? What kind of company keeps a coroner under contract?

Quinn tossed three ceremonial shot glasses of scotch down the drain, made a pot of coffee, and hopped on the stationary bike. Pedaling himself into a soaking sweat, he cleared his mind.

Walter and Zed were at the station before they came to Bob McConnell's office. They collected everything from the evidence room and they specifically asked for her backpack and her phone. Fig said they seemed to be in a rush. They also kept asking if anyone had touched or gone through her backpack, repeating this question multiple times. Walter and Zed asked if anyone had tried to log onto her laptop. Fig telling the two men they had no reason to go through her things - they just bagged everything up for her next of kin.

Quinn felt that there was not something wrong with these events, as much as there was just nothing right with them. At all.

Arriving at the station at 8:00 a.m., Quinn muttered good morning to Rose and marched into his office, yelling for Fig. Rose curiously looked on as Fig shuffled into Quinn's office, closing the door behind him.

Quinn asked Fig if he'd been able to get into Pippa's phone.

"No, boss. I really didn't even have a chance. And her phone was pretty banged up. I'm not sure it even works anymore. And those creepy guys walked through the doors as soon as you'd left."

"And they kept asking about her backpack?"

"Yeah. It was weird. Those two guys asked if anyone had been messing with it. I said no. We bagged it up and sealed it along with everything else for transport to next of kin."

Quinn sat down, staring into a dark PC monitor screen. Fig stood, silent, wondering to himself if his boss was on the verge of having another blow-up.

Pangea wanted her phone. They wanted to know if anyone touched her backpack. They didn't ask about the accident. They just cared about her things. Why? Company secrets? Pangea worked on a lot of things. Things for the Department of Defense, for instance.

Quinn stared at the monitor screen as it flickered to life. What have I gotten myself mixed up in here? He felt like he was falling behind in a race, and Pangea had left the starting blocks well before the starting gun had even gone off.

"We're taking a drive, Fig."

"Where too, boss?" Fig asked, perplexed.

"The deceased's house."

"Chief, what is going–"

Quinn cut him off. "No time for questions, Fig." Pushing his chair back, he abruptly stood. "72 hours, Fig. It's been 72 hours since the wreck. We've wasted enough time."

QUINN AND FIG PULLED up in front of Pippa's quaint yellow and white-trimmed house, fully expecting to be greeted by more Pangea "representatives," if you could even call them that. The house, however, appeared to be empty. Stepping out of the SUV, they walked up the path to the front door.

"Can we do this, boss?" Fig asked. "Don't we need a warrant or something?"

Ignoring Fig, Quinn kneeled, carefully examining the front door latch. "Hmmm," he muttered. "As I thought." Reaching into his pocket, he pulled out a pair of latex gloves, stretching them over his hands. "Gloves, Fig," he muttered, his fingers feeling the latch.

Cocking his head, Fig cast a perplexed stare.

"Don't you carry gloves?"

Fig shrugged.

"I've clearly failed you." He nodded toward the police SUV. "There's another pair in the truck. Go put them on."

Fig dashed off down the path as Quinn pressed down on the latch, the door swinging open with a creak.

Fig ran back to Quinn, sliding the gloves over his hands. "Wow, she left the door unlocked? Or has Pangea been here already?"

Quinn remained silent.

From behind trimmed evergreen shrubs beneath the front window came a yowl and a hiss. Oscar, eyes wide and terrified, bolted between the two men, slid on the wood entrance flooring, and darted off and out of sight.

"Shit!" Fig yelled. "A cat!"

Quinn looked up at Fig with a smirk. "Yes, Fig, a cat. Top-notch police work, big guy."

The two stepped inside the house and looked around. The home appeared clean and orderly. Pulling out his penlight, Quinn panned it around the house. Fig switched on the lights.

"Turn them off, Fig. We'll see more with the penlights."

Quinn walked into the kitchen. Coffee maker. Microwave. Air Fryer. He went through the kitchen drawers. Their penlights swaying about in the dusky house like spotlights during a London blitz, they made their way into Pippa's bedroom.

"What're we looking for, boss?" Fig asked, whispering.

“You can talk in a normal voice, Fig. There’re no bad guys here.”

Stepping into the bedroom, Quinn noticed Pippa’s framed white bed was in disarray, blankets and sheets piled haphazardly at the foot of the bed. Dresser drawers were partially open, her underwear and shirts stuffed inside in balls. Judging by the rest of the house, it seemed unusual her bedroom would be such a mess. He carefully went through her drawers. Opened her closet. Moved skirts and slacks left and right. Examined framed photos on her dresser. Pippa cuddling with Oscar. Pippa with the posse in Las Vegas. Pippa with her parents at her graduation from MIT.

Searching under the bed, Fig made out a pair of eyes glistening under the beam of his penlight. Oscar lay on the floor, ears flat against his head and fangs bared.

“Poor cat.” Fig said, trying to coax Oscar out of his place of safety with clicks and whistles. “Must be starving. Reminds me of a dog I used to have.”

“It’s a cat, Fig.”

Fig grunted as he tried to reach Oscar under the bed. Oscar growled. “I know, but a pet’s a pet, you know, and this is someone’s pet.”

Quinn walked back to Pippa’s bed, plopping down on its edge. Kicking at the pile of blankets, mindlessly panning his penlight along the ceiling, he knew someone had been to her house, and it hadn’t been Pippa.

“What’re you thinking, chief?” Fig asked, giving up on Oscar.

“I dunno, Fig. It’s odd.”

“What’s odd?”

“Someone was here.”

Fig stood up from the floor and brushed his pants. “You think someone broke in?”

Quinn shrugged. "Or she left the door unlocked, and forgot to bring in her cat."

"But you don't believe that, do you, chief?"

Leaning over, Quinn gazed at the floor. "First rule of police work, Fig," he said with a thoughtful voice. "Before you can prove what something is, you must first prove what it isn't. And I can't prove that the victim didn't forget to lock her door. I can't prove that she didn't forget about her cat." He scratched his head. "She could've been late for work."

"Are you getting a hunch, boss?" Fig asked, a tinge of enthusiasm in his voice.

"More like a feeling, Fig. Did you look behind the house?"

"Yeah, nice view."

"That's coyote country, Fig. No half-assed decent pet owner is going to let their dog or cat roam around out here unattended. We have pet warnings on our website, for Christ's sake."

"What else are you thinking?"

Quinn turned to Fig and pointed toward the front of the house.

"The door latch is all scratched up. And those scratches are fresh. I've seen enough picked locks in my time to know that someone picked that lock. Someone came here. Someone spooked that cat."

"Why would someone break in?" Fig asked. This was a real mystery. Something really nefarious. And Woodrock just didn't have nefarious things. Not since Mary Glover vanished way back in 1964.

"I'm not sure, Fig," Quinn mumbled.

Pangea was in an awful hurry to collect Pippa and her things, he thought. Why does a Fortune 500 technology firm send out Frick and Frack to collect everything? They were more like janitors than professionals. Zed looked like he'd put more bodies in the morgue than he'd retrieved. Walter had the IQ of a box of rocks. Why were they so specific about the cellphone? And the backpack? They asked Fig if anyone touched it. Why would they care, unless both those items contained some very sensitive confidential company information?

Quinn sighed. It could be as simple as that. Company confidential information and Pippa was just absentminded or in a hurry. But why then would someone come here, break in, and search her house? To Quinn, this seemed to be some sort of cleanup operation. To look for something, or to make sure something wasn't here. What actually killed Pippa? The accident? A mysterious pair of hands from the backseat of her car? And how did Pangea even know Pippa had perished? It was as if they knew before he did.

Quinn smacked his thighs and stood. "Give Rose a call, Fig. Tell her to send the SPCA out here to collect the dumb cat."

Fig whipped out his phone, dialing Rose back at the station.

What was Pippa telling him that night? Envy? They're all dead? What did that mean?

Fig put his cellphone on his chest. "Rose says you're a cruel SOB."

Quinn, confused, squinted at Fig. "What?"

"Hold on, Rose, hold on." A reluctant Fig looked at Quinn. "She says you're not taking that poor woman's fur-baby to pet prison. It just lost its mom." Through the phone's speaker, from ten feet away, Quinn listened to Rose, chattering to Fig at lightning speed.

"Okay, okay…geez, okay, Rose," Fig pulled the phone away from his ear. "She says you go spend the night in pet lockup, and if no one comes to collect you, then-" Fig stopped and turned a light shade of red. "Okay, I'm not repeating that."

Quinn shook his head in disbelief. "It's a stupid goddammed cat, Fig. What the hell does she want me to do with it?"

Fig relayed that question, then put the phone in his pocket. "She'll take it in for now. She already has two cats. She's coming over here to pick it up."

Quinn thrust his hands at Fig. "Jesus, why didn't she just say that?"

Echoing through the stillness of the house came the sound of a large truck. The truck's gears shifted down, and the engine groaned, followed by a *beep, beep, beep* as it backed into the driveway. The truck let out a hiss and went silent, then the truck's doors slammed shut. Voices of men rang out from the driveway. Someone pounded on the front door.

Quinn looked toward the front of the house. "Well, they're here. As I suspected."

"Who's here?" Fig asked.

"Pangea's movers. They're getting all her stuff. They'll have her house cleaned out and on the market by the end of the week."

"Wow," Fig said. "These guys don't mess around."

Quinn walked out of the bedroom. No, they don't. Not in the slightest.

CHAPTER 14

THIS IS A DREAM, Samir Singh had thought, many years ago. This is a dream and I'm just awakening. Or this isn't a dream, but it should be.

Born into poverty in a village in the north of Punjab, it may have indeed seemed a dream to Singh, strolling through the ivory-draped Fitz Randolph Gate, into the University Chapel, and past the particolored brick and vanilla mortar of Blair Hall. With spring standing on the precipice of summer, the university grounds dazzled with bird's songs, and the rich fragrance of freshly cut grass filled the air. Having completed his studies at Princeton, a proud Singh strode with his family, feeling as if he'd ascended to heaven.

Two decades before this day, penniless and illiterate in English, Samir Singh's parents arrived at the U.S. Customs and Immigration. His father a simple laborer in Punjab, his mother working a farm since the tender age of nine, the family arrived with nearly no formal education. With such few skills, finding any work in their adoptive nation would be grueling, tedious, and often discouraging.

But in just fifteen years, the Singh family built one of the largest trucking companies in New York State. Singh's father never had time to dream any American dreams, and nothing about America was ever dreamlike. Success was all about hard work, aggressiveness, and outsmarting the competition - learning that from the first day he'd arrived.

America was about opportunity, not dreams of fancy. Seizing every opportunity that crossed his path was how his family flourished.

Navi, Samir's younger sister by three years, was his sole sibling. A rare gem on this earth, long flowing hair fell about her shoulders like fine, midnight tinsel. Her smooth, coffee-brown skin sparkled in the sunlight. A broad smile radiated the brilliance of a star from beneath chestnut eyes. Indeed, Navi was stunningly beautiful and shared as much of, if not more, the intellect and deep thoughtfulness as her brother. Whenever he and Navi were together, Samir Singh felt as though time had stopped - their adoration for one another being an unbreakable bond, forged by a deeply felt love and mutual respect.

Now, just hours from commencement, under a flawless blue sky with his wonderful parents and rare-gem sister, Samir Singh strolled through the Princeton campus, transcending this world and into one of dreamscapes.

The after-graduation party at a rented ballroom in Kendall Park was an Indian extravaganza. Thrown by people who cherished celebrations, more food and drink was provided than anyone could ever possibly consume. Indecipherable chatter and laughter filled the room. Chatter from family, friends, local business leaders, and politicians. Samir gazed adoringly at Navi, flowing through the room like an ethereal spirit. Meeting guests. Elegantly shaking hands. Flashing her heart-seizing smile.

He sensed his phone buzzing in his pants pocket. "My love," his mother spoke. "I am so sorry we're running behind, but your father needed to go to the hotel for his medication."

"No worries, mom. Take your time. Guests are still arriving, and it's always best to be late. It'll be a grand entrance."

In the background, his father shouted. "Proud of you Samir, so proud!"

Shoving his phone in his pocket and striding through the room, he struck up conversations on politics and economics. Ty Keller, the revered senator from Pennsylvania, congratulated him on his graduation and Singh apologized for his parent's lateness.

An hour passed. Then two.

The chattering in the large room fell into nervous whispers. Texting his mother and father multiple times, he received no response.

Then came the blood-curdling scream. Whirling around, he watched horrified, as Navi collapsed.

Sprinting to his sister as she lay on the floor, legs curled, head propped up with one hand, long black hair draping over her face like a stage curtain, Singh knelt beside her as she sobbed and mumbled incoherently. All around her, a concerned crowd of guests gathered to see what had happened.

Next to her thigh lay her phone. Picking it up, he read the screen. Every muscle and every tendon going rigid, he dropped the phone to the floor.

A SCENT OF SICKNESS and antiseptic wafted through the hospital waiting room.

Navi rested her head on her brother's shoulders. Their father's closest friends and business partners tried their best to console the two siblings. Telling them how strong their mother is. How she would fight and fight and fight.

A surgeon sidled into the room with detectable reluctance. They did their best, he said, but their best wasn't good enough to save their mother. Her trauma was just too severe. She'd lost too much blood. The next step would be to harvest her organs.

The first responders declared their father dead at the scene. A driver, smashing into their parent's sedan at nearly 100 miles per hour, was now sitting in the county jail. Driving under the influence of drugs and alcohol, or so a police officer explained to them.

And Navi screamed and screamed…

SINGH'S EYELIDS FLUTTERED OPEN. A rushing wind. A soft, electric hum. A deep throbbing of turbofan engines. He looked down at his right hand. Gripping the armrest with iron force, he felt he could just snap it off.

Where was he? Princeton? The ballroom? The hospital? 40,000 feet on his private jet?

That was it, 40,000 feet in his jet. Not that nightmare passing below him.

He gazed thoughtfully through the oval window, the world below hidden beneath a long pearl cloud-deck stretching for hundreds of miles. That world. Poor and rich. Starving and fed. Touchable and untouchable.

Jill, the sole flight attendant, eyed him with consternation.

"Sam, are you okay?" she asked. "You were really tossing and turning and mumbling something while you were napping."

Singh nodded. "I'm fine, dear. Can you bring me a fizzy drink? My stomach is bothering me. I need a fizzy drink."

Jill smiled and stood, moving into the galley to fetch sparkling water.

He closed his eyes and thought, air squeezing through pursed lips like a pipe venting excess steam. That fucking e-mail. Now Jupiter's moving Iron Hand up by two months. He's panicking. Too many security mishaps. The specimens are misbehaving. We're not ready. Stop dwelling. It's not the end of the world.

Feeling a buzzing on his hip, he pulled his phone from his pocket, seeing no call. Reaching into his other pocket, he retrieved the secure comm device.

Red Lancer:

Cleanup on aisle four complete. You're welcome.

Kilimanjaro:

Did they get the backpack and her phones?

Singh tapped his fingers and waited. He could almost sense the wheels grinding away in Red Lancer's simplistic brain.

Red Lancer:

Phones? As in plural?

Jesus, Samir thought. I thought these guys were pros. He typed his response.

Kilimanjaro:

She would have had a work phone and a personal phone. One plus one equals two. You can do math, can't you? Or do you just kill people?

Jill arrived with a sparkling, clear drink. He gulped it down.

Red Lancer:

I enjoy my work, so you better stop screwing up. We went through her house. We did not find any other phones. Her place was clean. We found no compromises. My guys asked her friends if they had anything of that woman's. They said no. If there's a second phone it had better turn up, Sammy boy.

Singh gritted his teeth. Sammy boy? Sammy boy?

Kilimanjaro:

Do you have the coroner's report? What did it say?

Red Lancer:

Our Chicago coroner finished. Blunt force trauma.

Red Lancer:

Dead

Red Lancer:

From

Red Lancer:

Crash

Kilimanjaro:

What about the local coroner? In Woodrock?

Red Lancer:

Who cares? The chief of police gave my guys a tough time, though. He's pissed off because we took his chief power away.

What? Why were the local police giving anyone a tough time? Somewhat alarmed by this, Singh tapped the device.

Kilimanjaro:

Does he suspect foul play?

Red Lancer:

There is no foul play, idiot. She died in a crash. We have everything we need. They can't prove anything else. They may have done a tox report, but it'll come back clean.

By that point, Singh became startled. Then the device buzzed again.

Red Lancer:

The cops were at the woman's house snooping around when the movers arrived. But I wouldn't worry about it.

Kilimanjaro:

Okay, good work.

Red Lancer:

Gee, thanks! That means so much to me!

Slamming the phone down onto the armrest, he raised his hand and flipped it off. He *really* hoped he met this Red Lancer someday. But as he leaned back in his seat, anxiety swept over him in a long rolling wave, his heart pounding in his chest as if it were trying to flee its cavity. Red Lancer is wrong. If a coroner were diligent and competent, there was something they could find.

But security was Red Lancer's job, not his. And Red Lancer really enjoyed killing people. A man so arrogant, so self-absorbed, he wouldn't see an elephant if it were sitting on his chest. Singh tried to visualize what Red Lancer looked like - tattooed, long hair, missing teeth, empty eyes. Patient zero for a Dunning-Kruger study. Too stupid to realize he's stupid.

These new revelations, however, left Singh shaken. The Woodrock chief of police visiting Pippa's house seemed suspicious. But his visit could also have a perfectly rational explanation and Singh knew next to nothing about police procedures, his only knowledge of criminal justice stemming from TV crime dramas. Maybe it was time to learn more about what the Woodrock police knew about the "accident." He needed to know what they knew, and he couldn't trust that sociopath Red Lancer to perform such a delicate task.

And then there was this phone business.

She must have a second phone. And if the woman had a second phone, he needed to find it, and ASAP.

Hastily leaving his seat, Singh dashed past a curious Jill and to the cockpit. He told the pilot to refuel the jet and file a return flight plan immediately after landing in London. "Where to?" asked the captain, surprised by the sudden change in plans.

"The Pangea plant in Woodrock," an emphatic Singh exclaimed to the pilot. "And we have no time to waste!"

CHAPTER 15

LOOKING SKYWARD, FIG ARCHED his back and stretched. From high overhead, a large cargo jet banked right and headed west, filling the early morning air with tranquility-crushing rumbles and whines. "The fourth one I've seen this morning," he muttered to Quinn. "Yep, Boeing 767. And yesterday a big ol' 747 took off from there."

"I know what they are, Fig," Quinn mumbled as he looked on, the dull rumbling of the plane heard, but no longer seen.

"What kind of company has its own airport anyway, boss?" Fig asked.

"A rich one. A rich one who has its own private coroner."

Fig glanced at Quinn. "What does that mean?"

Quinn shook his head. "Nothing. Forget it. Let's go to work."

As they entered the station, Fig suddenly stopped, his attention drawn to the large TV monitor at the rear of the station. Tuned to CNN, a reporter stood at the edge of a broad, grassy field - the streaming Chyron below reading *private commuter plane crashes near Boulder, Colorado.* Thick black smoke rose from a field, drifting over the countryside. A privately owned Saab 340 just fell from the sky after leaving Boulder. Both pilots are dead. No other fatalities were reported.

"That's why I don't fly on small planes," he told Quinn.

A stone-faced Quinn beckoned Fig inside, shutting the door behind him. "Listen, Fig. From now on, I don't want you talking to any of the other deputies about the Kurtz Curve accident, okay? And nothing about what we saw at the victim's home."

Fig nodded. "Sure, but what did we see? A maybe-picked lock and scared-shitless cat?"

"Exactly, Fig, that's all we've seen." Quinn aggressively scratched his scalp, puzzled by all that'd been happening. "And this stuff that's been happening with Pangea, I know you think it's odd, but just keep it to yourself. You're to speak of the fatality, accident, or details about the victim to absolutely no one. Am I clear?"

Fig nodded. "Clear, but confused. You've something you're not telling me?"

Quinn turned to the window, thoughtfully gazing out at Main Street. "I might, I might not. Just be diligent, okay? I'll keep you in the loop. The only people allowed to discuss the fatality on the Kurtz Curve are me, Bob McConnell, you, and Rose. I'll get her up to speed on this. Whatever this even is." He threw his head back, squeezing his eyes shut. "Ugh…maybe I'm just being paranoid."

That statement from his chief surprised Fig. "Is that what you were back in New York? Were you a paranoid detective?"

Quinn whirled around and faced Fig. "What?"

"Were you a paranoid detective?"

"Of course not," Quinn replied with a deep scowl.

"Okay then," Fig said. "You're not a paranoid chief either."

The slightest of smiles edged Quinn's lips. Fig's reassuring comment was just what he needed to hear.

Rose called into the office from her desk. Squinting out onto the department floor through partially shuttered blinds, Quinn saw Rose sitting at her desk and holding the phone to her ear.

"For the love of god," he muttered. "I don't know why she does that." He told Fig to get Rose into his office.

"Rose," Quinn asked as she ambled into his office and shut the door. "Why do you call me from your desk? I'm ten feet away."

An eyebrow of Rose's arched upward. "You think I only get one call at a time?"

Quinn relented. "Yeah. Okay Rose. What is it?"

"Someone from Pangea hasn't been to work since last Thursday. No one can reach him. They're asking if we can do a welfare check."

With disbelief, Quinn looked at Fig. "What is it with these people? Can't they keep track of anyone?" Rose and Fig both shrugged. But Quinn felt a strange, uneasy feeling in his gut. The feeling that usually never failed to warn him of an impending doom.

"Fig, grab Beth and go check it out."

Fig turned to the door to carry out Quinn's orders, and Quinn stopped him. "Hey, you guys be careful, okay?"

"Sure thing, boss," Fig replied, puzzled.

"I mean it. I want Beth backing you up, okay?"

Fig snapped a quick salute. "Aye, aye, chief," he said and scampered through the door.

Watching this scene unfold with interest, Rose sat down across from him. "Ronan, what's wrong?" She asked. "What's going on here?"

Quinn exhaled, closing his eyes while massaging his temples in wide arcs. "What I'm about to tell you is between you, myself, and Fig. Okay?"

Rose, his confidant since day-one at Woodrock, was a walking Hallmark Card. Her silver hair pulled into a tight bun, deep wisdom lines spread outward from bright emerald eyes along high bony cheeks. Bedazzled in artsy jewelry from faraway lands, wearing long flowing cotton dresses and flats, she exuded a long-lost class and dignity. One bony cheek a touch higher than the other, her right lip curled slightly upward in perpetual cynicism. And amazingly fit for sixty, she ran marathons and became an avid golfer, winning the Seniors category of the Bulldog Golf Classic three years running. On her 60th birthday, the station presented Rose with a TaylorMade graphite driver and a new Nike golf bag. Indeed, Rose was fit, intelligent, and therapist-level trustworthy. Studiously searching a somewhat troubled Quinn, she gave him her full, undivided attention. He did not disappoint.

Pippa's accident wasn't right, he told her. Her car had been out of control for an entire mile. Bob McConnell found signs of strangulation and she appeared to have defensive wounds on her neck. Wounds similar to those one would find on a victim trying to fight off an assailant. And when he arrived at the scene of Pippa's accident, he saw a truck parked on the shoulder. A light gray Toyota pickup. When he moved in behind it, the truck sped off. And Pangea, as Rose knew, moved awfully fast collecting Pippa's remains and personal items. Too fast. Impossibly fast. He couldn't figure out, for the life of him, how they knew of her accident so quickly. How they got a judge to sign off on release forms on that same day. How they'd obtained signatures from her grieving parents all the way in San Jose.

Something else bothered him. Why were they so specific about her phone and laptop? They questioned Fig repeatedly about whether anyone had touched them. And someone had broken into Pippa's house. He was sure of it. The door latch appeared picked and picked by a pro.

Walter and Zed came to mind. But Quinn felt another party may be responsible.

"Walter and Zed aren't the clandestine type. They're muscle men. Intimidators. I have experience with this, Rose. Mobster modus operandi."

Rose's bright emerald eyes widened. "Yowzah."

"There's something else," Quinn added, leaning back and crossing his arms. "Something I've told no one."

Rose tilted her head, wearing an expression of near maternal concern. "Are you sure you want to tell me all this? I'm not a police officer."

"Which is exactly why I'm telling you this, Rose. Sometimes I just need wisdom. And you have wisdom."

"Okay, Ronan, if you say so. What is it?"

Quinn sucked in a deep breath, trying to say something, yet seemingly reluctant. This was, well, just bizarre. "She wasn't in her car when I got there."

Like she'd received a mild electric shock, Rose shot up straight. "What?"

Quinn nodded. "Yep, she could still get out. There's more." What was Pippa saying? He thought, staring at the ceiling and feeling transported back to that night of the accident.

"Well, what is it?"

"She was still alive."

Eyes growing wide like tea saucers, she thrust her head toward Quinn. "Seriously?"

"Serious as a heart attack, Rose. I did chest compressions, and she regained consciousness. She spoke to me."

"Jesus, Ronan. What did she say?"

Quinn replayed the scene in his mind. Those eyes. Pleading with him. Desperate. Then they seemed to accept fate and just faded away into death.

"Ronan?"

Quinn snapped back to the present. "She told me they're all dead."

Staring at Quinn in stunned amazement, Rose's head snapped back. "Who's dead?"

Quinn shrugged. "No clue. And she kept repeating the word envy."

Searching Rose's staccato blinking eyes, he wondered to himself. What is she thinking? Am I crazy? A looney bin candidate? "So, what're your thoughts? I need to know, Rose."

"Envy," Rose muttered, eyes narrow in thought. "They're dead. One thought comes to mind."

"That's why I'm talking to you, Rose."

"When people are dying, when they're transitioning from this world to the next, random memories can pop into their heads. It happens often. Something from their childhood, or something they've seen or heard that was just tucked away somewhere in their consciousness. When my father passed away, his last words were that he had forgotten to lock the car. He had Alzheimer's. He hadn't driven a car for years."

"Yeah," Quinn replied. "That could be it. So far, I have a 'could be this or could be that' for everything. But my gut says everything is wrong."

"Go with your gut, Ronan. You're an extremely experienced man."

"I think Fig may have been telling me the same thing."

Rose stood. "Fig worships you. It wouldn't hurt to listen to him from time to time."

"Fig worships me?" Quinn replied quizzically.

"Ronan, please. And Beth thinks you're a superhero. And the rest of the deputies would lie down in front of a train for you."

Quinn shook his head. "I don't want anyone lying in front of trains. I need them to stay sharp and be safe." He turned to his monitor and began typing. "By the way, how's the stupid cat doing?"

Hands on hips, Rose's dark brows furrowed into a frown. "That adorable cat, Ronan, is eating but mostly hides under the bed. He's confused and misses his mom."

"Good to know." He looked up at Rose, that uneasy feeling bubbling back to the surface. "Rose, don't tell anyone about this, okay?"

"Your secrets are always safe with me." Rose said with a subtle wink.

"I know," Quinn replied, tapping at his keyboard. "That's why I tell you these things."

Rose left the office. Turning back to the window, he looked out onto the street to see Fig and Beth climbing into a patrol car, reversing, and speeding off.

PULLING UP TO A SMALL, single-story home, Fig and deputy Beth Sawyer parked their patrol car and gave a quick assessment. Yellow dandelions and prickly weeds mottling a dying lawn, the house appeared quiet and undisturbed.

"Well, seems like no one's home," Beth said.

Fig thought back to Quinn's warning. Unclipping the shotgun from the dash, he radioed the dispatcher that they were on the scene.

Beth's head snapped back. Curiously, she watched him check the shotgun for shells and snap the barrel back into place. "You think we're going to need that?" She nodded at the gun as Fig sucked in a breath.

"Hope not," he replied.

Beth reached over, clutching Fig's hand. "What's going on here, Fig? This is just a welfare check, right?"

Fig leaned across Beth, gave the home a once-over, leaned back, and looked into her eyes. "Hope so. Go around the side and see if you can see anything. Then come back and we'll knock on the door."

Beth studied Fig. "Okay. Whatever you say." She opened the cruiser's door.

"Beth," Fig added as she stepped out. "Stay alert. Please be careful."

"Will do," she replied with a quizzical expression.

As Beth carefully made her way around the side of the house, Fig stepped up to the front door with the pump-action shotgun clutched in his hands. To his right, neighbors gathered on the street, observing this odd scene. Beth reappeared from the side of the house, peering back over her shoulder and analyzing something. Then she rushed back to where Fig stood.

"See anything?" Fig asked.

"We have a window ajar and there's an odd smell coming out of it. I can hear a TV." Stepping up and pounding on the door, Fig identified himself as a police officer, to no response. He identified himself again, banging on the door, then stepped back. He handed the shotgun to Beth. "I'm calling the chief."

As Fig spoke into the phone, Beth faced the street as more curious onlookers gathered. A young woman held an infant, bouncing it up and down in her arms. Beth wondered if they knew something she didn't.

"Okay, boss. Got it." Fig thrust the phone into his pocket.

"Chief says we have probable cause. Enter the home. Weapons out. He's on his way here and called for backup." Fig jogged back to the patrol cruiser, pulled a flat steel bar from the trunk, and jogged back.

"Are you shitting me?" Beth gasped, watching him wedge the bar into the door frame.

"Beth," Fig nodded toward the street. "Back up and cover my six. Watch my corners."

Adrenaline coursing through his veins, Fig prepared to kick in the door. The only door-kicking and home-entering he'd ever done had been at the Old Ghost Town - the federal government giving their approval to the Woodrock Police to use the town as a training area for anti-terrorism and hostage rescue. Training that didn't exist until Quinn had arrived.

Fig cleared his head, then gave Beth a nod. She aimed the shotgun at the door as Fig pried at the door frame, wood splintering and cracking. Rearing back, he kicked at the door four times before it surrendered to his foot.

Fig burst into the house, swaying his service weapon left to right. Following close behind, Beth aimed the pump-action at everything resembling a corner.

An overpowering, rancid scent greeted them. Like someone left the fridge open and everything inside went rotten. Feeling light-headed as this pungent odor hung in the air like an invisible fog, he moved into the living room while Beth cleared the house. He noticed the TV was still on, tuned to a sports channel - analysts bickering over some trade between the Giants and the Astros.

Moving with measured caution through the room, Fig approached a man slumped over in his chair. A limp, alabaster arm dangling over the side, a Colt.45 lay on the floor.

"Gun! Gun! Gun!" yelled Fig. Beth scrambled into the room, aiming the shotgun at the back of the man's head. Carefully, Fig moved forward, kicking the gun off to the side. Then he swung around and faced the man in the chair.

"Oh, shit."

Screeching to a stop in front of the house, Quinn arrived at the scene with two more units following behind. Deputies scrambled from their cruisers, pushing the looky-loos back away from the house. Quinn noticed Beth standing on the lawn, doubled over and vomiting.

"Beth! Are you okay?"

She nodded and extended a thumb. "All good, chief. House is clear." Vomit spilled out of her again as Quinn rushed into the house.

An overpowering and smothering stench filled his nose and mouth as he hurried through the shattered front doorway. Moving into the living room, he saw Fig standing next to a recliner, pressing a cloth against his nose and mouth, his freckled face an odd shade of both pale and rose.

The television blaring, a broadcast replayed a home run from a Red Sox game. Quinn told Fig to turn the TV off and check the rest of the house. "You bring gloves this time?"

Fig barely managed a nod.

"Good, put them on."

Quinn pulled on his latex gloves, moving his hands gently around the man's head. Like maroon icing on a fleshy cake, dried blood coated one side of the man's face, a gaping hole in his head. To the left of the recliner, Quinn observed blood and brain and skull fragments coating the carpet. On the coffee table lay a single sheet of paper. Removing his pen from his pocket, he slid the sheet toward him. *I'm so sorry,* it read, typed and printed from a computer. *If I hadn't left, she might be alive. I can't live with myself. Please tell her family I'm sorry.* Confusion riddling him, he tried to decipher this suicide note. If I hadn't left, she might be alive? Who might be alive? Quinn shouted for Fig and another deputy to search the house thoroughly. "We may have a second victim, guys! Search every room!"

In the kitchen, he found a wallet, a stack of unpaid bills, and a badge of some sort. Spreading the wallet open, he retrieved a driver's license. *Christopher Hadley*. The photo, he noticed, matched the victim in the room. He picked up the badge, carefully examining the name and photo. *Chris Hadley. Security. Pangea Dynamic Solutions.*

Quinn was perplexed. Pangea security? I'm sorry? She wouldn't be dead? What is all this? An ecstatic Fig rushed into the kitchen, interrupting his thoughts.

"You're not going to believe this, boss," he gushed. "Come check this out." He beckoned Quinn down the hallway of the house and to a rear doorway.

Hurrying after Fig, the two dashed into the garage. Stunned, Quinn's jaw dropped. He couldn't believe his eyes.

In that garage, cluttered with boxes and tools and reeking of oil and grease and dust, sat a light gray Toyota pickup. Identical to the truck which fled the scene of Pippa's accident.

Quinn placed his hands on his hips and looked over the Toyota. "Well, I'll be damned."

Quinn stayed at the scene until an ambulance transported Chris Hadley's body to the morgue. Directing evidence collection, he told his deputies to leave no stone unturned. "And please guys, keep your gloves on."

Arriving back at his office at 6 p.m., he began typing up a report, then paused, falling into deep reflection. There were many things wrong with this scene, he thought. No tipped over bottles of booze. No anti-depressants scattered everywhere. No messy, disorganized house. Nothing that pointed to chronic depression. And someone leaving the scene of an accident, though kind of fucked up, is not an occurrence that usually drives people to take their own life.

Quinn had investigated more than his fair share of suicides in New York. He'd seen traumatized veterans fall victim to the relentless pain and suffering that comes with PTSD. People living their lives on that ledge often drank heavily. They turned to medication to help ease their pain. They had lost their jobs. Had given up on self-care and housekeeping.

Quinn knew what mental suffering looked like, and Chris Hadley didn't appear to be the suffering type. He seemed young and fit. Good looking. Had a decent job with Pangea. And based on the preliminary search of the home, he didn't seem to drink much, smoked a little pot now and then, and wasn't taking medication for, well, anything.

This didn't add up, he thought. Chris Hadley witnesses Pippa's car go off the road. Stops to assist. Flees when Quinn arrives. Then, judging by the state of his corpse, 48 hours later, he types up a half-assed suicide note on his computer, prints it, and shoots himself while watching ESPN?

What did he see? What saddled him with such intense guilt that he took his own life? Did they know each other? Were they romantically involved? That both he and Pippa worked for Pangea seemed to be slightly south of a coincidence.

Quinn was unsure what Hadley's motives were. But one thing was certain. In a web of suspicion, Pangea Dynamic Solutions had grown into a menacing spider clinging to its center.

AT 8 P.M., QUINN powered down his computer. Pulling a bottle of Advil from his drawer, he downed them along with a half-bottle of water. Like a startled mouse, his cell phone buzzed on his desk. He picked it up and looked at the screen.

Rose R.

What now? Tired and drained, he just wanted to go home, flop down on the couch, and listen to a classic rock playlist. "What's up, Rose?" He asked, cradling the phone and powering down the PC.

Over the phone, he heard Rose's heavy breathing. Almost hyperventilating. The type of rapid breathing when someone is in fear for their own safety. Alarmed, he shot up from his desk.

Rose was in danger.

"Rose, what's wrong?" Quinn asked in a soft, assuring voice.

"Ronan," she whispered, her voice trembling and trying to stave off panic.

"Rose? Are you okay?"

"Ronan," she pleaded. "You need to come over. Please? Come over right now."

"Rose, speak to me. What is it? What's wrong?"

"It's the cat."

What? Quinn thought. Seriously? "What about the cat?"

A brief, tense silence followed, and then suddenly Rose shouted. "He's fucking talking to me!"

Part 3

The Night of the Wasp

Chapter 16

Madison Sheppard searched the desert through the dusty windshield of her black Land Rover. Ahead lay an expansive, bleak valley floor. In the heat-hazed distance, rocky peaks clawed their way into a parched blue sky. It was there that the black asphalt highway disappeared over a hill, on its way to Tonopah.

Glancing at the map on the flat-screen below the dash, the blue GPS arrow chased invisible prey, telling Madison everything but directions to her destination. She smacked the screen. Pounded on the dashboard. Tried frustratingly to knock some sense into her global positioning system. The arrow froze. Then it spun in a tight circle and zoomed off the screen.

"You fucking piece of shit!" Madison shouted. "Of all goddammed times!"

She continued speeding north along the highway, an unforgiving landscape of sand, snakes, and tumbleweeds stretching for miles on either side of her. Like the shimmering surface of a lake, a heat inversion caused Madison to slow as the highway seemed to vanish from sight. An occasional car whizzed past her, shaking the Rover as they sped on to Las Vegas.

As an exasperated Madison high-tailed it across the valley, a small collection of trailers forming a rather disorganized semi-circle appeared on her left. An apparent victim of some enraged pterodactyl, a green, heat-scorched Mazda Miata convertible sat parked in the center, its soft-top shredded and torn. A blue, 2015 Ford F-150 sat next to a plastic swimming pool with no water and a 3-inch layer of dirt.

Madison slammed the brakes, swerving the Rover into the lot and skidding to a stop in a plume of dust and sand. She looked at her cell phone. Zero bars and no service.

"You've got to be kidding," she muttered. "Where am I, the damned moon?"

Stepping out of the idling Rover, stinging heat and bone-dry air greeted her immediately. Panning around the small complex, she observed a wood picket fence lying flat on the ground, and a thick coil of rusted barbed wire. Three faded powder blue trailers, umber streaks of dirt and dust streaking from their screened windows, squatted ahead of her. The place looked like a scene from the horror film *The Hills Have Eyes*. She brushed off her jeans. "Jesus, what a dump," she muttered. "What do these people even do out here?"

Stepping up to the middle trailer, Madison tapped on the screen door. After a moment, she impatiently tapped again. The door creaked open, a pair of eyes gaping at her through a 3-inch gap.

"What you want?" Grumbled a man's voice from the darkened interior of the trailer. His eyes traveled down to her desert boots, then up the skin-tight jeans wrapping her athletic thighs and to her untucked, loose-fitting shirt. Then his eyes met hers. "You lost?"

"Is it that obvious?" Madison responded in a light, girlish voice.

The door creaked open, and the man stepped out into the daylight. Looking like a living scarecrow, his skin taut and pocked with red pussy sores, the odor from his sebaceous scalp drifted into Madison. Malodorous stale beer and unwashed socks soon followed. Madison, fighting back the urge to gag, felt her eyes watering. Vapid eyes moving past her, he locked in on the chugging Land Rover.

"I'm having trouble with my GPS and my phone has no signal," Madison said, glancing around the complex.

"Yeah, that happens 'round here a lot," he replied. "It's weird. You some sort of tourist? You're not one of those dipshits who wanna see Area 51, are ya?"

"Oh my god," Madison gushed. "I can't hide it, can I?" She tilted her head. "I'm Madison, by the way."

"I'm Scrug," he responded.

Scrug? She thought. His name is Scrug? Perfect.

Scrug folded his arms. "Yeah. I get at least two of you types a week. It'll cost you twenty bucks."

Madison brushed her shirt to the side to retrieve some bills from her back pocket, revealing a holstered Glock 19.

Startled, Scrug stepped back. "Hey, you a cop?" he asked, pointing wide-eyed at the pistol holstered on her belt.

Surprised, Madison glanced at her hip. "No," she laughed. "I'm a woman out in the desert asking a stranger for directions. I like the protection."

Drooping his shoulders, Scrug sighed relief. "Wow, that's so cool." He stepped past Madison, pointing back in the direction from which she'd come. "Okay, turn 'round, go back 'bout twelve miles. You'll see a dirt track that leaves the road and goes across the valley. That'll take you up to a ridge." He threw Madison a stern look. "And man, when you see them helos and black Suburbans, it's time to stop. Take your fucking selfie and turn your ass around."

Madison handed him a folded one-hundred-dollar bill. "Thanks, you've been helpful."

An astonished Scrug stared at the bill as if she'd handed him keys to a casino vault. "Wow, thanks!" he exclaimed. Then his expression grew serious and his eyes narrowed. "I'm not kidding, lady. When you see them, stop. Those assholes shot the tires out on my truck once because I got too close. Locked me up for a night. Didn't even replace the wheels."

Madison smiled. "I'll be fine," she said. "I can take care of myself."

"Yeah," Scrug mumbled, scanning her from head to toe. "I can see that."

Madison tore out of the lot in the Rover, leaving Scrug and his trailers behind in a cloud of dust. Twelve miles later, as Scrug promised, she found a rutted track leading across the valley and into the mountains. No wonder I missed it, she thought. It's just a dirt track. She glanced at the flat screen in the Rover, the blue GPS arrow meandering around in a circle as if it were playing musical chairs.

"Useless!" Madison shouted. She switched off the map and turned on some music. Oddly, with all that seemed to have gone haywire with her phone and GPS, the satellite radio still worked. The high vocals of Adele streamed from the speakers.

And who are you hiding from?

It ain't no life to live like you're on the run.

Madison switched the music back off. "God, I hate that woman."

THE DRIVE ACROSS the valley, along a deeply rutted dirt road, was brutal. Eventually reaching the base of the mountains, she stopped. Squinting through the dusty windshield at the serpentine road twisting its way up the bleak, rocky mountainside, she contemplated turning around.

"Fuck it."

She pushed the accelerator, winding her way upward along a steep dirt trail, trying not to imagine the long tumble back down the hillside - rolling, flipping, and smashing into boulders all the way back to the valley floor.

After what seemed like an eternity, the steep, winding road straightened out and she bumped and chugged her way onto a broad ridge. The earth falling away for thousands of feet on either side of her, another broad flat valley lay ahead. In the hazy sunbaked distance, buildings appeared - some tall and broad and others flat and narrow. A long asphalt runway stretched outward from the small cluster of buildings.

She leaned forward in her seat, enjoying the panorama. Then the Rover shook, and a deep *thumping* sound pounded her eardrums. Dusty cyclones swirling around her, she leaned as far forward as possible and looked above her. A gray Air Force HH-60U Ghost Hawk helicopter hovered 50-feet above, a helmeted crewman training a mini-gun on the Rover and ready to shred her if she attempted escape.

To her left, a black Suburban sped along the ridge, skidding to a stop in a cloud of desert dust. The doors flew open and four men in black t-shirts, tan cargo pants, and desert boots moved toward her, their scoped rifles all pointing right at her head.

Wow, Madison thought. Scrug's been on-point with everything so far. She sat back in the seat, placing both hands on the steering wheel, and staring straight ahead, remained motionless. One of the security men tapped the glass of her driver-side door, shouting instructions over the deafening blades of the Ghost Hawk. He commanded Madison to turn off the Rover and roll down her window, then place both hands back on the steering wheel. Madison complied, and the security man leaned in through the open window. Inspecting a photo in his hands, he then carefully studied her face.

"Wow, thanks for the dramatic reception!" Madison shouted over the din.

The man shouldered his rifle and waved at the Ghost Hawk. Banking steeply, the helicopter turned and headed back to the valley. He tapped his wristwatch. "You're late!"

FOLLOWING THE BLACK SUBURBAN across the valley and through multiple security checkpoints, Madison drove into the heavily guarded Groom Lake Proving Grounds, classically referred to as Area 51. She brought the Rover to a stop, switched off the engine, and stepped out into a relentless sun. A sun that, to her, seemed to have moved closer by ninety million miles.

"Jesus," she said to the man who'd approached her on the ridge. "How can you stand all this damned heat? And don't even tell me you get used to it."

"Well, ma'am, we get used to it." Technical Sergeant Groves responded with a charming grin.

Her face twisting into a frown, she flipped him off, then shielded her eyes as the Ghost Hawk landed and wound down. From next to the Ghost Hawk, the whine of a jet turbine grew louder, emitted from a sleek-looking black helicopter. Dressed somewhat impractically for a desert in all black, a muscular, chiseled, meticulously groomed man with jet-black hair and a precision-trimmed goatee waited next to an open door. To Madison, he could very well strip for bachelorette parties as a side gig.

"There's your chariot!" TSgt Groves shouted through cupped hands. He pointed Madison toward the gleaming black Augusta Westland helicopter.

As the helicopter wound up, she noticed no markings on the fuselage of any type. Not even an FAA registration number. The spinning rotors made a whooshing sound, not at all like the Ghost Hawk, whose thumping rotors seemed to beat the air into submission. Uneasy and anxious, Madison shivered. She turned back to Groves. "Where're we going?"

Groves shrugged.

An anxious Madison looked at the stripper-guy waiting for her next to the helicopter. She turned back to Groves. "Aren't you coming with me?"

"No, ma'am. I'm not," Groves responded. "And I don't know where you're going, and I don't want to know where you're going." He waved her on toward the black helicopter. Cautious and unsure, Madison reluctantly plodded over to the Westland. The muscular stripper-guy took her hand, helped her step inside, followed her in, and latched the door.

As the helicopter deftly lifted off, Madison felt as if she were leaving her stomach behind on the ground. She waved to Groves, turning her head just in time to see the stripper-guy spreading open a black hood. Swiftly, he yanked the hood down over her head. His large hands moving around her waist, he unclipped her holster and yanked the Glock 19 free.

"What the fuck!" She yelled.

"Quiet," he said in a deep, masculine voice. "Or we'll turn this bird around and kick you right back out. You'll get your weapon back when we return."

Madison defiantly crossed her arms. "Fine then," she said grittily. "Like I'd be able to see where we're going, anyway. Everything looks the same out here."

"Just a precaution, ma'am."

"By the way, do you know who I am?"

"Yes, I do," the man responded. Then he fell quiet, and all she heard was the soft thumping of blades and the hum of electronics.

45 minutes later, her stomach was floating up toward her throat as the helicopter suddenly descended. She felt a jarring force as the Westland touched down, and the stripper-guy unceremoniously whisked off her hood. An Air Force colonel in desert fatigues opened the door and helped her out.

"What's with all this Mission Impossible bullshit, colonel?" A frustrated Madison asked, wincing at the bright sunlight.

The colonel grabbed her elbow and pulled her away from the helicopter. "No one knows this place even exists," he responded. "I have to wear the stupid hood as well. C'mon, we have lunch ready."

The colonel escorted Madison toward three double-wide trailers. A large, steel, brown and tan camouflaged building rose high above her, and she estimated the structure to be roughly the size of a high school gymnasium. A diesel generator roared from behind a corner.

She had no clue where she was anymore. Nevada, Utah...California?

Not that she was any geography whiz.

MADISON ATE A MEAGER lunch of grilled cheese on white bread, potato chips, and a bland looking complimentary pickle. She made small talk with the colonel and three Pangea employees, none of whom she recognized.

Taylor waxed on about flight testing back at the Groom Lake Proving Grounds. With adolescent enthusiasm, he described two heavily modified F-22 Raptors he'd been putting "through the ringer." Or at least that's how he described it.

"This new electronics suite will triple the air-to-air capabilities of the Raptor," he said with a gleam. "All new look-down, shoot-down radar, data computers, and countermeasures. No adversary can match it. One Raptor will equal three." He took a large bite of sandwich and spoke as he chewed. "But it can't shoot down even one of your little bastards, can it?"

Madison wiped her lips with a napkin. "I wouldn't know, colonel. I haven't seen one yet."

Taylor nodded. "Well, let's stop wasting time. Hell, you've probably traveled a few hundred miles today."

Madison pushed her chair back and stood up. "Maybe next time you boys can give me a lift from the airport. I'd wear a hood from Vegas to Seattle before I'd drive through that nightmare again."

"Sure," he replied as he stood up. "I'll ask the President."

THE SMALL GROUP PROCEEDED across a large blacktop pad, Madison noticing odd geometric patterns of white lines with small orange and green concentric circles.

"What're those lines and circles, colonel?" Madison asked, curiously.

Taylor glanced over his shoulder as they reached a large steel door. "That's where we train them." He punched in a code on a keypad, and the door unlocked and opened with a clang and a grind.

A blast of frigid air immediately doused Madison as she stepped inside the enormous room, her head rotating around as she examined the structure. Rows of incandescent lighting bathed the room in white light. Soundproofing foam lined the walls and ceilings. A polished, sterile looking floor spread out before her. To her left, she noticed a desk with an open laptop lying on it. A lanky, brown-haired kid with dark-rimmed glasses, maybe all of twenty-five years old, stood at the desk tapping keys on the laptop. He noticed Madison watching him and introduced himself as Rich Hansen. Madison nodded.

"Sorry about the cold," Taylor said in a dark, monotone voice. His mood shifting from Pollyanna to pessimist, Madison sensed he wasn't entirely pleased with this job. He'd rather be chilling with his cool F-22's than training uncooperative Pangea specimens.

Directly across from her, on the far wall, three insect-like creatures with rounded humps on their fronts lay silent and motionless on the polished floor. About fifty feet from them was another, alone and separated from all the rest. She tried to get a sense of what they appeared to be. About five feet across and perhaps three feet long, they had smooth gray skin. Four separate wings spread outward, and on the edge of each wing was a wide, hollow cylinder. Their amber eyes seemed to look right past her and at the wall behind.

"Fuck me," Madison stuttered. "They look creepy."

"They don't need to be pretty," Taylor responded. "They're practically invisible and nearly silent. They just need to fly and communicate."

Madison's head snapped around. "Communicate?"

Taylor nodded and turned to Rich, the programmer. "Rich, get a program 12 spun up, will you? To show Ms. Sheppard?"

"A program 12?" Madison asked, confused.

Rich tapped frenetically on the laptop and the specimens hummed to life - a quiet, gentle, mesmerizing hum. Then they rose into the air and hovered.

"Ms. Sheppard, meet the Air Force A-88 Wasp."

"So, these are just drones?" She asked. "Like you can buy on Amazon?"

Taylor shook his head. "Oh no. You aren't buying these on Amazon."

Soon, all four Wasps were hovering above the floor in a harmonized, soft, and nearly undetectable whirr. Like soldiers on parade, the group of three rotated to their right, synchronized, moving quietly toward the sole Wasp at the far end. Now wearing a sheepish grin, Rich had moved away from his laptop, watching this scene unfold.

As the Wasp procession moved along the wall, Madison noticed a dark red crown stenciled on the hump of the lone Wasp at the far end. "So, um, colonel, who is actually controlling these?"

Taylor pointed at the crowned Wasp. "She is. The Queen."

Madison cocked her head. "Um, Queen?"

Taylor explained to Madison that the group of drones was like a collective, with the Queen being the master. In fact, he said, they functioned much like bees. The drones were always under the direction of the Queen, and they would defend her at all costs. Anxiously, Madison watched the Queen moving through the room in near silence. Now forming a conga line, her three subjects spun left and right, scanning the walls, the table, the laptop, and moving toward the door. All the while, they were reporting data in real time back to the Queen. She collected this data, compiling a picture of what Taylor referred to as "The Battlespace."

Madison shuddered. The Queen's eyes, now a bright, glowing yellow, seemed to stare straight at her.

"She's checking you out," a cautious Taylor muttered. "To see if you're a friend or foe."

Madison erupted. "What! What do you mean checking me out?!" She shot a wide-eyed look of horror at Taylor. "She's looking to see if I'm a target?!" On instinct, she swept her shirt back and placed her hand on her holster, only then remembering she'd surrendered her pistol to the stripper-guy in the helicopter.

"Yeah," Taylor said with caution. "I wouldn't do that."

The Queen sped across the room toward Madison. Her glowing eyes pulsating, she actually appeared angry.

"They learn. They remember. This is cutting edge Artificial Intelligence. Developed by your company, actually. And the more of them in a group, the smarter they become. Imagine these in the thousands, gathering gigs of data, constantly evaluating the battlespace around them. Determining the predictability of the enemy and the probability of their operations. And all autonomously."

Staring with wide-eyed apprehension as the Queen hovered just two feet away from her, Madison froze. Noticing her wide-eyed expression, Taylor turned to Rich. "Nest them please."

Eyeing the Queen with caution, Rich returned to his laptop and typed codes and instructions.

"These little shits are going to put Air Force Recon out of business," Taylor added with a deep sigh.

"So, this is where all our money goes," Madison said, scrunching her lips and shaking her head.

"They'll get the job done," Taylor replied.

Madison watched the Wasps move to the far wall. The Queen, moving off by herself, seemed to think she was too important to mingle with her little workers. Then the humming ceased, and all the Wasp's eyes dimmed to a dull amber.

Taylor studied Madison. "You know, the way you guys are using these things-"

Madison looked at the colonel with glacial blue-gray eyes. "Yes?"

Taylor looked incredulous. "Well, it's illegal. A big time Geneva Convention no-no. We've already had one incident and-"

Madison shrugged. "I have no idea what you're talking about." Her phone buzzed. What? I have cell service here? Here?! She looked at the screen and groaned, throwing her head back in frustration. "Sam, you pain in the ass." She turned back to Taylor. "Thanks for the show-and-tell, but I need to get back."

Astounded, Taylor cocked his head back. "What, now?"

"Yup, now." She shoved the phone in her pocket and tilted her head, flashing a girlish grin of flirtation. "Say, you guys' mind throwing a bag over my head and flying me to the airport?"

Chapter 17

In the pitch black of a moonless night, Quinn coasted to a stop in Rose's driveway.

Thrusting his head back, he dragged the palm of his hand down his face. Is Rose losing her mind? Am I losing mine? Why on earth did Rose think a cat was talking to her?

Exhaling a long, deep breath, he stepped out of the SUV and hurried up the path to the house. Tapping on the door, it swung open with a clatter and Rose stood in the doorway wearing a blue silk nightgown and pink slippers. Her expression was that of someone who'd just witnessed a hatchet massacre. Trembling hands clutched her birthday gift, the TaylorMade graphite driver, with a white-knuckled death grip.

"Jesus, Rose," Quinn said, reaching out and gently pulling the golf club from her hands. "I don't think you need this anymore."

"I'm not crazy, Ronan," Rose said, her voice quivering. "I know what I heard. Will you come in? Please?"

Quinn nodded, following Rose through the door and into her home.

The house was a midwestern Louvre. Soft recessed lighting illuminated the works of Parisian street artists, obscure watercolors from Eastern Europe, statues from the heart of Africa, and rugs from the Orient. Her mortified eyes searched Quinn's, as if trying to read his thoughts.

"Where's the cat?" He asked.

She grabbed his hand, leading him into her living room where, squatting indifferently on a fine woven rug purchased at a Bangalore bazaar, sat Oscar. Staring intently at the ceiling as if he were searching for a new constellation, he'd lick a paw or scratch behind an ear at random, but otherwise remained motionless.

"Okay. What did he tell you?" Asked Quinn, watching Oscar behave like any cat would.

"It was just a word at first. 'Cold.' Then there was silence, and then I heard where, dark, bright, and it's beautiful."

Folding his arms, Quinn watched as Oscar became distracted by an insect buzzing around his furry head. The cat looked like, well, a cat. There seemed to be nothing unique or spectacular about him. Just a cat distracted by a bug.

"When I heard the voice, Oscar was staring at me, Ronan. And I was like 'oh my god, the cat's talking to me.' The words came again. Cold. Where am I? This place? Like he was asking me why he was here. So, I called you."

"Rose, I mean–"

Rose shook her head. "Don't, Ronan, just don't. I know what I heard. And when the voice came back, after I called you, Oscar began meowing. I don't think he's talking to me at all. Someone else is. The voice sounded like it was coming from, well, everywhere."

"Everywhere?" Quinn asked.

"All around me. And the voice is from a woman."

"Huh," Quinn grunted. "That eliminates Oscar."

"My other cats are scared out of their minds. They're hiding under the bed," she said, gesturing down the hall to her bedroom.

"Oh? Really?"

"Yes…oh really. I'm clearly not the only one who heard her. So, I'm not so bat-shit looney now, am I? Would you like some tea?"

PLOPPING DOWN ON THE couch next to Quinn, she handed him a steaming cup of Earl Grey, tucked her feet up, and slurped tea. "Dear god, Ronan," she said. "Please tell me my house isn't haunted. I can't deal with a ghost."

Quinn sipped tea. "Rose, I think you'd get along just fine with ghosts."

She gazed at Oscar as the cat-medium rolled onto his side and seemed to drift off. "Maybe my wild days are catching up with me now."

Quinn turned to her with an arched brow. "Wild days? You? What on earth are you talking about?"

Rose rested her head on his shoulder. "My dear, I lived what I call a 'very fluid life' back in the day."

Quinn couldn't help but laugh. "Do tell."

"Well," she explained. "In the 80s, when I lived back in L.A., I worked for a large and influential law firm. We had these 'office parties' and by parties, I mean, yowzah…serious parties. Cocaine. Pills. Booze. Raunchy sex in offices." Rose slurped some more tea, and her eyes grew distant with recollection. "Oh, I had some wild times back then. But oh my, did I get burned out or what? When I caught John cheating on me, in our own house no less - the swine - I called it quits. Left LA for Florida. Bounced around for a while. Wound up here. Looking for a fresh start. Just like you."

Quinn placed his arm around Rose, pulling her close, noticing Oscar was now fast asleep.

"So, you worked for a law firm and everyone did drugs? How'd that work?"

"Well, funny thing. We charged $800 an hour to defend our clients from drug offenses, and that paid for our drugs." She covered her mouth and let out a soft giggle. "Those crazy Eighties."

Quinn leaned forward, placing his tea on the coffee table. "Rose, I think I'm in over my head on this whole deal." His shoulders slouching, he moved his head in a circle, trying to release a deep, exhaustive strain. "I'm wondering if I should turn everything over to the State Police. Not like I have much to turn over. Nothing but supposition and hunches and feelings."

Rose's head snapped to face Quinn. "Seriously? Over your head?" She twisted her body around on the sofa, facing him. "Ronan, listen to me. When you came to us, you were a train wreck. But I didn't see a wreck. I saw a man who'd lived more lives than any of us could imagine. You'd seen and done things in Afghanistan - things back in New York - that none of us could ever imagine. You came here, and you changed this department. You changed us. Why do you think the city council voted for you to be their new chief? Because you're a leader. I just don't think you realize it sometimes. You may think you're over your head, but I don't believe it for one second. You're built for this sort of thing. And we'll deal with anything that anyone throws at us, and we'll do it together."

"Well, I really screwed up in New York," he said with a twisted, pained expression.

"So what?" Rose said. "That's in the past. I hope someday you'll be able to put all that away somewhere and live in peace. I can see that tortured look in your eyes sometimes. It makes me want to cry."

"Don't cry. I'm fine."

Rose patted his knee. "Will you spend the night with me?"

"Well, Rose, what'll everyone think about the chief spending the night with his assistant?"

"They'll think that chief sure is one lucky son of a bitch." She stood and stretched. "I'm going to bed. I hope you don't mind sleeping on the couch." She left the room, returning with a blanket and pillow, kissed his cheek, then strode off to bed.

Tossing and turning, Quinn attempted comfort on a sofa he was much too large for. He studied Oscar, curled up on the floor, sleeping. Oscar hadn't moved from that spot since Quinn arrived.

"Are you going to talk to me or what?" He muttered to the snoozing tabby. Exhaustion taking hold, his eyelids dropped like curtains to the floor of a stage. "Dumb cat…"

PUNGENT DUNG-SMOKE WAFTED through the icy air as Gunnery Sergeant Quinn kneeled on a makeshift wooden platform attached to a crumbling, ancient stone wall.

Quinn hated this village, and he hated this position. Too open. Too easily surrounded. Indefensible. Through the artificial green light of his night vision equipment, he scanned a broad open field. Ghostly shapes moved with slow deliberation from the tree-line a hundred yards from his position. Silent, but not unseen.

"Shit," he muttered, turning to the lieutenant. "We're about to be contacted. What's with the gunship they promised us, LT? Are we getting air support or what?"

The LT turned to the radioman. "Hey, radio Green Dog. Get some air support before we're overrun."

Thunk, thunk, thunk. Quinn heard the telltale sound of mortars firing.

"Incoming!" he shouted. "Gomez, get on the sixty!" Rushing along the wooden platform, he tapped on every other Marine's shoulders. "I want you assholes on the south wall!" Surveying the scene again through his night vision, he observed at least a hundred Taliban taking up positions. Rifles cracked in the distance. Bullets whooshed past his head. Flashes from exploding mortar rounds lit up the primitive homes of the village. "Return fire!" he ordered.

Glancing behind him, he saw villagers assembling outside their homes, watching the battle unfold. "Are you people nuts?! Get back in your homes!" He scrambled down the ladder, frantically pushing villagers back to safety. Shouting in the Pashto dialect, he pleaded for them to return to the safety of their homes, then scrambled back up the ladder. "LT, are we getting fucking air support or not!?"

Shouting into the radio, the LT called out grid positions. "Gunny Quinn! We have air assets inbound! I want flares and strobes on the target!"

Quinn nodded, and hurrying along the platform, he shouted orders to his Marines. "I want flares and strobes on the Talis! We've got Apaches inbound, hot!"

In the far distance, over the din of battle, the comforting sound of helicopter rotors cut through the crisp night. Moments later, two Apache attack helicopters crested the tall ridge to the east, then dropped toward the earth, moving toward the fight at high speed.

Quinn ran to the LT, tapping him on the shoulder. "I'm heading to the south wall." Scrambling along the platform, he noticed a villager standing alone. Then, to his amazement, the villager darted toward the wall, halting at a spot just below the LT's position. What the hell? He thought. What is that in his hand? Before Quinn could even process what this villager was clutching, a hot streak of light from an Apache pierced the blackness of night.

The Apaches are firing on us! Quinn thought in desperation. Firing on our position! He looked down at the villager. This man is no local. He's Taliban. A Taliban clutching an IR strobe light, directing the Apaches to fire on their own troops.

A Hellfire missile seconds from hitting the lieutenant's position, Quinn could do nothing to stop it.

"*CHIEF? CHIEF?*"

Quinn's eyes shot open like a screen sucked into a roller.

Where am I? He thought, his eyes moving across a dimly lit ceiling. What is this place? Afghanistan? Am I back in Helmand Province? Slowly, he regained his senses and came to realize he was on Rose's couch. His heart pounded so hard in his chest, it seemed it would just snap its restraints and scamper off.

"Ronan?"

Quinn sat up. Massaging his eyes and gathering his bearings, he looked over at the Indian rug from Bangalore spreading out across the hardwood floor. Oscar, squatting and neck stretched outward, seemed fixated on the ceiling.

"Rose," Quinn grumbled. "What time is it?" Rubbing his eyes, he glanced at the hallway leading to Rose's bedroom.

Eyes wide and body rigid like a marble statue, Rose stood quietly at the entrance to the hallway. Nodding toward the ceiling, she placed a finger to her lips.

"What?" Quinn mumbled, confused.

"Mr. Quinn?" A voice, like that of a young woman, filled his ears.

"Mr. Quinn, I can see you. I can see Oscar."

Quinn shook his head. This can't be happening. "Who are you?" he asked, unsure who or why he was asking. This all seemed so confusing.

"What…what did you do to me?" The voice asked again. The tone of the question sounded rhetorical. *"Where am I? What is this place?"*

Quinn turned to Rose and shrugged. Rose shrugged back.

"I'm so cold."

"Where are you?" Quinn searched the ceiling, but this voice emanated from everywhere.

"I don't know. It's really weird. Like I'm moving through a corridor. The voices. I can hear the voices."

Cautious and quiet, Rose moved into the room, searching the ceiling. "Whose voices, dear? Whose voices do you hear?"

"All of them. All who came before me. What is this place?"

"Who are you?" Quinn asked again. "Do you have a name?"

"Hello?"

Once more he asked for a name, hearing only silence. Rose tried reconnecting with the voice, but with no success. With a prolonged stretch, Oscar arched his back, yawned, then trotted daintily toward Rose's room as if nothing had even happened.

"She's gone," Rose muttered. "Oh, damn it."

Quinn stood and stared at Rose with astonishment and dismay. "She knew my name, Rose," he said from behind bewildered eyes. "She knew thc cat's name. She knew our names."

Quinn, confused and unsure, looked as if he were wandering through a dark forest with no compass. "You don't think…" he gasped to Rose. "You don't think that voice is Pippa Simpson's, do you? The accident victim?"

Gliding gracefully to her boss, friend, and confidant, Rose gently took Quinn's hands. "I don't know, sweetie. But I know two things for sure."

"What's that?"

"Well, I'm not crazy, and I have a haunted cat in my house. Who's going to believe that?"

CHAPTER 18

AT 2:30 P.M., BATTLING a westerly crosswind, Samir Singh's private jet touched down at the Woodrock Pangea airfield. Thanking Jill and the pilots for their flexibility as the Gulfstream's turbofans wound down, Singh rushed through the cabin door, down the steps, and into a blustery afternoon.

Placing soft foam protectors in his ears, he stood on the massive aircraft parking ramp, absorbing the entire scene. Jet engines howled, diesel trucks roared, and tugs and loaders chugged in a dizzying industrial discord. Loaders fed a 747 through its gaping maw, the giant jet swallowing cargo like a starving beast. A large 767 cargo jet rumbled past him, taxiing for takeoff. This airfield, fortuitously abandoned by the Air Force decades before, had become Singh's most prized acquisition. But all this activity will draw its share of attention, he thought. Aviation enthusiasts tracked aircraft flights from their PCs, and just for kicks. An odd hobby indeed, but one that the Iron Hand team needed to be constantly aware of. All this activity at his Pangea complex could give the impression that South Dakota was launching an invasion.

A black Chrysler pulled up in front of his jet, the rear door swung open, and Singh stopped dead in his tracks. Madison, sweeping her golden mane over her shoulders, stepped through the door and rushed to Singh, holding him in a tight embrace. As she held him, Singh could only wonder why she was meeting him here to begin with.

"I told you I was coming here!" He shouted over the racket of jets, trucks, and cargo loaders. "But I didn't expect you to be here to greet me! I thought you were in Chicago!"

Madison released him and took a step back, her glacial stare piercing. "And you're supposed to be in London!" She shouted over the din, her blue-gray eyes narrowing with suspicion. "Don't tell me you have a girlfriend in South Dakota!"

"I could be so lucky!" he replied.

"She wouldn't be!" Madison sneered.

"That's why you're my one and only, Madison!"

She thrust her hands to her hips. "I'd better be!"

The two slid into the backseat of the sedan and closed the doors. The noise of airfield activity muted in the car, Singh twisted around, studying Madison while she tied her hair off into a twisted updo.

"But seriously," Singh asked. "Why'd you come here?"

"What does it matter?" Madison said. "I wanted to see you. And if you recall, I'm the Senior Vice President of Operations. We're moving into the midyear, and you're spending an awful lot of money on things I don't understand. So, I was coming here anyway, just a few days sooner than I'd planned."

Singh shrugged. "Well, it's good to see you. I missed you for the whole two days we spent apart."

Madison extended her middle finger. "You're such a dork." Turning and gazing through the window as the sedan moved across the ramp, she watched a scissor-lift load containers into the rear of a large, white 747. "What's with all the planes?"

"Moving product to market," Singh replied, marveling at the busyness of his prized real estate.

"Sam, why do we make so many drones?"

"Drones?" Singh stuttered.

Madison turned in her seat and faced him. "Sam, please. We're making and shipping drones and we haven't seen a dime. You're putting me in the red. Who're they for?"

"Why does it matter? As long as someone is buying them?"

She turned back to the window, watching jets and containers flash past. "I have a confession to make," she said, her voice trailing off.

Singh's throat tightened. She's seeing another man.

"I went to Area 51. I went to go see these drones for myself. I wanted to see what we're spending so much R&D on and getting nothing in return."

Singh's head snapped toward Madison so fast he could've broken the sound barrier. "Wait. What? You went to Area 51? How'd you know about Area 51?"

Madison faced him and held up her phone. "Location tracker, Sam. You go to Vegas and then you vanish on a highway in some shit-stain part of America."

Singh gaped at her phone like she'd just shown video footage of him robbing a 7-11. Then he fell into a quiet frustration and anger. "Putting you not trusting me aside, those drones are highly classified. You have no clearance for that. How'd you even get into Area 51 in the first place?"

Madison, with a subtle shake of her head, seemed disappointed by Singh's questions. "I worked for the DOD before I came to you, Sam. Remember? I still have connections within the department."

Singh crossed his arms, looking dejected. "Why didn't you just ask?"

"Because of right now, Sam. 'I have no clearance. I don't belong.' Blah blah blah."

"Did they take you to the site?"

"I have no clue where it is. They stuck a bag over my head. Why do you ask? Are you going to have to kill me now?"

Singh sighed. "No, of course not. Don't be silly. And honestly, I don't know what they're for either. I just build them."

"Okay then, Sam." Madison replied. "You tell those bastards to pay for them as well."

Moving into the multi-storied garage and parking, they stepped out of the sedan and walked through the garage toward the elevators.

"I'm sorry if I'm being too nosey, Sam, but fuck. We're going to go broke if you don't have buyers lined up for those drones. And if they're all going to the Air Force, you'll eventually need to tell me why, because I have a feeling that you're not being straight with me."

"When I know, you'll know. You handle the business and I'll handle the sales." He stopped and caressed her cheeks, studying her eyes. "But don't do that again. I won't kill you, but someone else just might."

Madison stepped back, an expression of horror twisting her face. "What? Who?"

"Never mind. Just be honest with me. Next time please ask, okay?"

Madison, still shaken by the 'kill her' comment, checked her phone. "We have a three-o'clock with Kim Cho and her team in corporate."

Singh glanced at his watch. "Okay, just give me a few. I have to go see something first."

Madison tilted her head. "See what?"

"Oh, the office of the woman employee who died last week. Just want to pay my respects." Singh turned and hurried through the garage toward the elevators, leaving a dumbfounded and speechless Madison behind.

A RUSH OF CHILL air tingled the back of her neck as the cluttered laboratory hummed and whooshed.

Sitting quietly on a tall metal stool in the frigid laboratory, Kisha peered through the lenses of the temperamental radioscope and scribbled notes on a pad of paper.

She closed her eyes and threw her head back, sucking in a deep breath and dabbing a tear meandering along her cheek. Her heart ached. A bruised, pulsing muscle in her chest that felt as if someone had punched it in a brawl. Pippa's team was an emotional mess. Barely speaking to one another. Walking through the halls like depressed zombies. Preet, Pippa's boss, had taken over the role of managing the team, but he was no help at all. That man couldn't produce an emotion if there was a gun to his head.

A soft tapping came from behind her.

Startled, she spun in her chair and faced the door. She couldn't believe her eyes. The CEO of Pangea, who'd probably never even seen the inside of Building D, let alone a lab, stood at the doorway with a sparkling, million-dollar grin. Stumbling off her stool and brushing her lab coat, she fixed her hair and fiddled with buttons.

"Please, please, relax, um, Kisha, is that correct?" Singh said in a calm, calculating voice.

Still in shock, looking as if the Dalai Lama had just walked through the door, Kisha nodded. He approached her and they shook hands. Then Singh scanned the lab but, oddly, not with much curiosity. He seemed to feign more interest than to actually show any. Hands clutched behind his back, he gave himself a tour of the lab, bending over inquisitively, making soft *mm-hm's*, strolling about the room like one would stroll through a rose garden on a Sunday morning. He ambled back to Kisha.

"Your work here is very much appreciated," Singh said, his expression turning more serious. "I want you to know that your team is valuable. So valuable, in fact, I have no clue what you guys even do here." His broad smile disarming, impeccable teeth, bricks of pearl, Singh's dark eyes searched hers as if expecting some response. He glanced around the chill lab. Seeing a stool, he slid it up in front of Kisha with a metallic screech. Reaching out and taking her hands, his eyes arched into sorrowful ovals.

"I want you to know," he said solemnly. "That I heard about the tragic accident with your manager. I want to express, on behalf of the board of directors and the leadership team, our condolences."

Kisha's heart tightened as she fought back an urge to collapse to the floor and weep at his feet. Please, Kish, she thought to herself, don't get all melodramatic. Don't go all Macbeth on him.

"I've heard nothing but wonderful things about her," Singh continued. "From her boss, and all the way up the chain. She was an incredibly bright woman."

Kisha wiped an escaping tear from her cheek. "Yeah, she was like super smart and goofy as well. She was a great boss. Best I ever had."

"Well then, she's certainly more popular than I am," he said, shifting his gaze around the lab. "Kisha, is there anything in her office she may have left behind? I know it was gone through, and thoroughly, as I understand, but anything they have missed, or anything you may have found that you want me to send back home to her mother and father?"

Puzzled by this question, Kisha sat erect. What is he looking for? Why is he really here? "No, nothing was in there. I looked."

"Are you positive?"

Of course I'm positive, Kisha thought. Like I'd forget something like that. "Positive. They cleared everything out, like the very next morning. It really bothered us. These security guys just boxed everything up. They made it seem like she wasn't even a real person."

Singh slapped his thighs. "Bastards!" Teeth clenched, he looked down at the floor, disgustedly shaking his head. "Yes, well, procedure, I suppose. I'll look into that. That's just not right. Oh, a new radioscope." He stood up from the stool, leaning over Kisha's shoulder, carefully examining the scope. "How's it working out?"

Kisha became suspicious of this entire surprise visit. The very direction of this entire conversation. He's fishing, she thought. Fishing for something that he thinks she knows.

"It breaks a lot," Kisha replied, leaning away from him as he hovered over her.

Singh sat back down on the stool. "I'll tell Purchasing you need a replacement." Once again, Singh burrowed deeply into her eyes, Kisha shifting uncomfortably on the stool.

"Did Pippa ever mention what your work goes into?"

Kisha shook her head. "No."

"Did she ever mention or ask you about anything? Like a name, or a project, or something along those lines?"

"Like what?" Kisha replied, puzzled. "She went to meetings a lot. I'm sure she knew what we were supporting."

Singh nodded impatiently. "Yes, I'm sure, but nothing about a special project?"

Kisha studied Singh's narrowed, darkened eyes. "Well," she said in recollection. "The day before her crash, she asked me about something.

Something 'hand'? Big Hand? Something like that. I really don't remember. Is that what we're working on?"

Singh shook his head, resting his hand on her shoulder. "No, Kisha, she must've been referring to something else. Something we don't do here."

"You know," Kisha added thoughtfully. "She asked if I'd heard about someone going missing. That I remember for sure."

Singh's eyes snapped back to hers. "Really? Who?"

Kisha shrugged. "I don't know who. She never said the name."

Singh stood up from the chair. "You know what, Kisha?" He smiled and clasped his hands together. "Forget I even asked."

Glancing beyond Singh's shoulder, Kisha noticed a woman standing alone at the lab door. Someone she'd seen around the campus and on Kim Cho's boring PowerPoint slides. Madison Sheppard, the executive VP. Kisha grew immediately annoyed, and Madison hadn't even spoken yet. Acting pretentious and bothered by having to mingle with the ordinary boat rowers, Madison's dark red matte lipstick highlighted her impertinence.

Singh glanced over his shoulder and then returned to Kisha. "Uh oh," he said, cupping his hand next to his mouth and falling into a whisper. "The real boss is here."

To Kisha, this entire episode felt condescending. Like she was just some doofus intern.

"There you are." Madison tapped her watch. "We have a team to meet."

Singh leaned into Kisha. "I'm very sorry about Pippa," he whispered. "Forget about my questions, okay?"

Kisha nodded. "Of course, Mr. Singh."

His eyes bore into hers. Feeling uneasy, she shifted on her stool.

"I mean it," he whispered in a dark, ominous voice. "Forget I ever asked."

Kisha nodded again. "Um, okay."

SINGH AND MADISON WALKED briskly down the hallway of Building D, Singh glancing into Pippa's darkened office as they passed by.

"I thought you were visiting the dead woman's office," Madison said with a crisp edge to her voice.

"Well, I saw Kisha in the lab and wanted to give her my condolences."

"Well? What did this Kisha have to say?"

"Nothing," Singh responded. "She said nothing, except what a wonderful woman her boss was."

Madison threw Singh a fierce sideways glance. "Great. I'm sure she was really wonderful."

Madison took the elevator up to the corporate offices after Singh told her he needed to make some calls back to London.

"3 pm, Sam. Meeting at 3. Stop making me go hunt for you."

He pecked her on the cheek. "I enjoy playing hard to get," he replied.

"Yeah, okay," Madison said with a glimmer and an impish smile. "If you're not giving me wine and bending me over in the shower tonight, then I'm dumping you."

"Okay, I'll see if I'm available," he chortled.

Madison flipped him off. "Dork."

Walking through the halls of the Pangea complex, searching for an empty conference room, Singh came across a darkened office and slipped inside. Plopping down on a chair, he whisked the secure comm device from his pocket, tapping in a code. Jupiter's odd, tinny voice came through the speaker immediately.

"Yes, Sam?"

Singh leaned back in his chair. "I'm at the Woodrock plant. We're moving specimens out in plane-loads. What about the other locations? Are they moving out also? As scheduled?"

"I thought you were in London," Jupiter replied in a metallic, male Alexa voice. "Why did you come back?"

Singh shifted in the chair. "Well, Red Lancer said that the local police gave his guys a hard time. Do you think we moved too fast? It could raise questions."

"Questions?" Jupiter shot back. "From some redneck cop in Woodrock? What sort of questions?"

Singh gritted his teeth. "Gee, I don't know, like maybe why we took her body away so quickly. The coroner hadn't completed his autopsy and Red Lancer's guys, who I'm sure are tip-top, were pretty clumsy."

"Red Lancer informs me we may not have everything of hers. You said she had two phones."

Singh leaned back, slapping his hand over his eyes. "I said she 'may have.' Not 'she had.' Normally, people have a work phone and a personal phone. But it's probably not a big deal. At least we have her work phone."

"If you're comfortable with it, then I'm comfortable with it," Jupiter said. "But I want you to make sure. You know, zero hour is going to come fairly quickly. I'm moving the project up again. We have two months before Operation Iron Hand goes live."

Singh rubbed his forehead. "I know that..."

"Are you having second thoughts? If you are, you need to tell me now, and let me know why you're having them. You're my number two, and you are my son, so please tell me how you feel."

Singh hated that conciliative tone. He only ever had one set of parents and they were both dead. But Jupiter felt it made things more relatable, and by doing so, kept Singh in a constant state of appeasement. Like a son continuously trying to win a dismissive father's approval.

"I will, I promise. Also, the woman has mentioned nothing, that I can tell, about Iron Hand. So, I'm satisfied that there've been no further compromises. The woman didn't even know what she was looking at. Let's keep that in mind before you send Red Lancer out there assassinating everyone. There've been questions raised about his previous little job."

"We have to do what we have to do."

Singh leaned into the phone. "Yeah, well, keep a leash on that freak. What was he thinking? The Simpson job could've shown up on a tox report."

"I'll speak to Red Lancer. He wanted to see how well Genesis performed for himself."

Singh shook his head. "Why does he care? He's a janitor. He needs to remember that. And we're lucky we got to her backpack in time. Someone else could've died and this thing wouldn't be so secret anymore, would it? He's worse than a moron. He's a sociopathic moron. This whole affair got more complicated than it needed to be."

"I'll speak to him. Be well, Sam," and the call ended.

Singh shoved the device into his pocket. Be well? *Be Well?* I'll feel much more "well" when I learn what the Woodrock Police Department knows, he thought. He needed to know everything they did. Did they think she was murdered? Did they recover a second phone?

Singh had done his research into Ronan Quinn like he would prior to any business negotiation. A decorated Marine and former New York homicide detective, he was no redneck cop. But he was no shining star either. Heavy drinker. Assaulted his wife. Divorced. Fired from the NYPD. A real fall from grace.

It wouldn't be hard to get information from this guy at all, he thought. With dazzling charm and years of closing business deals behind me, I'll make quick work of this former hero turned burnout.

KISHA WATCHED SAMIR SINGH and Madison Sheppard vanish down the hallway. She pulled her cellphone from her back pocket and typed a message.

You'll never guess who just popped in to see me.

Santa Claus?

Better than Santa. The big boss.

Well, isn't that interesting?

It was kind of weird, TBH.

Talk later?

Yup. Ciao for now.

CHAPTER 19

SHORTLY AFTER DAWN BROKE, Quinn left Rose's house, making his way back home under slate gray skies and an unusually chill, damp morning. He nearly drove right past his own home, so preoccupied he was with the previous night's events.

A ghost? Really? A ghost?

Standing in his kitchen, he poured three glasses of scotch and dumped them into the sink. His three Hail-Mary devotion of a forever struggling addict. Then he walked to his bedroom, undressed, and slipped into shorts and a t-shirt. Dropping to the floor, he grunted out 200 pushups. 200 sit-ups. 20 pullups. Gasping, he jumped on the stationary bike and set it to the maximum. Pedaling with vigor, he switched on the TV.

The Dow dropped 500 points at the opening bell. *So what?*

The President signed a bill allowing an additional $1 billion in defense spending. *Like we need more of that.*

The Chinese Navy and American Navy were having a standoff in the South China Sea. *Screw China. Go Navy.*

Temperatures in Bangalore, India, soared to 130 degrees. Thousands were dead or dying. Paris hit 110 degrees. *Jesus…*

A plot to bomb the White House was foiled. The accused bomber, a retired schoolteacher, claimed lizard people ran the government.

According to this hysterical educator of kids, the lizards were coordinating an invasion of earth with other lizards in another universe, using the Washington Monument as an intergalactic radio antenna. *Maybe we're overdue for an asteroid strike. Even the dinosaurs weren't this damn stupid.*

Quinn completed his workout, shaved, ironed shirts, and tried to create some sense of his world. What a life arc. A wealthy Boston kid joining the Marines, to Woodrock ghost-whisperer. Why was this spirit from the afterlife even talking to him in the first place? The more he thought about the voice, the more he thought of Pippa. That voice. Those words. Well, they seemed very Pippa-like.

LATE BY MORE than an hour, Quinn drove to the station. Passing Rose's desk, she muttered *good morning*, and he returned a muted *good morning* in return. He asked Fig to step into his office.

An eager Fig, his hometown now shrouded in the greatest mystery since aliens abducted Mary Glover in 1964, hustled inside and closed the door. Swaying left to right in his chair, finger propping up his chin, Quinn's expression was one of detachment.

"You okay, boss?" Fig asked.

Quinn slowly focused on Fig, his vision penetrating the awkward deputy as if he weren't even there.

Ronan Quinn had grown very weary of the *could have been this and could have been that* theories. Feeling as if he were being dragged down a street behind a horse, he needed to get up, brush himself off, and begin taking command. To stop being reflexive. To be proactive. It was time to look at the facts. Look at the evidence. Forget about ghosts and afterlives and invisible stranglers.

Fiddling with his fingers, Fig shifted uncomfortably. Quinn continued staring intensely at Fig, like he was pulling some energy force out of him.

What was Pippa like as a person? Was she a bad driver? Was she mixed in with the wrong people? Bad boyfriend? Did she belong to a cult? Did she know Chris Hadley? Were they in a relationship? Is that what the suicide note was all about?

Quinn shattered the silence. "I need you to find out who her friend circle was, Fig."

Fig jerked as Quinn suddenly spoke. "Who's friend circle?"

"Pippa's friend circle," Quinn replied.

Fig threw Quinn a confused look. "You mean the victim?"

"Yes. See if any of her friends are Pangea employees. I want to speak to them first."

"Okay, boss." Fig replied. "Cal Barber is dating someone at Pangea."

"Who? Cal who?"

"Cal Barber. He's the real estate guy. You know, the billboard, 'see a Barber get a price cut?' He's in my weekend shooting club."

"Oh yeah," Quinn chortled. "Really great slogan. Get on it, please?"

Fig rushed out the door.

Quinn slumped into his chair. Fig needed to contain his enthusiasm. The last thing he needed were the other deputies asking questions. Absent-mindedly chewing on the cap of a blue ballpoint pen, he spun around in his chair.

Asking Pangea for information would be about as fruitful as getting a sea sponge to talk about its feelings. And Quinn felt uneasy about approaching Pangea at all. They were inching up the rungs to the top of his suspect list. But then how do you make the world's largest and wealthiest tech company a suspect? And suspects in what? A maybe murder? A possibly faked suicide? Should he uncover a crime - a crime committed by a Pangea employee or employees - he was going to punt this whole thing over to the FBI. This wasn't a matter of being in over his head. This wasn't a question of competency. This was just a matter of jurisdiction and resources.

So, the question remained. How could he interview Pippa's friends without setting off alarm bells and raising red flags of suspicion? That possessed furball feline, that's how. Oscar was the perfect bait, and he needed to earn his keep.

Rose opened the door and peeked inside. She had an odd, perplexed look on her face.

"Ronan, Mr. Singh is here. He wants a meeting with you."

"Mr. Singh?" Quinn asked, puzzled.

"You know, the CEO of Pangea."

Quinn leaned way back into his creaking leather office chair. Why in the hell is the CEO of Pangea here? He glanced through open office blinds and to Rose's desk. A lean, dark-skinned man in a Patagonia vest and cargo pants tapped away on his cell phone. Not exactly how I thought a CEO would dress, he muttered. Keeping a low profile? Quinn felt suspicious.

"Send him in."

Rose stepped out, directing Singh to his office. Striding in with a charming grin, Singh carried the demeanor of someone reconnecting with a long-lost friend. Which he clearly wasn't.

"Good morning, Chief Quinn!" An ebullient Singh thrust his hand outward. "If you're busy, I can come back another time."

Quinn pushed his chair back. "Nope, I'm free. I have nothing going on of any real importance right now." The two men shook hands with vigor, neither wanting to be the first to release his grip.

Singh stepped back, studying Quinn as Quinn studied him back. For a moment, they stood in silence - two bull elk sizing up each other's antlers. Quinn's imposing stature had little effect on the much shorter and slender Sam Singh.

Quinn broke the awkwardness. "So, what brings the CEO of Pangea to Woodrock?"

With a pretentious grin, Singh asked if he could have a seat, slid the chair back, plopped down, and crossed his legs. "Oh, you know, just checking up on our Pangea plant. I don't get out much."

"Really," Quinn replied. "What can the Woodrock Police force do for you today? We don't have any of your people locked away. Not that I know of, anyway."

"Oh my, nothing like that." Singh examined the walls, eyes moving from one framed photo to the next. His eyes landed on the silver-framed photo of Alexx and Beatrice, positioned at the corner of his desk.

"Oh, is that your wife?" Singh asked. Quinn had the sense Singh knew of his marital situation just as much as he did. Observing Singh's body language, the CEO seemed confident, yet coy. Was he about to be interrogated by Singh? Because this is how interrogations start - searching for emotional tripwires.

"I'm divorced," Quinn responded flatly.

"Oh, I'm sorry," Singh responded with feigned sympathy. "I, myself, have never been married, you know. Just never had time for it."

"You don't say." Quinn leaned toward Singh, placing his hands on the desk. "Can you please get to the point? Why are you here?"

"Well, I do pop into Woodrock from time to time. You know, to see how my town is doing."

"Your town?"

"Well, I sort of view Woodrock as one of my most prized creations. I mean, this place was just a dusty little town. Now you have a Walmart and a Target and a–"

Quinn cut him off. "And a Starbucks on every corner, I get it."

Singh made a circling motion of approval with his index finger, then pointed at Quinn. "Precisely."

This is such bullshit, Quinn thought to himself. What does this guy want? Why is he being evasive?

"So," Singh continued. "I want to apologize for any misunderstandings there may have been between your department and my employees regarding the retrieval of Ms. Simpson's remains after that dreadful accident. I understand you were, well, somewhat annoyed by our very efficient process. We have employees all over the world. We make guarantees that in the event of unfortunate accidents, such as the accident Ms. Simpson had last week, that closure comes swiftly to their families."

Wow, Quinn thought to himself. This is some next-level grade-A bullshit. Just like Walter and Zed over at Bob's office, he keeps repeating the word 'accident' like he's pulling some Jedi mind trick. Singh was trying to see if he thought the "accident" was suspicious. This *is* a damned interrogation.

Singh moved his eyes to the wall on the right. A framed, folded American flag with red and gold sergeant's stripes flanking either side hung on the wall.

"Oh. You were in the military?" Singh asked, his eyes focused on the flag.

"Yeah," Quinn replied, turning to look at the wall hanging.

"Well, thank you for your service."

"Unnecessary," Quinn said, as he turned back to face Singh. He could almost visualize Singh's mind winding around and around like a Ferris wheel. Then Singh threw a curveball.

"And I understand you were also a New York detective?"

Quinn's head jerked back. This is totally a goddammed interrogation! And this bastard had done his prep work! Quinn ground his teeth so hard he could bite through steel. "Yeah, I was a detective," he responded abrasively. Where in the hell is he going with this? Singh was putting him on defense. And it was working.

"Oh," Singh continued. "And I understand you were let go. That's very unfortunate. Is that how you wound up here? In South Dakota? I mean, this is an odd place for New York detectives to wind up."

Rock-jawed and red-faced, Quinn stood up, brushing his pants and looming over Singh like the granite face of a cliff. Singh shot up from his chair, trying to match this maneuver.

The two men glared at one another in what appeared to be a sort of Mexican standoff. The silence was deafening. Neither man heard the busy department floor, or the cars cruising up and down Main Street.

"Well, chief, I'm sorry if I may have offended you," Singh stuttered.

"Apology accepted," a glowering Quinn said to a retreating Singh. He called for Rose to please see Mr. Singh out of the office.

The two men shook hands in a half-hearted conciliatory hand shake. Like a deer in the headlights of a car, Samir Singh appeared stunned. His attempt to back an alcoholic burnout into a corner and wriggle some information free had been a misfire. Singh had expected Quinn to stumble over his words. To feel intimidated by Singh's superior intellect and education. To blab away about what he knew about Pippa Simpson's death. But Quinn had been on Singh's side of the table a hundred times. It was how he himself, as an interrogator, had delicately sliced information out of suspects like a surgeon. Quinn knew this and slammed a metaphorical door on Singh and slammed it hard.

Quinn gave Singh nothing. But Samir Singh gave Quinn plenty. Leaving his business card on the desk, Singh told Quinn to ring him anytime - day or night - and walked dejectedly through the door.

What a ginormous, pretentious prick, Quinn thought. Thanks for letting me know I'm on the right track.

CLIMBING INTO THE LAND Rover, Singh slammed his head back and slapped his hand over his eyes.

"Fuck, fuck, fuck," he muttered. "That could've gone better."

He leaned forward, pounding the steering wheel in frustration. Starting the Rover, he backed out and drove back down Main Street and to the highway. A musical ringtone echoed through the vehicle and Madison's name appeared on the Rover's screen. Crap, what now?

"Hey, what do you need?" He asked, defeated and exasperated.

"What do I need?" Madison tersely replied. "That's how you answer my call? Really? What's with you these days, Sam? You've been a real jerk lately. I just wanted to know when you were coming back to the facility. I'm heading to Chicago tomorrow and wanted to make a little time for us. Is that okay?"

Singh pursed his lips, exhaling in a long, slow release of air. "Sorry, my dear. Just a lot on my mind."

"How'd your meeting with the police go?"

Like the Hindenburg in a lightning storm.

"It went well. The chief was very gracious. Let me call you when I get to the office."

"Okay, but I'll warn you," Madison said sternly. "I've reserved a room for us tonight and you're going to fuck my brains out. Got it?"

I'm not in the mood for that, he thought. Not in the mood at all. "Got it. I'll call you when I get back to the facility." He ended the call, reflecting on his meeting.

Samir Singh, a Princeton graduate, billionaire, and expert deal-closer, expected to find a burned-out failure in Ronan Quinn. Phoning it in until his retirement. Sweating out a night of drinking. Cowing to Singh's prowess. Giving him the goods on Pippa's death. If there were any goods to be had at all.

Singh knew all about the Helmand Province debacle, the school shooting, and the Central Park murders. He knew about the Operation Scorpion blow-up in New York and that Quinn had been told to resign from the NYPD and not asked. He thought all this math added up to an emotional wreck. A human being weakened by tragedy and stupefied by liquor.

But Quinn was clean now. His skin was clear, his eyes sharp, and his body was in fine, physical shape. Strangely enough, Singh actually liked and respected him. This man fought his demons and came out on top. In a certain way, Singh even envied Ronan Quinn. Not everyone can escape their past.

But Singh also felt Quinn was hiding something. He sensed it. Quinn slammed the door on him way too quickly. He knew exactly why Singh was there. Quinn didn't think Pippa's death was an accident at all, and though he didn't realize it now, his fate was now left entirely in the hands of Samir Singh.

Ronan Quinn had become just another loop that may need closing.

TRANCELIKE, QUINN WATCHED SAMIR Singh step into his flashy black Land Rover. After a few moments of Singh smacking his steering wheel in anger, he backed out and drove off.

Singh wanted to humiliate him. Make him feel doubt. Question himself. Get him to blab about Pippa's death when it got to that point. Maybe that behavior worked in business negotiations, but it didn't work on him. He slammed an invisible door hard on Singh and gave him nothing. But that man was doing some serious fishing. Bait, line and sinker.

Rose scurried into his office, closing the door.

"Wow, that didn't last very long. He seemed so cheery and charming. I thought you guys would've talked for hours." Rose, expecting a response, received none. Quinn seemed lost. Staring out into the world in a deep, meditative state.

"Ronan? What did he say?" Rose asked again, insistently.

"It wasn't what he said," he muttered with a thoughtful quietness. "As much as what he didn't."

"Oh? What was that?" Rose asked, curiously.

Quinn spun around in his chair. "Rose, he said nothing about Chris Hadley. The Pangea security guard. The guy who took the forty-five caliber Tylenol."

Rose tilted her head. "Maybe it slipped his mind?"

Quinn leaned back, running his fingers through his hair. "Rose, I get the feeling that nothing slips this guy's mind. And I don't recall Pangea rushing to Bob's office to haul off Hadley's body. This 'swift closure' stuff is a bunch of horseshit." He turned to his monitor. "I'm going to stay the night at your place again, if that's okay with you. I want to get to know our Amityville cat a little better."

"I would love your company, all things considered." She turned to walk out the door. "And he's a very sweet cat!" She yelled as she shut the door behind her.

"If you say so," Quinn mumbled absentmindedly. He started sorting e-mails, trying to get his mind focused once more on the day-to-day work of the Woodrock Police.

Chapter 20

Carried aloft on soft fluttering wings, bats swooped for insects. Cicadas chanted their forest songs. Crickets chirped. Burbling and gushing, a swift stream sliced through the woods. The night teemed with life. Then, as if a giant hand had pressed down on the hills, the world fell silent.

Skin sparkling like diamond dust in the moonlit bedroom, Yetunde rested her head on Simon's chest as he lay awake, wondering where all the sounds of the forest had vanished off to.

When the forest fell silent, Simon became alert. Poachers were not uncommon here. And if it weren't the poachers, it was the loggers' slaying trees in the dead of night for a growing lumber black market. Or Boko Haram, an ISIS offshoot, may be prowling nearby. Cruel, barbaric, ideologically starved. They came for the girls and left everyone else for dead, selling flesh to pay for beds, weapons, and food.

When the forest went silent, these were the monsters that came in from the dark.

But all Simon heard was silence. As if God had thrown a blanket over the forest and told everything to hush. Pushing a mumbling Yetunde over, he sat up. There was something else. A gentle humming from outside the window. The sound faded into silence.

Simon slipped on his sandals, quietly tiptoeing past small Fara and unusually tall Gimbya, sound asleep in their cots. Stepping outside and onto the street of the village, he searched to his left and right for the source of the odd sound he'd heard.

What am I seeing? He thought. There? Toward the village center?

Perhaps fifteen yards from where Simon stood, hovering in the air, he made out the outline of a shadowy creature. The mysterious thing hummed toward the open space at the center of the village, carried aloft by four large wings sticking out from the body. Circular hands, or perhaps feet, made up the tips of each wing. Its oddly smooth skin reflecting the moonlight, the creature halted and, with stunning agility, spun in the air and faced him. Simon took an abrupt step back. He'd never seen such a thing before. Appearing annoyed, the creature's two glowing eyes glared right through him, causing a chill to run down his spine.

Simon drew in a deep breath, approaching the beast with trepidation. Perspiration dampening his forehead and tremors rippling through his hands, he drew closer to the creature. This was no bat, and certainly not some unknown species of giant insect. Its unblemished skin was too perfect, and its wings did not flutter or flap. Yet, somehow, it could still maneuver. And those rings on the tips of the wings are not appendages, he thought. They must be a propulsion system of some sort. This was not an animal. This thing was, in fact, a man-made machine. In moments, the soft hum grew in size. Glancing over his shoulder, he saw four more machines moving in behind him. With deliberate caution, he stepped toward the village center, the machine in front of him retreating and the four behind following. Curious if the glowing eyes might be cameras, he raised his hand and waved.

"Hello?"

The lights of the homes in the village flickered on, the recently silenced forest now filled with the mechanized whirring of technology. Mosi the Elder, stumbled through his door clutching a rifle. Skin weathered like an old dry tree and half blind, he squinted at Simon wandering into the village center with his new mechanical friends.

"What is this?" Mosi growled, wagging his gnarled finger at the machines. "What is going on?"

"Mosi, please, stay calm," Simon whispered.

As the villagers gathered, more machines appeared. The sheer number startled Simon. He estimated forty, perhaps even fifty, were now encircling the small village like a squadron of planes. He instinctively ducked as Mosi fired a warning shot into the air.

"Stop it!" Simon whispered. "What's wrong with you? Don't be such an idiot. These aren't animals. You will not scare them off. I don't know why they're here, so let's not provoke a fight."

"Quiet!" Mosi shot back. "The big man from Lagos!"

"Shush!"

"Simon…" a villager asked. "What are they? If they're not animals?"

Simon studied the machines. "I don't know. Maybe something from the military. They could be drones."

"Drones?" someone whispered. "What's a drone?"

The ever-stubborn Mosi, too old to listen, too old to care if these hovering things were bats, bugs, drones, or airplanes, lowered his rifle, took careful aim and fired. His shot was wide by yards as the machine darted to the side.

What occurred next, in this quiet village nestled in a forest in the south of Nigeria, took less than three minutes. The machine ahead of Simon flew at Mosi with shocking speed. In mere seconds, he was clutching and clawing at his throat as if he were being strangled by a python. He fell to the ground in agonizing pain, writhing and rolling and kicking and tearing at his own flesh.

Screams of women and shouts of men filled the village as panic erupted. The drones split up into small teams, systematically hunting down human beings. Seeking any shelter, villagers ran as the drones chased after them with falcon swiftness. The victims could not shut their doors in time. They could not close their windows fast enough.

The drones anticipated each villager's movements as if they read their very minds. They predicted how each villager would react. How fast they ran. Their probability of certain actions. The drones had created a blueprint of the entire village and a profile of every villager in just minutes. They knew every door. Every window. Every plausible opening to every house. Panicked human beings stumbling and falling, Simon watched in horror as they succumbed to an excruciating, horrible death - strangled by the unseen hands of a mass murderer. Simon tore off his shirt, slapping it over his mouth and nose, and sprinted back to his home.

He'd somehow evaded the drones, at least for now. Numbers were in his favor. There were two hundred villagers and only fifty or so drones. However, *time* was not in his favor. He knew they'd come hunting for him. And soon.

Standing at the door as Simon ran to her, Yetunde clutched a sobbing Fara. Gimbya, her arms to her side and lips sucked in tight, trembled. Rushing his family through the house, Simon led them out the back door and off the porch, where they fled for the tree-line. Telling the girls to pull off their tops and cover their mouths, Simon led them into the dark, silent forest. Following the rumblings of the nearby stream, the family blindly felt their way through the trees in near darkness, stumbling over roots and tripping on rocks, finally reaching the water's edge, gasping and out of breath. Simon told them all to not make a single sound.

"They can hear. They can see in the dark," he told them in a soft whisper. "We must stay quiet."

"Simon?" Yetunde asked, fear giving an edge to her voice. "What are those things?"

He shrugged. "I think they're military, whatever they are."

The frantic screams of villagers carried through the night, and Yetunde sobbed. Friends, families, and neighbors suffering a terror none of them could've ever imagined.

The screaming from the distance ceased, plunging the forest into a stark and eerie silence.

Simon, straining to listen, barely made out the faint sound of drones moving through the trees. In seconds, the drones emerged from the forest, moving across the rock and clay river bed toward them. Four drones broke away from the group and, with shocking speed, zoomed toward the small family. Simon scanned the riverbank. Four more drones were moving to their position. Over his shoulder, another four approached.

Surrounded, their only chance was the stream.

"Cover your mouths. We're going to make a dash for the stream. If we can stay underwater, maybe they won't see us. We'll let the current carry us away."

Yetunde gasped. "Simon, Fara can't swim!"

"Hold her tight. Don't let her go. We need to move fast." He looked at each of their mortified faces. "Ready?"

They nodded.

"Go!"

Simon grabbed Yetunde's hand as Yetunde clutched Fara, and Gimbya grabbed onto her mother's arm. Turning toward the river, a defeated Simon faced a drone hovering over the swift water, its yellow eyes penetrating the dark. To Simon, it seemed as if it were gloating.

"Do these things read minds?" He muttered to himself. Spinning around, he searched for another escape route. But with drones now hovering around them in every direction, any chance of escape had all but vanished. A harmonious wavering and warbling noise, like an orchestra playing a victory overture, filled the damp night air. There was nothing he could do and nowhere to go. Machines of death, he thought. Machines built in some far-away land by morally corrupt people of immoral wealth. But why? He thought. Why us?

"My love, what do they want? What are they?" Yetunde sobbed.

"Cover your mouths," he said softly. "Everything will be just fine."

Simon pulled his wife and daughters close to his body. Twenty yards away, a solitary drone hovered, watching the entire scene unfold. "Incredible," Simon muttered in wonder. "It's giving them orders."

The warm skin of his beautiful wife pushed into him. "Orders to do what?" She whispered.

"Close your eyes, my love. All of you, just close your eyes. We'll be fine."

In a matter of a minute, Simon and his family lay motionless on the bank of a rushing stream, their contorted corpses bathed in the light of a pale African moon. 300 yards away, an entire community lay dead.

The machines disappeared into the night. Their mission complete.

CHAPTER 21

CURLING UP ON THE soft cloth loveseat in her Manhattan penthouse, Navi Singh gazed thoughtfully at the towering skyscrapers through a large, panoramic window. A low winter sun moving across a hazy orange and powder blue sky, she listened to the muffled sounds of honking cars and rushing ambulances far below her.

Turning her attention to a framed photo of her parents, she said she'd see them soon. From her laptop, she drafted an e-mail to her brother Samir. They should get together for coffee, she wrote. She missed him terribly, and just wanted him to know she loved him. After drafting and sending a flurry of messages to friends and colleagues, she strode into the kitchen. On the granite counterspace, she crushed an entire bottle of sedatives with a steak knife, funneled the powder into a 2016 Chateau Lafite Rothschild Bordeaux, drank the bottle dry and at 3:36 on a cold Tuesday afternoon, fell quietly asleep and died.

Navi Singh battled her lurking demons for 411 heart-shredding days following the death of her parents, killed by a speeding Cobra GT helmed by a blistering drunk.

On the 412th day, Navi lost her war.

She was just 23 years old. Her stunning beauty, her radiant smile, her fathomless intellect, were forever gone.

Today was the tenth anniversary of Navi's suicide.

Soberly gazing through the window of the Gulfstream, Singh's thoughts were of his sister. The hole she'd left inside him felt as deep as an ocean trench. Abandoning him on this horrendous world with no one but a faceless, metallic voice on a speaker. If she'd just told me, he thought. If I'd known, I could've helped. How did I not see her pain? Why did she hide her feelings from me? I had no idea.

No. Idea.

He missed his sister. He missed his mother. He missed his father. All taken from him because of one careless, selfish, stupid human being. Sipping tea, he let the warmth and gentle sweetness of chamomile soothe him. Closing his eyes, he tried to focus.

Valuable time had been lost. Lost because of that stupid, ill-advised talk with the Woodrock police chief.

And time they did not have. And there'd been problems.

The specimens, the drones, the Air Force A-88 Wasps, the whatever they should be called by this point, now numbered almost two million. The speed of production had been nothing short of miraculous, and as Singh zoomed like Mercury across the Atlantic in his private jet, the Wasps were now finally being deployed. But not before everything had been ground to a halt first. Two months earlier, under a bright desert sun, the Iron Hand team discovered a flaw. An easily overlooked flaw, but a terrifying flaw indeed.

Peaking at a relatively tepid 95 degrees, the test and evaluation team didn't consider the temperature that day to be all that high - not for the high desert. For five hours, Rich Hansen rewrote code and fine-tuned the complex AI of the Wasp drones from his laptop as a bright sun rose high into a cloudless sky. The Wasps, constantly arguing and bickering with one another, behaved more like a flying mob of anarchists than $45,000,000 worth of supremely intelligent killing machines. Just rewriting the software embedded in the Wasp's little silicon brains cost hundreds of hours in labor.

So, on this warm April afternoon, at the top-secret test range named Juliet Tango, Rich adjusted lines of code as Wasps rested quietly under a brilliant desert sun for five long hours. While the Wasps waited for Rich to finish his work, their stealthy black skin absorbed the heat. The black-top pad on which they rested absorbed even more - reaching 128 degrees under a cloudless blue sky. The heat warped the Wasp's thin wings and cooked their little minds like bread in a toaster. This process, as Rich would later describe it, turned the Wasps into *polycarbonate serial killers.*

On the fifth hour of sunning themselves like weekend beachgoers, the squadron of Wasps rose from the blacktop pad, humming their way across the desert in perfect formations. Their mission? Seek and destroy a hundred artificial targets scattered over a fifty-mile radius. But instead of accomplishing this directive, most of the Wasps crashed.

And the Queen went rogue.

Wandering aimlessly into mountains and canyons, heat-stroked drones fell to the earth like drunken birds - emitting strange, eerie sounds as they struck the ground. But four drones remained relatively airworthy and the Queen, her little processor brain mildly cooked, took it upon herself to re-write her own mission and plot a new attack. Shanghaiing her surviving troops, she gave an all-new directive. The small drone re-bellion assembled, then hummed their way across the desert to some mysterious location.

As desperately as Rich tried to get the drones to return, the Queen, to his horror, ignored his commands. Traveling nearly sixty miles across the valley floor on uranium batteries, the rogue Queen and her subjects appeared at a sheep farm and in a matter of just minutes, 37 animals lay dead in their pen. The Queen had written her own mission, found a new target, and convinced her subjects to commit animal genocide.

The last thing the Iron Hand team needed was some plucky backpacker stumbling upon a Wasp, posing for selfies with the odd creature, and uploading them to social media. HH-60 Ghost Hawks at the Groom Lake Proving Grounds, 200 miles away, launched on a desperate search and recovery mission. Searching mountains, dry riverbeds, and steep canyons, the crews collected dead or dying Wasps, not understanding what these strange things they were collecting even were. They'd seen many hush-hush things in Area 51. But large drones shaped like giant insects, with sinister glowing eyes gaping at them, were certainly not anything they'd ever encountered before. Some of the Wasps, still displaying a base form of function, emitted an odd squeal as crews dragged them into the Ghost Hawks. Sounding like a child in pain, their cries led to more than a few sweat-filled nightmares in the coming weeks.

Singh was furious over this disaster, as was Jupiter. And as if he needed more headaches to deal with, Singh had to talk Red Lancer out of assassinating Col. Aiden Taylor and the helicopter crews. With a professional aviation saboteur on standby, Red Lancer suggested crashing all the helicopters into the ground with the airmen inside. Singh shook his head with disgust. Not only disturbing, he thought, but wildly impractical. Red Lancer is a bull in a china shop.

But after the initial shock wore off, this mishap turned out to be a blessing in disguise. The team, performing the first operational flying tests in winter time and in much cooler conditions, had never evaluated the Wasps under high-heat temperatures. With Iron Hand now scheduled to launch by the end of summer, an unforeseen departure from the Iron Hand script may have occurred, catching the team flat-footed.

Modifications to the Wasps were certainly in order.

The real belle of the ball in this disaster was the Queen. While the heat had knocked many of the Wasps out of commission, a few had retained enough functionality to keep operating. But the Queen, to everyone's shock and horror, had taken operating to a whole new level. She became sentient. Self-aware. Achieving a level of consciousness, independent thought, and complex problem solving the team had never expected. Rich, stating the obvious, suggested their AI programming be dialed back a bit.

Singh and his team of engineers went back to the drawing board to develop a solution. The Wasps in manufacturing, or to be manufactured, required a special heat-reflecting coating. As for the prototypes at the test facility, the team imposed a limitation of one hour outdoors before launch. If the prototypes exceeded one hour, they were to be shuffled back into the chilly environment of the gymnasium-sized test structure.

Then there was this issue of the poor, doomed sheep. Just five drones had snuffed out 37 sheep in minutes and sent a grizzled old rancher into a fit of hysterics. A level of efficiency that surprised even the Iron Hand team. Soon after the incident, Jupiter's investigators arrived at the ranch to question the old rancher who, to everyone's dismay, had spilled his horror story to a journalist and an amateur blogger from Las Vegas. Chattering away almost nonsensically, eyes projecting both shock and grief, the rancher's story landed on the internet for the world to read. Alien robots, he claimed, had killed his sheep in a practice run for an invasion of earth. And be warned, he said. Humans are next up on the menu. The old man was hysterical, inconsolable, and not entirely wrong.

Shortly after, a counter-story appeared. An official DOD statement professing the sheep had died of anthrax. Red Lancer, a meticulous sociopathic assassin, ensured the old rancher never spoke of the incident ever again. Soon, The Great Sheep Massacre of Nevada moved away from the mainstream, and into the realm of UFO mythology and conspiracies.

Iron Hand narrowly avoided disaster, but a disaster with multiple silver linings.

First off was the sheep. Bound by a kind of macabre rule of ethics, the Wasps targeted only human beings. So, scientists improved and centralized the Wasp DNA targeting, ensuring they would never chase after anything but people fleeing for their lives. Engineers and chemists developed a heat reflecting coating, testing it with great success. Rich and his team re-wrote code to keep the Wasp Queens and drones from ever reaching complete self-awareness. Iron Hand was back on track. Now Singh was winging his way to London to implore his contractor to double their efforts at shipping the new coating to Pangea plants. Disasters. Delays. Leaks. An increasingly irate and panicked Jupiter was demanding Iron Hand be launched in two months. Not the six months as planned.

Jill left her seat at the front of the jet and moved to where Singh sat. She made a comment that he seemed very distracted.

Of course, I'm distracted, he thought. Today is the anniversary of Navi's death, and the UK contractor is falling behind. "Thanks, my dear," Singh replied with a shallow smile. "Just a lot on my mind."

Jill said to let her know if he needed anything, moving to the front of the cabin where she sat, flipping through a magazine.

Singh's secure device buzzed.

Rich's self-assigned codename, *HashtagGoblins*, came up on the screen. Rich, often frustrated with the Wasp's knack for misbehaving, referred to his high-tech progeny as "little fucking goblins" more than Singh cared to hear.

"Sam!" Rich panted and gasped into Singh's ear as if he were running. "We have a real big problem here!"

Singh told Rich to calm down and tell him what was wrong.

"I'm in Nigeria doing the tropical field test. All was going well and then the Queen left the reservation!"

Singh shot up in his seat. "What do you mean? Where'd she go?"

"She took the little fucking goblins out to some village in the southeast, so we drove out there. She killed everyone, Sam! Everyone! People, Sam! She killed people! What the hell are we going to do?"

Singh, in complete disbelief, tried processing what Rich was telling him. "Did you try to nest them?"

"No response!" A panic-stricken Rich shouted. "Just like Nevada! I thought the new batches had been upgraded! Are we screwed or what!?"

Singh rubbed his forehead so hard his skin felt raw. "Rich, calm down. Take photos and get the hell out of there. Where are they now?"

"No clue, Sam," Rich replied, panting over the phone as if he'd just run a hundred-meter dash. "We can't pick them up on the receiver any longer."

"Okay," Singh said, tapping his fingers on the armrest. "They probably nested somewhere. But you need to re-establish an uplink with the Queen and then shut her the hell down. Got it?"

"Got it," Rich stuttered.

"And you guys better find every last one of them. How many were in the test?"

"Fifty," Rich responded.

"Fifty?"

"Yeah, fifty."

"Why did you need fifty, Rich? What the hell?"

"You tell me, Sam. I just work here. I don't plan these things."

Singh drew in a deep breath and exhaled. "Okay, Rich. Take photos. Then I want you guys to get out of there ASAP."

Ending the call, Singh threw his head back against the rest and groaned. What is this? Amateur hour? Who mixed up the Wasp types? Barely able to control the rage taking hold, he punched a code into the device and Jupiter answered.

"Yes, Sam?"

Singh turned his head, facing away from Jill. "What the hell just happened in Nigeria? Someone sent specimens that weren't modified and they went rogue. Again!"

Jupiter remained silent for an insufferable amount of time, with Singh impatiently tapping the arm rest waiting for an answer.

"They didn't act autonomously, they acted under a program," Jupiter's metallic voice responded.

"What!?"

Jill's head snapped up from her magazine.

"Don't raise your voice to me, Sam. Settle down. It was a functional test. Now we understand the true capabilities of Iron Hand."

"Wait," Singh leaned forward, dropping into a whisper as Jill went back to her magazine. "So, you're telling me this was all planned? And I take it from my conversation with Rich that he didn't know about this program, did he?"

"Of course not. The man was upset over a few dead sheep. His job is writing code and programs. He doesn't know what Iron Hand even is. He still thinks he's working on some secret military thing."

"Well, Jupiter," Singh said, his voice shaking with frustration. "Rich knows now. And the United Nations and the Nigerian military are all going to find out and when they get there, they'll find everyone dead. Don't tell me that won't hit the news cycle."

Jupiter grumbled. "Red Lancer has that taken care of."

Singh bit down on his lip. "Oh, that's great, Red Lancer, wonderful. That man has the IQ of an eggplant."

"We planned it well in advance. An attack by the Chadian Air Force on a suspected Boko Haram target. Who gives a damn about that? The U.S. and the U.N. will shake their hypocritical fists in anger, and, of course, we've destabilized Africa which hasn't been stable since imperialism. So what?"

"Wow, that's a really great plan," Singh grunted. Why was I left out of the loop on this? He thought, irritated and annoyed.

"I'm going to be in Aspen. As we draw closer to zero hour, I think we should meet, in person."

Stunned, Singh slammed back into his seat. For the first time since that life altering phone call between him and Jupiter, the call placed to him the day after Navi died, he was finally going to meet this mysterious figure. The mysterious figure who'd made Samir Singh into the man he is today. The mogul of a tech empire. This was an astonishing development.

"We can meet there," Jupiter added. "Let's talk about ensuring all the specimens are getting their modifications. Let's talk about plans and contingencies. It's getting close and I'm getting anxious."

A jubilant Singh replied as if Jupiter had asked him to the prom. "Okay! I'll be there in two days!" He replied. "But I have a scheduled meeting with the Horsemen first."

"I know you do," Jupiter said in closing. "I'll see you in Aspen after your meeting."

The device went silent.

Suddenly, to Singh, everything had a fresh new gleam. After an entire decade, he'd meet this man who'd given him so much. The man who'd pulled him from the abyss of despair. The man behind the curtain. The man who'd help create Singh's empire. The man who shared the same view of the planet as he did. Who, like Singh, felt everyone but them was out of touch. That civilization was a speeding car heading for a cliff. Like an orphan about to be reunited with a parent, his enthusiasm bordered on child-like glee.

The secure device buzzed.

HashtagGoblins:

Singh clicked open the three attached photos. The white flash of Rich's camera captured a visceral horror. Tongues protruded grotesquely from saliva-caked mouths. Eyes bulged with terror and suffering. Gaping with revulsion at the peaceful villagers who'd died at the hands of fifty Wasps, a thick nausea formed in his stomach. Studying the third image intensely, a heart-wrenching pain shot through his chest as if someone had struck him with a spear.

On the banks of a frothing stream, Rich had captured the image of a man clutching his wife and daughters on a clay riverbank, frozen in death. A sudden, rogue wave of emotional grief washed over and through him.

This emotion was all too familiar. The same emotion he'd felt releasing Navi's ashes into the frigid winds on the icy summit of Kanchenjunga. No air was as pure, no world so barren, as a summit on the roof of the world. Navi had been the essence of purity, and the world would forever be barren without her.

Singh held the device up to his face, gazing mortified into the screen as if he were standing on that very riverbank and staring down at the very people he'd murdered. Just as he had with Pippa, studying her photo the night before Red Lancer murdered her, Singh felt conflicted. These emotions were so confusing. Why do I even care? What the hell is wrong with me?

Glaring at the crumpled bodies of an innocent family, he snatched the airsickness bag from its pouch and vomited.

A stunned Jill shot up from her seat and rushed to his aid.

Chapter 22

Fig stuck his head through Quinn's office door. "Hey, boss. I've got Emma Massey in the interview room. She's one of the victim's friends."

Quinn's eyes snapped away from the PC monitor. "What? Here?"

"She didn't want to talk on the phone. She wanted to meet us in person."

"Okay then, I'll be there in a minute," Quinn replied, standing and gulping down a cup of coffee.

The previous evening at Rose's house, the maybe-ghost of Pippa never materialized. Awake for most of the night drinking tea, the two sat, eyes glued on Oscar, like a pair of naturalists observing a snow leopard. But the voice from beyond performed no encore. No sequel to their previous stage engagement. Perhaps they were busy zooming through their mysterious corridor in some other dimension.

Regaling Quinn with fascinating globe-trotting adventures, Rose gave spontaneous lectures on her collection of artworks. Then, at one point, she dashed through her kitchen and returned with her TaylorMade graphite driver. Demonstrating golf skills to an amused Quinn, she swung at an imaginary ball from the exquisite Bangalore rug with grace and precision. Shielding her eyes from a make-believe sun, she tracked her imaginary ball along its imaginary trajectory.

"Right down the fairway, baby!" She exclaimed.

But now, as he prepared to meet Emma, Quinn couldn't help but wonder if the conversation he and Rose had with the maybe-Pippa Simpson ghost had been a one-off. A fluke. Perhaps even a mini-Mandela effect. He and Rose, both under great stress, convincing one another they'd talked to ghosts when in fact they hadn't. I'll rationalize all that later, he thought. I have an interview to do.

Striding into the interview room, Quinn softly closed the door. Fig, sitting at the table, scribbled notes down on a pad. Wearing an apple-green strapless dress, slight of frame, her light brown hair trimmed short into a crewcut, an edgy Emma Massey sat across from Fig. Through pouting hazel eyes, she glumly peered up at Quinn as he slid a chair back with a screech and sat down.

Quinn, studying Emma, noted that this was a young woman in peak physical shape. A former track and field star at Brigham Young University and chronic marathoner, Emma was unabashedly ultra-competitive, competing in races all over the world. But this healthy, bright-eyed woman seemed fidgety. Anxious. Troubled. Hands clasped together, resting on the table, her fingers weaved through fingers turning knuckles into snowcapped peaks. A pair of anxious pupils darted between him and Fig.

Quinn thanked her for coming to the station. She could've just spoken on the phone, he said. Fig merely wanted to discuss finding a new home for Oscar, and maybe get some additional friends to contact. After that, the police would close out Pippa's file.

"Really?" Emma responded. She lurched forward, thrusting her hands across the table. "A police officer called me to ask if I would take Pip's cat? Then asked me if I would provide a list of her friends?" Glowering, she sat back and crossed her arms. "You didn't call me just to ask about Pip's cat."

Quinn glanced over at Fig. With raised brows, Fig looked as surprised as Quinn felt.

Quinn looked at Emma. "Okay, Emma, if it's not about Pippa's cat, then why do you think Deputy McClure called you?"

Emma stared directly at Quinn. "Because, chief, you don't believe for a single moment that Pip died in a car accident."

Quinn's head snapped over to Fig and Fig's head snapped toward Quinn, both looking like Thor's hammer had fallen from the sky and landed on the table.

"Well, um," Fig stuttered. "Why do you say that, Emma? We know each other. You can talk to me."

"You know my boyfriend, Fig."

"Well, we've met a few times."

Emma's slender, trembling fingers opened and closed and stretched outward. Jesus, Quinn thought. This woman is terrified.

"You can trust us, Emma. We're the police," Fig added in a calm and even voice.

Emma thrust her head forward, brows arching, hazel eyes widening. "Trust you? Look, a few days after Pip's death, I received a call from a masked number. I normally don't answer those because they're, you know, scams. But this person kept calling and calling, so finally I answered." Emma's eyes drifted to the rear of the room, recollecting that voice on her phone. "There was this strange, creepy guy on the other end," she said between quivering lips. "God, it gave me serious chills. He asked if Pippa had shared anything with me about her work, or if I had any of her things. That if I did, I needed to meet with him at the Old Ghost Town, that night, alone, to discuss it and hand over anything I had of hers that could be company property."

Quinn leaned forward. “And what did you say, Emma? Did you have anything of hers?”

Emma, agitated and nerves raw, threw her arms up. “Of course not!” Settling into her seat, she let out a long breath. “Not anything work-related.”

Fig glanced at Quinn and turned back to Emma. “Emma, what did you say to him?”

“I told him I had nothing, and I wasn’t telling him anything more. I ended the call. I wasn’t giving that creep any information, and no way was I meeting him at the Ghost Town. What if he wanted to murder me? Guys, I was so scared I nearly flushed my phone down the toilet. Kim said she got a call also, and it freaked her out. I can tell you one thing; she’s not coming to see you guys. She’s scared.”

Quinn looked at Fig, leaning back in his chair. Fig was thinking. Processing. The young deputy didn’t have the complete story yet. Quinn kept things from him. Now he wondered what was going through Fig’s mind. He thought he’d let Fig continue. Untainted by theories and speculation, Quinn felt Fig could query Emma better than he.

“Here’s another thing,” Emma added. “The night before Pip died, she texted me, all excited like. This guy had asked her out on a date. She was really buzzing about it.”

“Did she text you on her way home?” Fig asked.

“Who, Pip? That woman was the most annoyingly safe driver I’ve ever known. She would never text while driving. She would lecture us if we did.”

“Did she meet this guy? Did they have a date?”

Emma shook her head. “Pip would normally not date people from work. It was one of her rules. But she had a serious thing for this guy.

We all called him her guard crush. She was thinking of meeting him for coffee. You see, Pip hadn't dated for a while and I think she was just looking for a fling."

Did she say guard crush? Quinn thought. Guard? As in, security?

Fig scribbled down notes, then looked up at Emma. "So, you said she wouldn't date anyone from work, but yet this guy was a coworker? At Pangea?"

"Well, kind of," she replied. "He was a contractor. A guard at the complex."

Was? Quinn thought. As in, no longer a guard?

"Do you know his name?" Fig mumbled, while scribbling.

"His name was Chris. Chris Hadley."

Fig's head shot up. Briefly locking in on Emma's eyes, a stunned Fig's head snapped around to Quinn as if she'd stabbed him with a pencil. Emma studied Fig's reaction with a subtle nod of her head. "Yeah," she said with slow deliberation. "The guy who, quote-unquote, killed himself."

Fig, immobilized in disbelief, stared wide-eyed at Emma.

"You guys get it now, don't you?" Her eyes darting between Quinn and Fig, she studied their expressions.

"Get? Get what?" Fig stuttered.

"Pip, the safest driver in the world, dies in a wreck. I get a creepy phone call from a hidden number asking me if I had anything of hers and to talk about work stuff. To meet him at the Ghost Town. Probably to murder me and stuff me in his trunk. And the guy that asks Pip out? Chris? He kills himself after Pip died?" Scrunching her lips, Emma slid back in her chair. "Oh, please. Give me a break." She turned to Quinn.

"Now you get why I came in. Why I didn't want to talk on the phone. I wanted to see your faces when I told you this stuff. This was no accident guys, and I think you know that already. That's why Fig called me. And I'm really sorry about Pip's cat. She loved that little rascal. But I'm more afraid something is going to happen to me. I'm heading out-of-town tomorrow."

"Where to?" Quinn asked.

"I'd rather not say. I'm sure you can understand that. I've entered a marathon. I need time to think, and I need to get the hell away from here."

"Listen, Emma," Quinn said, attempting to reassure her. "If you feel concerned at all about your safety, let us know and I'll send an officer." He handed Emma his business card. "You can always call me directly, day or night."

"Thanks, chief, but you'll have to forgive me if that doesn't comfort me much. Pangea, well, we're a big company and we're a huge defense contractor. They probably have, you know, 'people'. Pip knew something she wasn't supposed to. I just know she did. And I think those bastards at Pangea killed her because of it."

"Let's be careful not to speculate, Emma," Quinn said as Emma stood up to leave. "I understand your concern, but it's best you keep all this to yourself for now."

Emma quietly nodded, a tear streaming along her cheek as Fig escorted her out of the station.

SWAYING IN HIS CHAIR, lost in thought and nibbling on a ballpoint pen, Quinn didn't even notice Fig was standing in the doorway.

"Boss?" Fig asked as he stepped inside and shut the door.

Quinn spun in his chair and faced the young deputy. "Fig, that woman is terrified," he said, nodding to Fig to take a seat. "Let's look at what we know. First, Pippa wasn't texting on the road. Second, she and Mr. Hadley knew each other more personally." Thinking through all the events that'd transpired, Quinn fiddled with the cap from the pen. "So Hadley followed Pippa home until she had her accident? Then he fled the accident scene when I arrived and shot himself out of guilt the following night, sober, in front of the TV? Fig, there're enough links here to make a chain, considering everything else."

"Everything else, boss?"

"Pippa may have died from something other than just a car accident. That was Bob's initial assessment."

"Well, what did she die from?"

"Strangulation," Quinn said in a level, matter-of-fact voice.

His eyes squinting, mouth parted slightly to speak words he couldn't even form, Fig gaped at his pen-gnawing police chief. *Strangulation?*

"And we both know someone broke into her house," Quinn continued, ignoring Fig's baffled face. "I'm certain of that now, based on what Emma told us." Quinn paused. Thinking, organizing, laying down the evidence groundwork like railway ties under a train track. They already took her phone and laptop. What else would they be looking for? "Someone, aside from us, is reaching out to Pippa's friends. Asking questions. Trying to set up meetings. Probably Walter and Zed. So, Emma may have been right to be afraid. And Hadley asked Pippa on a date? The night before her death? I find it hard to believe that's just coincidental. He was planning to interrogate her, Fig. And I believe Hadley stopped at the accident to get something from her car. I imagine her phone and backpack. What Walter and Zed were so desperate to get their hands on. When I showed up at Pippa's accident, Hadley panicked."

Fig put his notepad on the desk, jotting everything down.

"Good idea, Fig. Capture all this."

Leaning back, Quinn gazed at the ceiling. "And another thing. I've seen enough suicides to know that Hadley's was staged. Someone did not want that man saying anything. Saying anything to us. Because, rest assured, we'd have found him eventually and brought him in for questioning for fleeing the scene of an accident. Clearly, they hadn't expected I'd arrive at that scene."

Fig looked up from his scribbling. "They? Who's they?"

"Precisely, Fig. Who are they? Who wanted both of them dead? And why? And why is Hadley still chilling in the morgue? This bullshit Pangea peddles about quick closures is just that. Bullshit. They whisked Pippa away so fast Bob barely even got an examination in. This all smells of a coverup, Fig."

Face cracking into a boyish grin, Fig's freckles vanished in a flushed face. He looked as if he'd just discovered penicillin. "So, boss," he gushed. "What you're saying then is-"

Quinn smacked his hand on the table. "Yup! This is no longer an accident investigation. This is now a homicide. Or, rather, homicides. And yes, I have a hunch before you ask. I think Hadley killed Pippa. Then someone killed Hadley. And we need a motive, and right now we don't have one."

Fig drew in a long breath, blowing air through a pair of ballooning cheeks. "Holy shit, boss. You going to call the State Police? Or, maybe, the FBI?"

"No, Emma was right. Pangea is a huge defense contractor. We don't need this to get out, not yet. It may be homicide, but our case is flimsy. So, for now, we follow the facts, gather the evidence, and build a case. Got it?"

"Got it, boss. Wow, a real homicide. I've never had one of those before."

"Yeah," Quinn dragged his hands across his face. "Don't get too excited. Pippa is dead, and nothing we do is going to bring her back."

Fig tilted his head. "Chief, just one question. Why do you call the victim by her name? Is that something you normally do?"

Quinn hadn't even realized he'd been doing that. What was he supposed to tell him? Pippa came back to life? That he'd tried to save her and couldn't? That she spoke to him that night? That she spoke to him from the great beyond? This had become personal. No, it wasn't normal. But then, what was? What was normal about anything right now? "No. It's not normal, so just keep thinking of her as the victim. Because that's who she is now, and not who she was."

Fig nodded, asked if there was anything else, and Quinn reminded him to not share any of this with the other officers.

"The guys are asking a lot of questions, boss. Like, why we're spending so much time together? They think I'm a kiss-ass."

Quinn couldn't help but laugh. "Oh, Jesus Fig. Just tell them we're drawing up new training stuff. It's a project."

Fig nodded and dashed through the door. Thrilled, excited and energized, he was Fig McClure - detective at large.

But Ronan Quinn now faced a dilemma. He needed a lot more resources than one enthusiastic deputy and an art-hoarding assistant. But who? The State Police? The FBI? How was he going to question witnesses if they were all too terrified to talk? And Walter? Zed? Samir Singh? How's he going to bring them in for questioning? Quinn rubbed his head, feeling as if he were stuck on the traffic meridian of a freeway at rush hour.

And Quinn couldn't play dumb for very much longer, either. Samir Singh had paid him one suspicious visit, and he expected more to come. Playing aloof isn't a long-term ploy. Pangea will see right through that charade. Even Pippa's friends were questioning her death, which meant by now everyone was.

Gossip in this town traveled like a bullet train.

A SULLEN EMMA MASSEY moped out of the Woodrock Police Station, stepping into her small, blue Corolla, as Yousef looked on.

Sliding further down into the seat of the sedan, pulling his cap over his brow, he maintained as low a profile as practically possible. Reversing out of her spot, Emma turned and sped away down Main Street.

Yousef switched on the sedan, following the Corolla, staying three car lengths behind her. Emma braked at the stoplight, turned left on the green, and drove to the highway - heading north to the Pangea-built subdivision and home.

Yousef grabbed the secure comm device from the passenger seat. Following her onto the state highway, he carefully typed a message.

Talon:

The girl is heading back to her house.

Red Lancer:

How long was she talking to the police?

Talon:

Long enough. Want her gone?

Red Lancer:

Not there.

Talon:

Where then?

Red Lancer:

She's flying to Salt Lake tomorrow. She's signed up for a dumb marathon.

Talon:

Do it there?

Red Lancer:

Yes. Discreetly.

Talon:

Sure she's going to Salt Lake?

Red Lancer:

You underestimate me. Can you make it look not obvious?

Talon.

I have something for that.

Red Lancer:

Great. Good luck.

Chapter 23

At 6 p.m., Quinn arrived back at Rose's quaint home and parked. Stepping from the SUV and into a warm and still early evening, he closed his eyes and took a moment to savor the peace of the prairie. The rich perfume of fresh alfalfa drifted from a neighboring field. Red-breasted robins and black-capped chickadees chirped about the day's events. Fluttering swallows went about their evening diving for insects. Quinn loved this time of the day, but would love it even more if it weren't for the throbbing pain in his temples. Greeting him at the front door, Rose led him into the living room and he let himself fall onto the couch.

"I have a Godzilla-sized headache," he groaned, massaging his forehead and the back of his neck. "Any word from our ghost?"

Rose shook her head as she walked back to the kitchen to fix some tea and retrieve some aspirin. "Nope."

Leaping onto the couch in a series of clicks and chirps, Oscar stretched, curiously sniffing Quinn's thigh, then crawled onto his lap.

Rose leaned up against the doorframe to the kitchen, gazing warmly at Oscar pawing Quinn, pleading to have his fur stroked. "Aw, look at that. He loves you, Ronan."

He groaned. "I hate cats."

"You hate cats?" Rose gasped, clutching her chest. She strode across the room and sat down next to Quinn, placing the tea on the table. "Why do you hate cats, Ronan?"

"We had a cat once. Peppers. One day, I came home from school and my goldfish was missing. Nowhere to be found. Peppers murdered my goldfish. He tried many times to murder our parakeet. Peppers was a real bastard. So, yeah, I hate cats."

"I'll forgive you for now," Rose said with a grit in her voice. She reached behind Quinn's neck with long supple fingers, kneading taut and tense muscles like dough.

"Oh my god, Rose," he groaned. "You're an angel."

"Rough day at the office?"

Leaning over to the table, he popped the aspirin into his mouth. "Rose, we've got a lot to talk about. Let me get you caught up."

He told Rose about the meeting with Emma. She seemed fragile. Terrified. Someone had called her. Quinn suspected that someone had been Walter or Zed. Probably Walter. And Emma seemed right on point. Pippa's accident was no accident at all. She suspected everything that Quinn did. But the real mind-blower was Chris Hadley. Emma said the two casually knew each other, with Hadley asking Pippa on a date the night prior to her death.

Now the puzzle pieces were fitting together. Quinn was certain Chris Hadley murdered Pippa Simpson. He was most certain Hadley planned on retrieving something from Pippa's wreck, something of great importance. Quinn's hunch that Hadley's suicide was no suicide at all was now emerging as a fact. Mysteriously, Bob McConnell had found no gunpowder residue anywhere on Hadley's hands when he examined his body. McConnell was certain Hadley hadn't fired the Colt.45 into his own head.

Quinn suspected, to almost certainty, that someone ordered Pippa's death, then ordered Hadley's death because Quinn had seen him at the scene. A coverup. A cleanup. Whatever it should be called. And Hadley asking Pippa on a date the night before the murder? Even then, someone was suspecting Pippa of something. They'd tasked Hadley to set up a meeting with Pippa. To ask questions. To interrogate. To retrieve something they thought she may have.

"Then someone changed the plan." Quinn said. "Deciding to just kill her outright. These were executions, Rose."

Rose gasped, slapping her hand over her mouth. "That poor, dear girl!"

Quinn nodded. "Yep, poor Pippa. Very professional. Very mob-like. Whoever these people are, they know how to cover their tracks. If I hadn't happened upon the scene when I did, Hadley-the-assassin may or may not still be alive. I blew his cover."

What Quinn hadn't figured out yet was how Hadley actually killed Pippa, and why? Had Pippa stolen something? Was she a thief? A corporate spy? He highly doubted this. She didn't fit the espionage bill.

And Pippa's death by strangulation was still puzzling. McConnell's tox report came back from Dallas clean. No alcohol. No drugs. No peanuts or bee toxins. But McConnell found something odd. Her blood contained an extraordinary amount of lactic acid, similar to what blood produces during a rapid, traumatic loss of oxygen to the brain. But with no brain to examine, McConnell was stuck - hamstrung by Walter and Zed's zeal to whisk her off to Chicago. But McConnell was pretty sure something was depriving Pippa of oxygen well before the crash. And the injuries to her neck were consistent with someone trying to fight off an attacker.

"They killed Pippa. And the why is either on her phone or on her laptop, and we have neither."

"But who?" Rose asked. "Who's the 'they' in this crime?"

"Pangea. They did it."

Stunned, surprise lighting their faces, Quinn and Rose faced one another. Oscar leaped off Quinn's lap, scurrying to the center of the room. On the Bangalore rug he squatted on his haunches, turning his attention to the ceiling, ears flattening, then perking up again.

As he and Rose looked around the room, Quinn wasn't sure what to do or say next. So, he asked her directly. "You're Pippa, aren't you?"

"Yes."

"Are you a-" Reluctant to categorize Pippa as a poltergeist, Quinn stumbled over his words.

"No, I am not a ghost," she responded.

"Well, dear, what are you then?" Rose asked.

"I'm not sure. I don't know what I am or what I am not. I'm an energy, I think. A consciousness. This place I'm in. It's strange."

Quinn scanned the ceiling. "Describe it for us, Pip. Can I call you Pip?"

"Yes, Mr. Quinn, please do."

"What do you see? Do you see us?" Quinn asked.

"I see you, Mr. Quinn. I see Oscar. Oh, Oscar, you brat. Are you okay?"

"I'm taking very good care of Oscar, dear," Rose said.

"It's always so cold here. I feel like I'm trapped. And I'm moving really, really, fast, like, down a corridor."

Quinn visualized speeding down a corridor at his old high school in Boston, metal lockers and people and classroom doors whizzing past him.

"I see the most beautiful light. On one side, I see this blue. On the other side, I just see darkness. And billions of people are all talking. And I can hear every one of their voices, as if they were just one person."

Quinn shook his head. This is absolutely bananas, he thought. "Pip, can you tell me why Pangea would kill you?"

"Envy…Envy."

"Envy, Pip? What does that mean? Envy?" Quinn asked, straining his neck as if he were sneaking a peek into Pippa's alternate universe.

"I don't know. Memories. They just come and go. Like fragments of glass. They pass me in the corridor. Passing me so fast. I see mom and dad, are they okay?"

"They're very sad, Pip." Rose replied, her eyes glistening as she fought back tears.

"Envy. Envy. Envy."

The floor suddenly trembled and shook. Rose's collection of fine art rattled and clanged.

Pippa's soft, sweet voice now boomed through the house like a clap of thunder. *"ENVY!"*

Through this entire strange, and now somewhat startling episode, Oscar did not move.

"Pip? Pip? Why are you envious? Who are you envious of?" Rose asked as calmly as she could. "Pip? Pip? Are you there?"

Falling back, Quinn and Rose sank deeply into the couch. So still they sat, a chattering of spider's feet running along the floor would've reached their ears.

"She's gone again," muttered Quinn, finally exhaling a slow, long breath.

Her hands trembling, Rose clutched them together to make them stop.

"Ronan," Rose muttered.

"Yes, Rose?"

"I'm absolutely freaking out right now. Are you?"

"Oh yeah, Rose," Quinn whispered. "I'm about as freaked out as I've ever been."

Glancing at her Apple Watch, Emma checked her pulse, blood oxygen levels, and completed miles. All the metrics modern microchip technology can provide.

On pace for a personal record, she and a small group of runners rounded a bend on the highway as the sun beat down on her from between puffy white cumulus. The scents of pine and bark and musty forest soil filling her senses, she ran through the cool, parched air of Utah, sneaking peeks from the highway and across the valley below - The Great Salt Lake, and Salt Lake City, in the distance.

Pippa's memory, still fresh in her mind, provided motivation. This run was for her. For her memory. And the adrenaline had not left Emma. Not even here at the 24th mile. Perhaps Pip was watching from the great beyond, cheering me on, Emma thought. Pippa's energy flowed through her, encouraging her to push herself harder, to make this race count, to forget all her troubles back in Woodrock.

The highway straightened out, and Emma picked up her pace. The clot of runners thinning now, she trudged on toward the finish, a singular being - alone - no one existing but her.

You can do this, Emma, she thought encouragingly. Screw the altitude. Pick up the pace. Make the top ten. You're almost there.

Stumbling across the finish line 25 minutes later, an exhausted Emma doubled over, gasping for air and trying her best not to vomit. Exhaustedly, she looked up at the runner's board. Sixth overall in the women's category. She glanced at her watch again. Personal record! After gathering her breath, Emma strutted around the parking lot slapping high-fives with the other women runners. Then she collapsed to the ground, lay on her back, and covered her face. Steadying her breathing, she began her long road to recuperation. After stretching out her tired and sore muscles, Emma agreed to meet with a group of ladies for drinks later on in the evening.

Then she left for her hotel.

AT 6:30 P.M., AN EXHAUSTED Emma arrived at the Hyatt Regency in Provo.

Struggling along the hallway, leg muscles twitching and cramps painfully gripping her calves, she reached her room. After a few swipes of the key-card, the latch clicked, and she pushed the door open, rushing in and collapsing onto the bed like a sack of potatoes.

After just a few minutes of sprawling on the bed, debating whether she wanted to go out for drinks, a loud rap came from the door. "Jesus Christ," she muttered. "Go away! I'm busy!"

"Ms. Massey?" Came a muffled voice, followed by more rapping on the door. "Ms. Massey? I'm with hotel management."

Emma groaned, rolling off the bed and stumbling to the door. Peering through the peephole, she saw a handsome man in a dark suit and pink silk tie standing in the hall. "Ms. Massey?"

Emma unlatched the door and pulled it open. Standing before her, a tall, attractive man of middle-eastern descent, and with a sexy UK voice to boot, flashed her a pleasant smile.

"Hello," Emma said to the man. "Can I help you?"

The man produced a small wicker basket loaded with drinks. "Yes, I have brought a complimentary energy drink and some ice-cold bottled spring water, compliments of the hotel. Congratulations on your marathon."

Emma's head snapped back. "Marathon? How'd you know I was running a marathon?"

The handsome man seemed confused by this question. "You put it on your guest card. We're giving away free drinks to all the runners. Please. These will help with your recovery."

Emma shrugged, taking the wicker basket of drinks.

"Is everyone here as charming as you?" Emma said, smiling broadly.

The man shrugged. "Not everyone, but I try."

Emma thanked him, closing the door behind her. Walking back to her bed, she grabbed the remote from the nightstand and turned on the TV.

Wow! She thought. He was right! These drinks are ice cold! She twisted off a bottle cap, searching through TV channels, settling on an episode of *90-day Fiancé*. Gulping down the drink, she leaned up against the headboard.

Moments after she finished the bottled drink, Emma felt an unusual tightness in her chest. A tightness that grew with every breath. A tingling sensation moved through her left arm. The Apple Watch displayed an insanely rapid pulse.

What the hell? Emma thought, panicking. Am I having a heart attack?

Rolling to her side, she reached across the nightstand for the phone but her arm went numb, dropping toward the floor like a limp noodle. Desperate, filling with panic, she used her good arm to grab the phone, but just as she reached it with her outstretched fingertips, a searing pain shot through her like a bolt of lightning. Clutching her chest, Emma doubled over, knocking the phone to the floor.

Fuck! Fuck! Fuck! She thought, her mind racing. I'm having a goddammed heart attack!

Emma fell to the floor and, with a fumbling hand, attempted to dial the front desk for help. A voice came across the receiver, and Emma tried to speak, but she couldn't form words. Saliva filling her mouth, her jaws froze in paralysis. Groaning and struggling to climb back onto the bed, she pulled the lamp off the nightstand with a crash.

Terror occluding her brain and her consciousness fleeing, Emma's face went rigid. A second searing pain shot through her from heart to head. Her vision tunneled, her arms and legs folded inward, fingers curling tightly as her mind peeled away down to its primal core. Emma's final thoughts faded away into darkness, her breathing ceased, her heart went still, and thirty seconds later, her life was no more.

Two minutes after Emma's sudden death, the door latch clicked, and Yousef hurried into the room, kneeling and checking for a pulse. Emma's skin cooling and feeling no pulse, he gathered the empty bottle and unused drinks, dashing from the room in haste, gently closing the door behind him.

Two hours later, Yousef was on a plane and flying back to Woodrock, sipping a Columbia Valley merlot, relaxing in first class seating, and catching up on world events from his phone.

Part 4

Compromised

CHAPTER 24

KENDRICK STANZ RAN DOWN the brightly lit 4th floor hallway of CIA headquarters as if his life depended on it. Cheap leather shoes *patting* on thin carpeting, apologetically bumping into grumbling colleagues, he clutched a lime-green folder in his left hand. The seal for the National Reconnaissance Office on the front cover, SECRET/SCI, in bold, black stencil on the back, Kendrick rushed along the hall, apologizing and carrying America's most crucial intelligence in his hands like a live grenade. The folder's purpose was clearly labeled. No plausible excuse for confusing its sensitivity with, for instance, the CIA cafeteria's special of the day, or even the President's travel schedule, would ever be accepted, let alone even entertained.

This was crucial intelligence, and time was of the essence.

Darting from the hall and tapping on the door to the SIO's office like a Jurassic woodpecker, Kendrick twisted the chrome handle, stumbling inside before anyone had given him permission to enter.

Senior Intelligence Officer Barb Dent's expression, as Kendrick burst in uninvited, was that of wide-eyed surprise and teeth-grinding fury.

Recruited straight out of high school, Barb Dent was a CIA legend. All of 5'2 and 110 pounds, with burning brown eyes and wavy dark brown hair, Barb was never one to shy away from opportunities to lace people up with a flurry of colorful adjectives and suggestions of self-sex acts. Earning the titles of both *maverick* and *cast-iron bitch*, she embraced the latter of the two wholeheartedly. And to understand Barb Dent's pathological hell-bent crusade against terrorism in any form or fashion, one needed only to observe the maze of scar tissue on her back from dozens of skin grafts. In 1998, on just the 14th day of her first overseas assignment, a 22-year-old Barb would find herself trapped under the burning rubble of the Nairobi Embassy. An explosive laden truck had exploded in front of the building with a force of 15 metric tons, leaving Barb with third-degree burns on her back and shoulders, a fractured skull and spine, and a year in rehabilitation.

What seemed to be centuries since that horrible day, Barb now led the Central Intelligence Agency's investigation into a chlorine gas attack on a quiet village in Nigeria. A suspected air attack from nearby Chad, the CIA Director had tasked Barb with finding the truth.

Sitting across from Barb, the deeply creviced face of Bob Evans, a chain-smoking career intelligence officer with the CIA's APLAA office, snapped around to face this interloper.

Kendrick, the former hacker turned CIA analyst, stood before the furious SIO and the weathered Evans, waving his green folder of secrets.

"They didn't do it!" Kendrick gushed, doubling over, catching his breath.

Barb's eyes darted to Evans, then back to Kendrick. "Who didn't do what?" She asked, her brown eyes burning into Kendrick like torches. Evans shifted around in his seat, expecting an explanation.

"Well? Who didn't do what?" she asked, again. "I'm in a fucking meeting here."

"Chad didn't gas the village in Nigeria!" Kendrick stood and tried to slow his breathing.

"Jesus, Kendrick, you're panting like my fucking Labradoodle. Did you run here? How do you know they didn't do it?"

Sliding a black-and-white image out of the folder, taken from a satellite hundreds of miles above the earth, Kendrick placed it on her desk. "I know they didn't because the NRO has been watching the Boko Haram cells in that region. What do you see in the first picture?"

Placing her eyeglasses on, Barb whisked the image off the desk and studied it. "Um, trees, a bunch of homes, so what?"

"That's the village. The time: 2234 hours. Now, what else?"

She pulled the satellite image closer. Glowing in the infrared, ghost-like figures stood scattered throughout the village. Most seemed to concentrate around the village center. "I see people. Looks like they're having a town meeting or something."

"Right, and here's the same village," Kendrick said, pulling a second image and placing it on her desk. "This is fifteen minutes later."

Barb saw those same people, but now they lay sprawled on the ground and scattered in a much wider and disorganized pattern, like they'd been running or fleeing from something. The villagers' bodies cooling in death, their infrared glow had dimmed. "I see dead people. We already knew that." She looked up at Kendrick and shrugged.

Kendrick slid a third picture toward her. "And what is that?" Kendrick said, tapping the photo with his finger. Barb eyed him from over the rims of her glasses, wondering where this was all heading.

Picking up the photo with a deep, impatient sigh, she studied it. A bright blob with long blades protruding outward flashed over the top of the village, clearly at high speed. "Okay, a helicopter. The helicopter that gassed the village."

"Barb, the time. Look at the time."

Her eyes moved to the top corner of the photo, her brows arched, and her glasses slid down the bridge of her nose.

"Wait, is this…"

"Yes, it is. That helicopter, the one that gassed this village, flew over it twenty minutes after everyone was already dead. The chlorine traces found at the site, the chlorine that was dropped on the village, well, they dropped it *after* whatever already took place killed these people."

Whisking off her glasses and tossing them onto the desk, she studied Kendrick. "So, who was flying the helicopter if the Chadians weren't? And why would they drop gas on dead people?"

Kendrick, eyes locked on Barb's, slid a fourth picture across the desk.

"What the fuck am I looking for, Kendrick?" She muttered, her eyes moving around the image.

"That." He leaned over, tapping at the right side of the photo. "In the distance. That 747. Look what they're pushing out its nose."

Her eyes widened. "Jesus, a fucking helicopter." Barb thrust the images at Evans. "Bob, check these out."

"Yeah," Kendrick continued. "So, I contacted our Black Site in Lagos, and they dug into customs. There's no record of a helicopter, of any type, being delivered into or shipped out of Lagos. Nada, Nothing. It's gone. And so is the 747."

Barb leaned back in her chair, sliding a purple bow off her ponytail, and rearranging her wavy brown hair. "Would it be too much to ask that you know who this 747 belongs to?"

"A company called Global Carrier."

"What do we know about them?"

"They're contracted out to Pangea Dynamic Solutions. Their entire fleet. And have been for a month."

Snapping her fingers, she shot a look at Evans. "Hey, Bob, isn't the Bureau working an investigation on Pangea?"

"Yeah," Evans mumbled as he examined the photos. "Some contracting funny business with the DOD. They've been working on it for a while. Been digging into Pangea's overseas operations. Also-"

Barb lifted her shoulders. "Also, what?"

"Well, I guess they have an embedded source who's been feeding them something about some mysterious operation. And Pangea's been shipping out drones by the thousands."

"Drones?" Barb asked, wrapping her hair back into a ponytail and sliding the bow back on. "What sort of drones? And shipping to where?"

Evans shrugged. "That's all I know."

Barb scowled. "What the fuck good are you, Bob?" She turned back to Kendrick. "So? Where'd this 747 originate from?"

"Dublin, Ireland."

"And do we know where this 747 is now? Is it back in Ireland?"

The analyst lifted his shoulders. "Don't know, it's missing."

Barb's eyes darted back and forth between Kendrick and Bob Evans. "Wait. What? It's missing? Kendrick, it's a fucking 747, not a set of car keys. How the fuck does a 747 just go missing?"

"There's more," Kendrick continued.

Barb blurted out a restrained laugh. "There is?"

Kendrick nodded. "A 767 from the Pangea facility in South Dakota landed in Dublin two days before the attack. There was a cargo swap from the 767 to the 747. I tried to pull up the cargo manifest, but couldn't get in. Classified. Top Secret. Access denied."

"What?" Barb squinted at Kendrick with an expression of befuddlement. "Classified by who? Us? And what about the helicopter? Where'd that materialize from? You can't ship one of those inside a 767." Her eyebrows arching in disbelief, she turned to Evans. "What the fuck, Bob? We're the CIA, goddammit. Who's classifying this shit? Better yet, who's seeing it? What're your fucking thoughts?"

Evans groaned and frowned. "I think we need to give the Bureau a call. Pangea's their baby. They need to know what we know, and we need to know whatever the hell they know."

"Great," Barb muttered between gritted teeth. "The fucking FBI. Just what we need." She leaned back in her chair. "Okay, Jack Fitzgerald and I go back a while. Set up a call with him today, will ya, Bob?"

Evans nodded. "Will do."

She turned back to Kendrick. "As for you, mister, we need to find out what *actually killed* those poor bastards in Nigeria if it wasn't chlorine gas. Get our Black Site on that, ASAP. We need to find someone to do an autopsy, but in the dark. Get a body, you hear me, Kendrick? Get a fucking body. And find that fucking 747. I want some no-shit, actionable intelligence. Not a bunch of suppositions and guesses."

"Yes, ma'am."

She turned back to Evans. "Well, any other fucking thoughts, Bob?"

Evans pulled a wrinkled pack of Lucky Strikes from his pocket, stuck a cigarette in his mouth, and rolled it around between his lips. "If Kendrick can find out all this, so can someone else. We better get this right, Barb, or this shit will blow up right in our faces."

Kendrick suddenly realized he'd left something out. "Oh crap, there's something else." He pulled one final image from the folder and handed it to Barb. Eyeing him with doubt and impatience, she snatched the image, looking it over. Four figures, bright with infrared heat signatures, stood in the village. A fifth figure headed toward the tree line and a nearby stream, where four more bodies lay on its banks.

"Who the fuck are these guys?"

"Don't know, Barb. They arrived about two hours after the attack, and they left about a half hour later. They're not U.N. The U.N didn't arrive until the next day. These guys were there hours before anyone even reported the attack."

Barb studied the image, slapping it down on the desk with a *whap!*

"Well, guys," she said, her lips curled into a twisted grin. "We all love a mystery. That's why we dedicate our lives to this miserable fucking agency."

THE DEPUTY DIRECTOR OF the FBI pushed the button on the speakerphone, ending a call with Barb Dent and Bob Evans.

Tall, black-haired, and still hanging onto boyish good looks even at forty-five, Jack Fitzgerald looked like an accountant who modeled for GQ as a side-gig. Sharp, intellectual, and seasoned, the former white-collar crime fighter cut his terrorism teeth on a domestic terror plot many years earlier when he met his future wife, Anna, a former district attorney who lost her left leg and right eye in a bomb explosion. Now serving as a partner in a high-powered D.C. law firm focusing on human rights cases, she jokingly referred to herself as Anna Blackbeard.

Across from Jack, sat former federal prosecutor and agent in charge of Operation Cobalt, Grady Freeman. A former linebacker at Nebraska

State University and graduate of Georgetown Law, he was a physically imposing man. But Grady's appearance was deceptive. With a talent for disarming detractors through prolonged stares and silence, his voice was deep, yet soft and articulate. A Barry White meets James Baldwin style of speaking that gave the impression some other human being was inhabiting his body.

Operation Cobalt, an investigation into the shady bookkeeping of Pangea Dynamic Solutions, had been moving along for the better part of a year. Pangea received billions of taxpayer dollars from the Department of Defense. Dollars approved by the House and Senate, and spent on developing innovative AI and surveillance drones for the Air Force.

Pangea, in four years of receiving money from the DOD, had delivered all of 100 of them.

Where was the money going? According to Sam Singh, the CEO, the money was going into development and, as a spokesperson claimed, there'd been delays. Many delays. Yet the production of drones soared and the money poured in from the DOD, and nothing was being pushed through the door in exchange. Grady Freeman and his team were now rapidly approaching the tipping point of secret grand juries, search warrants, and subpoenas.

But Operation Cobalt just got flipped on its head by the CIA. Based on this call, Pangea seemed to be involved in something much darker than bilking tax dollars.

"Wow, Jack," Grady said with a sigh of exasperation.

"Wow, what?" Jack replied, steaming his glasses and wiping the lenses.

Grady shrugged. "Well, I mean, that all seems kind of thin, doesn't it? Pangea sneaking a helicopter into Nigeria and gassing a village? Why on earth would they do something like that?"

Jack continued wiping his glasses. "You think this is actionable intelligence? Or do you think our friends at the agency are just guessing? Or maybe trying to divert attention because they're covering something up?"

"Well, they do have that history," Grady added.

"Oh yeah," Jack replied. "I have personal experience with these bozos from way back." Placing his glasses back on, he leaned toward Grady. "But why, of all people, places, and things, would they choose Pangea? Bob seemed pretty certain about this. He's been in that business for a long time. And I've known Barb Dent for years. She's, let's just say, very direct. Not someone who'd get caught up in some coverup. What more do you have on this Hand thing you talked about on the call?"

"Iron Hand?"

"Yes, that's it."

"Not much, really," Freeman replied. "We know it exists. We also know it may have something to do with these drones they're shipping out."

"But to where, Grady? Where are they shipping these drones? Do we know if they shipped any to Nigeria?"

"No, not really."

"Get on that, okay?" Jack asked.

Grady nodded, scribbling on his notepad.

Jack studied Grady as he captured notes. "Anything from Cobalt you need to brief me on? Now that I'm getting pulled in? This would be a good time to get me up to speed."

Grady flipped through his notes. "Yeah, a few, actually. But I don't know their relevance yet."

"Okay," Jack said. "Firc it at mc."

Grady flipped a page on his notebook. "A couple of deaths at Pangea's Woodrock manufacturing facility in South Dakota have grabbed the attention of Local Law Enforcement."

Jack tilted his head. "Deaths?"

Freeman nodded as he reviewed his notes. "Yup. Pippa Simpson, a scientist who headed up their global innovation department, drove her car off the road and died."

"What's suspicious about that?" Jack asked.

"We're not sure, but it appears some of the victim's friends think it is. One spoke to LLE. That's all we have on that for now."

"Okay, go on."

"A security guard committed suicide after the accident. I guess he may have been at the scene."

"At the scene? The guard was at the scene? Then killed himself? Seems odd, doesn't it?"

"We agree with that, Jack. We're digging a little further."

"So, what do you have on this guard?"

Grady ran his finger along his notes. "Name is Chris Hadley. Former Spec Ops. Army Ranger, Delta Force, clean arrest history."

Jack's head snapped back. "Delta Force? That's who Pangea hires to check IDs in South Dakota? Who the hell do they expect to show up at their gates? The local chapter of the Taliban?"

"Also, this is interesting," Grady continued. "The very Sam Singh himself went to the police chief and spoke with him a few days after the two deaths. We don't know what they talked about, but it wasn't long, and when he left, he didn't seem too happy."

Jack picked up a pen, twirling it in his fingers. "Not happy? What do we know about the chief?"

Grady ran down his notes. "Ronan Quinn. Former detective. Came in from New York. Been their chief for about-"

Jack cut Grady off. "You've got to be kidding me."

Grady looked up from his notes. "You know him?"

Twirling the pen with his fingers, Jack leaned back. "Well, I know of him. Got let go for leaking a name to the press. The guy messed up a joint investigation we had with the NYPD."

"Wow," Grady chuckled. "Can we trust him?"

"I'm not sure," Jack replied thoughtfully. "Heavy drinker. Assaulted his wife. Got let go from the force after he blew up our operation. But he was a highly respected detective for a while. Ex-Marine. Silver Star recipient. He's their chief of police, you say?"

"Yeah, he is."

"Well, he sure must've cleaned up his act," Jack muttered, his mind lost in thought. "How the hell does a New York homicide detective wind up in South Dakota? Does that seem weird?"

Grady shrugged. "You want me to send a team to Woodrock and set up surveillance on Quinn? See what they're working on?"

Jack gave a high-browed response. "Seriously, Grady? You want to get a warrant from a judge to spy on Local Law Enforcement? Good luck with that. And in any case, that's far exceeding the scope of Cobalt. Who's your mole?"

"Yeah, Whitetail. That's where all this is coming from. They also brought this Iron Hand thing to us. Whatever the hell it is."

"Okay, have Whitetail keep tabs on Quinn for now. We may need to pull him in. But Grady, I don't want a bunch of agents sneaking around Woodrock until we know more about Iron Hand. What it even is. We need to know if it ties into the Nigerian mass murder Barb and Bob were talking about."

"Okay, Jack, anything else?"

Jack gazed at the ceiling, twirling his pen. He stopped, scribbled on a post-It note, and handed the note to Grady.

Grady, puzzled, looked at the name Jack had written. "Who's Miá Perez?"

"She was Ronan Quinn's supervisor, the one who fired him. She's a captain in NYPD Homicide now and a former Marine like Quinn. They were good friends. I want you to call her and see if she's kept in touch with him. Try to get a feel for Quinn. See if he's someone we can trust if we need to."

Grady stuffed the note into his pocket. "Okay, then what?"

"I trust your judgment on this, Grady. You've been on Operation Cobalt from day one. If you get good vibes, put Whitetail in touch with Quinn. Let them trade information. I want to know what he knows every step of the way."

"You got it."

Jack held up his finger. "And I don't want Quinn contacting anyone about anything. Not the State Police. Not Homeland Security. Not anyone here at the Bureau. Everything gets channeled through Whitetail. Keep this clean and simple. I want the connection strictly between Quinn, Whitetail, and us."

"Okay, anything else?"

"Grady, we're going way beyond Cobalt's scope here," Jack said, leaning back, absentmindedly twirling his pen. "If we get Quinn and your source, this Whitetail, talking to each other, you think Whitetail might blow their cover? What if Quinn knows them?"

"Jack," Grady said, cocking his head. "I don't even know who Whitetail is."

CHAPTER 25

THE TIRES OF SAMIR Singh's prized Gulfstream-650G, struck the asphalt of a LaGuardia Airport runway at noon on a warm, muggy, New York Friday.

Rushing down the steps, the two big turbofans winding down from a scream to the clacking of fan blades, the thick odor of heated asphalt and jet fuel greeted him. He dashed to his waiting limousine.

Displaying equal parts skill and patience, Ramon, the hulking driver with the smooth, waxed scalp, weaved the limo through stop-and-go Friday congestion. Tapping the wheel and bobbing his head, he mumbled along to the lyrics of Drake's *Way 2 Sexy* playing on the radio.

I'm too sexy for Milan, too sexy for Milan, New York or Japan.

Following along with Drake's rhythm, subconsciously tapping his knee along with the beat, Singh gazed outside. Fighting New York traffic through the power of blaring horns and profanity, Zombie motorists honked and shouted. He closed his eyes and focused. A meeting with The Five Horsemen, the council of Jupiter's most trusted advisors, was on the afternoon's agenda.

As Jupiter's number two, Singh oversaw this council. With their grim dystopian title, the Horsemen directed a much larger and more diverse group known as The Apostles. Further yet down the organizational chart were The Disciples, a large assortment of scientists, military brass, and other critical figures who'd signed onto the idea of Iron Hand. The Disciples included Red Lancer as well, along with their highly trained teams of assassins, and somewhere in a murky organizational basement resided Red Lancer's low-skilled, disposable assets. If the titles of this organization seemed straight out of the Old Testament, it's because they were. Jupiter, for some mysterious reason, liked to keep things biblical. Perhaps it made Iron Hand seem more prophetic than pragmatic. Maybe he was attempting to brush Iron Hand with some sort of misguided romanticism. Whatever his motives were, they worked. His followers were true believers.

After fighting abrasive New York drivers for an hour, Ramon pulled the limousine into a multi-storied covered garage adjacent to a rather ordinary looking, five-story building in Queens. This mundane structure headquartered a little known, mostly ignored Think Tank, named *The Center for Earth First.* Composed of scholars, scientists, bipartisan government leaders, and burned-out university professors, this miserable collection of humans, as Singh referred to them, spent their days quarreling over ways to save humanity from its rapidly approaching demise. Ways that no one at Earth First could agree on, let alone society itself. Getting eight billion people to agree on anything was as conceivable as teaching poker to penguins.

Singh felt for these poor sods at The Center for Earth First - creating pie-in-the-sky solutions to environmental challenges, and then reality crashing down on their heads like a planet-killing asteroid. The futility of it all, he thought, making his way across the cluttered first floor. The brightest people in the country, huddling in meeting rooms, brainstorming, spit balling, and connecting hypothetical dots on whiteboards with dry-erase pens. They'd get more joy planning an invasion of Switzerland with leprechauns riding unicorns than feverishly working on readily dismissed solutions. Laughed out of boardrooms and senate chambers like blathering idiots, their most recent study forecast a bleak future. Mass starvation. Tribalism. Wars consuming the world. Refugees flowing from regions no longer habitable, like ants fleeing a flooded basement.

No one at Earth First, nor the Horsemen, Apostles, Disciples, or even Singh knew who Jupiter was. But this mysterious Jupiter, over several years, had cultivated a cult-like trust despite his physical absence - a trust nurtured through fire and brimstone speeches, and through very generous monetary donations. In Jupiter's world, money walked, talked, sang a tune, and quoted scripture.

The poor, overworked, frustrated people at Earth First hadn't the slightest inkling of the super-secret project named Iron Hand. If they had, despite being ignored and shunned and laughed out of rooms, Singh felt they'd resign en masse in protest. Not even these lost souls would agree with something so dark and preposterous. More critically, their reports and studies were crucial to Iron Hand's effectiveness and ultimate success. Losing that analysis, if they all walked out, would cause Iron Hand to go blind. And Red Lancer to go bananas at the prospect of 'silencing' so many people.

Meandering through the maze of cubicles and people, Singh reached the elevator. Stepping inside, he pressed a button for the fifth floor. Affixed to the wall next to the floor-button panel read a very ominous message.

"Restricted Area. Approved Personnel Only. Use of Deadly Force is Authorized."

For some strange reason, someone had pasted a cutout of the unfortunate Kenny from the cartoon *South Park* on the elevator wall.

Moving up the floors, the elevator dinging and rattling, Singh took in a deep breath, nervously smoothing his pants and jacket. Jerking to a halt, the elevator hissed and a small camera lens next to the doors glowed an odd lime green. On an LCD screen next to the camera, instructions appeared. If he failed to follow the instructions, or if the instructions he followed led to a failed authorization, the elevator would drop Singh to the bottom of the shaft like a stone.

1. ***Place eye in front of camera***
2. ***Keep chin level with floor***
3. ***Do not blink***
4. ***Wait for three beeps***
5. ***Elevator doors will open upon successful scan***

Singh performed the tasks, waiting for what seemed to be an eternity to find out if a database approved, or rejected, his eyeball. The elevator buzzed, and the doors slid open in a *whoosh*.

His hasty steps reverberating through a long featureless hallway, Singh hurried toward the two steel doors and desk where the sole guard on duty, Karma, patiently waited. Thick eye-lash extensions fluttering, her broad grin captured in cherry-red lipstick, Karma slid a sign-in sheet toward Singh. Her large, rosemary-green eyes studied him as he pulled the sheet closer.

"You look lovely today, Karma," he remarked, scribbling his name on the sheet.

"Oh my, thank you Sam," Karma replied with a warm smile. "It's so good to see you again. Everything going well?"

"Swimmingly," he muttered, writing the time and date on the sheet.

Her fingernails polished in glittery-green, Karma's left hand held the sign-in sheet steady for Singh as he wrote. Slung beneath the desk, a

Honey Badger PDW rifle aimed for Singh's midsection, Karma's right hand and a glittery polished finger resting against the trigger. Singh always felt a touch of anxiety during these moments, knowing a glittery trigger finger was just a flinch away from ripping his torso in half. Karma pulled the sign-in sheet toward her, studying Singh's signature and comparing it to one on an index card. She released her grip on the rifle beneath the desk, pulling her right arm back into view.

"Do you ever get bored, Karma?" Singh asked, watching her press a blue button on the desktop.

"For your sake, Sam, you'd better hope not. They're inside waiting for you." She tilted her head with a dimpled smile, batting her eyelashes. "Have fun!"

From behind her, the two steel doors slowly opened, where the Five Horsemen awaited him.

Karma watched Singh walk through the steel doors. Another press of the blue button, and the doors closed behind him.

A MUCH DIFFERENT SAMIR Singh stormed from the room three hours later. Muttering a half-hearted farewell to Karma, he stomped down the hallway toward the elevator.

Not only has Iron Hand gone down a completely new path, he thought, frustrated and angry. Jupiter has not informed me of this change! Why was I excluded from this decision? And this new direction? What the fuck!

Feeling like he could rip the elevator from its cables and heave it Hulk-style across Queens, Singh simmered with anger. Recalling those condescending grins from the Horsemen, hearing their patronizing tone, the tables had turned and the great Sam Singh finally learned something second-hand for a change. He thought he heard their snickering as he left the meeting room. The Horsemen, under direction from Jupiter, had tossed him from his throne.

What the hell was this all about? He thought as the elevator took him to the main floor. And the Nigeria op? Excluded from that as well? What the hell is happening? The elevator whooshed open, and he stormed his way through the chatter and talking of the Earth First war room. Is this why Jupiter wants to meet with me in Aspen? Am I being pushed off to the side? Set out to pasture? Was losing my temper over the miniature genocide in Nigeria getting me pulled from the project?

My project?!

Hurrying along the covered walkway to the garage, he saw Ramon leaning up against the limousine, watching videos on his phone and chuckling like an enormous child. Ramon saw an enraged Samir Singh approaching, shoved his phone into his pocket and opened the door.

"Everything okay, boss?"

"No," Singh responded testily, sliding into the rear of the limo. Ramon closed the door, hurrying to the driver's seat. The limousine swerving and speeding down each level of the garage, Singh heard the buzzing of his secure device.

Red Lancer:

Wasps worked like champs in Nigeria! Those things really kick ass, don't they?

Singh frustratedly shook his head. I'm not in the mood, idiot. He typed his response, hoping Red Lancer would just go away.

Kilimanjaro:

Yes, they sure do.

Red Lancer:

Jupiter says your boy, Rich, may not be fully on board. He really freaked out.

Kilimanjaro:

Leave Rich alone. Nothing better happen to him. He's just a programmer, and a damned good one. We need him.

Red Lancer:

Not my call, bro.

Kilimanjaro:

Yes, it is.

Red Lancer:

Had to take care of someone at Woodrock. She was talking to the police there. Heart attack. Who knew being a runner was so hazardous to your health?

Singh fumbled with the device and it tumbled from his hands, falling to the floor of the car. What!? What the hell is he talking about!? He scooped up the device, frantically typing.

Kilimanjaro:

Who was talking to the police? Someone from Pangea? Why would you have to kill her? What the hell?

Red Lancer:

I think you're getting soft. Should I be concerned?

Singh threw his head back. "Fuuuuck!"

"You okay, boss?" Ramon asked, glancing into the rearview mirror.

Singh drew in a deep breath and nodded. "I'm fine, Ramon. I'll be alright." He typed…

Kilimanjaro:

Why don't you just kill the whole damned town while you're at it?

Red Lancer:

That thought has occurred.

Singh tossed the device down onto the seat. Fuming, he glared out the window of the car as they made their way past shops and stores. What a nightmare, he thought. No one respects me. I'm nothing to them. It's time I recalibrated with Jupiter. I need to right this ship.

Up ahead, as the limo approached an intersection, Singh saw something of interest. "Ramon," he said, leaning forward and tapping the mammoth human on the shoulder. "Stop at that little store up ahead. I need to grab something."

Ramon turned onto the cross-street, parking the limo against the curb. "Whatcha need, boss?"

"I'm picking up some vodka. You're free to join me when we get back to the hotel, if you like."

Ramon gave Singh a shoulder bouncing tee-hee chuckle. "Sounds like a plan, boss. Sounds like a real, good plan."

LEAVING LAGUARDIA AND THE Horsemen behind, the sleek Gulfstream 650's landing gear retracted into their wells at 9:15 a.m. the following morning. The jet banked left over the Hudson River before climbing and turning to the north.

The outskirts of New York City fell far below him, and in minutes webs of highways and grids of small towns appeared beneath the Gulfstream's wings as it turned on a northwesterly heading over Pennsylvania. Passing 10,000 feet, the jet sped up, pushing him back into his seat, and soon the Gulfstream was speeding toward its final destination of Aspen, at a swift Mach .90.

Singh pulled the shade down on the window and reclined his seat. His head throbbed and his mouth felt as dry as a desert. The previous night, he and Ramon had stayed awake until 2 a.m. Swilling vodka. Talking Mets baseball. Watching videos. Debating the meaning of life. Eventually, Ramon's hulking physique flopped onto the hotel sofa like a walrus, passing out in just seconds. Singh remained awake, curiously observing Ramon, wondering to himself if he could ever be as free and joyful as this enormous man. Polite. Sensitive. Funny. Carefree. Just a simple driver. Living his best life. Watching sports and hanging out with his friends and hitting the nightclubs on Fridays. He envied this gentle giant. But he didn't envy what lay in wait for Ramon. Soon, this gentle giant will be fighting for his very life...and, more than likely, losing it.

Jill approached, asking if he'd like a fruit smoothie. Singh asked for spring water and some aspirin instead. Returning from the forward galley with his water, she dropped the aspirin into his palm and took her seat at the front. Exhaustion and sleep deprivation won him over. His head rolled to the side and his eyelids snapped shut. The whooshing air across the skin of the jet and the dull throbbing of the engines faded away into nothingness.

THUMP. THUMP. BANG!

Singh's eyes flashed open.

Thump. Thump.

Glancing over his shoulder toward the rear of the jet, he wondered if loose baggage was tumbling around in the rear cabin. He turned to Jill. Her face looked as pale as a white cotton bedsheet, eyes wide with terror and confusion.

Thump. Bang! Bang!

Sensing the jet arching over, he suddenly felt weightless, and the sound of air rushing across the fuselage grew deafening as the plane's airspeed quickly increased. Approaching a velocity that would soon tear the jet to pieces, Singh's beloved Gulfstream 650G now hurtled toward the earth like a meteor.

In just over a minute, the jet would impact the earth at the speed of sound, with Samir Singh, the crew, and his jet vanishing in a massive fireball.

CHAPTER 26

THE GULFSTREAM DOVE TOWARD the earth, transitioning from airplane to projectile in just seconds. What is going on!? Singh screamed inside his own head.

The wing's spoilers, used to create drag and slow the jet down, extended into the airflow with a loud rumble. The jet abruptly leveled off, slamming Singh back down on his seat.

Thump! Bang! Bang!

As quickly as the jet leveled off, it just as quickly nosed over, diving toward the ground once more. Jill grasped the armrests of her seat, legs flailing above her head like she was performing a gymnastic routine, praying she wouldn't be tossed about the cabin like a rag-doll. The plane's vertical trajectory shallowing once more, Jill tumbled into her seat in a heap of flailing arms and legs. Unstrapping himself, Singh stumbled forward.

"Jill! Are you okay?" Unfolding her arms and legs, he pulled back her hair and looked her over. She nodded, gathering her wits, locating her seatbelt and snapping it together.

"I'll be fine, Sam," she stuttered, extending her thumb. "Go find out what's wrong."

Singh nodded, dashing through the galley and opening the cockpit door.

In front of him was a scene of complete chaos.

Through the windshield, the greens of rural Pennsylvania rushed toward them. He glanced at the captain. Pulling the yolk back into his stomach, he was strained to the point of bursting. The first officer alternated between frantic radio calls and reading off emergency checklist items. A loud clacking sound from the overspeed warning reverberated through the cockpit, and the roar of the wind was deafening.

"What's going on?!" Singh shouted.

"We have a jammed stabilizer, Sam! Nose down! I've managed to get the nose back up a bit, but we're still descending like a son of a bitch!"

Singh pulled the foldaway jump seat out and strapped himself in. "Can you override it!?"

The first officer shook his head. "No, electric trim isn't working, and neither is emergency!"

"Because it's jammed, Rob!" Yelled the frustrated captain. Singh's personal and most trusted pilot of eight years was nearly hyperventilating and looking as red as a beet. "Nothing is going to un-jam it unless it just frees itself up by some goddammed miracle!" The captain took a moment and glanced outside. "Get us radar vectors to the nearest airfield, Rob! And tell them we need a long runway!" Pointing at the landing gear handle, he directed the copilot to lower the landing gear. "Rob! Rob! Drop the gear! I can't slow her!"

Giving the LCD screens in front of the pilots a quick study, a grave situation displayed itself in alarming colors and numbers. The airspeed lit up in bright red, the jet flying well beyond its design limits. The altitude wound down so fast it was barely readable. The artificial horizon, painted entirely in tan, displayed a steep dive toward the ground. Even to the most novice of observers, these basic indications foretold doom.

Grabbing onto the small handle protruding from the instrument panel, the copilot slammed it down. From behind him, the sounds of doors and panels being ripped away as the landing gear extended outward from their wells reached the cockpit. My jet is going to smack into Pennsylvania at the speed of sound, he thought. They'll be lucky if they find an intact finger.

Thump. Thump.

Singh felt a shudder through the airframe. The jet was disintegrating.

But after a few seconds, waiting for imminent death, he realized it wasn't disintegrating after all. The jet was leveling off!

"Goddammit," the captain muttered, the strain on his face from exertion causing veins to pop out of his neck. "Rob, I'm getting some pitch control back. Holy shit."

"Bill, what can I do? How can I help?" Singh asked.

The horizon, once obscured in their near vertical descent, now appeared ahead of them as the nose of the jet slowly rose.

"I'm getting some control back, Sam. I don't know how, but the stabilizer freed itself up just enough to give me something. Look outside. See if you can spot a place to set this girl down. Rob, call ATC, give them our position, and tell them we're making a forced landing." The pilot shook his head in frustration. "Too fast. Too fast. C'mon you bitch, slow down."

They were still descending rapidly. Nothing the crew could do would stop that. The horizontal stabilizer at the rear had freed itself momentarily, but not completely. "Do you think we can still land, Bill?"

"I don't know, Sam. But I'm not giving up yet. I still don't have full elevator control, but if I can get enough power from the engines near touchdown, I can arrest the descent enough for a maybe survivable god-dammed impact."

Singh nodded and patted him on the shoulder. "It's for moments like this that I'm glad I hired you, buddy." A large pasture with a long road running perpendicular to it, appeared ahead and to the right. "There, Bill. Two o'clock. About three miles. See it? See that pasture? It looks pretty smooth and there's a road next to it."

The captain glanced outside. "Got it." Yanking the wheel left to right, banking the jet steeply from side to side, the pilot tried to slow a sleek plane designed for speed. "Flaps, Rob. Start inching the flaps out."

"You want throttles back up?" the first officer asked.

The captain shook his head. "Not yet, Rob." He looked over at Singh. "Sam, go get strapped in and check on Jill. This landing's going to be a bit bumpy."

Singh nodded, smacking the two pilots on their shoulders. "Good luck, guys. We know you can do it." Folding the jump seat back up, he headed into the cabin.

Jill, in the forward seat, mascara and tears streaming down her face, stared wildly into Singh's eyes as he checked on her. All alone in the cabin while Singh was with the pilots, she'd heard roars, thumps, bangs, pieces of the jet being torn away, and the plane shuddering and shaking. Isolated and cut off from everyone else, poor Jill had sat still and alone, waiting for death to arrive at any second.

"Are we going to die?" She asked, lips quivering and her eyes searching his.

"We're not dead yet, my dear." Singh replied, mustering a forced smile. "Hang on, put your head between your knees."

Managing the bravest of smiles, she reached and held Singh's hand. "Hey, Sam, that's my job."

Singh kneeled. "So, here's the deal, Jill. Bill's going to land us in a field. It'll be just another minute or so. Get ready."

Jill, alarmed, mouth gaping, gushed. "A field? What's our chances?"

He took his seat and pulled the belt as tight as it could go. "About fifty-fifty," he told her as he opened the window shade, watching trees and telephone poles rush past. "I hire only the best." He couldn't tell if that made her feel better or worse. "Stop worrying about me, dear. I'll be fine!"

Jill nodded and thrust her head between her legs.

The engines throttled up slightly, and he could see the flaps now in their fully extended position. Trees flashed past him. In the distance, he saw homes and barns and other buildings.

The engines spooled up into a scream. This is it! Keep fighting boys!

Then, an earsplitting bang, and Samir Singh's world went dark.

"SAM. WAKEUP, MY DEAR brother."

Navi? Is that Navi's voice?

"Don't let the darkness win. Be the truth and the light. You are a Sikh."

Navi?

Singh's eyes snapped open.

The jet was no longer moving, and he was shocked to find he was still alive in an intact cabin, but the cabin was quickly filling with smoke.

The fumes of burning composites and jet fuel stung his eyes. Frantic, he fiddled with the clip on the belt and freed himself from the seat.

Choking on acrid smoke, he stumbled toward Jill. Doubled over in her seat, she appeared to be unconscious.

Singh shook her. "Jill! Jill!"

Moaning, Jill muttered something about being late for a concert. Singh shook his head, unstrapped her, and with all his strength, dragged her semi-limp body through the narrow galley. Pulling the emergency release for the cabin door, it fell outward, but only halfway. Smoke smothered him. His lungs burned. His eyes were watering so badly, the world became a moisturized blur of toxic gray and black. Pushing Jill through the opening, he climbed over her, making his way outside.

Brilliant orange flames roiled into the sky, mixing with black, pungent smoke. Sheared off by trees, the left wing of the jet was nowhere to be seen - wiring, twisted aluminum, fractured composites, and twisted tubing being all that remained. The landing gear, torn away on landing, was somewhere in the field behind them. The troublesome tail, broken off, lay on its side.

Grabbing Jill by her collar, he dragged her across the stubby grass field and away from the jet. A rather large farmer-type in blue-bib overalls materialized from only who knew where, sweeping Jill up in his arms like she was a pillow. "C'mon," he yelled over his shoulder at Singh. "Before that thing blows up!" In a stunned daze, he watched as two bicyclists rushed toward him - the woman rider grabbing his wrist and urging him to run away. The fire, spreading from the right wing and engine, now encompassed the entire rear of the jet and, having just begun their flight from New York, much of the fuel load for the trip still sat in the tanks. Singh yanked his arm away.

"What're you doing!?" She shouted.

Sprinting back to the jet, he crawled across the ladder and burst into the small cockpit.

Leaning across the center console, the blood-soaked captain was desperately trying to free the copilot, slumped over in his seat, unconscious. "Bill," Singh pleaded. "Get out. Please. We're right behind you."

The captain, half blind with blood from a gnarly gash on his head, stumbled through the door and Singh reached over, unsnapping the copilot's harness. Struggling to get any sort of leverage, he fought mightily to remove the copilot from his seat. Burning heat filling the small cockpit, the fire was now halfway through the cabin and half a minute from reaching the two men. There would be no way that he could make the door in time.

But Singh knew his jet. Being the consummate perfectionist, he'd gone through flight training with the pilots and attended Jill's training courses for flight attendants. Each crew member had to know the jet, front to back. So did Singh.

Dashing into the forward galley, he pulled a smoke hood from the cabinet, snatched the fire extinguisher, and pulled the crash axe from the wall. Slipping back into the cockpit, he tore open the bag for the smoke hood, pulling it over the copilot's head and shoulders. Taking the axe, he swung at the pilot's side window with all his might. He swung and swung and swung and swung - the axe burying itself into the glass. With such little room, he struggled to achieve a full swing, but it was just enough. He reared back and kicked the remaining glass free. Mountaineer and triathlete, deceptively strong for his size, he dragged the 200-pound copilot toward him, across the console and into the pilot's seat.

Fire now engulfed the forward galley. Pops, snaps, and cracks of flames filled his ears. The exit was now blocked by flames. He had seconds to act or fire would burn him and this young pilot alive. Pulling off his shirt, he covered his mouth and nose, took the fire extinguisher, and filled the small cockpit with a deadly halon. It would buy him seconds. But seconds were all he needed.

Squeezing past the copilot, he pushed himself through the window, reached back inside, and yanked the copilot free from the plane. To his surprise, the two bicyclists, braving the heat, assisted him. Then the big burly farmer jumped in, lifting the young pilot up with no effort, and ran off to where Jill and the captain now lay. Singh half-stumbled away from the crash and, seconds later, the entire Gulfstream vanished into flames.

Safely away, he fell to the grass next to his captain. Thick, black, billowing smoke rose into the sky, travelling over the countryside for miles in an ominous dark cloud. Numbering close to a hundred by now, onlookers gathered around the scene. Many of them were just standing around, filming this exciting event on their phones. One idiot was taking selfies with the crash behind him, making silly faces at the camera. He suddenly broke into some sort of odd dance. What the hell? Singh thought.

"That was some goddammed landing, wasn't it?" Muttered the battered captain, the woman bicyclist wiping blood from his face.

Singh wrapped his arm around his captain, pulling him close. "That sure was, Bill." In a dreamlike trance, he watched as fire and police arrived. Paramedics rushed across the field toward him.

SITTING AT THE REAR of an ambulance, pressing an oxygen mask to his face, Singh gazed upon the smoldering ruins of his Gulfstream. A young paramedic checked his pulse. Another draped a blanket over his shoulders and applied clips to the cuts on his head.

Singh pulled the mask away. "How's our first officer?"

The paramedic shook his head. "Not too good. He's getting airlifted. He has a lot of head trauma."

"And Jill? Our flight attendant?"

"Concussion. She's banged up, but she'll be fine." The medic finished reading Singh's pulse. "Dude," he said with a look of astonishment. "Your pulse rate is barely ninety. You realize you were just in a plane crash, right?"

Singh nodded, gazing at the scene.

Of course, he knew he'd been in a plane crash. And by some miracle, they were all alive to talk about it.

But this was no accident.

Iron Hand could launch whether he was dead or alive. The Wasps were fully tested and ready, deliveries to nests were on schedule. His utility as the architect and planner now diminishing to zero, he'd become Red Lancer's most favorite asset - the disposable one. His anger over Pippa Simpson's death, and the attack on the village, had given Jupiter enough doubt over Singh's loyalty to add his name to Red Lancer's list of targets.

For the first time in Samir Singh's life, he had no value. He may have survived a plane crash, but he was now a dead man walking.

JUPITER ERUPTED IN FURY. "What the hell happened?!"

"Well, the pilots pulled off a miracle. That's what happened," Red Lancer replied grittily.

"They didn't pull off a miracle. The job was lax. Your man didn't do it right."

Red Lancer sat back in the chair, staring into the dark void at the end of the room. "Hey, Jupiter, he took care of the plane in Colorado. A jammed stabilizer, historically, is pretty fucked up. But these guys pulled it off. I'm actually impressed."

"Well, I'm not!" Jupiter boomed. "Next time I ask for a plane crash, I expect a smoldering crater and an accident the NTSB will fumble over for years!" Jupiter fell silent, and a long awkward pause followed. "Do you think he suspects anything? Do you think he suspects me?"

"Knowing Sam, probably." Red Lancer unwrapped a pack of chewing gum and thrust in a stick.

"Where's he now?" Jupiter asked.

"Somewhere in fucking Pennsylvania. He's in the hospital. That's all I know."

"Maybe we rushed this," Jupiter mumbled.

"Hey," Red Lancer leaned forward. "We don't need him. Not anymore. Production is soaring and deployments are on schedule. His work's done here."

"I know. I'm bringing you into the Apostles now. You'll help with final planning and deployments. But security is still your priority. Find him."

Red Lancer nodded. "I've got people headed his way."

"Good," Jupiter said. "Do it right this time. And get to him before he finds help. He has resources. He has friends. He might go to the press."

Red Lancer leaned back in the chair. No more sabotage, no more heart attacks. It was time for a good, old-fashioned murder. The irony in all this was that without Samir Singh, Iron Hand wouldn't even exist. Now, Iron Hand could exist just fine without him.

Oh well, Red Lancer thought, typing a message to Yousef on the secure device.

Fuck irony.

Chapter 27

Beth stuck her head into Quinn's office. "Boss, you need to see this. Samir Singh's plane just crashed."

"What?" Looking up at his deputy, a stunned Quinn stopped typing. "Is he okay?" He stood and hurried after Beth to the station floor. Everyone had dropped what they were doing, transfixed by the story on CNN. Someone shouted to turn the TV volume up.

"The plane dropped thousands of feet in just minutes," a reporter said. "It's a miracle anyone survived. One pilot is in serious but stable condition, and the captain and flight attendant are hospitalized, but expected to make a full recovery. We have reports that Sam Singh, the CEO of Pangea Dynamic Solutions, was on board. Witnesses are telling me that Sam Singh pulled two of the crew members to safety, risking his own life to save theirs…"

"Huh," Quinn muttered to Beth. "Saved lives, did he? I would've never guessed he had it in him, the colossal prick."

"Stop being so judgmental. He saved those people's lives."

Quinn looked down at Rose, now standing next to him. "I didn't see you there."

"I was born ninja," she replied with that curled lip and a gleam.

Quinn looked back at the giant television on the wall. "He's still a prick. And he's still on my list of suspicious Pangea people. He's at the top of that list, actually. This doesn't change a thing." His cell phone buzzed, seeing Fig's name on the screen.

"Yeah, what's up?"

"Hey, chief, Emma Massey? The woman we interviewed? Pippa's friend?"

"What about her? Does she have more to tell us?"

"Chief, she's dead."

Wait… what? Emma? Dead? "How? Do they have suspects?"

"Don't know Boss. I just heard about it from someone in my shooting club. Cal is having a total breakdown. She was running a marathon in Utah. I took the initiative and called Provo PD. Not suspicious. Seems she had a heart attack or something."

Gripping the phone in a crushing grip, it nearly shot out of his hand. A dark rage rose inside him like a dragon from a slumber. "Not suspicious? Fig, that's a bunch of bullshit. I want you to get on that medical examiner and stay on him. I want to know the cause of death as soon as he rules it. Not a second later." Quinn ended the call, shoving the phone in his pocket, his jaw muscles clenched with anger.

Rose grew immediately concerned by her boss's expression. "Ronan? What is it? What's happening?"

"Emma Massey is dead," he muttered.

"What? Oh, my god. Where? How?"

"Yesterday, in Utah. Heart attack, I guess. She was a runner, for Christ's sake. That woman was as healthy as they come."

Rose pondered that statement for a moment. "Maybe she had a blood clot or an aneurism? Perfectly healthy people have died that way."

Frustrated, Quinn placed his hands on his hips. "C'mon Rose. I mean, I appreciate the alternative theories… but c'mon. She talked to us, and two days later she's dead."

Quinn turned back to the television at the rear of the station. The story moved on from Samir Singh's crash to the standoff between the U.S. Navy and the Chinese Navy in the South China Sea. "And now that prick Sam Singh's jet has crashed."

Rose tilted her head. "You think there's something suspicious about that?"

"Rose, it's high time we assumed nothing is a coincidence. That nothing is just suspicious. Someone placed hits on Pippa, Emma, and Chris Hadley. And, for whatever reason, Sam Singh has made his way onto their list."

QUINN STOOD AT HIS window, reflecting on Emma's death.

Cars and trucks motored past. People hurried along the sidewalk. Some were talking on their phones. Others chatted. Some just meandered past his office. All minding their own business. Living their lives. Dealing with their own problems. Celebrating their own successes.

Is my town at risk? He thought. The town I'd sworn to protect with my life? And how long before someone connects the dots? How long before people draw their own conclusions about this spate of deaths in their idyllic community? Who else is going to get killed? Me? Rose? Fig? Beth? Anyone who even utters a thought or suspicion? A journalist, hungry for a story, is bound to ask questions. And did these people, whoever they are, want their very own CEO dead? Is it even Pangea? Could this be a terror plot against Pangea itself? All that weekend-warrior anti-terrorist hostage-rescue training at the Ghost Town may soon pay off, he thought.

Needing fresh air and time to think, he left the station at 10 a.m. Driving along the highway and around the Kurtz Curve, two distinct rows of black rubber skid marks crossed the lane. Vanishing off the shoulder, and out to the emptiness of the flat grassland below, those marks represented the last moments of Pippa's life.

He left the highway, driving to Pangea's first metal security gate at the main entrance to the enormous facility. Pulling off onto the grass, he exited the SUV, walking across the driveway to the barbed-wire crowned fence-line. He stood, staring into the facility through cyclone fencing, wondering what mysteries the complex held.

What was happening in there? Someone in there knows something. He listened to the rumbles of jet aircraft and growls of diesel trucks. What company has its own airport? What company has their own coroner?

A thunderous roar startled him. Shielding his eyes from the sun, he looked up as a cargo jet flew right over the top of him. The jet climbed into the sky, banked left, and headed eastward. Watching it fade into the distance, he turned his attention to the panorama from his vantage point high atop the bluff. Below him, the Old Ghost Town sat in a stark, silent contrast to the bustling facility above it. The old, run-down buildings seemed to stare back at him. Judging him. Asking how many more people will die under his watch.

He turned back to the fence and abruptly stopped.

"Morning, chief."

A Pangea security guard in full tactical gear stood on the other side of the fence-line, hands resting on his hips. Quinn's vision moved past the guard and to his right. Kneeling in the grass with a high-powered rifle, a second guard trained his rifle's scope onto Quinn's chest.

"How can we help you today?" the guard asked, a broad, belittling smile crossing his face. The guard slid his hand down to his sidearm, unsnapping the holster.

Are these idiots really going to shoot me!? Quinn thought, alarmed. Are they going to shoot a peace officer? "Just stretching my legs," he replied, then turned back toward the SUV. The sniper kept his rifle trained on Quinn the entire time.

"Oh, okay, chief," said the guard, eyeing Quinn. "Stretch your legs, but go do it somewhere else."

Quinn stopped and turned to the guard. "I'm outside the fence-line, dipshit," he growled between clenched teeth.

"Don't care," the guard responded. "That's still federal land you're standing on. If you don't leave, we'll have to take necessary precautionary actions."

Necessary precautionary actions? Like shooting the Chief of Woodrock Police to death? These were uncharted waters for Quinn. His authority being tested. But then, he thought, they'd tested my authority since day one. Like when the Pangea goon squad showed up with signed letters from judges and waivers from Pippa's parents. These guards were just as big of assholes as Walter and Zed. But unlike those two halfwits, these guards were professionals, and likely ex-military.

"Fine," Quinn said, waving his hand in a gesture of peace. "Leaving." But peace was not the emotion he felt at this moment in time.

COMPLETELY SHAKEN BY WHAT'D occurred at the Pangea fence, Quinn cruised around town, allowing his temperature to cool. He had lunch at

Dave's Cafe. Talked with a few Old Timers over at Dollie's. Kept himself distracted. Tried not to dwell on the smug, patronizing young Pangea guard.

But who were these people? Training a high-powered rifle on a police chief? And if they'd shot Quinn, what consequences would they face? Would Pangea tell some fable about the chief breaking into the facility? It seemed Pangea could take any implausible story and make it plausible. And this had not been Quinn's first trip to the complex either. He'd been inside many times. Taken tours as guides bragged about Pangea's technological achievements. He couldn't recall seeing any guards dressed in tactical gear hauling high-powered rifles marching around the place.

At 2 p.m., still visibly irritated, he told Rose he was going to need her to hold his calls. Slumping into his chair, he groaned. I came all the way out here into the middle of nowhere, so I wouldn't have to deal with shit like this, he thought. Oh, go ahead, Ronan, you tool. Throw yourself a pity party.

Ding!

Quinn whisked his phone off the desk, reading the screen.

Miá:

Hey, heads up, the FBI called me this morning. Wanted to know your background. Asked if we still talked.

Ronan:

Really? Are they offering me a job?

Miá:

I don't think so. He was fishing.

Ronan:

Fishing?

Miá:

Yes. He asked how I thought you'd been doing in Woodrock.

Ronan:

What did you say?

Miá:

I said you're kicking ass.

Ronan:

Lol. Ok.

Miá:

Is something going on out there? Do we need to talk?

Ronan:

Can't now. But we'll talk later, okay?

Miá:

Okay. Whatever it is, stay safe and watch your six, devil dog. xxxooo

Ronan:

Roger that.

Quinn placed the phone on the table. Why was the FBI talking to Miá? Why would the FBI want to check on him? Does this have something to do with all that's been happening here, at Woodrock? And Utah? And on Sam Singh's private jet? Because if these happenings since Pippa's death were merely coincidental, then the universe is on the brink of destruction.

He switched on his PC and the monitor flickered to life. Clicking on e-mails, he thought back to Miá's text messages. He needed an outside opinion. He needed a pair of reasonable ears. Ears like Miá's. Rose made a great confidant, but she was no detective.

"I don't need to drag Miá into this hot mess," he mumbled aloud. "Not yet."

He exhaled deeply and scanned through e-mails. Messages from business owners. Complaints from ranchers about property lines. Status of investigations into shoplifting. A missing dog. The FBI wanted lists. State Police bulletins. He arrived at an e-mail from a strange sender. Someone named John Smith. *John Smith? Jane Doe? Alias?* He clicked open the e-mail, and a rectangular box appeared on his screen requesting the code sent to his phone. What? To my phone? A code?

Ding!

He pulled the phone toward him and examined the screen.

Code: 738596.

Quinn sat back in his seat. What the high holy hell is this?

Ding!

Unknown:

Open the e-mail.

Unknown:

Please.

Quinn spun in his chair, searching the street. An occasional, benign looking Woodrockian, or Woodrockite or whatever they were, lazily strode past his office. He peered into parked cars and scanned rooftops.

Chief Quinn:

Who is this? Are you spying on me?

Unknown:

That's illegal.

He thought back to the conversation he'd had with Miá just moments earlier. About the FBI asking questions. Questions about him.

Chief Quinn:

Are you FBI? Homeland? ATF?

Unknown:

Open the e-mail. It has an expiration. Stop wasting time.

Chief Quinn:

How can I trust you?

Unknown:

We'll worry about that later. Open the e-mail. You need to see what I sent you.

Unknown:

You're only getting this once.

CHAPTER 28

A BURNING ZEAL TO solve Pippa and Emma's murders consuming him, Quinn elected to continue down this odd path on which he was being led.

Was this mysterious e-mail and clandestine phone person involved in his case? Or was this something entirely different? A prank, perhaps? By this point, Quinn didn't even care. He starved for information. Ached for it. Longed for any adhesive that would make his evidence stick to something. Once more, he turned and searched the street outside. Either someone was spying on him through his window, or someone was spying on him through his phone. Who would have the technology to pull off such a stunt?

Pangea, of course. Or, he thought again, maybe a 'three-lettered agency.'

Shrugging off all risk that came with opening mysterious attachments from the internet, he typed in the code, waiting for who knows what. Answers. Confessions. A laughing clown on his monitor. He waited, impatient and nervous, as a little blue thinking cyclone spun on the screen. The e-mail opened, revealing two files titled Vid1 and Vid2 embedded into the body of the message. In the upper right-hand corner of the e-mail, a clock counted down from 30:00 minutes.

From: John Smith

To: Ronan L. Quinn (WPD)

00:29:55

Vid.1 Vid.2

Whatever he was about to witness, he had thirty minutes to witness it - or perhaps thirty minutes before someone hacked his entire station. Shaking his head, he went with his gut.

With finger twitching caution, he clicked Vid1. A black and white surveillance video appeared on his screen, and at the bottom right corner was a date and a time. The video, taken from inside a dark office, seemed to show nothing. Leaning into his monitor, he searched for anything of any interest at all. What, exactly, am I looking for? He thought.

Wait.

Jerking back into his seat, Quinn couldn't believe his eyes.

Pippa Simpson strolled into the office and switched on the lights. The time was 07:45:23, and the date was the day prior to Pippa's death.

Leaning closer to the screen, he followed her movements intensely. She dropped her backpack on the floor, slid her laptop into the docking station, and hurried from her office. She returned around three minutes later with either a mug of coffee or tea, shuffled papers around, and placed her phone on her desk. Yawning as she gazed at her screen, Pippa mindlessly typed. Stopped. Typed. Read. Typed. Moved her mouse around.

What precisely am I watching here? Quinn thought, baffled. From the angle of the camera, her screen was visible, but the video was too grainy for him to make out what was on it.

Then something very odd occurred. Abruptly, Pippa sat straight up in her chair. For a few moments, she remained frozen, and Quinn sensed she'd read something that caught her off guard. Leaning forward, she ran her finger down the screen, then sat back, undid her ponytail, wound her hair around, and tied it back up. Leaning forward once more, she moved and clicked her mouse.

Then Pippa did something Quinn found to be highly peculiar.

Reaching for the cell phone on her desk, she held it up in front of her and snapped a picture of the screen. Then she put the phone down, her head turning to look outside her office, seeing if anyone was observing her. She reached in front of her and switched the monitor off. Leaning back in her chair, Pippa sat still for a moment before switching her monitor on once again, then her shoulders slouched. She seemed relieved.

The video ended.

Glancing at the clock on the screen, it wound down past 25 minutes.

He opened Vid2. The time read 19:45:22, the date showed the following day. The day that Pippa actually died.

In this video, she packed up her things, disconnected her laptop, typed something on her phone, stuffed the laptop into her backpack and, turning off the office lights, left her office. The video ran for a couple of minutes, with a perplexed Quinn staring eagerly into a darkened office. What am I waiting for now? Three minutes passed, then Pippa rushed back in.

"What the hell?" A stunned Quinn said aloud to no one. "You've got to be kidding me." Sweeping up his phone, he frantically dialed Fig.

"Hey, boss. What's up?"

"Where the hell are you?"

"On my way back from a shoplifting. You need something, boss?"

The time on the e-mail ticked past twenty minutes. "Get your ass back here ASAP," he urged Fig. "And grab Rose and both of you come into my office."

He slammed the phone on the desk, scrolled the video back to the beginning, and ran through it again.

FIG AND ROSE RUSHED into Quinn's office with ten minutes left on the soon-to-be self-destructing message. "What is it now, Ronan?" Rose asked, looking at a fully focused chief staring at the monitor.

Quinn beckoned them both to stand behind him and watch his screen. He had something to show them. "Guys, watch these videos. Tell me what you see. I want to know if you see what I'm seeing."

Confusion crossed Fig's face. "Videos? Videos of what? Where're they from?"

"This is security footage from Pangea," Quinn replied.

"Really?" Rose asked. "Where'd you get those from?"

"Don't ask," he replied, opening Vid1.

"Wow, they like to watch their people, don't they?" Fig muttered.

"A lot of companies do this, Fig."

Vid1 began.

Rose gasped, slapping her hand over her mouth. "Oh, Ronan, I'm getting teary. Seeing her alive like this. That beautiful girl."

Quinn nodded. "This is the day before she died. Watch."

After Fig and Rose witnessed Pippa's odd reaction to whatever she'd read on her screen, Fig asked why she'd taken a picture. "Why not just take a screenshot? Print it?"

"Exactly, Fig. What did she see? What was it that made her so nervous? What was it she saw that made her want to save it in a place nobody would find? Or think to look for?"

The video ended. Rose stood straight, scratching her chin. "How weird."

Then Quinn opened Vid2. "Now watch this one and tell me what you see."

Leaning closer to get a better view, Rose and Fig hovered over Quinn like they were watching a football match on TV.

On Vid2, Pippa turned out the lights and left her office for the night. Three minutes later, she rushed back in. Typing something on her phone, she then stuck it into the waistband of her skirt. She shoved folders around her desk, looking for something, and then pushed a folder off to the side.

"Wait," Rose asked, her slender finger pointing at the screen. "Am I seeing what I think I'm seeing?"

With the video paused, they saw Pippa reaching for something. Something shiny. Something rectangular. Something that folders and papers had covered. Something that Pippa Simpson absentmindedly forgot in her rush to leave work on a late Friday evening to start her weekend.

"What's that, guys?" Quinn asked.

"Another phone," Rose muttered.

"That's right, Rose. A second goddammed phone."

Quinn leaned back and placed his hands behind his head. "Whatever Pippa saw on her computer that morning, Pangea killed her for it. And someone sent this video to me so we could see this. Someone wants us to know she had a second phone. And this someone does not believe Pangea has it or they wouldn't have sent this to me."

"This person wants *us* to find it. Don't they?" Fig asked.

"Bullseye, Fig. This person or persons needs us to find this phone for them."

"But who?" Fig asked.

Quinn shrugged. "No clue."

Rose pondered this, tapping her chin again like a sleuth deciphering a clue. "Someone at Pangea wants to help us find the killer. A friend, perhaps. Or a whistleblower."

Quinn thought back to Mia's advisory about the FBI asking about him. Then, shortly after, he gets Vid1 and Vid2 from a John Smith. "That's a distinct possibility, Rose. This person has access to some very high tech. And clearly, they have access deep inside Pangea."

"Samir Singh?" Rose asked. "I mean, he came to see you. He seemed interested in what you knew."

"Let's not start throwing spaghetti at the walls. We need facts. And Sam Singh is still a suspect as far as I'm concerned."

"Why are they using us?" Fig asked.

Quinn turned, looking up at a wide-eyed Fig. "Easy. We're a dumb hick police station. Who's going to be watching us? We're also expendable."

The e-mail on the screen vanished and with it, the videos.

"Guys, the clown brothers, Walter and Zed, wanted her phone and wanted it badly. Someone watched the same surveillance video we did and saw her take a picture of her screen. But what I'm guessing, is they didn't think of watching surveillance from the night she died. Why would they bother? So, they think she took the picture with her work phone. They have no clue the second one even exists."

"What does that mean?" Fig asked.

"It means, Fig, that the second phone is still out there and we need to find it. And I mean, we need to find it, like, yesterday."

CHAPTER 29

THE FALL FROM GRACE for Samir Singh had been as meteoric as his Gulfstream plummeting from the sky. On this morning, one day removed from nearly perishing in a plane crash, he shuffled through hoodies on a sales rack in a Walmart, in some township, in some ignored part of Pennsylvania.

After the G650 crash, and after ensuring his crew's wellbeing, Singh left the local hospital and began hitting ATMs and banks, withdrawing as much cash as possible. After he'd withdrawn close to ten-thousand dollars, he cut up his credit cards, tossing the shredded plastic into a garbage can. It was cash only from here on out.

Harried by reporters and journalists since he'd left the hospital, every minute the media televised the billionaire Samir Singh, was another minute Red Lancer knew his location. Remaining in this picturesque town of St. Mary's, and in the public eye, certainly confused Red Lancer. But this was Singh's intention. Remaining visible and hiding in plain sight gave him a feeling of security - using the public as both protection and shield. But time was not on his side. Eventually, Red Lancer would get to him.

Eyeing the surrounding Walmart shoppers with caution, Singh pulled wool hoodies, a ball cap, jeans, and a pair of sneakers from their shelves. Then, after picking up a pre-paid phone, he paid the gawking cashier for his items in cash, and at the young girl's request, also an autograph. "We don't get a lot of famous people here," she said.

"You don't say," he impatiently replied.

Dashing from the store, he immediately headed for a garage on the other side of town.

An hour later, he reached a car repair shop on the far side of St. Mary's. His black hoodie pulled over his head, he arrived on foot and incognito, asking the garage owner about a used subcompact he saw advertised in the local newspaper.

"It's a bit beat up," said the owner, looking at Singh head to foot with curiosity. "But it's got a good motor. Say, aren't you the billionaire from the plane crash?" He asked with a wry smirk, wiping grease-stained hands on a filthy rag.

"Not anymore, I'm not. Here's an extra thousand for your silence," Singh replied.

"Hiding from the old lady now, eh?" The owner chuckled while counting the cash. "Been there buddy."

"OH...MY...GOD!" MADISON screamed over the pre-paid phone. "I've been trying to reach you!" Her voice trembled and crackled, followed by a good deal of sobbing. "You have no idea what it's been like seeing you on the news and not being able to speak with you. The hospital said you checked out. Sam, this is breaking my heart," she said, breaking out into full on waterworks over the phone.

Madison Sheppard was his only hope now. The only human being he trusted. She knew nothing about Iron Hand. Only Air Force drones, ledgers, and balance sheets.

"Can I come and get you?" She pleaded.

"I'm going to be at the Holiday Inn tomorrow. You can meet me there. Is that okay?"

"Why don't I just send a jet to pick you up and we'll meet in New York?"

"If you don't mind, I'd like to stay away from airplanes for a little while. There's a municipal airport here. Fly in and send the jet off. Get a rental car and meet me at the Holiday Inn. Tell absolutely no one you're coming here."

"I don't understand," Madison replied in a quivering voice. "What's happening? And what number are you calling from?"

"My phone melted, along with the plane I used to have, so call this phone. Please, Madison, just don't ask questions. I love you."

"Oh, Sam," she responded, her voice shaking. "I love you too, baby."

"Okay, see you soon," and he ended the call.

Singh lay back on his bed in a stale, musty room in a sketchy motel off the side of a highway. Closing his eyes, he fell fast asleep.

Sliding down into the driver's seat of the compact that smelled of cigarettes, weed, pine freshener, and amassed body odor, Singh watched a car park in front of the entrance to the Holiday Inn.

Madison, her angelic golden hair flowing behind her, dashed inside. Cautiously scanning the parking lot, he was relieved that, so far, no one had followed her. He dialed Madison's phone, telling her to come back outside. That she'd see a white car flashing its headlights in the parking lot, and that would be him. Watching Madison step back outside, her hand pressed to her forehead, scanning the lot from behind her large bees-eyes sunglasses, he nearly broke down. Seeing his lights, she waved enthusiastically and strode toward the car.

"Oh, please, Madison," Singh muttered. "Don't make a scene. Don't attract attention." He pulled his ball cap down further onto his brow.

Opening the creaking passenger door, she peeked in and froze. "Yuck, this car smells funky," she said, pinching her nose. Peering at Singh from over the top of her glasses, she squinted at his hat. "Bass Pro Shops? Really? And is that hoodie from Walmart?"

"Park your car," an impatient Singh replied. "Leave your bag in the trunk and hand me your phone."

Madison stared at him, tilting her head in a perplexed look. "Sam…"

"Just do it!" He stretched out his hand, gesturing for her phone. Reluctantly, she gave it to him and he smashed it on the dashboard.

"Sam! What the hell!"

"Just go park the car! Hurry! Before they spot us! They've been tracking your phone!"

Madison jumped into the car and he backed out, screeching from the parking lot and onto the street.

"What's going on, Sam?" Madison asked, dabbing tears from her cheek with a tissue. "My luggage, my phone, please, please tell me. And who is 'they'? Who's tracking us? Why are we doing this? Please, Sam, talk to me? Can't we just go back to the hotel and chat?"

"We're not going back to the hotel. We're going to a different one."

"Really?" Madison quipped, wiping tears off her cheek. "Is it as luxurious as this car?"

"Better." He checked the rearview mirror and sped onto the highway. "It has a coffeemaker."

Racing south on the highway toward a mysterious destination, he glanced at Madison as she studied him through puzzled blue-gray eyes. "You look beautiful. The most beautiful thing I've ever witnessed in my entire life." He focused back on the road. "But right now, no one can know where you are, because if they do, they'll know where I am."

He checked his mirrors and turned to her. "And then we'll both be dead."

DRIVING FOR TWO HOURS along the winding highway, Singh pulled into a rundown, single-story motel named *The Shady Inn.* A name that meant something entirely different on the day they built it; the tall, yellowed, weather-beaten sign, missing two letters, read as *The Sad Inn.* The place itself looked half deserted, littered with empty bags of fast food and paper cups and the odd abandoned shoe, having seen more than its share of truly shady things in its far-from-glory days. But *The Shady Inn* seemed to be just the kind of shady Singh now needed.

Singh held Madison tightly in the shower, letting the warm water and her soft, smooth skin wash everything from the past twenty-four hours down the drain. The burns on his hands, received from rescuing the copilot from the crash, still pulsed with pain. He removed the bandages, tossing them to the sink. The pain kept him alert and awake. He'd apply fresh bandages later. But for now, the combination of water and cheap motel bar soap on his burns kept his adrenaline flowing.

After quietly holding each other under the steam of hot water, they finished showering and toweled off. Madison plopped down on the bed, drying her hair.

"Okay," she said, draining water from her ear. "Now that we've showered, can you tell me what the hell is going on?"

Singh paced in front of Madison, giving her a high-level account of what Pangea intended the Wasps for. Their true capabilities. Their missions. Iron Hand. Madison Sheppard, his Executive Vice President of Operations, was neck deep in the program without her even knowing it. He was unsure how she was taking the news. Her lips thin, eyes wide, she looked catatonic. Understandably, Madison seemed to be in a complete state of unblinking, rigid-muscled shock.

"You were using me..." she muttered. Her eyes moved to his, narrowing into a glare. "You fucking used me."

"No, it was never like that. Don't even think that. Not for a second. I didn't tell you because I needed to protect you. You could deny everything and plausibly. An accomplice to nothing. And if it worked, you would see the brilliance of Jupiter's plan. But..."

She lifted her shoulders. "But what?"

A reticent Singh sighed, and his chin fell to his chest.

Madison's eyes lit up into a gleam. "But... you're reconsidering."

He lifted his head and sullenly nodded.

"All those years of hard work and commitment to this... this plan or whatever the hell it is, and to this Jupiter character, and you're willing to throw that all away?"

Singh nodded.

"Why? What changed your heart?" She asked, quiet and subdued. "You can tell me these things, sweetie."

"I guess when something is a vision, you imagine the goal, you evaluate the cost-benefits, you visualize success. But then, suddenly, one day, you realize you'd left out one important detail." He sat next to her on the bed, held her hands, searching her eyes. "You realize you forgot about the consequences. And those consequences have dreams, and families, and lives to live." Sighing deeply, he hung his head. "The plan is flawed. There must be a better way." He turned and faced her. "Navi spoke to me."

Madison's head jerked back.

"Yes, Madison, I heard her voice. After the crash. She was trying to tell me something." He thought back to her cryptic message. *Don't let the darkness win. Be the truth and the light. You are a Sikh.*

Madison stood, dropping her towel to the floor and pulling her clothes back on. "You're doing the right thing, Sam." Snapping her bra in place, she swept her hair back and smiled. "And Navi was telling you the same also, I'm sure of it. So, I hope you're going to talk to the authorities about this. Or go to the press."

Singh nodded. "Yes, that's where you come in."

A soft buzzing sound, like a sound of bees, came from beneath the pillow. Confused, he glanced at Madison. She tilted her head, hearing the sound also, her eyes questioning. The buzzing sound, muffled and barely audible, came once more from underneath the pillow. Reaching across the bed, he pulled the pillow back. A black secure comm device lay on the bed, and once more it *buzzed.*

"What's that?" His head snapped to face Madison. "Why do you have a secure comm device? Who gave it to you? Were you hiding it…"

Madison lunged at Singh. "Yes! It was in my bra, Sam!" A strange smirking grin split her face as she rushed at him. "I hid it with my magnificent tits!"

Singh leaped from the bed to face her, but she spun on her right foot, landing a blow to his chest. Stumbling and gasping for air, he tried to tackle her, but she spun again, landing a kick to his jaw that snapped his head around like a tether-ball.

Singh tried to strike back, but Madison danced around on the floor, landing a flurry of punches to his jaw and ribs. Then she thrust forward, wrapping her arms around his neck, and burying a knee deep into his sternum.

He collapsed to the floor in a heap as she danced around him like a boxing ballerina. Unable to focus, his world spun in circles.

Grumbling and cursing, Madison stopped and moved behind him. The motel phone dropped from the desk with a *clang*. Rolling over, he tried to push himself back up, but her knee dug into the back of his neck.

"Oh, no you don't," she growled. "You're not going anywhere."

"Madison," he groaned. "Why're you doing this?"

"Shut up," she grunted impatiently.

"I can't believe you work for Red Lancer."

"I said shut up. Jesus, dude."

"Tell Red Lancer he can go fuck himself." He felt her long fingers brush against his throat. Then she wrapped the telephone cord around his neck tightly and pulled it.

"You can tell her yourself."

"What?" Singh choked and gasped as she began strangling him.

Pushing her knee deeper into the base of his skull, she bent over and whispered softly into his ear.

"I am Red Lancer."

He couldn't believe it. He couldn't believe the words she'd just whispered into his ear. His heart sank, and despite impending death, he felt an immense sorrow - the deep, knifing sorrow when confronted with the betrayal of a lover. Closing his eyes, Samir Singh let fate take its course. His mind wandered to a weathered stone monastery on a barren windswept hill, brightly colored prayer flags fluttering in an icy breeze. A place of peace. A place where Navi, his mother, and his father awaited him.

He held in a final breath, resisting the primal urge to exhale and draw in another, allowing himself to drift into unconsciousness.

The cord squeezed tighter and Madison Sheppard, aka Red Lancer, grunted and groaned, choking Samir Singh to death in a filthy motel room at The Shady Inn.

MOTIONLESS, SINGH LAY FACE-DOWN on the musty floor as a gloating Madison pulled the secure comm device she'd hidden amongst her self-proclaimed magnificent tits, and dialed a number.

"He's gone," she said on the call. "Had to do it the hard way. The crafty bastard made me leave my stuff behind. I didn't have my Glock, but boy, it sure was a great workout. You were spot on, though; he was going to talk." She glanced around the room. "Jesus, this place looks like the fucking Bates Motel. He couldn't have picked a better place to be murdered if he'd tried. I'll call back in a bit. I'm getting dressed."

Tossing the device onto the bed, she leaned over to grab her socks.

Singh's hands quickly closed around her ankles.

Before she could react, he yanked her feet out from under her, dragging her onto the floor. In complete shock that Sam Singh was still living, Madison tried to jump to her feet, but he laid a series of punches to her jaw and nose. Stunned, she fell to the floor. He drove his foot into her ribs and fell to his knees, grabbing a handful of hair and yanking her head back. Still managing a creepy, psychotic grin on her bleeding face, he swiftly flipped her onto his chest, wrapping his legs around her like an anaconda, and pulling his arm tight against her throat. Madison grunted and struggled as he choked the life from her.

Completely overlooked by Madison, Samir Singh had climbed the highest peaks in the world and competed in Iron Man races. In all that time, he'd learned to adapt to low oxygen environments. To conserve air. To pace his breathing. Having perfected the art of meditation, he let his mind travel to places that brought him peace and serenity. While

Madison was gleefully strangling him with a cord, he lowered his heart rate, conserved his air, and entered a state of transcendental hibernation.

Lacking those same skills, Madison went unconscious. Spasms rippled through her body, and after a brief final struggle on the stained and moldy carpet, she went limp.

LEANING AGAINST THE BED in panties and bra, her hands and feet tightly bound, Madison regained consciousness with a groan.

"What the fuck, Sam?" she said, looking down at her underwear. "Are you going to rape me now?"

Singh sat behind her on the bed, securing the long telephone cord around her neck. "Now, where would be the fun in that?" He climbed off the bed, kneeling before her. "That lovely cord you tried to strangle me with is now tied around your throat with a slip knot. The more you struggle, the tighter it gets."

"You know what, Sam?" A defiant Madison said. "You weren't even a good lay."

He gave the cord a gentle tug, the noose tightened slightly, speckles of blood appearing as it dug into her skin.

Madison rolled her eyes. "Sam, if you're going to kill me, just do it. Or don't you have the balls?"

He stood, studying her bloodied face. She didn't even seem afraid. What a sociopathic bitch, he thought. "I'm not killing you, dear. If anyone kills you, it will be you." He tapped the cord, ensuring tension. "If I were you, I'd not move a muscle, or speak, or even flinch. The more you move, the tighter this gets." He glanced at his watch. "Judging by the time, you have about 14 hours before housekeeping arrives." Leaning forward, he kissed her gently on the cheek, then jammed a sock in her mouth. "Consider this my parting gift. So long, my dear."

Pulling the Bass Pro Shops hat tight over his head, he heard the secure comm device buzzing and vibrating on the nightstand. He placed the device in his pocket and, turning once more to the room, looked at the back of Madison's head. She remained perfectly still.

Stepping outside into a muggy afternoon, he placed the "Do Not Disturb" sign on the knob and headed for his car. I may not have any friends or allies left, he thought. But I haven't shown my entire hand. I still have one ace left up my sleeve. I just pray this ace can be trusted.

A car with its windows lowered a few inches for ventilation, sat parked four rooms down from his. He slipped over to it, slid the device through the space in the rear window, and carefully dropped it onto the floor of the car beneath the passenger seat.

"Track that, assholes."

Chapter 30

Jack Fitzgerald slammed the phone down on the receiver.

They've got to be kidding me, he thought. Unbelievable. Who the hell do these people think they are? Smacking his forehead with his palm, he growled and raked his fingers through his hair. Taking a deep breath, he dialed Grady Freeman.

"What's up, Jack?" Grady asked.

"Operation Cobalt just flatlined."

"What?" Grady stuttered.

"The director called me. Todd Sykes told the director that in the interest of national security, Cobalt needs to be, as he put it, paused."

"Wait, Todd Sykes?" Grady's voice moved up an octave in frustration. "*Thee* Todd Sykes? Chair of the Senate Arms Committee?"

"That's the guy."

"With all due respect, Jack, isn't this obstruction?"

"Grady, you show me a senator who's seen a jail cell for obstruction, and I'll show you my ten-year-old daughter's SAT scores."

Grady fell silent for a moment, then seemed to accept the situation. "Okay, okay. What do we do now?"

"We'll talk later. Meet me at my office at 3. We'll get the director in here and find out what the hell is going on."

"Okay," sighed Grady. "Well, like I always say, you can never trust a guy named Todd."

"Right?" Jack chuckled. "Okay, talk soon," and he ended the call.

Absentmindedly twirling a pen with his fingers, he swayed left to right in his chair. How odd was this? Two days after he gets a call from Barb Dent and Bob Evans at the CIA, the senate folds up the Pangea investigation. An investigation only a handful of people even knew existed.

The door to his office swung open and Elliott Handel, his assistant, strode into the office, handing a manila envelope to Jack. He took it from Elliot, noticing a strip of tape with the words *Eyes Only* sealing it shut.

Jack flipped the envelope over. "Who's this from?"

Elliott shrugged. "Came from a courier. We've scanned it. It's clean. Weird, though, it just has a note in it."

"Thanks, Elliot," Jack muttered, inspecting the front and back of the envelope, waiting for Elliot to leave the room and close the door. Grabbing an envelope opener out of his desk drawer, he sliced through the tape, turned the envelope over, and shook it. A small square of pink paper, with a note handwritten in purple ink, floated onto his desk.

Stay off your phone. Do not write e-mails. Do not use any electronics regarding anything related to our call the other day. Come have a hot dog with me at the National Mall at noon. Monument end. You only.

- Barb D.

Leaning back in his chair, Jack flipped the note over. Barb Dent flew all the way up here from Langley for a hot dog?

Well, he thought, this can't be good.

JACK LEFT HIS OFFICE at 11:30 am and headed over to The National Mall.

Striding alongside the glimmering Reflecting Pool and bathed in a warm sun, he moved toward the Washington Monument while taking a moment to absorb a beautiful summer day. I should come out here more often, he thought, gazing up into a deep blue sky. Pigeons flapped and fluttered about, looking for scraps. Tourists strode along the broad pathway posing for photos. Barb approached, clutching a white paper bag, and throwing him an enthusiastic wave.

"Hot dog, Jack?" She opened the bag and peered inside. "We have mustard with no relish, or mustard and relish."

"I'm not all that hungry, Barb," Jack replied gruffly.

"I asked you here for a hot dog, Jack, so you're eating a fucking hot dog. I'm a slave to appearances."

Jack stared into Barb's recessed eyes. Those narrowed, glimmering brown beauties burned into him like diamonds cutting glass. Fine, he thought. Reaching into the bag, he pulled out a foil-wrapped hot dog. Mustard, no relish.

"Sorry, I didn't get drinks," Barb apologized. "Can you believe these were five fucking bucks apiece? For mashed cow bits?"

"Thanks, Barb, for that," Jack mumbled as he bit into the hot dog.

The two walked alongside the pool. "Jesus," she exclaimed, looking up at the blue sky above. "Nice day, isn't it?"

Jack chewed. "Yup."

Barb took a bite of her own hot dog. "So, how's Anna? How's Ashley?"

"Anna made partner at the firm. Ashley just turned ten." Jack stopped and faced her. "Why are we here, Barb? Why the handwritten note? Budget cuts? Should we hire the pigeons?"

Barb beckoned him to keep walking. "I have three things," she said, brushing crumbs off her blouse. "First, we have four dead bodies from the village in Nigeria. Some family. We did an autopsy."

Jack threw a questioning glance at Barb. "How'd you get hold of four bodies?"

"We're the CIA, Jack. We fucking stole them." She took another deep bite as they walked along The Reflecting Pool. "So, something interesting," she said, voice muted by dog and bun. "The UN guys found these bodies next to a river. A few hundred yards away from the village. They had no signs of chlorine on them. None. Nada. Zippo."

"Interesting. What'd they die from?"

Barb stopped and turned to Jack. He patiently waited for her to finish chewing and finally, Barb gulped her hot dog down. "Acute strangulation."

"Wait," Jack stuttered. "Acute strangulation? Someone gassed a village, then chased a family down to a river and strangled them? On what planet does that make sense?"

Barb held up a finger. "Fake gassed them, Jack. The villagers were already dead, remember? It gets better."

"It does?" Jack asked in disbelief.

"No bruising on this family's throats. No external signs of an assault. But they scratched the hell out of their necks, so they died fighting off something. And their tracheas had trauma. Their blood? Loaded with lactic acid."

"So, what I'm hearing you say, Barb," Jack clarified in a not-so vague sarcastic tone. "Is that someone fake-gassed a village, saw a family escape, ran after them, then strangled them? But not with their hands? With what then? The force? Did you put out an APB for Darth Vader?"

"I note your fucking sarcasm, Jack," Barb replied. "But let's stay serious here. Two hours after the attack, someone showed up at the scene. We have no clue who these guys were."

"Did they kill the family?"

"Nope. Satellite imagery showed the family dead well before these assholes arrived."

"Do you know who they are?"

"No fucking clue. The UN didn't arrive until the following day. Our assessment is these guys weren't there to help. They were looking for something. We just don't know what."

Jack looked toward the monument as the two continued walking. This was all so bizarre. The villagers die from some mysterious force? A helicopter sprays their corpses with chlorine gas? A family escapes, dies also, but with no gas traces on them? Then someone shows up looking around for something? Evidence perhaps? Or perhaps covering something up? This math was one plus one equals eight.

"Second thing," Barb continued. "We found the 747. It landed in Kazakhstan. We only know this from satellite imagery because it never filed a flight plan. Your friends at Pangea chartered a jet to Lagos, unloaded a helicopter that we suspect gassed a village… suspected because our analysis showed the same helicopter type and not necessarily *the* same helicopter and…" Barb took another bite, wiping a smattering of mustard from the corner of her mouth. "The 747 mysteriously caught fire while sitting at the airport and burned to the ground."

"Jesus, Barb." Jack said, incredulity in his tone. This sounded more and more like a coverup operation.

"Oh, just wait, there's more. Let's keep walking. Some shit-stain is probably listening." Barb said tensely, her eyes shifting and scanning the crowd.

Jack glanced at Barb. "Listening?"

"Why do you think I asked you to meet me here in a crowd of fucking tourists? We've been compromised."

Jack stopped, staring at her with a wrinkled brow. She beckoned him to keep walking.

"Yup," she continued. "Someone got through our firewall. They hacked our network and targeted files on our Nigeria Op and Pangea. Our dork ex-hacker analyst seems to think it was an inside job."

"So, you mean…" Jack stuttered.

Barb nodded. "Yup. If we've been compromised, you've been compromised. Strange, your little Pangea operation getting canned the day after we get hacked, isn't it?"

"How'd you know the senate killed Cobalt?"

"Jack," Barb raised an eyebrow. "Don't be such a dork."

Looking past Barb, Jack gazed thoughtfully at the shimmering waters of The Reflecting Pool. "So, that's why the written note."

"Yup." Barb stopped, scanned the mall, took another bite, and looked up at Jack. "Look, Jack, I'm a fucking spy. I work for a fucking spy agency. We have a very gray, oblique, non-linear view of the world, meaning everything is always on the table. So, when something smells funky, we pry into everyone's fucking business. But now someone is prying into mine. You can be goddammed sure I'm going to find out who." She crammed the last bit of hot dog into her mouth.

Jack thought for a moment. "We don't have to totally shut it down. We still have our mole. And we have Ronan Quinn."

Barb coughed as she swallowed. "Who? Ronan who?"

"He's the chief of police at Woodrock."

"What?" Barb stuttered in disbelief. "The chief of Woodrock police? Are you shitting me? We're hedging on some hillbilly cop?"

"No one knows he's working with us, Barb. Including him. But he's in touch with our mole, and they're feeding each other information. He's had a couple of suspicious deaths. Both Pangea employees."

"Don't forget also," Barb added, holding up her finger. "That Sam Singh's jet nosedived into the Pennsylvania countryside two days ago."

Jack took a deep breath. This is all so strange. The timing of it all.

"Oh," Barb reached into her pocket. "One more thing." She handed him a small photograph. "Guess who showed up in Atlanta a week ago?"

He examined an airport surveillance picture of a tall man in a running suit, carrying a large backpack. "Yousef?"

"Yup, Yousef. The for-hire fucking hit-man from Damascus. A few days ago, he was in Salt Lake for some god only knows reason why. Now he's gone again."

"Barb, are you telling me everything?" Jack asked, suspicious that she was telling him everything but, yet, not everything.

"Of course I'm not telling you everything, Jack. What the fuck do I do for a living? Look, if he pops up somewhere, I'll let you know. But I suggest y'all find some way to talk to each other because Big Brother's listening. Meanwhile, me and Bob and our geek analyst are going to keep pursuing this Nigeria thing. We're going to dig up more info on this smoldering 747. Get our sources to figure out what all these overseas shipments from your Pangea buddies are for."

"Thanks for the heads up, Barb."

"Jack," Barb said, her eyes arching in worry. "I have a terrible feeling about all this. The dead family confirms our suspicions that chlorine gas wasn't the culprit. Someone or something strangled an entire village. We have to assume it was a chemical or biological agent of some sort. We just don't know what it is or where it came from." She searched Jack's eyes. "I think this Iron Hand thing Grady mentioned is some dark, nefarious scheme. I sure hope your Mayberry sheriff in South Dakota's up for this."

"So do I."

Barb took a deep breath and looked up at the sky. "It's almost romantic, isn't it?"

"What's romantic?" Jack asked, surprised.

"Us. You and me. Caught up in some sneaky skullduggery with our fate in the hands of some redneck small-town police chief. There's a certain romance to that."

"Well, write a novel about it, Barb." Jack tossed his leftover hot dog into the trash bin. "And don't underestimate Quinn. You guys do your stuff, and we'll do ours."

Barb nodded. "I hear that." She dropped the hot dog wrapper into the bin.

"And Jack," she said sternly.

"What?"

"We protect the homeland." Barb Dent turned on her heels and hurried back along The Reflecting Pool, vanishing into a sea of tourists.

Chapter 31

Attentively sitting on Rose's soft patterned sofa, Rose and Quinn watched every flick of Oscar's tail and every scratch behind his ear as he went about being just a typical cat. Sitting on his haunches on the prized Indian rug from Bangalore, he rolled over, writhing on his back and scratching an unreachable itch. Rose deduced this Indian rug was some sort of Medium. A portal to the great beyond. Blessed by an ancient guru in the mysterious Orient. Oscar, the occidental cat, had been chosen as some sort of channel to the afterlife.

"Look at him," Rose said, nudging Quinn while he flipped through news articles on his phone.

"What?" Quinn muttered.

Rose nodded toward Oscar, now sitting on the rug, his ears perked, chirping at the ceiling. Tilting his head, his fluffed tail swayed left to right like a furry serpent, seeing something or someone his two human counterparts could not.

"Pip, is that you? Are you here?" Rose peered up at the ceiling space above Oscar. "Dear, can you hear us?"

"Yes. Hello brat. Hello chief. Hello Rose." Pippa's voice filled the room. Such an unusual sensation it was. A sensation that she was inside of them as much as she was out.

"Pippa," Quinn asked, leaning forward on the patterned sofa. "We know you had two phones. We need to find the phone that you didn't use for work. Can you help us find it?"

"I'm not sure. I can't remember where I had it last. In my car? It's so hard. Memories are so fleeting. I can capture some. They are slowing..."

"Did you keep it in your backpack? Because we didn't see it with your things."

"I can see them. There's... something. They're all dead."

"Who's dead, dear? Who are they? Where can we find them?" Asked Rose.

"All but one. It's so cold. I'm always cold."

Leaning forward and hanging his head, Quinn dreaded what he needed to tell her. Ghost or not, he felt compelled to tell Pippa what she may or may not know. Something he'd been asked to do hundreds of times in his life.

"Pippa, Emma has died. We think she may have been murdered." A deep guilt boiled away inside him as he fumbled for words. "We think they killed her because she spoke to us about your death. Because she suspected what we suspected. The more you can remember, the more I can protect your friends."

A hush fell across the room. Windows gently rattled in the wind, the house groaning ever so slightly.

"I can remember her. I can see her. She was so pretty. So, kind."

A low rumbling came from beneath Quinn and Rose's feet. The floor, moving in shallow undulating waves, lifted the heavy marble table in front of them six inches into the air. Quinn and Rose, eyes agape and lips cinched, feeling very small, helpless and insignificant, watched as the table slammed back to the floor.

Bam!

A painting at the far end of the room slid down the wall. A cup fell to the kitchen floor and shattered. Quinn and Rose gripped the arms of the sofa as if it would just fly them out of the house and into space.

"ENVY!" Pippa's voice filled the house like rolling thunder.

The waves on the floor fell into a low rumble, then subsided entirely. Oscar, legs and paws flailing on the floor, scampered off to the safety of Rose's bed, taking cover with her other frightened cats.

"You must find it. It has… something. The voices are talking to me. They're… helping me."

"What are they helping with?" asked Quinn between gasps of frantic breath.

"They're helping me to navigate this strange place. To use my energy. That's all I am now. I'm just an energy. All I am…" Pippa's voice drifted off into an unseen void beyond any comprehension of the two living beings witnessing this event.

"Pippa, is there anything else you can tell us? Can you remember what was on your phone? Is it the picture of your computer screen? What was the picture of?" Quinn asked in frustration. "Pip? Pippa? Are you there?"

Silence.

Rose slowly turned to Quinn. "Ronan," she muttered. "That woman is really pissed off." She sunk back onto the sofa and crossed her arms. "You know, if she's just some sort of energy force, maybe she uses that energy to speak with us? Maybe she needs to, you know, recharge?"

"Recharge? Like plug into an outlet?"

"No, silly. Or maybe… oh hell, I don't have a clue how any of this works," she said, biting her lip and fiddling with her fingers.

Quinn moved off the couch and stood. "I need to go back to my house and get some sleep. Can you manage without me for a night? Can you go stay with someone?"

"I don't think Pippa means us any harm," Rose responded calmly, yet still shaken. "But I'll go bunk with Beth tonight. Spin some tale about fumigating for cockroaches."

Quinn stretched. "Ok, great idea." He turned to Rose. "You know, if Emma was in fact murdered, I wouldn't want to be in the shoes of the killer." He pulled his jacket on, looking above him and scanning the ceiling. "Because if Pip gets ahold of them, they're totally and completely screwed."

Pop. Pop. Pop. Pop, pop, pop, pop, pop.

The sharp bangs of firecrackers reverberated throughout a hallway of an indeterminable length. To an experienced ear, like Detective Ronan Quinn's, these were no firecrackers. These were the repetitive firings of an assault rifle.

Quinn unholstered his service weapon. Running along the narrow hall, he saw the door to a room appear ahead of him. But instead of drawing closer, the door moved further away. He ran faster. The door moved further. He was gaining no ground. He pushed harder but his legs, like they were made of large down feathers, had no strength. No matter how fast he ran, he couldn't reach the door. He shouted as loudly as possible. No sound came from his lips. No air filled his lungs.

Pop pop pop pop pop pop.

The hall evaporated, and he stood in a large, open space. Materializing before him as if out of thin air, children appeared. One after the other. Ten. Twenty. A hundred. A thousand. The boys all wore blue trousers and white shirts and the little girls wore long, pink dresses. Obscured in a grainy haze, he was sure they had faces but couldn't make them out.

Where am I? He spoke, but no words came from his lips. He lowered his service pistol, and a boy and girl stepped forward. The girl's face came into view, a familiarity about her he couldn't quite place. "Hello Ronan, will you play a game with us?"

Quinn couldn't speak. He had no voice.

"Would you like to play a game?" The boy asked.

A stain appeared on the children's chests, spreading outward and in every direction. Standing in this open space, Quinn watched in horror as all the children became drenched in bright red.

"We wanted to play a game, Ronan. We just wanted to play a game. We didn't want to be shot."

"Why didn't you save us, Ronan? Why didn't you save us?"

The girl's face became clear to him.

Beatrice. Beet honey. No. No. No. Every girl, hundreds, no thousands, all took on Beet's form. And the boy's face… was his own.

He screamed, but no sound left his lips. He screamed again…

QUINN SHOT UP FROM his bed as if someone had launched him from a rocket launcher. Pounding so hard and with such rapidity, his own heart echoed through the room. "What the hell was that?" He muttered to himself.

Rolling out of bed, he stumbled to the bathroom, running the faucet and splashing cold water on his face. He felt tired. Worn. Exhausted. And with exhaustion came his demons. Lying in wait in the dark recesses of his mind, they sprung on him like predators pouncing on weakened prey.

He toweled his face dry and stepped into the kitchen. Sliding the bottle of scotch out of the cabinet, he poured three glasses and dumped three glasses down the drain. Then he placed the bottle back into the cabinet. Oh, how he would love to drown those dreams with liquor. Sighing deeply, he pushed his arms against the sink and stretched. Gathering his wits once more, he walked into the living room, mounting his stationary bike.

"You are in so much pain, Mr. Quinn, so much has happened in your life. Would you like to talk to me about it?" Pippa's soft voice echoed in the room. *"I can feel it. I can feel this sharp pain and I think it's coming from you."*

"What!?" A startled Quinn's foot slipped from the pedal and his leg shot outward. "Pip? Pip? Is that you?" He scanned the room.

"I can see you. I think we're connected to each other by something. Like Oscar. And my mom and dad."

Quinn shook his head. "God, Pip, you scared the living crap out of me! How'd you find me?"

"I think you did something to me."

"What did I do to you, Pip? You keep saying that? What do you think I did?"

"I see my phone. It's in a very dark place. I'm trying to see better, but it takes a lot of energy."

Quinn shook his head. "Don't worry, we'll find it, Pip."

"I hope you can rid yourself of your pain someday, Mr. Quinn. It feels horrible. Like needles."

"It is horrible, Pip. It really is."

He waited in silence, sitting motionless on the bike. After five minutes had passed, she still hadn't reappeared, and Quinn felt a wave of disappointment wash over him.

For the first time in over a decade, he felt he'd finally found someone he could speak with. About Helmand Province. About Maya Angelou Elementary. About Central Park. Things he'd held back from Alexx. Things he'd held back from Miá. Things he'd held back from the therapist. All that he'd kept bottled up inside, readying to explode like an IED.

FIG ARRIVED AT THE scene of Pippa's murder the following afternoon.

A furnace of heat blasting him as he stepped from his Dodge Hemi, he walked to the side of the highway, peering down the steep hillside of Kurtz Peak. Pulling his Kansas City Royals ball cap tight over his head, he slid down the loose scree of the hill in a cloud of dust and falling rocks until he arrived at the ledge where Pippa's orange Subaru had come to its final resting place.

Carefully, he stepped around loose rock and shale, looking over the rock ledge, and down the remaining steep hillside. Yikes, he thought. I hope it's not down there. He turned back to the accident scene. Shoving and kicking brush and switchgrass aside and tipping over shattered shale and stones, he found nothing that resembled Pippa's phone. He dialed Quinn back at the station.

"Boss, there's nothing here. Even if I found it, remember we had that massive storm the next night. It would've gotten soaked. And it's been two weeks. The sun would have cooked it. My guess is it got cannon-balled from her car. If it's anywhere, it's at the bottom of Kurtz Peak.

Probably smashed to bits." Fig waited for Quinn to respond. "Chief? Are you still on?"

"Go to the yard. Go through her car. I have a feeling it's still in there."

Fig cocked his head. "You do? I don't see how that's possible."

"Fig, just go to the yard. Go back through her car. And keep maintaining a low profile."

Fig shrugged. "You got it, boss." He shoved the phone in his pocket, scrambling back up the hillside to the highway above.

FIG ARRIVED AT *GARY'S Wrecking Yard and Parts Emporium* an hour later. Littered with the corpses of cars and trucks in various stages of dismantlement, the place was like some seedy underworld of dead automobile organ donors.

The wrecking yard's owner, Gary Towers, cleanly shaven and wrinkled like a Shar Pei, immediately recognized Fig. He ambled his way over, studying Fig with curiosity the entire time. Wiping his grease-stained hands, he grunted and tipped his hat back. "Hey there, Fig. What brings ya here? Need parts for that piece of shit Dodge you call a truck?"

"No Gary," Fig replied with a chuckle. "Need to peek around the wrecked Subie that got towed in a couple of weeks back."

Gary looked over his shoulder at Pippa's Subaru. "That Subie?"

"Yup," Fig said.

Clicking his tongue and running it along the inside of his cheek, Gary's glimmering eyes scanned Fig. "How come you ain't in uniform today? Working on your day off?"

Fig smiled and shook his head. "Oh, geez no, Gary. The chief made this casual dress day."

With a blank, unblinking expression, Gary stared at Fig, then spit a dark glob of tobacco onto the ground. "Casual dress day? Jesus Christ, Fig, you sound like one of those corporate morons at Pangea." He thumbed over his shoulder at Pippa's Subaru. "Take a good look. She's getting torn down in a couple of days." Gary turned and stomped toward his dust-stained office trailer. "Casual dress day," he grumbled. "Jesus H. Christ." He stepped into the trailer, slamming the door behind him.

Fig hurried over to Pippa's Subaru. Hands on hips, he looked over the wreck. "Well, here we go."

Pulling on the crumpled door, it relented with a loud creak and a sharp metallic crack. Then, lifting a penlight from his pocket, he lit up the inside of the car.

"Can see more with your penlight, Fig," he muttered. "Whatever you say, chief."

Sweating from the heat and cursing, he pushed his way inside the Subaru, inspecting the underneath of the passenger seat. He crawled over the top of the center console, searched the back seat, and went through the glove box.

The seats, twisted oddly in the crash, angled slightly toward one another, pushing against the center console. Fig shoved his hands between them and into the thin gaps, stretching his wriggling fingers outward and through the sliver of space. He pulled himself out of the wreck, yanking his cap off and wiping sweat from his forehead.

Look harder, Fig.

Pulling the switchblade knife from his pocket and flipping out the blade, he went back inside the car. Grunting and groaning, he slid the blade into the painfully narrow space.

Clink.

Fig's head jerked up. What was that? He thought. He tapped the blade on something hard and smooth. Trying to push whatever it was with the knife-edge, the knife just kept sliding off. He jammed his hand into the space as far as it would go, rubbing the device's surface with the tip of his finger. Jesus, it's jammed in tight, he thought. He rocked the seat back and forth. "C'mon dammit!" Leaning over the seat, he jammed the knife-blade once again onto whatever this thing was.

Thunk.

Pulling his hand free, the flesh on his knuckles torn and bleeding, he scrambled around to the back seat. Shining the penlight beneath it, light reflected off the glistening flat metallic case of Pippa's cellphone lying on the floor of the car. Ecstatic, Fig felt as though he'd just found a Spanish gold doubloon. He hurriedly dialed Quinn.

"I got it, boss! Her phone was in her car! As you guessed!"

"Does it still work?"

Fig turned it on, and a *low battery* symbol appeared on the screen.

"Yep, sure does. Just needs to be charged. I think it needs a passcode, though."

"Okay, bring it here," Quinn replied. "We'll see if we can figure that out. I'm headed back to my house to grab something and will meet you at the station."

"Pip, we have your phone. Can you remember the passcode?" Quinn glanced desperately around the living room. "Pip, can you hear me?" Impatient, he paced back and forth.

Nothing. Where is she? Where does she vanish off too?

"Oscar." Pippa's voice filled the house.

"Your passcode is Oscar? The numbers? The code for the phone?"

"Yes, Oscar. But... not Oscar. Turn the word around. It's different."

Quinn felt his face flush with irritation and frustration. "Pip, will you ever be able to remember more than just fleeting memories?"

"Is Kisha okay? How is Kisha?"

Quinn shook his head. "Pip, I don't know who Kisha is, but if we don't get ahead of this, more people may die."

"Oscar, but not Oscar. Please, keep Kisha safe."

"I will, I promise."

Then Pippa was gone once again. Jesus, he thought as he headed for the front door. This is nuts.

THE THREE STOOD IN silence, staring at the phone lying on Quinn's desk like it was the fossil of some newly discovered dinosaur. Watching as it charged, each of them couldn't help but wonder what mysteries lay inside of it. The phone buzzed to life and, to no one's surprise, Oscar's fuzzy mug appeared on the screen.

"Okay," Quinn said, eagerly rubbing his hands together. "Let's see what we have here."

"And what if we can't get in?" Fig asked. "Then what do we do?"

Quinn shrugged. "I guess we get the FBI involved then. Send it off to some lab. Never hear about it ever again. So, let's put our thinking caps on. I know the passcode uses Oscar's name." Quinn tilted his head. "Oscar, but not Oscar. What did she mean?"

"Who's she?" Fig asked.

Quinn and Rose glanced at each other. Fig was still out of the Pippa-poltergeist-loop.

"I'll tell you later, dear. Let's think about the code," Rose said. She thoughtfully tapped her chin. "Hmm. Oscar, but not Oscar. I think she's saying Oscar is an anagram."

"Anagram…" Quinn said. "Of course."

Fig shrugged. "What's an anagram?"

Quinn fell down into his chair. Each hour was something new. Each hour, a new mystery. He closed his eyes while Rose explained anagrams to Fig.

"Oh," he said, enlightened. The two sat down, scratching word combinations on notepads.

Anagram…

Closing his eyes, Quinn let his mind wander. Across Woodrock. Across the Plains. Over the Appalachians. Into New York. Across a broad ocean. Into the desolate mountains of Afghanistan. Memories, not unlike Pippa's, passed through him like beams of light. New Jersey. East Rutherford. His home. Young Beet in Sponge Bob pajamas. Alexx screaming.

He shuddered as he recalled those nights.

Lifting a lamp. Heaving it at a petrified Alexx. Wait… Alexx? Who is that?

Quinn's eyes flew open like unrestrained window blinds into rollers. "Give me the phone." He leaned over his desk and thrust out his hand.

"You got something, Boss?"

"C'mon, hand me the damned phone."

Laying his own phone on the desk, he looked at the dialing pad, matching letters associated with numbers. He was short by one number. One digit.

That looks like an L... He scribbled on the pad, swept up Pippa's phone and entered a code. *227167.*

"Got it." He shoved the phone across the desk to an astonished Rose.

Gazing at his scribbles, Quinn's face displayed an odd emotional torment. Not excited. Not celebratory. The expression a lost child separated from his parents would have.

OSCAR. CAROS. CAR1OS.

He now knew Carlos, his sworn imaginary foe. The foe who took on the shape of Alexx during his alcohol-drenched nights.

But Carlos wasn't his sworn enemy. Carlos was his guide to this very place and this very moment in time.

Part 5

Operation Endor

Chapter 32

Iron Hand. Jupiter. Red Lancer. Specimens. Incident. Security 1000%.

The screen-grab of Pippa's computer monitor stored on her phone, and the e-mails that she snapped a picture of, made as much sense to Quinn, Rose, and Fig, as it all had to Pippa the day before her death. However, one thing was certain to Quinn now. Sam Singh's fingerprints were all over this. He sent the e-mail that Pangea killed Pippa for reading.

Glancing through the brief, head-scratching e-mail, reality quickly settled in.

This operation, Iron Hand, didn't appear to be a local jurisdiction thing, whatever it even was. After all, Pangea Dynamic Solutions sat on federal land, and Emma Massey's still suspicious death occurred in another state entirely. Quinn announced to Fig and Rose that he was finally handing everything over to the FBI. Now, with Pippa's phone, he felt he had the missing link. He could turn everything over to the Feds without sounding like a complete lunatic.

"I'm really proud of you guys," he said. "It's time we put this in the hands of the right folks. They have the resources for this. I don't."

Fig looked dejected. Rose nodded, morose. To Quinn, the two of them looked as if they were sending their only child off to college. But the further he'd dived into Pippa's death, the more he felt Rose, Fig, and his entire town were in danger. And Quinn couldn't stand the thought of anyone else being hurt or killed. It was time to fish or cut bait.

He was ready for bait cutting.

But Quinn's large stature, physical fitness, and vast resume of experience belied a simpler truth. The mind can only process so much chaos. How much free-weight he could bench or how many artificial hills he could speed up and down on his stationary bike mattered little to his overtaxed mind. Brains have their own set of physical limitations and his had reached a limit. He was teetering precariously on the edge of mental collapse.

"We did good things here, guys," he said as he leaned over his desk. "But we need to go back to our day-to-day work. We won't be letting it go entirely. We'll still support the FBI in any way we can."

Shortly after breaking the news to Rose and Fig, Quinn sat down at his desk. He typed up his plan to pass the Pippa Simpson, Chris Hadley, and Emma Massey cases off to the FBI. His phone *dinged.* The mysterious person who'd led Quinn to the videos from Pangea appeared on his screen.

Unknown:

Did you find it?

Chief:

Yup. In her car. I'm packaging everything up. Turning this over to the FBI. This isn't a case for the Woodrock Police.

Unknown:

DO NOT DO THAT

"Oh, for Christ's sake!" Quinn shouted. He threw his head back and groaned. That last message, in all caps, annoyed the chief yet even more.

Chief:

I don't even know who you are. You don't have a say in this. I don't know why you wanted us to find the phone. But we found it. Goes to the feds buddy.

Unknown:

We need to verify each other.

Chief:

What? Verify each other?

Unknown:

Go to the website for the Federal Bureau of Investigation. Select the Washington D.C. field office. You'll see a number to report a crime. Call it.

Chief:

I'm confused. I thought you didn't want me to call the FBI?

Unknown:

Tell the agent you want to speak to Grady Freeman.

Chief:

And?

Unknown:

Tell him you have a deer problem.

What? Quinn thought. Am I getting pranked?

Chief:

A deer problem?

Unknown:

Yes, a deer problem. He'll tell you that deer can be troublesome, but you have the wrong number. Then he'll hang up.

Chief:

This is bananas. Then what?

Unknown:

You wait. You'll receive an overnight delivery. In it will be a note. Follow the instructions.

Chief:

Jesus. Seriously?

Unknown:

Just do it. You're wasting time. Things are happening that you don't know about.

Chief:

What's happening?

Chief:

???

Chief:

Hello?

No response came after that.

Quinn rocked in his chair, chewing on a ball-point pen cap. This is crazy. Don't contact the FBI. Do contact the FBI. What the hell? He thought through the possibilities here. He wasn't being sent to just any

Joe Blow in the FBI. They gave him a name. A specific FBI name. Maybe the FBI was in on this. They used his department to obtain that phone. Which means someone already knew what was on it. Something worth killing Pippa for.

He so wanted to disconnect from this thing and just go back to normal. Back to the joys of patrolling. Back to hearing stories from the Old Timers at Dollie's Tavern. Simplicity. Stability. Quinn drew in a deep breath.

"Screw it."

He followed the instructions that the mystery texter gave him. A woman answered and asked if he needed to report a crime. Quinn told her he did, but needed to speak to Grady Freeman.

"Okay. Hold on. I'll put you through."

As if he'd been waiting for this very call, Grady answered the phone immediately.

"Hello? Is someone there?" Grady asked.

"Yeah," Quinn replied, massaging his forehead. This was all so dumb. "I have a deer problem."

"Deer can be troublesome, but you have the wrong number." The phone clicked and went silent.

Quinn held the phone in his hand. What just happened? Deer can be troublesome? That was precisely the answer he was told he was going to get.

Chief:

Done. This Freeman guy told me deer can be troublesome.

Chief:

You there?

Chief:

?

What sort of secret-squirrel bullshit was this all about, anyhow? Quinn thought, frustrated. Fine then. I guess I'll just wait.

He left his office and headed to Dollies for some chitchat with the Old Timers.

QUINN ARRIVED AT THE station at 7 a.m. the following morning. The breeze felt cool and crisp and overhead, through a slate gray overcast, the rumblings of yet another cargo jet leaving the Pangea facility.

Quinn told Rose good morning and waved to the deputies. Enjoying a Pippa free night, Quinn managed five hours of solid, uninterrupted sleep. The most he'd had in weeks. As he sat down at his desk, Rose stepped inside, laying an overnight Fed Ex package onto his desk. "Sleep well last night, Ronan?"

"Oh yeah," he muttered as he opened the envelope.

Quinn turned the envelope upside down. A new cell phone and a note fell onto the desk, along with a business card for Grady Freeman. Grady had scribbled over his phone numbers with a sharpie.

Okay, guess I won't be calling him. He read the small note. On it were instructions he was very familiar with from his time in the Marines. COMSEC procedures:

Do not call anyone. This phone has an encryption app that has been setup for your use. Text 2193329988. Password is KING. Authentication is ABLE. Your Identification is BUCK. Theirs is WHITETAIL. Proceed with these. In order. All responses must be correct. After authentication, you will receive further guidance. Do not use any other phone.

G. Freeman.

Quinn let out a half-restrained laugh. "Buck? Whitetail? Are these clowns the FBI or the Park Service?" Sweeping up the new phone, he turned it on and sent the first text. He knew how this all worked:

Buck:

Password is KING

2193329988:

KING acknowledged. Authentication is ABLE.

Buck:

Identification is BUCK.

2193329988:

Identification is WHITETAIL.

Buck:

What now?

219332998:

Welcome to Operation Cobalt. Or what used to be.

Buck:

Why can I only speak with you? What's with notes in packages?

219332998:

We've been compromised.

Buck:

Who?

219332998:

Everyone. It's our show now, Chief.

AS THE MESSAGING CONTINUED back and forth, Quinn gave the highlights of the e-mail he'd found on the phone.

Buck:

Sam Singh is on the e-mail.

Whitetail:

Not surprised.

Buck:

What's iron hand?

Whitetail:

We're working on that.

Buck:

It mentions iron hand depends on Jupiter. Any idea what that means?

Whitetail:

No clue.

Buck:

Red Lancer?

Whitetail:

Nope.

Buck:

GLNV? JT? Specimens?

Whitetail:

Specimens? Interesting.

Buck:

I don't want to come off like a dick, but I'm tired of texting this crap to you. There's no context. Can't I just send it to you? The screenshot?

Whitetail:

You need to be briefed. We want to meet you. Can you travel?

Buck:

I don't like the idea of leaving my people behind so a short trip.

Whitetail:

Can you go to D.C.?

Buck:

I thought you were compromised? I don't think that's a great idea.

Quinn placed the phone on the desk. He could tell where this conversation was going. If they had, in fact, been compromised as Whitetail claimed, the last place the FBI would visit was Woodrock. Going to D.C. seemed to be an equally foolish preposition. And if they were who they claimed they were, they'd be able to figure out the meeting place.

Ding!

Whitetail:

Hello? Where?

Buck:

If you're really the FBI, you'll figure it out. I'm leaving this afternoon. Nothing had better happen to my people.

Whitetail:

I'll keep tabs on them. But under no circumstances will I blow my cover.

Buck:

Why am I helping you?

Whitetail:

Because you want to find who killed the Simpson woman.

Whitetail:

You also don't have a choice.

Quinn called Rose into his office. "Rose, I have to leave town this afternoon."

Rose's eyes widened into a gleeful look. "Wait… is this?"

Quinn cut her off and held his finger to his lips. A subtle smile widened on Rose's face. The FBI dealt them back in before they even dealt themselves out. He scribbled onto a note and held it up for Rose to read.

People may be listening. We need to stay quiet.

Quinn gathered his things up. "I'm flying down to Orlando. My grandma's in the hospital."

Rose nodded.

"Pippa's memorial service is tomorrow. I need you to find someone for me." He scribbled a name and some words on a piece of paper and handed it to Rose.

Rose read the note and tilted her head, her eyes questioning.

"I promised," Quinn said.

Rose nodded approvingly.

Quinn stepped around the desk. "Don't worry," he said, placing a gentle kiss on Rose's cheek. "It'll all be over soon. I promise." As he rushed out, he stopped and turned back to Rose. "Oh, I'm leaving Fig in charge. Don't let it go to his head."

As QUINN PACKED, HE tried contacting Pippa to squeeze every piece of information from her before he left. After an hour of fruitless attempts, never clear on where she gets shuffled off to in her afterlife corridor, her soft voice filled his home.

"*Where are you leaving too, Mr. Quinn?*"

"I'm meeting with the FBI, maybe."

"Did you find Kisha?"

"We will. Pippa, is there anything you can tell me about the e-mails on your phone? There isn't a lot to go on." Shoving clothes into a suitcase, he spoke to Pippa, as one would speak to a common acquaintance.

"*One thing is a picture. Yes. A picture of a thing or things. They're dead. A man. He looks like a cowboy. He's alive. A desert. I remember a desert. Envy. Envy.*"

"Pippa, what do you mean when you say envy?" Quinn panned around the room. He always expected, or hoped, Pippa would show herself. Materialize out of thin air. "Who is it you envy? Samir Singh?"

"I don't know. Also, I see something floating. It's staring at me. It looks..." Pippa's voice faded.

"Looks what?"

"It looks evil."

She vanished.

Folding his clothes and gathering his things for his trip, Quinn felt melancholic. When she spoke, he felt a pull, a tugging, like he and Pippa had some physical connection. He never wanted to lose her. The only being, or ghost, or spirit, or energy, or angel, who truly understood his pain.

THE MEMORIAL SERVICE FOR Pippa Simpson, organized and paid for by Pangea, was a beautiful affair.

Now, two weeks after her death, many from around the globe - managers, friends, colleagues, and plant workers - gathered at the lovely, ornate Baptist church on 4th and Elm to pay tribute to one of their most beloved employees. A bright, charismatic young woman with a future was gone, and all too soon. The sky had dawned a flawless azure. A mild, early summer sun bathed the town in warmth. The chirps and caws of birds seemed more eloquent and musical than ever. But a dark pall hung over the beautiful church.

Whispers about the strange death of Emma Massey filtered through the mourners. Whispers of shock and whispers of suspicion. With the suicide of Chris Hadley in the picture, it would only be a matter of time before suspicion became fear.

Rose and Deputy Beth shuffled along with the crowd to the granite-stepped entrance as people filed into the church. The two women scribbled their names into a guest book and took seats on the third-row bench. The church filled quickly, forcing some mourners to stand against the walls at the rear. It would take a miracle to find this Kisha person Pippa had asked Quinn to keep safe.

Fifteen minutes into the ceremony, their solution presented herself.

Kisha took the stage as a guest speaker and spent eight minutes talking about Pippa. Wiping away tears, she went on about Pippa's humor. Her intelligence. Her team oriented managerial style.

She told a story from the last day Pippa was alive, and Pippa giggling in a meeting for reasons no one will ever know. Soft weeping broke the silence in the church. Rose gently elbowed Beth, nodding at Kisha on the stage. Glancing at the deputy, she saw Beth's cheeks glistening with moisture as tears streamed from her eyes.

After the ceremony drew to a close, the two women made their way out of the church, searching for Kisha in a throng of morose people. Rose felt Beth's elbow tap her ribs. She glanced behind her, seeing Kisha make her way out of the church entrance and down the steps.

"I'll meet you back at the station, Beth. I don't want Kisha seen speaking to a deputy." Beth nodded and headed for the patrol car.

Rose pushed her way back through the crowd like a fish swimming upstream, stepping up to Kisha and embracing her. Kisha returned Rose's gesture, but with a puzzled look.

She stepped back. "Do I know you?" Kisha asked.

"No, but we have a mutual friend," Rose replied with a warm smile and soft eyes.

"Oh? You knew Pippa?" Kisha asked, still puzzled.

"Here." Rose took Kisha's wrist and opened her hand, placing a piece of folded paper on her palm. "The chief's condolences. He apologizes for not being able to attend." Rose embraced Kisha and released her, following the crowd out of the church and toward her car.

A rapid clicking of high heels striking the pavement came from behind Rose as she made her way to her car. Spinning around, she saw Kisha storming toward her. She grabbed Rose's wrist, forcefully yanking her arm outward, peeled Rose's fingers apart, and slapped Quinn's note onto her opened hand.

Glaring and fuming, Kisha growled between gritted teeth. "You can tell Chief Quinn I'm not going anywhere. Not until you people do your fucking jobs and find out who killed Pip."

Kisha spun on her heels and stomped off, vanishing into the crowd while a dumbstruck Rose looked on.

MIÁ AND PEPE CUDDLED on the leather sofa in the living room of their luxurious brownstone in Crown Heights. Stuffing the salty popcorn in her mouth, Miá rested her head on Pepe's shoulder, the flickering light from the television illuminating their faces.

As Miá crunched popcorn, a tattered zombie bit into a woman's neck. Blood shot out of the victim like spray from a whale's blowhole, globs of Hollywood blood even striking the lens of the camera.

"Ew, so gross," Miá muttered. "How can you watch this stuff?" She peered up at him. A grin spread across his face, staring at the screen as if he were being transported right into zombieville. Sighing, she nestled back on his shoulder. "Jesus, you're like a child sometimes." Her cellphone on the table dinged.

Ronan:

Hey, what's up? Where's my vanilla muffins?

Grinning, Miá tapped on her phone.

Miá:

Hey devil dog, patience is a virtue. So, what's going on? I haven't heard from you in days. What did the FBI want? Is everything okay out there? We never talked.

Miá awaited Quinn's response, watching the wavering little dots on the message bubble.

Ronan:

I was just thinking. Remember that time in Kandahar? That time you and I got lost and had no clue where we were?

Miá tilted her head, a mystified expression crossing her face. She sat up.

"What's wrong, love?" Pepe asked.

"It's Ronan," she mumbled. "He's asking me about a time he and I got lost in Kandahar."

He shrugged. "What happened?"

Miá fell back onto the couch, gazing confusedly at the wall. "Nothing happened. Ronan and I never served together in Kandahar. We were in different units and in Afghanistan at different times." She tapped the phone.

Miá:

Oh yeah! Good times!

Ronan:

Cool. Me too. I'm back at the old post. Let's catch up sometime?

Miá:

Sounds good! Take care!'

Miá leaned forward, placing the phone on the table. "Ronan's in trouble."

Pepe sat back. "What is it? Where is he?"

Miá looked at Pepe. "He's outside our house."

YOUSEF JAMMED A CROWBAR between the door frame and the door, wrenching it back and forth until the frame cracked and splintered. He glanced left and right, searching for curious onlookers. What a dump, he thought. The dimly lit parking lot of The Shady Inn was nearly empty, and only a few of the rooms had their lights on. Even the manager's office had closed for the night.

Glock out and raised, he reared back and kicked the door. It burst open, slamming hard against the wall. Yousef swiftly entered the pitch-black room, swaying his weapon left to right, rushing past the bed and clearing the bathroom. He switched on the light, then walked back out into the room.

A sock stuffed in her mouth, Madison greeted him with a steel-piercing glare and a taut telephone cord cutting into her throat. Holstering his Glock, he pulled a knife from his pocket and cut the cord. Madison slid to her side, falling onto the floor with a thud. He rolled her over onto her back, removing the sock stuffed into her mouth, then sliced through the binds on her feet and hands.

"Can you move?" Yousef asked.

"No, I can't move," Madison choked. "Why you ask?" She moved her tongue around her cheeks, trying to form saliva. "Because I've been stuck here for eight fucking hours." Coughing, she looked up at Yousef with a scowl. "What the hell took you so long to get here?"

Yousef pulled a blanket off the bed, sweeping it over her shoulders. "He tossed your secure device into the back of someone's car. We eventually figured you probably weren't driving to Pittsburgh."

Madison managed the mildest of smirks. "Sam thought of that?" She rubbed her jaw. "That sneaky son of a bitch."

CHAPTER 33

WITH WIDE-EYED ASTONISHMENT, Miá fell back against the sofa. Pepe, lost in thought, scratched his balding scalp. "Holy cow, Ronan," Miá said in a rhetorical, unsure voice. "Murder? Ghosts? Secret agents?"

"And don't forget Carlos," Quinn added, sitting in a chair across from the two. He leaned forward, resting his arms on his thighs, bowing his head.

"Ronan, you need to understand something here," Miá said, but in a calculated and cautious voice. "This is a lot to take in. Are you… have you been…"

"No," Quinn's head snapped up. He knew where Miá was going with this. "I haven't touched a drink since I left here. It's been over four years. Rose and Fig and the dumb cat can back all this up." He felt as if Miá, his sister-from-another-mister, was dismissing him. Treating him like a patient suffering from an addict's psychosis.

"Ronan, you hate cats," she added, struggling to make sense of Quinn's bizarre Woodrock tale. She turned to Pepe. "What do you think, babe? What're your thoughts?"

His face a blank, unreadable slate, Pepe studied Quinn. Quinn shifted uneasily in his chair, awaiting a verdict.

"I believe him," Pepe said. "I believe everything he said."

Quinn sat back in his chair, folding his arms across his chest. "Well, thank you for that, Pepe." He turned to Miá, his lips scrunched, brow raised, and wearing a look of victory and salvation.

"Look, Ronan," Miá pleaded. "We're homicide detectives. We deal with facts and evidence. This… everything you've told us…with all due respect, sounds more like a campfire story."

Quinn pulled the phone Grady had provided from his pocket and thrust it at Miá. "They sent me this phone with an encrypted app. And that's COMSEC verification, Miá. I haven't seen this since I left the Corps. This isn't someone pulling my chain."

Miá scrolled through Quinn's conversations with the mysterious Whitetail, muttering to herself as she read them. Quinn retrieved a folded sheet of paper from his other pocket and handed that to Miá as well. "And this is a printout of the e-mail from Pippa's phone. Tell me what you think."

Miá carefully read through the e-mail.

Re: Iron Hand

From: William K. Hendrickson

To:

Bcc:

Rich,

Specimens are now in final development. I expect all specimens will be ready for deployment in two weeks. The specimen batch A322 has successfully completed testing GLNV and is eager to go.

– Bill

Re: Iron Hand

From: Samir Singh (CEO)

To:

Bcc:

Rich, et al.

JT and GLNV specimens performed beyond all expectations. Well done! Gentlemen, specimens must stay contained, out of sight, at all costs. There is still work to be done at JT. I shouldn't need to remind you that after the NV incident, security is 1000% of our focus. Red Lancer will handle any compromises. Iron Hand must go in Q4. Jupiter is dictating this time, so we must all do our best.

Regards, Sam

Leaning across the coffee table, Quinn tapped the paper Miá held in her hands. "Whitetail, my contact, says they don't know what this Iron Hand thing is. But they said, quote - things are happening - unquote. They're still looking into it. They also told me the FBI's compromised. I feel I'm their boots on the ground at Woodrock now. The Feds can't be seen snooping around, or the whole thing may go up."

"What thing, Ronan?" Miá asked. "Iron Hand? This is a tech company. I'm sure specimens and Iron Hand may just be corporate lingo for a project. Your victim, this…"

"Pippa Simpson," Quinn added.

"Yes, her. Maybe she was all caught up in some corporate espionage and they killed her for it."

"So, you agree with me now." Quinn sat back in his chair with a smirk. "You agree she was murdered."

"Oh, Ronan," Miá rolled her eyes and sighed, returning the phone. "Look, you're exhausted. Why don't you crash here, and we'll take a fresh look at everything in the morning."

Ding!

Quinn stared at the screen of the new phone. "Hmph," he grunted and handed the phone back to Miá. She read the screen.

> **Whitetail:**
>
> We believe we know where you are. A jogger, 6'2, 230 pounds, African American, Adidas runner's outfit will jog down the sidewalk in ten minutes. If you are where we think you are, flash your living room lights twice.

Handing the phone back to Quinn, Miá scowled. "So, we're the safe-house now, are we?"

"Look, Miá," Quinn replied, searching her eyes. "I can leave. Right now. I was never here. This is yours and Pepe's decision to make, not mine."

Miá turned to Pepe. "Babe, what're your thoughts? You'll be in on this as well now."

Pepe stood, raised his arms to the ceiling, and stretched. "I'll go get some coffee started."

BENEATH RADIATING CONES OF street-lamp lights, Miá saw the jogger approaching in the darkness. Pepe turned the living room lights off, then on, then off, then on once more. Miá opened the door, hurrying along the front path to the street and peeking inside her mailbox. She brushed past the jogger on her return to the house and then walked through the front door. “I told him to meet me at the back door,” she muttered as she flashed past.

Moments later, following closely behind Miá, Grady Freeman walked into the living room. Pepe poured everyone cups of coffee as a round of introductions flowed. Grady thanked Miá for her help.

“How’d you know he’d come here?” Miá asked Grady while he pulled his hoodie over his head, tossing it over the chair.

“It was a guess,” he said. “The Deputy Director knew you and Quinn worked together. I called you to discuss Ronan’s background, to get a vibe on him, and after that, I got Whitetail and him talking. It also helped that we knew he was flying to New York.”

“Oh? And how’d you manage that?” An annoyed Quinn asked. “You guys break into my PC? Download some spyware?”

“No, Ronan,” Grady responded as he sipped some coffee. “Whitetail followed you to the airport.”

“Oh. Okay. I’ll buy that,” Quinn responded, glancing at Miá.

Miá appeared to be struggling with everything transpiring during this odd evening, gaping at Grady like he wasn’t real. To Quinn, she was still at the starting line after the starter’s pistol had gone off. From him showing up at her house unannounced, to Pippa’s ghost, to an FBI special agent arriving at her house, announced via text by a mysterious deer.

AFTER SOME MORE COFFEE, and settling in, it was time, said Grady, to get to work. “You have the screenshots from Simpson’s phone?” He asked.

“First things first,” Quinn said. “Who’s Whitetail?”

Grady shrugged. “We don’t know their identity. They’re a mole in Pangea that we’ve been working with for a while. They feed us information, bits and pieces mostly.”

Miá looked puzzled. "Well, if they're a mole, then they must be an employee, right? They sent Ronan security footage from the complex, which means they have access. So, who put them there? If it wasn't the FBI?"

Grady shrugged.

"Well Grady, maybe I'm asking the obvious here, but how is Ronan supposed to trust this Whitetail?"

Grady slurped some coffee, giving a nod of approval to Pepe. "We've corroborated all that we got from Whitetail. You see, Pangea and Samir Singh have been under investigation for some time. We have a fraud case open on Pangea, and we've been digging into their business ops for a year. We were so close. I was just getting a grand jury ready to go. Now, we're getting a sense that something else is going on there. Can I look at the e-mail?"

Quinn handed it over to him.

"Iron Hand?" Miá asked.

Grady shrugged. "Maybe." Reading Pippa's e-mail, muttering to himself, he looked up. "There were three attachments. They wouldn't happen to be on the victim's phone also, would they?"

Quinn shook his head.

"Bummer," he said, as he continued to read. "This Red Lancer must be their security service. And what would they be doing that coincides with Jupiter?" He asked, clearly puzzled. "What do planets have to do with anything? Is this some weird pagan thing?"

"I wondered about that also," Quinn added.

"Guys," Miá said, glancing between Quinn and Grady. "Let's use our brains here. Jupiter isn't just a planet. Jupiter is the Roman God of Sky and Thunder. The king of the gods, actually. He's a big deal."

Quinn smacked his forehead. "Of course. Jupiter is a code name. A person who's higher up the food chain than Sam Singh. If Singh is the CEO, then who could he be answering to? Who's higher than him?"

"These abbreviations. Codes perhaps?" Grady scratched his scalp. "They seem to be places. JT? GLNV? NV?"

Quinn sat straight and suddenly shouted. "Stop!"

Everyone in the room, deep in thought with their thinking caps on, jerked at Quinn's sudden outburst. "What did you say?" Quinn demanded. "Repeat what you just said, Grady."

"What? JT? GLNV? NV? You have something to share with us?" Grady responded, puzzled.

Quinn looked awake, alert, and giddy. I can't believe it! He thought. Pippa wasn't saying envy! She was repeating letters!

She was saying NV!

Having never actually heard these letters repeated to him, he'd only casually glanced at them on Pippa's e-mail. In stunned silence, 3 pairs of widened eyeballs waited for Quinn to explain himself.

Looking at each of their stunned expressions, he explained. "Look. Pippa wasn't saying the word envy. She was saying the letters N-V. She kept repeating it. NV, they're all dead. N…V..." Quinn, clearly teetering on the brink of madness to his stunned audience, looked up at the ceiling and blew Pippa a kiss.

"What… is… going… on?" Confused, Grady glanced at Pepe and Miá.

Quinn leaned forward. "NV. They're all dead. Pippa said this to me before she died, Grady. Her last words. And she mentioned a desert. So, here's what I'm thinking. NV is Nevada, which is very much a desert. What they're saying in this message is they tested these specimens in

Nevada. But something happened." He thought back to his last conversation with Pippa's ghost. "We need a PC, Miá. Can we use your PC?"

Miá hurried from the room and returned with her laptop. Quinn stretched his fingers and typed into the search bar. *Nevada. Dead. Cowboy.*

He closed his eyes and imagined a desert. Things. Dead things. Cowboy. He erased his search and typed *Nevada, dead livestock, mystery.* Several hits resulted from his search, but one grabbed his attention.

Rancher Who Claimed Aliens Killed His Sheep Dies from Suicide.

A distraught man in a photo, wearing blue jeans, a plaid shirt, and a white Stetson hat, pointed at dozens and dozens of fluffy dead sheep. He claimed to have seen giant flying demons with glowing eyes leaving the area after a loud commotion came from his sheep pen. Aliens, he said to the reporter, from Area 51 - some 110 miles south of the ranch. The government sent people to investigate, concluding the sheep died from anthrax. Two days later, the old grief-stricken rancher shot himself in the head with a rifle.

"Suicide, my ass," Quinn growled. "And Pippa mentioned floating things. Things that looked evil."

Grady leaned over Quinn's shoulder, reading the article. He sat back in the chair and re-read the e-mail. "This incident in Nevada they refer to in the e-mail must be this. This ranch thing. So GLNV is Nevada as well." Grady now looked distraught, and he looked up at Miá.

She understood exactly what he was thinking and nodded in the affirmative. "Groom Lake."

"Groom Lake?" Pepe, thoroughly confused, looked for understanding. "Where is this Groom Lake?"

"Area 51, Pepe," Quinn added.

"Oh," Pepe said thoughtfully. "Where they keep the aliens."

AS THE ROOM WEIGHED this new understanding in silence, Quinn spoke up.

"So, they murdered this rancher, just like they murdered Hadley. They were covering something up."

"But covering up what?" Miá asked, gazing at the ceiling in thought, gently tapping her chin with her long, green-nail-glossed finger.

"Well," Quinn said. "This incident in Nevada. Something went wrong. Like Pepe here, when someone says Area 51, they think of aliens. So, these things that killed the rancher's sheep were something he'd never seen before." Quinn paused as he organized his thoughts. "What if these were weapons the Air Force is testing? What if these weapons carry some sort of nerve agent?"

Grady nodded. "Keep going."

"Well," Quinn continued. "Our coroner said Pippa died from strangulation and there were defensive wounds all over her neck. Yet there was no one in the car but her. So, what if some sort of toxin killed her? A chemical or biological agent? The same agent that killed the sheep? And they used it on her. Like a test, to see if it worked." He glanced around the room. A stunned Grady, mouth agape, stared unblinking at Quinn.

"What?" Quinn asked.

"Strangled? She was strangled? But no one was in the car?"

"I know it sounds ridiculous but…"

"And she was a Pangea employee. And killed for this e-mail," Grady now looked like he was solving quadratics on a chalkboard - adding everything up.

"Grady," Miá tilted her head. "What is it?"

"Was there a tox report done?" Grady asked.

"Yeah, it came back clean but..."

"High levels of lactic acid? Lactic acid and nothing else?"

Quinn nodded.

Grady sat back, closed his eyes, and rubbed his forehead. "What I'm about to tell you guys is classified at the highest level." He glanced over at Pepe, waiting for the boutique baker to leave the room.

Miá noticed Grady's look. "He stays. There're no secrets in this house," she said in a stern tone. "He's in this now, just like the rest of us."

Grady turned to Quinn. "Last week there was a chlorine gas attack on a village in Nigeria. Everyone...dead. The U.N. blamed the incident on the country of Chad, but as it turns out, it wasn't Chad after all. We have some evidence, well, more of a theory actually, that Pangea overflew the village with a helicopter to make it look like the Chad military gassed the village. I say *look-like* because when the helicopter overflew the village, the villagers had been dead for at least twenty minutes. Someone wanted us to believe it was a gas attack, when in fact it wasn't. Which means something else killed them. The CIA got ahold of four bodies, found by a river. A family. They found no traces of gas on them."

Miá shook her head. "So, what killed them?"

"They died of acute strangulation. With no bruising or signs of trauma, except their tracheas were crushed, and they'd scratched the hell out of their necks. Just like your victim at Woodrock."

Everyone in the room sat back with a collective breath flowing from their collectively pursed lips. Grady pointed at the laptop on the coffee table. "Those sheep died. All of them. Like the villagers."

"But how?" Miá asked.

"Pangea is under investigation for fraud because the Feds have paid billions of dollars for drones. For drones that were never delivered. The Air Force has received just one hundred of them. Yet Pangea's building thousands and shipping them all over the world."

"These specimens in the e-mail," Miá added. "A super creepy name they're giving these drones, I bet. And this means the Air Force is in on this."

"Also, we've been hacked," Grady added. "And so has the CIA. Our investigation into Pangea just got canned by the Senate Arms Committee. The Air Force is testing these things. Jesus Christ, guys, this is internal. Someone in our own government is conspiring with Pangea. And maybe the Nevada sheep thing was a test gone wrong, but I bet Nigeria was a test gone right. There's going to be an operation. A big one. In the fourth quarter. And this Jupiter person is behind it all."

"Iron Hand," Miá muttered.

Grady nodded. "Yes, Miá, Iron Hand. And we may be too late. Ronan, you need to get back to Woodrock ASAP. You and Whitetail need to monitor Pangea. You're going to need to nab Pangea workers for speeding or jaywalking or anything. Start asking questions, start interrogating."

"What're you guys going to do?" Quinn asked.

"We're going to find out who in the military knows about this and why this is being done in Area 51. Someone at the Pentagon knows. I've got to get back to DC and get all this to Jack and Barb. And more than anything, we need to find Sam Singh and bring him in. He's off the grid."

"Off the grid?" Miá asked.

"After he checked out of the hospital, he disappeared," Grady stated. "That, to me, is not a good sign. He's either in hiding, or he's dead."

"Do I get any help?" Quinn asked. "I mean, we just have twenty officers. Pangea has a small army up there. You'd better not hang my people out to dry, Grady."

Miá stood up, brushing off her pants. "I'm going with him."

"Miá," Grady said. "Give it some thought first before you get involved in this."

"I already have," she responded. "I have vacation time on the books and I'm already involved. We leave tonight."

She walked out of the room, shouting from the hallway. "And I'm bringing Marge!"

"Marge?" Grady asked, confused. "Who's Marge?"

Quinn grinned. "Marge is a family friend."

They both turned to a forlorn Pepe.

"Pepe, are you okay with this?" Quinn asked.

Pepe drew in a deep breath and rose. "Keep her safe, Ronan." Then Pepe ambled into the hallway to speak with his wife.

AFTER STAYING THE NIGHT at Miá and Pepe's house, Grady caught the first flight to D.C. at 6:05 a.m. Speaking to Jack through a burner phone, they set up a meeting with Barb Dent for 10 p.m. that night.

To everyone that worked with her, Barb had two readable expressions. Giddiness when she spoke of her beloved Labradoodle, and fury when things weren't going as planned. Her expression now, as Jack and Grady stood before her, was as blank as a virgin whiteboard. She sat erect on a park bench with a thousand-mile stare, swatting away mayflies and swirling clouds of gnats on a warm, still, Washington D.C. night.

Jack and Grady waited for her thoughts on the now earth-shattering Pippa Simpson e-mail. On Pippa's death, uncannily similar to that of the villagers. On the sheep massacre in Nevada, also uncannily like that of the villagers. On the Drones. Area 51. Jupiter. Sam Singh. Everything tied together and served to the seasoned SIO as a conspiracy du jour.

She swept off her glasses, rubbing her eyes, watching the swirling eddies of the dark Potomac. "Fuck me," she muttered, handing the mind-blowing Pippa e-mail back to Grady. "Fuck... me. And you still don't know the whereabouts of Sam Singh?"

Jack and Grady both shook their heads.

"We've got limited resources," Jack said. "Since this seems to be internal, and we've been compromised, we can only use Grady's Cobalt team for now."

Barb, her eyes subjugated and dark, peered up at the two men. "Guys, did we completely miss the boat on this thing or what? How'd we get so far behind these ass-hats?"

"Barb," Jack replied, trying to reassure her. "You can't keep something like this under wraps for this long without compromising people high up. We're talking about Pentagon level, Homeland Security, Congress. Maybe even the damned White House. We're not to blame here."

"No, Jack, we are," Barb said with disgust. "It's our job to protect the Homeland from enemies, both foreign and domestic. Even if domestic means our own fucking bosses." She sat back, folding her arms across her chest. "Okay, guys. What the hell do we do? Is this thing going to kick off or what?"

Grady nodded. "We have to assume it is. But it's my assessment that Singh was supposed to be eliminated by this Red Lancer security team. It's my assessment also that Singh may still be alive. I assess he's travelling to Woodrock. Jack and I think he may be willing to cooperate."

"Why Woodrock? Why would he cooperate?" Barb asked.

"Someone sabotaged his jet. The timing is too odd, and he's gone into hiding. They tried to kill him because he's threatened to talk, or maybe he just knows too much. He can ID every perp involved in this op. Whatever the reason, he's a danger to Pangea and whoever else is involved. He'll want to find someone he thinks is the least likely to be compromised, and he'll want to be near his facility."

"The Mayberry Sheriff?" Barb asked with a raised eyebrow.

"Yes, Ronan Quinn," Jack added. "Someone tried to assassinate Sam Singh. He's certainly looking for his pound of flesh. He's not your average billionaire."

Barb chuckled. "What, exactly, is an average billionaire?" She looked up at Jack. "So, this is a lot of supposition, Jack, and none of us has much in the way of concrete, actionable intelligence. What's the probability that Singh's heading for Woodrock to spill his guts to the Mayberry Sheriff?"

"About 70 percent," Grady said.

"I concur with Grady. 70 percent," Jack added.

Barb stood and brushed off her pants. "Well, that's damned near certainty in this business. And if that's the case, we have to go on the assumption that Sam Singh represents an existential threat to Iron Hand, whatever the fuck it is. So, we have to assume it's going to launch within the next 72 hours."

"We agree," Jack responded.

"Okay then," Barb said as she straightened up. "I'm sending a flash message to our embassies overseas. We're going to raise the terror threat level up a notch. But drones? Nerve agent? What am I supposed to tell them, Jack? We don't even know where this Iron Hand thing is going to start yet? Or who they, or we, or who the-fuck-ever is even attacking?"

"Tell them to be prepared for anything, Barb," Jack placed his hand on her shoulder. "We're out of time."

Chapter 34

The report of suspicious activity at the Old Ghost Town came across the radio in the early evening. Beth acknowledged the call, speeding along the highway toward the abandoned enclave left to prairie wildlife.

Beth, looping around the Kurtz Curve, gasped at the beauty unfolding before her. The Old Ghost Town sat silent and stark, the glass Pangea buildings on the bluff above it shimmered in the early evening sun. Tall prairie grass undulated in a light breeze, like waves on a golden sea set against a deep cerulean sky.

This time of year - early summer - was Beth's favorite. She and Fig would pack lunches, rendezvousing at Blanche Pond or on the banks of Spanish Creek. Fishing for Bluegill and Smallmouth Bass. Making love in the grass. Talking about life after, and outside of, Woodrock.

Beth was the first female deputy ever hired by the rapidly growing Woodrock police force. Quinn's predecessor, staunchly against hiring women, had run the Woodrock police department like a slap-happy white-boy frat house until relenting to the mayor's pressure for more diversity. Beth arrived soon after, and the all-male police club did not greet her arrival warmly.

Except for Fig.

He treated her with respect. Like a colleague. Like a professional. After two years of working side-by-side, Fig blurted out to her one evening

- his inner voice uninhibited by alcohol at the Woodrock 4th of July square dance - that he'd been madly in love with her from the day she walked through the doors of the station. They spent the night together. Then, after a few months of meeting in secrecy, Beth realized she'd fallen for him as well. Fig was kind, smart, a bit goofy, and honest to a fault. That was Fig in a nutshell.

The two kept their relationship out of the station and away from work. Quinn had no idea the two were secretly dating and, for now, they intended to keep it that way. Much in the same manner that Quinn had kept his friendship with Miá private in New York, Fig and Beth did the same, keeping gossip and perceived conflicts of interest at bay. No one had a clue about their feelings towards one another. No one except for Rose. Hiding anything from Rose was futile. That woman missed nothing.

Beth pulled off the highway and descended the rough, cracked and potted road that led to the main security gate for the ghost town. A small white sedan was parked on the flat gravel lot where the cyclone fenced gate led into the town. Beth pulled up alongside and stepped out of her patrol car. Walking around the mysterious vehicle, inspecting the interior through the windows with her flashlight. Beth called it in, asked for the dispatcher to run the vehicle's license plates, and told her she was proceeding on foot.

"Careful, Beth," Jackson Davis responded. "Keep an eye out for the bogeyman. Over."

"Ha, ha," Beth responded. "I'm living a Scooby Doo episode every time I come here. Over."

Beth pushed the rusted gate inward, and the gate resisted her intrusion with a *squeal* and a *clang* and a *rattle*. Doves fluttered off, a pheasant bolted from behind her, and a family of northern bobwhites scooted and bobbed across the dirt-covered street leading into the town. They're so adorable, Beth thought, as they vanished behind the old commissary.

But this place still gives me the creeps.

Walking along the street past the old failing buildings, a sudden vision flashed through her brain. A vision of being in an old western movie. Pistol slung on her hip, striding up a dirt-covered main street to a saloon, unsavory characters in black hats waiting to spring on her from cover. Even a couple of tumbleweeds bounced across the street.

A faint noise, like a creak, or the sound of an old board bending underfoot, came from behind her. She glanced over her shoulder. For a split second, she swore the figure of a man - or something - slipped behind the wall of the Post Exchange.

"Hello?" Beth called out. She turned, walking at a brisk pace toward the corner of the exchange. "This is the Woodrock police. You're trespassing."

Beth's pulse rose, she unclipped her holster and pulled her flashlight, shining the beam on the corner of the building. She didn't like this at all. The figure she'd seen was as black as night. Was that even a person? A ghost? A spirit?

Clutching the grip of her service weapon, holding her flashlight high over her head, she swung around the corner. A moment of confusion caused her to freeze, unsure if she was looking at a human being or a supernatural presence.

So many presumptions someone has when they enter a place preceded by the word *ghost*. A place where urban life had once thrived, now inhabited by coyotes and snakes and gophers and bird nests and beehives. Seeing only a dark shape, Beth's ghost-biased brain hesitated, because she saw only a shape. A shape moving toward her. In that second long delay that took her to rationalize what she was seeing, she froze. But instinct and training overrode her fear. Reflexively, she drew her service weapon. But that brief hesitation cost her dearly.

In the fading light, and for a brief second, she thought a pair of eyes were peering through a tightly drawn black hood. A muzzle flash lit up the narrow space between the two buildings, and a bullet struck her in the chest, lifting her off her feet and throwing her backward.

Why is this happening? Beth thought. What did I do to deserve this?

She hit the earth in a cloud of prairie dust and dirt on a street named after some random army captain who'd done some random heroic thing during the Spanish-American War.

BETH'S EYES SNAPPED OPEN. Struggling to breathe, searing pain shot through her as she gasped for air. She tried reaching for her pistol, resting just beyond her outstretched fingertips, but the assassin kicked the pistol off to the side. The killer, looming over her, was holding a Glock 19 and pointing it right at her head.

Then the hooded assassin placed his pistol behind him, tucking it into his belt. "Take shallower breaths," he said as Beth gasped for air. An odd voice, she thought. Educated. Precise. Not one that she expected from a cop killer. A cop killer that baited her into coming to a ghost town for an early evening murder.

The assassin kneeled, ripping her shirt open, and pulling at the Velcro on her service vest. He tapped the thin Kevlar with his finger. "Your vest caught it, good."

What the hell kind of cop-killing ninja-assassin is this guy? She thought. Is he taking me hostage? "Why'd you shoot me?" She gasped.

"Never mind that."

"What?" she said incredulously. "What do you mean, never mind?!"

The strange man grabbed Beth's wrist, pulling her up into a sitting position. He dusted her off. "You have a Kevlar vest, right?"

"How'd you know I had a Kevlar vest on?" Beth asked in a voice trembling with desperation.

The mysterious man's head moved back as if this question surprised him. "I assume all you police officers wear Kevlar. Am I wrong?"

"You assumed?!" Beth blurted out in astonishment. "You assumed?! You moron, you could've killed me! What do you want? What do you want from me? Are you the one who called in the disturbance? Is this a trap?"

The man removed his hood, and confusion swept over her. "Mr. Singh? Mr. Sam Singh?"

Singh nodded. "Call your boss. I want him here. Alone."

Beth suddenly blurted out a pained laugh, slapping her hand over her mouth and suppressing further laughter.

"What? What's so funny?" A bewildered Singh asked.

"Oh my god," she said, composing herself. "This is totally a Scooby Doo moment." Grimacing, she massaged her chest. "Oh boy, this really hurts. Why didn't you just come to the police station?"

"Because everyone in the world wants to kill me, Deputy Sawyer." Singh looked around. "And that may also include your chief. So, in exchange for his trust, I give him you. I have nowhere else to go."

Finally catching her breath, Beth was pretty confident she had a bruised sternum. "Well, this is all a bit melodramatic, isn't it? Plus, he's in Florida."

"No, he's not. He got back last night. And he's with some woman. I don't know who, but she looks intense." Nervous and agitated, Singh panned around the dusty town.

"How do you know all this?" Beth asked.

Singh grew impatient. "Deputy, just call him. Now."

Beth reached into her pocket for her phone. "You know," she said, tapping the numbers on the screen. "The chief's going to be, like, super pissed at you for shooting me." She pulled the phone to her ear. "So, good luck with that."

QUINN APPEARED ALONE, AS requested, an hour after Beth had placed the call and told him that Samir Singh was holding her hostage at the Ghost Town, adding that Singh had plugged her with his Glock 19 and fortuitously had decent aim. She was fine, she added, though really sore.

Quinn said he'd be there in one hour, and he would be alone. His voice was deep and dark, indicating some sort of mayhem was soon to follow. Quinn would not take an assault on one of his deputies lightly.

Now Quinn stood in the center of the street as the sun sank toward the crest of Kurtz Peak. Quinn, the sheriff of Ghost Town, and Sam Singh, the cattle rustler, Beth thought. All she needed was a church bell ringing in the background.

"You okay, Beth?" Quinn asked.

Sitting cross-legged on the street, Beth extended her arm and gave a thumbs up. "I'm fine, chief."

"Sam, you shot one of my deputies." Quinn's voice drifted down the street like a growl from a pit bull.

"Chief," Singh said, his voice carrying a more panicked tone. "How can I be sure you haven't been working for Pangea? They can pull in anyone they want. I'll release her when I know I can trust you. I need assurances." Singh sighed. His chin fell to his chest in defeat. "The entire world has turned against me."

Beth rolled her eyes. "Oh, spare me."

"I'm not working for Pangea," Quinn responded, stepping cautiously toward Singh and Beth. "No one has pulled me in. I haven't been bribed or bought or whatever it is you're implying. I don't do that."

"I know, chief. I know you're a good man. That's why I'm taking a chance on you."

"A chance? What is it you want from me, Sam?" Quinn stepped closer, and Singh told him to toss his service pistol to the ground. To Beth's surprise, Quinn unclipped his belt and let it fall. Surely, she thought, the chief must have some secret gun stored somewhere else? On his ankle? In his back pocket?

"Chief, something's going to happen, something terrible," Singh said in a desperate, trembling voice.

"Iron Hand?"

Stunned, a jaw-dropping surprise lit Singh's face. "How'd you know about that?"

"Iron Hand?" Beth asked, glancing between the two men. "What the hell is Iron Hand?"

"A terrorist attack using drones and a nerve agent, Beth," Quinn answered.

"What?" Singh stuttered, wide eyed.

"Yup. We know all about it, Sam. Now, put the weapon down and let me come get Beth."

"I don't trust you. I apologize, but I still don't trust you."

To Beth, Samir Singh looked like he wasn't getting whatever reassurances he'd expected to hear.

"Look," Quinn said, stepping to just feet away from Singh. "Up on that hill behind me, right now, at 500 yards, Marge is locked in on your forehead."

"Who's Marge?" A befuddled Singh asked. His eyes moved past Quinn, out the gate, and up to the hillside, now hidden in shadow.

"Yeah, chief," Beth asked curiously. "Who's Marge?"

"Marge is a precision MRAD sniper rifle. Attached to Marge is a very capable graduate of the Marine Recon Sniper Course."

Quinn raised his right hand into the air. A whisper rushed through the still evening, and dirt and dust erupted just inches from Singh's feet. The sound of a hollow metallic thud followed one second after. Singh leaped back in shock.

Rushing forward, Quinn grabbed the Glock from Singh's hand, tossing it behind him. "If you couldn't trust me, you'd already be dead, asshole."

"Are you going to arrest me?" Singh asked, hands on his hips in defiance.

"Nope," Quinn said.

Beth cocked her head back in surprise. Nope? She thought. What does he mean, nope?

"We're going to talk. But first-" Quinn swung his fist, catching an unaware Singh right on the jaw. The former billionaire stumbled backward, falling to the ground on his rear. "That's for shooting Beth," Quinn growled between clenched teeth.

Beth looked over at the stricken Samir Singh and shrugged. "Told you he'd be pissed."

Chapter 35

"How many drones?" Quinn asked in brow-raised astonishment. "How many did you just say?"

Sitting across from Quinn and Miá in the small interview room, the beard-stubbled, red-eyed, odorous Samir Singh, studied everyone's expressions of shock and dismay. He sensed their judgement. He sensed their hostility.

Behind Quinn and Miá, stood Fig, Beth, and Rose. Beth winced, massaging the deep blue bruise spreading across her chest from Singh's bullet.

"One and a half million," Singh sullenly replied. "In the past six months, we've shipped one and a half million Wasps. We've delivered them to what we call 'nests' all around the world."

"Dear God," Miá gasped.

"Nests," Quinn grumbled. "That's cute."

"Sounds really creepy to me," Beth said, rubbing her chest.

Fig looked down at her, eyes arched in half-moons of worry. "You okay, Beth?"

"I'm fine, Fig," she replied, gazing into his eyes.

A broad grin crossed Rose's face as Fig and Beth had their tender moment.

Miá leaned forward. "So, this is your come to Jesus moment, Sam. Time to lay it all on the table. We need to get the message out."

"To who exactly?" He replied edgily. "Iron Hand goes all the way to the top of the U.S. Government. Why do you think I came here?"

Sam Singh's usual confidence, charm, and disarming personality had fled in a musty Pennsylvania motel room with chocolate brown drapes and mysterious carpet stains. The masquerade was over. A deeply cynical Samir Singh was all that remained.

"So, Iron Hand is an act of terror, right, Sam?" Miá asked. "Where is this going to start?"

Singh looked at a camera in the upper corner of the room. "Is that thing on?"

"We're recording everything," Quinn said.

Singh leaned back and exhaled. "Iron Hand will begin simultaneously in 4,000 locations around the world. At least, that was how it was supposed to be."

"Supposed to be? What is it now?" Quinn asked.

"First, let me provide some context," Singh said, looking up at the ceiling. "About ten years ago, we - Jupiter and I - began a think tank in New York called The Center for Earth First. Jupiter and I shared the same view of the world. Our human population is exploding. Crime is exploding. Wars and civil strife, all of it… exploding. While all this is happening, human beings are consuming more and more resources and faster than we can replenish. We're like, forgive the overused expression, locusts. We always have been. Throughout history. But things really went haywire when we entered the industrial revolution. At the beginning of the twentieth century, there were one and a half billion locusts. By the end of the century, there were six billion locusts. And just two decades later, we hit eight billion locusts. For thousands of years, the earth could replenish what we took, but now, there's so many of us, we have a negative balance on that ledger. A negative balance that is growing by the year."

Quinn held up his hand. "Wait, let me get this straight. Iron Hand isn't a political terrorist attack, but… a green one?"

"You could say that. So, the idea of taking some sort of action to bring attention to this crisis grew into Iron Hand when Earth First completed their first study seven years ago. Based on an accelerating consumption of resources, the amount of C02 and methane being released into the atmosphere, massive deforestation, wars over resources, civil uprisings, increasing temperatures and the rapid loss of arable farmland…" Singh's voice faded as if he had trouble finishing the sentence.

Miá glanced at Quinn, waiting for the climax of this horror movie. "What, Sam? What?"

"They projected four billion people will be dead within a hundred years."

Quinn leaned back, waving his hand at Singh. "C'mon. Give me a break, Sam. How come no one else is reporting this?"

Singh's eyes widened in astonishment. "Are you serious, Ronan? Okay, let's just think about that for a second. I come out and tell the world that their kids and grandkids could all be dead in seven decades. That this is a 911. That's going to start a worldwide panic, right?"

"Right," Quinn said.

Singh slammed his hand down. "Wrong! We'll be ridiculed! We'll get dragged through the mud!" His voice transcended into a jaw-clenching growl. "Suddenly we're getting plastered on social media. Alarmists. Idiots. Dumbasses. Conspiring with foreign agents, or kidnapping children in the night and drinking their blood or some bullshit like that. No one wants to hear messages, Ronan. They just want to kill messengers! And pretend everything is normal so they can live their blissful little lives and act like none of this is happening!"

"He has a point," Rose added.

"Ronan, no one on this planet has the stomach for action," Singh's pleading and desperate eyes searched everyone in the room. "We're all too entitled. Our petty freedoms are too precious. We don't have eight billion people, guys. We have eight billion fucking ostriches! Asses to the sky and heads in the sand!"

"We're too entitled?" Quinn said. "That's pretty rich coming from a billionaire. And you don't know this is all going to happen."

Singh sat back, looking at Miá, pointing his finger at Quinn. "See? This is what I'm talking about."

Miá quietly sat, analyzing everything that Singh had just unloaded on them. "So, Sam, Iron Hand, I'm guessing here, so cut me some slack, is killing those four billion people who your study projects to die in seventy years? To just kill them all now? And save what resources we still have?"

"You need no slack, Miá. That's it, precisely. Cut our losses now and try to rebuild." Singh said. "That's Iron Hand, in a nutshell."

"That's it." Quinn slapped the table, shoving his chair back and standing. "I've heard enough. The four billion dead is going to start with you." He glared down at Singh. "You're a dead man." Pushing the table to the side with shocking ease, he moved at Singh like an enraged bear.

Miá grabbed his arm. "Ronan! Please! Stop it!"

Quinn yanked his arm from Miá's grasp. "Seriously, Miá," he said, his face now expressing horror. "Think about it. Half the damned planet.

That's Pepe, and Beet, and Alexx, and who knows… maybe everyone in this room. This plan is totally fucked!"

Singh shot to his feet. "It's not fucked! It's perfect! It's not only perfect, it's necessary!"

Everyone in the room stood frozen in place. Beth covered her mouth, eyes wide, pupils like pin tops. Not just the shock of two men having a bull-elk-showdown settling in on everyone in the small room, but also this astonishing and brazen plan to wipe out half of humanity.

The two men glared at one another, trembling with rage. Singh, at least half a foot shorter, was not backing down, and neither was Quinn. Blueish veins pushed their way out of Quinn's neck, causing Fig to squirm uncomfortably. In those few seconds of high temperature tension, someone needed to pour water on this fire. Miá, the clear-headed and sensible person she was, gently grabbed Quinn by his elbow.

"Okay, let's keep our cool, guys. We've got work to do," she said calmly. The tables and chairs were all put back in place, seats taken, and a collective sigh of relief filled the room at a war averted.

"Sam, if you believe in this so much, why are you here?" Miá asked. "Why did you come to us? Because it seems to me you've had a pretty big change of heart." Miá's soft-spoken words and deep walnut eyes calmed Singh. Quinn, dark and brooding, plopped back down into his chair, folding his arms across his chest.

"Pippa Simpson. She started it," Singh said with a touch of guilt carrying his words. "When Red Lancer put the…"

"Red Lancer?" Miá asked. "From the e-mail?"

"Yeah, that's her," Singh replied. "My bitch ex-girlfriend. Her name is Madison Sheppard. A true sociopath, guys. She may or may not be dead. I don't know. She tried to kill me. Twice."

"The plane crash?" Quinn asked.

Singh nodded. "Yes, and then again, two days later, in a motel room."

"Sorry about that, Sam," Miá said.

"Anyway, I tried to stop them from killing Pippa," Singh continued. "You must trust me on this. And when she died, suddenly, there was a face. A human face. This bright, beautiful girl was gone. Then there was an operation in Nigeria which, let's be clear, I had no part of, but a lot of people needlessly died. A sick little test carried out by Madison and Jupiter."

Quinn nodded. "We know all about Nigeria. Continue."

Singh's head tilted with curiosity. "Oh, so you know about that, too? Anyway, I'm suddenly seeing people. Actual people. Those poor villagers. Just living their lives. We took it all away." Singh said sullenly.

"Let's not forget Emma Massey," Quinn added.

"Who?" Singh asked, puzzled.

"Never mind, Sam," Miá said. "So that's what changed your mind? Pippa and the villagers?"

"Yes, and no. I realized I can't play God - forgive the cliche. This is not my choice to make. I don't know who everyone prays to here, but they must look down on us, watching how we behave, disappointed in how we all treat each other. Disappointed in how we treat this incredible gift we've been given. This planet. But it's not my choice. Not Jupiter's. If the planet needs a course correction, I just need to have faith. Faith that we all wake up. Faith that we will do the right thing. I think that's what Navi was trying to tell me."

"Or we'll get another asteroid like we got when God course-corrected the dinosaurs," Rose stated.

Singh nodded. "Correct. Only in this scenario, we *are* that asteroid. Humans are the extinction level event."

"So," Miá said. "Just to recap. Iron Hand is a million and a half drones loaded with nerve agent and they're going to buzz around the planet and kill four billion people. Correct?"

Singh sighed. "That's reductive, but yes, essentially."

"So how?" Miá asked. "Is it just random? And if you're trying to save the planet, aren't you kind of killing the planet along with these people?"

"It's not random," Singh replied. "The Artificial Intelligence in these drones is incredible. Developed by our top people, including some work by Pippa and her team. They scan people, looking for certain traits, features, diseases, and physical defects. Because we've been collecting everyone's DNA - whether you knew it - for the past thirty years, we know exactly what traits we need for a successful, flourishing human race. We eliminate those that don't meet a certain set of criteria."

Miá fell back into her chair, letting out a whoosh of breath. "Jesus Christ, Sam, this is a cull. You're culling humanity. And what about this nerve agent?"

"Yes, Genesis-6. Highly effective. Purely organic. It attacks the upper respiratory tract, causing the neck muscles to swell and constrict with such force it literally strangles the person to death. However, it's non-lethal to animals. Though there was the Nevada incident with the sheep. But we fixed that. Again, it targets a specific DNA. After a few minutes, the organic compounds break down and eventually become neutralized. Gone. As if it never existed."

"Genesis-6?" Rose asked. "Like from the Old Testament? Like Noah?"

Singh nodded. "For whatever reason, Jupiter likes everything to have a biblical touch."

"As a practicing Christian," Beth said with indignation. "I find that to be pretty f'd up."

Rose looked thoughtful. "God was going to kill all people for their corrupt ways…" she said. "Clearly, this Jupiter character thinks he's God, and this Iron Hand is some perverse ark."

Once again, Quinn looked like he was going to explode. "You people are sick."

"It was for the greater good!" Singh exclaimed. "There's also another reason for my, how do you say, coming out of the cold?" He looked into the camera. "The plan has changed. The primary focus for phase one is the United States."

Quinn slammed his fist down with a *whack!* "What!?"

"This was never about saving the planet, Ronan. Never. It's all about power. Me? The poor bastards at Earth First? We were all used. All of us. I was so naïve after Navi died. So vulnerable. I believed everything Jupiter told me." Singh rubbed his forehead. "Jupiter and the Five Horsemen want to install a new government - some might call it a dictatorship - and hold the rest of the world hostage. A smaller population is much easier to control, right? They want a new world order. And the survivors will obey, or they will face the wrath of a Genesis-6 carrying Wasp."

"Well," Rose said with a sigh. "Power does corrupt."

Quinn, lips twisted in complete disgust, had heard enough. "Okay, Sam. So, who are these Five Horsemen? And aren't there supposed to be four?"

Singh nodded. "I hope you're recording."

General Kelly Hanna, Air Force Chief of Staff.

Todd Sykes, Chairman of the Armed Services Committee.

Traci Burch, National Security Advisor.

Dr. Jorgen Branson, Science Advisor to the President

Erhard Otte, EU Ambassador to the United States.

A deep hush of reality smothered the small room, everyone gaping wide-eyed like he'd told them a comet was striking the earth. Singh asked for a pad of paper, scribbling down the names of the Twelve Apostles. People inside the Pentagon. People in Congress. Foreign dignitaries. Ambassadors. This was not just a U.S. led assault. Nations were conspiring against one another. Nations were conspiring on themselves. All looking for a seat at Jupiter's high council in his new world order.

Singh tried to scribble down as many of The Disciples as he could think of. "Sorry," he apologized. "I may miss a few for now. I'm exhausted."

The room was silent and filled with collective shock over this plan. A plan which, at any moment, may be unleashed upon the world.

"Look, Jupiter keeps moving the launch up," Singh added. "He's been panicking over the thought of leaks since the Nevada incident. He knows I'm still alive. Either he'll launch, or he'll have Madison and her goons kill everyone I just wrote on this paper to cover it up."

Quinn looked at the list of names provided by Singh. "Unbelievable. The President is in on this?"

Singh shook his head. "No. I know he's not part of this. He has no clue. When and if Iron Hand happens, he's going to be removed from power. Probably the VP as well. I wish I could tell you the identity of Jupiter, but I can't. No one can."

Rose had a thought. "Sam, you said four billion people. Surely this can't be done overnight?"

Singh shook his head. "No, it would take some time. A long time. Years even. But the drones run on uranium so they could, theoretically, stay active for decades."

Beth said she was going to throw up and rushed from the room, with Fig following close behind.

Miá turned to Quinn. "You've got to get this to Whitetail, Ronan. We need Grady to see this."

Quinn nodded in agreement. "So, Sam, can we shoot them down? How do we go about destroying them? Or better yet, how do we stop these drones from taking off in the first place?"

"Yes, you can shoot them down with rifles. They're not designed to be strong. They rely on stealth and speed. But I need your help."

"Sam, please," Quinn replied with an eye roll. "Give me a break. Whatever we need to do, we need to do. Let's get on this ASAP."

"What do you need, Sam? What can we get for you?" Miá asked.

"It's a who. I need Rich. He's a genius with code."

"Where can we find him?" asked Rose.

"He's locked away. He was having second thoughts as well. But they may still need him, so I'm sure he's still alive."

"Where?" Miá asked.

For the first time since this conversation started, Singh looked relieved. Even managing a slight smile. "At a place only a dozen people know of," he said. "And lucky for all of us, I am one of those dozen people." He turned to Quinn. "Ronan, we're going to need helicopters and lots of people with guns."

Quinn sat back and folded his arms. "Good. It's about time the FBI joined our little party."

SITTING ALONE IN THE interview room, Singh massaged his temples. Miá walked in with two cups of coffee.

"So, I will not apologize for Ronan's behavior," she said, sliding a dixie cup of coffee toward Singh.

Singh clutched the cup, slurping a drink of sweetened, cheap, police station brew, his eyes rolling up into his head as if he were savoring 12-year-old brandy. "I don't expect one," he replied, placing the cup on the table. "I'd have a similar reaction if the shoe were on the other foot."

"Good," Miá said. "Ronan has seen some really awful things in his life. I suppose I'm partly to blame for that. I always thought he could handle it. The blood. The trauma. We all have our breaking points. I just made assumptions without following through. You know what I mean, Sam?"

Singh nodded. "Probably more than ever."

She studied Singh's face. "This Iron Hand thing. Pippa's murder. It's all triggered things from his past. Do you know how he received the Silver Star?"

Singh shook his head.

"A Taliban member infiltrated his lines. Quinn's platoon leader called in an airstrike, but this infiltrator had stolen an IR strobe light. An Apache helicopter launched a Hellfire missile on the infiltrators' strobe, thinking it was a targeted enemy position. The blast killed Ronan's platoon leader and a dozen other Marines. Ronan took command, and a firefight went through the entire night. Not only did he save his platoon from being overrun, he also directed villagers into safe buildings for shelter, saving dozens of villagers' lives. That's Ronan. He sees the big picture. He sees good and bad. And he genuinely cares for people, but everyone has a breaking point and I think I was the one who eventually broke him."

Miá's voice trailed off in recollection. "I should never have sent him to that school..."

"So, you were a Marine sniper," an exhausted Singh asked, tipping back some station coffee.

Miá snapped back to the present. "What? Sniper? No. I graduated from the Recon Sniper Course. One of the first women to do so and with top marks. I'm proud of that. But they don't allow women in the infantry, so I was never an actual sniper. However, someone thought I'd be a general someday, so it was a box to check and I was pretty eager to give that course a try."

"A general?" Singh was genuinely curious about Quinn's and Miá's lives. They seemed to be the first real people he'd talked to in years.

"Yeah. I was top of my class at Annapolis, so they had plans for me. I ended up checking off professional boxes and, after two tours, they sent me to the Pentagon. I hated it. I guess you could say I was a victim of my own success. Still, though," she tipped back her own coffee and slurped. "Not bad for La Niña del Bronx."

"Aren't you bitter, though?" Singh asked. "Being a trained sniper, but not being allowed to be one? Because you're a woman? I mean, you seemed to be a pretty good shot to me, thank God."

Miá nodded. "Of course, Sam. But just a little. There'll be Marine infantry women someday. Badass sniper-chicks sneaking around in ghillie suits. But it just wasn't that time. I was a Marine officer. I go where they tell me to go and I don't gripe about it. And if I'm unhappy, then I make a change. So, I did. I left and joined law enforcement. I love the Marines. I loved being a Marine. In the Marines, there's integrity and honor. Codes Ronan and I will always live by. See how that works, Sam?"

Singh nodded. "I do. More than ever. I'm going to be standing before a tribunal at The Hague, facing charges for conspiracy to commit genocide on a level that makes Attila the Hun, Adolph Hitler, and Pol Pot look like hobbyists."

Miá slid her chair back and stood. "You're doing the right thing now, Sam. We can't dwell on mistakes we've made in the past." She gulped the coffee down, crushing the cup and tossing it in the wastebasket. "You look like hell, so try to get some rest. Things are going to get busy in a hurry, and we all need to be on top of our game."

Chapter 36

Madison, her hands folded neatly on her lap, sat perfectly still on an orange crushed foam chair in the principal's office.

Mr. Bosko - pudgy, sweaty, awful brown toupee stuck to his scalp - scribbled on a notepad with a number 2 lead pencil. She glanced at the clock on the wall. 2:45 p.m. Her gaze moved beyond the principal. A bronze *Principal of the Year* plaque, from who knows how many damn years ago, hung proudly on the wall. Madison drew in a deep breath. She was just going to sit here and wait. She could wait for hours. Days. Years. Never speaking a word. Driving Mr. Bosko into complete and total madness.

Finishing his scratching and scribbling, Mr. Bosko leaned back in his chair. "So, what about this rabbit?" He asked.

Madison shrugged.

"Miss Sheppard, your classmates believe you put the dead rabbit in Claire Pickett's locker. Why do they think you did it?"

Again, Madison shrugged.

Staring into her eyes, he leaned forward. "Look, Miss Sheppard-"

"You can call me Madison," she said, batting her lashes.

Bosko gritted his teeth. "Miss Sheppard. Everyone in your class thinks you're behind the dead rabbit."

"Did you know she was pregnant?" Madison said, tilting her head, twirling a lock of hair.

"Who? Claire?"

"Yep. Knocked up, bun in the oven."

"Okay, so what business is it of-"

"So, a dead rabbit. You know. The rabbit died."

Mr. Bosko's forehead crinkled with confusion. "What? What're you getting at?"

Madison sat back. "Glad you asked. You see, way back in the day, they used to test for pregnancy by injecting a live rabbit with a woman's hormones. Then they killed the rabbit and dissected the poor thing just to see the rabbit's ovaries. Can you believe that?"

"I don't get your point, Miss Sheppard."

She leaned over the desk, giving the principal the best view of her breasts, her voice falling into a low whisper. "Imagine. The entire value of your life, the whole reason for your existence, is to be born, have food jammed down your throat, get pricked by a needle, then get whacked and sliced open. All just to find out if some rando-human you give one-hot-damn about is a prego. That's it. Born just to do that crap."

Mr. Bosko shifted uneasily, glancing at her exposed cleavage and lacy bra. *Gotcha,* she thought.

She leaned back, crossing her arms. "So what if Claire has a dead rabbit in her locker? Now she knows that everyone else knows what a little leg-spreading slut she is. I hope she carries the dead rabbit around for the rest of her life just so she remembers what a useless twat she is."

Eyes wide and unblinking, Mr. Bosko stared at Madison as if she were going to catch fire. His bloated face seemed drained of blood, looking as pale as an autumn moon.

"Did you, or did you not put the-"

Madison shot forward in her chair. "I won't tell anyone you want to have sex with me," she said, flashing her eyelashes. "I promise, Mr. Bosko. I'll do anything you ask." She silently mouthed the word. *An… ee…thing.*

Now Mr. Bosko's pale moon face turned crimson. She thought he might just explode right there. Bits of Bosko splattered all over his stupid *Principal of the Year* plaque.

Buzzing his secretary, she hurried in, closing the door behind her.

The skittish, wire-thin secretary, Nancy, wearing eye-glasses that went out of fashion in the last century, leaned over to Mr. Bosko. Whispering to each other, Nancy's head suddenly jerked back. Aghast, she turned to Madison. Madison's stomach tingled, and the hair on the back of her neck stood up. Seeing Nancy's mortified expression, a rush of power over these two completely useless people filled her.

"Oh my," Madison gushed, leering at Nancy from her high heels up to her hair-bun. "And you too, Mrs. Graves? A threesome? Here on the desk? Are we about to get our kink on?" She flashed a wink. "You totally look like a whip and gag girl to me."

Trying to restrain himself from reaching over his desk and strangling Madison, the deep breath Mr. Bosko drew in seemed to last for minutes.

"Miss Sheppard," he said through clenched teeth. "You've been expelled from two schools now. Maybe your little teenage-girl blackmail routine worked elsewhere, but it doesn't work with me. I'm calling your parents."

"What?" Madison gasped.

"I think you need to see a therapist," Nancy added, a slight tremble in her voice.

To Madison, Nancy actually looked sympathetic. Can you believe it? She thought. She feels sorry for me! "Please, not therapy," Madison pleaded, her voice trembling.

"What are you afraid of, Madison?" Nancy asked. "They can help you."

"Oh," Madison said. "I'm not afraid for me. I'm afraid for them."

Mr. Bosko and Nancy glanced at each other.

Madison nodded. "Oh yeah, I'll wreck their damn brains. They'll be drooling in straightjackets when I'm done with them."

Mr. Bosko and Nancy Graves stared at Madison like she was Satan incarnate.

Ha! She thought to herself, high and giddy with power. You guys are scared shitless now, aren't you?!

GAZING THROUGH THE GREEN light of a nightscope, Madison recalled the day she tossed Mr. Bosko and Mrs. Graves onto their dumb heads with sentimental warmth.

"What was it like?" Yousef asked Madison from the driver's seat of a darkened sedan, his articulate Cambridge accent snapping her from her recollections.

She turned, squinting at Yousef. "What was what like?"

"You know, being with Sam. What was it like having to be with him for so many years? Massaging his ego? Pretending to love him?"

Pulling the night scope back up to her eyes, she studied the Woodrock Police Station, a block away from where they sat. "It was an eight-year puke fest, if you must know."

"Oh dear. So, how did you cope?"

Madison faced him, her lips crinkling at the sides. "Well, I fucked a lot of men, and I fucked a lot of women, I assassinated some people, and I did Pilates every morning. That's how I coped."

Yousef shook his head, pulling his own night scope up to his eye. "That'll do it, I suppose."

They sat in silence, carefully watching the station. That idiot Sam Singh is inside, she thought. Blabbing away to that alcoholic, wife-beating loser police chief from New York.

"Have you ever thought of having children someday?" Yousef asked, peering through his scope. "They have a way of bringing perspective to your life."

Madison's head snapped around. "What?" She asked, incredulous and narrow-eyed. "Are you seriously asking me that? Are you seriously asking me if I want to reproduce? Do I seem like I could be a mother? To anyone? To anything? How long have you known me? The fuck, Yousef."

Yousef chuckled. "A while. Point taken."

"And you? You still talk to that offspring of yours?"

"My daughters? Yes, I visit them as much as I can. They live in London with their mother now."

"What the hell do you tell them you do for a living? They don't know you're an assassin, do they?"

Yousef peered through his nightscope. "I tell them I work freelance for National Geographic."

Her head snapped back, a look of disgust crinkling her nose. "Jesus, Yousef."

"What?" He asked.

She turned back to the windshield, raising the scope to her eye. "That's really pathetic."

Fig and Beth strode out of the station.

"Hey, we've got action," she said, tapping Yousef's knee.

Moments later, Rose and Quinn followed Fig and Beth, and Sam Singh and Miá followed them. "Yowzah," Madison muttered, a tinge of arousal rising in her at the sight of Miá. "Who brought the Latina goddess?"

The group stood on the sidewalk, chatting to one another, then split up. Quinn and Miá strode down the sidewalk with Rose, then Rose vanished behind the building. Fig helped Singh into the back of a patrol car. He and Beth got inside, pulled out, and drove down the street.

"How'd you know Sam would come here?" Yousef asked.

"I guessed. He told me he was going to talk to the authorities. I think he actually trusts this wife-assaulting alkie police chief. Where else would he go?"

The patrol car stopped in the street. "Where are they taking him?" She mumbled to herself. Rose's car pulled out from the lot, with Fig and Beth and Singh in the patrol car following Rose down the street and turning left at the lights.

"They're taking him to that old woman's house," Yousef replied. "I'd bet anything on it. That's the safe house."

Madison nodded. "I think you're right."

"Want me to take care of it?" Yousef asked, watching Quinn and Miá step into the police SUV.

Madison shook her head, grabbing her secure comm device from the dashboard. "No," she mumbled, tapping on the screen. "I need you with me. We're going back to the complex to talk with Jupiter and get our marching orders." She looked at Yousef, sweeping back her hair. "As much as I'd like another shot at that prick, Rocky can take care of this one. When the time is right, Sam's going to meet a very gruesome death."

QUINN AND MIÁ LEFT the station in the SUV, heading to the outskirts of Woodrock and to Quinn's home. Fig and Beth, meanwhile, followed Rose driving to her quaint home on the outskirts of Woodrock - the Sam Singh safe house.

After alternating showers, Quinn and Miá fell down onto the couch, exhaustion sweeping through their bodies. They talked for a half hour, discussing random topics ranging from New York crime to the premise behind Iron Hand.

"I kind of get it with Singh," said Miá, having a brief philosophical moment. "Pepe's been investing in making his bakeries all carbon neutral. A five-year plan. Cleaner ovens, biodegradable packaging, solar power for his stores. Even an all-electric fleet of delivery trucks. But it seems too little too late."

Quinn let his head fall back onto the couch and closed his eyes and groaned. "Don't even tell me you're taking his side. And saving the world isn't even the plan. More like enslaving it."

"Of course I don't support it, Ronan," Miá replied, winding her head around, relieving tension in her neck. "His plan is repulsive. But, you know, I get the frustration." She yawned and stretched, moving her jaw around. "Anyhow, we should get some rest."

Quinn agreed, offering his bed to Miá. He'd actually rather sleep on the couch, he told her. Miá went to his bedroom, and moments later the light went out. It took all of half a minute for Quinn to collapse into a deep slumber.

HURRYING ALONG THE PATHWAY, he rushed through the lush green woods as a glorious dawn broke over Central Park. Ahead, a circle of uniformed police officers stood. Drawing ever closer, their faces faded into nothingness. No eyes or mouths or features of any kind.

They parted, letting him pass.

Looking downward from the crest of a drainage ditch, two completely nude women were lying on the damp ground. Peaceful, even appearing to be asleep, they held each other's hands. Quinn leaped from the crest of the ditch like he was on the moon, following a tremendous arc, eventually landing at their feet. So tranquil they seemed. Just two friends, out for an evening jog.

But where are their clothes? Why are they asleep?

Suddenly, and to Quinn's horror, their necks split open, blood gushing onto the ground in large crimson pools. Then blood spilled from their wrists. Then from their ankles.

A pair of eyes opened, staring deeply into his. He froze.

"Where were you when we needed you, Ronan?"

The second woman's eyes shot open. "Yeah, Ronan. What is it you even do?"

"Mr. Quinn? Mr. Quinn?"

Quinn forced open his eyes, stuck together with an adhesive of mucus. He sat up, rubbing the gunk from his eyelids, his shirt soaked with sweat. His heart pounded in his ears.

"Mr. Quinn?"

"Pippa? Is that you?" Quinn looked at the ceiling.

"Yes, hello. Is everything okay? I sense something. An anxiety. A fear."

"Well," Quinn responded. "We know about Iron Hand. We know who killed you and Emma. And they plan on killing billions more."

A harsh silence fell across the room. Pippa seemed to vanish again.

Quinn added another thought. "You know, Pip, had they not murdered you, I don't think we'd have uncovered all this. And if it hadn't been for your pictures, we'd never have figured out the plan." He thought she might be gone again, whizzing down her mystical corridor.

"Do you know Sylvia Plath? I read a lot of her works when I was young. I have a collection somewhere..."

"The poet?" He asked.

"Remember, remember, this is now, and now, and now. Live it, feel it, cling to it. I want to become acutely aware of all I've taken for granted."

"I miss my friends and Oscar and mom and dad. Life can be gone in an instant. Live every moment, Mr. Quinn, take nothing for granted. Leave that place where your demons live."

Pippa vanished, and one wave of emotion cascaded over another for the next ten minutes. He realized he might never see Beet again, or Alexx, or Miá, or Rose. Any of them could perish in this operation. Pippa was right. This is now, and now, and now. He swept his phone off the coffee table, frantically texting Alexx. He told her to tell Beet her dad missed her and would see her soon. To tell her he loved her.

MIÁ STEPPED GROGGILY FROM the bedroom, leaning against the doorframe.

"Who were you talking to? I thought I heard talking earlier," she asked sleepily.

Quinn shrugged. "No one."

"Was it your ghost?"

"She's not a ghost," he said with a sigh. He fell back onto the couch, dragging his hand down his face. "She's a castaway. Deserted between two worlds." He looked at Miá. "And I think I may have been the one who deserted her there." They gazed at each other for a moment, then Miá nodded.

"You should text Pepe," he added. "You should tell him you love him. You may not get that chance again."

Rising from the sofa, he walked to the kitchen, pulling out the scotch and gazing into the twinkling golden fluid inside. He thought back to Pippa's poem. Back to the sad and melancholic Sylvia Plath. He unscrewed the cap and dumped the remaining scotch into the sink.

Down the drain to the septic system, or down the drain to hell. Quinn didn't care.

He was done being a prisoner to his own fallibilities and demons.

Chapter 37

Whitetail received a flurry of messages from Ronan Quinn and his team, bringing Iron Hand into full view. Passing everything along from a PC in a freezing room inside the Pangea complex, including Singh's video confession, the secretive mole now sat inside ground zero for the demise of humanity.

Iron Hand: Toppling the U.S. government and replacing it with something tantamount to a global dictatorship. Nations all over the world, overthrowing their own people's wills just so they can have a seat at Jupiter's New World Order Council. An enslaved human race, forever living under the threat of execution by Wasp drones zooming around for decades.

What the hell? Whitetail thought, finishing up with a final message. This is what the nations of the world finally all agree on? This shit!

It all seemed like some dark, dystopian Hollywood movie.

As if all that wasn't horrible enough, Singh came forward with additional terror. In an event now referred to as The Great Sheep Massacre, Singh spoke of something entirely alarming. In that episode, the Wasp Queen had become sentient.

Though Singh believed Rich had dialed back the AI in the Wasp's ultra-powerful processors to keep self-awareness from creeping back into the Queen's silicon brain, could he be certain? It seemed Singh had been out of the loop for some time. And buyer beware, Whitetail thought. Jupiter was not just any run-of-the-mill god in Roman mythology. The god-buck stopped with him. Whoever this person named Jupiter is, he sure has a pretty damned high opinion of himself.

The mysterious Whitetail's mission as a mole was complete. A new mission came to them from above.

A new directive from their even more mysterious superiors.

Barb Dent's sour mood after learning a terror plot had been brewing right under their noses, reached near-core-meltdown as she, Bob Evans, Jack Fitzgerald, and Grady Freeman watched the video footage of Sam Singh blabbing all things Iron Hand to a camera.

Sitting in silence for what seemed to be an eternity, trying to process what they were learning, Grady mumbled something about this all being some sort of dream. Like this wasn't happening.

"So," Jack said, breaking the silence. "We were right about this being an internal job. But Jesus, guys."

Senators, White House staff, ambassadors, generals, foreign governments - these were just the names Singh knew. Who knows how many others were working at levels beyond Singh's knowledge horizon? There could be hundreds of little worker bees doing the day-to-day grunt work. Like who was placing the drones in these nests all over the world? And 4,000 nests to boot? That must be at least hundreds of individuals.

The four had never felt so isolated in their entire lives. Who could they trust? Anyone at all? With nothing left but Grady's Operation Cobalt team as fire support, bringing Iron Hand down was a long shot inside of a longer shot. And Operation Cobalt had lived as a fraud investigation, a far cry from terrorism. Forensic accountants and lawyers made up most of the team, as well as two Gen Z analysts who thought K-Pop was real music and *Breaking Bad* was an old-timey TV show. They weren't exactly Army Rangers, but they would just have to do.

Barb named them *The Bean Counter Berets* and *Wonder Twins.* "We're all going to die," she quipped in a nerve-laced half-laugh.

Before anything else, Barb and Bob Evans needed to reach deep into their espionage toolbox and find out who in the DOD they could trust. In Barb Dent's oblique, gray-filled spy world, you win and lose trust in mere seconds. A quivering lip. A distracted eye. A bead of sweat. A shortened breath. Barb and Evans, in their years as intelligence officers in the field, had learned all the subtleties of human behavior. In the electronic frontier of texting, direct messaging, social media, and other electronic communications, people can tell you a blue sky is orange, a zebra is a goat, and a fish is a banana. They can lie from behind a curtain of anonymity, typing out mistruths on a keyboard without having to face the scrutiny of a sceptic. Iron Hand was an octopus with tentacles reaching every branch of government and in every wealthy nation. So, the two spies would have to depend on that millennium-old technique of vetting humans. Looking them in the eye.

They had mere hours to accomplish this feat.

Jack lamented that this whole operation was like flying a plane through the Grand Canyon at night with no instruments and no windows. And on top of everything else, this Pangea programmer named Rich, sequestered away in a super-secret site named Juliet Tango, needed some sort of half-assed rescue.

Well, maybe sequestered. Singh wasn't entirely certain of this detail.

DRIVING THROUGH SNARLED TRAFFIC on the Capital Beltway at 10 a.m., Barb and Bob visited old friends and colleagues. They interrogated without interrogating. Carefully studying their subject's intonation, voice cadence, breathing rate, and eye movement.

Barb specifically targeted three people from the DOD for their knowledge of military procurement. Two of them, as she suspected, were aware of the closely guarded and highly secretive A-88 Wasps. They pointed her in the direction of the lead officer in charge of A-88 Wasp testing and evaluation, Colonel Aiden Taylor. Taylor had been running the Wasp program for a year. He'd also been trying to leave that program for a year. Taylor, an ex-fighter jock forced to eject from failing F-16 Vipers twice, had wound up medically disqualified from flying. The Air Force assigned him as program manager for test and evaluation of F-22 Raptors, and then A-88 Wasps, which he viewed as both a demotion and a threat to certain Air Force reconnaissance programs. This Taylor guy, Barb thought, seemed unlikely to be involved in Iron Hand. He was a sentimentalist, not a terrorist. Blissfully unaware of what his program was being used for. She half expected him to be furious over being a patsy for some Fortune 5 tech firm planning mass murder. But her well-seasoned cynicism half expected Aiden Taylor to be an Iron Hand soldier. If that's the case, she'd shoot him in the head.

In the afternoon, they assembled at a motel outside of Washington, D.C., hoping to stay away from prying eyes and ears. The Bean Counter Berets and Wonder Twins arrived one by one, predictably confused. Jammed inside the motel room, they stood in stunned silence while Grady explained Iron Hand and what they were going to be asked to do to stop it. They were all qualified to handle firearms, Grady reminded them, so now was the time to put that training to use. Some accountants hadn't fired their weapons for six months, and even that was at a training range. Two attorneys were former military officers, so at least they had that going for them.

They began drafting a plan.

Col. Aiden Taylor was selected as target A, and Rich, the Pangea programmer, as target B. Sequestered at Juliet Tango, the secret complex tucked away 80 miles north of Death Valley, the team didn't have concrete intelligence that Rich was even there or even still alive. But what operation in history didn't come without some intelligence risks?

So, after an hour, with scribbled notes and circles and squares and squiggle lines on yellow college rule notepads purchased from the local Office Max, the plan came to fruition.

Phase One: Red Team. Barb, Jack, Bob Evans and four Bean Counter Berets would fly immediately to Las Vegas. Tonight. As soon as this meeting was over. No time to even pack a toothbrush.

After Red Team arrived at the airport, they would commandeer a Janet Air 737 and fly to Groom Lake - Area 51- under the guise of sending in replacement support personnel. Bob Evans and Air Force Brigadier General Frank Smith, who'd known Bob for three decades and vetted eyeball to eyeball, would handle the subtleties of convincing the secretive Janet Air of their plan. The general was heading to Las Vegas as they spoke.

Once at Area 51, if Air Force security didn't engage them in a firefight, Red Team would inform Aiden Taylor of his contribution to a genocidal conspiracy and Barb hoped Taylor was in fact in the dark on Iron Hand and wouldn't force her to put a bullet in his brain.

Banking on success, two HH-60U Ghost Hawk helicopters and Air Force security, along with Barb, Jack, and two Bean Counter Berets, would fly to the California test site and rescue Rich. The CIA can't operate inside U.S. borders, Jack explained, for the benefit of the lawyers in the room. This was purely an FBI operation, with the CIA attached as advisors.

"Not that any of that matters now," Bob Evans said gruffly, striking up a cigarette. "But we don't want you lawyer types freaking out."

Phase Two: Blue Team. Ronan Quinn and 17 of his officers who, thanks to Quinn's foresight, had trained at the Old Ghost Town for hostage rescue and anti-terrorism, would set up a command post in the abandoned town. There, they would stage and prepare for an assault on the Pangea facility. The remaining Bean Counter Berets and the Wonder Twins would support Quinn and this assault. Since Quinn and his force had been training in the town for years, they hoped the sight of his force milling around just two miles from Pangea wouldn't sound any alarm bells. Getting through the first gate would be easy, as long as Rich and Singh's security badges still worked. Getting through the second gate would require some firepower. But the plan was not to invade the facility, but to draw Pangea guards to the gate in defense. This would help set up the next team.

Phase Three: Orange Team. Coined *The Geek Squad* (Barb named them of course), this team would comprise Grady, Rich, Kendrick, and two of Quinn's deputies, with Miá providing air cover. Their primary aim was to insert Rich and Kendrick inside the Pangea complex via helicopter. Once they were in, Rich would hack into the network, accessing the programs running the Wasps all over the world. Miá would support Blue Team with firepower from the helicopter until Orange Team was ready for extraction.

Grady sent a quick message to Whitetail, requesting an escort to the server room. Whitetail's response was unequivocal. They could not blow their cover, especially now, but knew someone who was willing to assist. Someone highly motivated by Pippa Simpson's death.

After the room was filled with excited and nervous chatter, Kendrick brazenly interrupted everyone and declared this operation as *Operation Endor*. Endor being the rebel-held forest moon from the movie, *Return of the Jedi*.

"Jesus Christ, Kendrick," Barb gasped. "You were, like, negative twenty years old when that movie came out."

"Star Wars never dies, Barb," Grady pointed out.

"Ashley is obsessed with Star Wars stuff," Jack added. "Haven't you been keeping up?"

Evans smacked his hands together. "I fucking like it!"

Pushed up against the walls, the Bean Counter Berets all agreed to the name. One of The Wonder Twins had no clue what any of them were talking about.

Jack Fitzgerald made a final unambiguous point with alpine-lake clarity. Under no circumstances was Sam Singh to take part in this Op. Jack needed Singh alive to testify against Jupiter's Horsemen, Apostles, and Disciples. In any case, Barb and Bob still didn't trust him. Not any further than they could throw him.

After channeling this plan back and forth between them and Quinn through Whitetail, Red Team rushed to Dulles Airport, leaving for Las Vegas on an FBI private jet. The Blue and Orange Teams would head out on commercial flights in the early morning to meet up with Quinn and his team. No FBI jackets. Men remain unshaven and unprofessional. Women wear make-up and jeans. Don't look like law enforcement, Jack implored them. They were undercover now.

No one knew when Iron Hand was going to launch. Perhaps it already had. Since Singh was roaming around the countryside, Jupiter may have pulled the trigger in a panic. What a relief it would be, said Jack, if this Madison person and her assassins just smoked everyone involved in Iron Hand rather than launching it. Grady muttered something about disappointment at none of them seeing a day in court.

What the teams, and even Samir Singh to an extent, didn't know, was that many of the Wasps had not yet reached their nests. Jupiter had pushed the launch date up in his sweaty panic over information leaks, but not all the way to today, or even within the next two months. And Samir Singh was key in the design, development, and overall planning, but the Apostles determined and coordinated the Wasp's final nesting spots. Many of the deadly drones were still sitting harmlessly in warehouses across the globe, packed in crates labeled *Children's Toys,* making Iron Hand seem even more vile than it already was.

More than enough Wasps, however, were ready to cause chaos on a global scale, and certainly enough to topple the United States off her perch. The teams just had to be fast enough, and precise enough, not to force Jupiter's hand before they'd succeeded.

A difficult task indeed for an operation drawn up on a notepad in less than an hour, passed through a mysterious mole no one had ever seen, and not anything any of them had the time to train for.

CHAPTER 38

AT 5:48 P.M., ON A pleasant June Friday, Operation Endor - or what Bob Evans referred to as the "paper, staple, and glue Op" - kicked off. Red Team flew at maximum speed from Dulles International, to Harry Reid International, in an unmarked FBI jet, call sign *Skylight Four-One.*

Five hours later, the jet taxied in, creaking to a stop on the north parking pad of the airport, where Gen. Smith and a cigar-chomping Air Force chief master sergeant awaited the team. Shouting over the constant roar of departing passenger jets, the group went over Phase One. The chief - a superintendent of the security personnel at Nellis AFB - was certain that the security forces at Area 51 would cooperate if he were there.

"Those are my damned guys, sir!" the chief shouted. "I'll get them in line!"

"Right on time!" Gen. Smith yelled, as the scream of turbofans and blinding taxi-lights of a Janet Air 737 - the secretive air shuttle for secretive people who work at secretive bases - filled the noisy ramp. Callsign *Janet Five-Zero,* the 737 didn't even shut down. A ladder extended from the front passenger door and the team scrambled up and took seats in the cabin. Barreling down the runway 7 minutes later, Janet Five-Zero lifted off, hauling this hastily cobbled force to Area 51.

The X factor for this whole operation was Colonel Aiden Taylor. The beleaguered A-88 Wasp whisperer was part of Iron Hand or he wasn't.

Adding to everyone's angst, security personnel at Area 51 were trained to shoot any unauthorized personnel on sight. Not a single member - not General Smith and not even the cigar-chewing security forces superintendent - had authorization to set one boot down on the painfully restrictive air base.

For phase one to work, Endor had to be a complete and total surprise.

Sitting in the middle of the cabin, Jack and Barb were both lost in their thoughts as the jet made the short trip to Area 51.

"How long have we known each other, Barb?" Jack asked her, while she gazed into the night through the cabin window.

Barb snapped her head around, a curious expression crossing her face. "I don't know, five, maybe six years?"

Jack shifted around in his seat to face her. "Hey, is that story about you true? Did you really drug the son of an ambassador, tie him naked to a hotel bed, and threaten to kill him with a pair of high heels?"

Barb shrugged.

"That you'd drive a high heel right through his eye socket if he didn't return something he stole from the embassy?"

"You know I can't talk about operations, Jack," she muttered, turning back to the window. But after a few moments of staring into the complete darkness of a desert night… "They were ruby red stilettos." She turned back to Jack with twinkling eyes. "Prada's, actually. Never tell me I don't have good fashion sense. The son of a bitch wisely cooperated."

After a few moments of searching each other's eyes for reassurance, the fates of their own lives at stake, Barb spoke up. "Did you call Anna?"

Jack nodded. "Yeah. She's taking Ashley to my in-laws in Hawaii. Didn't know where else to go. How about you? Call anyone?"

Barb turned back to the window. "Yeah, but the Labradoodle never fucking picks up."

AT 11:45 P.M., JANET Five-Zero touched down at the Groom Lake Proving Grounds, Area 51. Taxiing into the parking ramp and shutting down, everyone onboard performed a quick weapons-check.

The two ex-military lawyers on the Red Team seemed unfazed by all this, much to Jack's relief. Even the two accountants, a former women's pole vaulter at Ohio State and a guy with thick glasses who could pass as a CPA poster child, checked their weapons with calmness and precision.

The general walked out through the cabin door first, followed by Barb, Jack, the chief master sergeant and the rest of the Red Team. Base security, which always met the Janet flights on the tarmac, at first seemed confused - unsure of whether they were to shoot these people or if this was an exercise to test their skills. Two of the intruders wore CIA windbreakers, four wore FBI windbreakers. There was a general, and also their cigar chewing superintendent from Nellis. Thinking this must be an exercise, the team's leader, TSgt Groves, told Red Team to lay face down on the hot asphalt.

Rushing to a perplexed Groves, the chief master sergeant pulled him away from the group, speaking with him alone. Grove's mouth dropped in shock as he looked over at the team now assembled below the 737.

The base commander arrived ten minutes later, followed by Col. Aiden Taylor. Standing next to the jet, fan blades *creaking* and *clanging* in a hot night breeze, Gen. Smith, Barb, Evans, and Jack delivered the grim news to Taylor. He was stunned when he learned of his participation in global genocide. A good sign for Barb, who was ready to shoot Taylor on the spot if he didn't cooperate. Then Taylor dropped to one knee, looking ready to vomit.

The general told the base commander that all communications needed to be secured for twenty-four hours. Emergency traffic only. Then he requested two Ghost Hawks and flight crews, plus the base security team. Tsgt Groves spun on his heels and gathered his force together. Ghost Hawk crews rounded up, they received briefings, and as the flight engineers readied their helicopters for flight, the pilots hastily assembled a low-level tactical mission to the ultra-secret site, Juliet Tango, just on the California side of the border.

Aiden Taylor told the group that roughly twenty Pangea security members would be at the site to greet them, as well as one Augusta Westland helicopter that was a hell of a lot faster than the Ghost Hawks. "It might be a good idea to disable the Westland," he said. Groves assigned that to two Senior Airmen and an Airman First Class who looked barely old enough to even shave.

At 12:30 a.m., the Ghost Hawks lifted off in swirling clouds of desert dust and sand. Bob Evans, a lawyer, and the CPA poster child remained behind. If Jack and Barb didn't return, they would take command of whatever remained of the Red Team.

FOR FORTY LONG MINUTES, the pilots flew nap-of-the-earth, hugging the rocky terrain to elude detection. The crews slipped on their Night Vision Goggles, then switched off their Ghost Hawk's beacon and strobe lights.

Jack peered through the open door of the helicopter, seeing nothing but blackness. He shifted uncomfortably in the webbed seat and glanced over at Barb. Her eyes closed and lips pursed tight, she looked as if she were meditating. He turned back to the flight engineer leaning outside, scanning the pitch darkness through his NVGs, talking with the pilots over the interphone. The engineer swung the mini-gun into place and turned to his passengers. "Five minutes!" he shouted.

Go time.

The two Ghost Hawks, *Casper One-One* and *Casper One-Two,* crested a knife ridge at 12:55 a.m. A Pangea guard, stationed just below the crest, ducked instinctively as the helicopters thumped just feet over his head. As the two helicopters flew along the other side of the ridge, he radioed his team.

Juliet Tango greeted Casper One-One with heavy fire as it touched down hard on the apron. Circling overhead, Casper One-Two sprayed the area with mini-gun fire as cover. Two security forces personnel fell immediately as they exited Casper One-One, hit by gunfire from the guards.

Bullets clanged as they struck the helicopter. The pole vaulter rolled her way to the door and fell onto the ramp. Wincing and shielding herself from gunfire, Barb shouted. "Son of a bitch!"

Pushed from behind by Jack, then shoved indignantly through the open door, Barb fell out and next to the pole vaulter. Overhead, more gunfire burst from Casper One-Two's mini-gun. With passengers out the door, a crippled Casper One-One lifted off and Casper One-Two landed, dropping off Col. Taylor and the remaining force.

Red Team moved across the ramp as fast as possible, with an intense firefight ensuing between them and the guards. As they pushed their way toward the trailers and a large gymnasium structure at the rear of the complex, Jack noted the helicopter Taylor had warned them about was missing.

Still under heavy fire, and now too close to the guards to receive air cover without being hit themselves, TSgt Groves commanded his team and the FBI agents supporting them to split in two and try a pincer movement. Then Groves followed Barb and Jack as they snuck around to the far trailer where Singh said they would keep Rich the programmer. Bursting through the trailer door, a guard immediately shot at them. Barb dropped to one knee, putting a round right through his forehead, creating a moment of incredulity for Groves.

Methodically moving from room to room, the three arrived at a closed office. Groves kicked in the door, finding Rich on his knees with a guard holding a pistol to the back of his head. The guard spun around, exchanging rapid fire with Groves. Groves cried out in pain, doubling over, clutching his right shoulder, and the guard fell to the floor like a sack full of stones.

Jack dashed into the office, yanking Rich up by his collar. "Are you Rich?" He asked. "Are you the programmer?"

As pale as bleached flour, Rich barely managed a nod.

Outside, the firing ceased. Jack helped Groves to his feet, and the four hurried back out of the trailer. The remaining guards, Jupiter's so-called superior force, had surrendered to a rather lightly equipped and inexperienced security team. This development did not surprise Jack. Private security was usually much less motivated than professional military security. Jupiter clearly didn't pay these guys enough. The pole vaulter suffered a wound to her leg and Aiden Taylor lay dead on the tarmac along with three of Groves' security team, with five more being wounded.

CASPER ONE-TWO TOUCHED down to extract Jack, Barb, Rich and the wounded. A bullet-ridden Casper One-One would remain at Juliet Tango with the rest of Grove's team and secure the site.

As Casper One-Two lifted off, Rich thanked them for the rescue. "But you should know!" he shouted over the beating of rotors. "Madison Sheppard and some Middle Eastern guy already came and left!"

Barb gritted her teeth. "Damn it all to hell! Yousef! And what did this Madison bitch want!?"

"All my codes for the drones!" he responded. "With those, they can launch Iron Hand! We must go back to Woodrock!"

Barb glared at Rich. "Please tell me you didn't give them away!"

Rich glanced between Jack and Barb. "Well, um, I kinda…"

"Goddammit!" Barb threw her head back.

Rich threw his hands up. "They were going to kill me!"

Jack put his hand on her knee. "Don't worry about it, Barb, we still have time!"

Barb turned back to Rich. "How far ahead of us are they!?"

"About two hours!" Rich yelled back. "But I have this!" He reached into his pocket, pulling out a slick, rectangular device.

"Your phone!?" Jack yelled.

"My secure comm device and my insurance! Say, how'd you know about all this, anyway?!"

Jack yelled back. "Sam Singh told us!"

A satisfied grin stretched across Rich's face, and he slapped his thigh. "I knew it! I knew Sam would shut this down!"

"I'd hate to be the bearer of bad news!" Barb shouted. "But we haven't shut down jack shit!"

A loud *clang* hit the side of the helicopter, followed by another. The flight engineer at the door whipped his head around.

"Heads down!" he shouted. "We're taking fire!"

THE AUGUSTA WESTLAND THAT was supposed to be, but clearly was not, at Juliet Tango, had been zipping its way back across the desert after dropping off Madison, Yousef, and twenty Wasp prototypes at the airport. The Westland crew, hearing the site was under attack, sped toward the site, but the radios from the base had since fallen silent. Seeing a lone Ghost Hawk flying low across the desert under the light of a rising full moon, the Westland crew put on their own night vision equipment, banking steeply toward the lumbering helicopter.

A door slid open, a high-powered rifle appeared, and a shooter opened fire.

"WHAT THE HELL!" CAPTAIN Mitch Myers yelled into the interphone. The copilot craned his head around, trying desperately to see behind the Ghost Hawk.

"Pilot to engineer," Meyers frantically asked over the intercom. "Are we taking fire? What the hell's going on back there?"

"Roger," the engineer's voice crackled back. "I think I see a helicopter at our eight o'clock."

An amber light illuminated on the instrument panel. "Hydraulic low light," stated the copilot.

"Engineer! Where is he!?" Shouted Meyers.

"Coming up on our left! He's at nine o'clock, co-altitude… break left!"

Meyers pushed the left pedal, thrust the collective forward and turned steeply into the Westland.

Clang! Clang! Two more shots struck the Ghost Hawk.

"For fuck's sake Jimmy! Where is he now? Keep the positions coming!" Meyers leveled off the Ghost Hawk. "Jimmy," he said to the flight engineer, "I'm going to slow down and let him come up on our left. Try to scare the son of a bitch off with the mini-gun."

Meyers pulled back on the stick and the Ghost Hawk pitched up and slowed. Then he thrust the nose down and leveled the helicopter.

Brrrrrrrrt. The sound of the mini-gun from the rear reached the cockpit.

Then… silence.

CLUTCHING HIS HEAD AND bending over in his seat, Jack heard the minigun go off and, with one eye, glanced at the door. The engineer was leaning through the door and Jack thought he'd fall right out. A bright orange flash filled the cabin, and for a moment, he thought they were all dead. Then the engineer thrust his arms into the air as if he'd just scored a touchdown. Wearing an expression of complete shock, he turned and extended his thumb to the startled passengers.

"Un-fucking believable!" he shouted. "I just got an air-to-air kill! In a goddammed helicopter!"

Any celebration of the greatest inadvertent air-to-air kill by a helicopter in history was short-lived as amber lights lit up the panel in front of the two pilots. The engineer moved forward to the cockpit, and the three crew members dove into emergency checklists and began solving lots of problems.

Putrid, oily smoke pouring from the engine nacelle, and a rather heavy vibration causing dismay amongst its occupants, a fuel-starved

Casper One-Two landed at Area 51 at 2:33 a.m. As the crew shut the tough old helicopter down, Jack, Barb, and Rich, rushed to Bob Evans and Gen. Smith, standing near the Janet Air 737.

"It's fueled and ready to go!" the general yelled over the scream of the 737's jet turbine APU. "The pilots have it from here on! They'll take you to Woodrock!"

"Holy fuck, did we get lucky," muttered Barb as they all took seats in the cabin.

Jack drew in a deep breath of relief. "Oh yeah, we did. But I think we met Jupiter's B-Team. The A-Team's waiting to greet us at Woodrock."

Jack's assessment was correct. The specialized security forces of Pangea, all former special forces, had assembled at Woodrock, leaving the now less-than-relevant Juliet Tango lightly guarded by some of Madison's basement level, low-paid security.

Phase one of Operation Endor had been an overall success through pure luck and good fortune. Soon, the time would come for Ronan Quinn and the Blue Team in Woodrock to prepare for the fight to save humanity. That fight would not be as easy, and there would be casualties.

Many casualties.

Chapter 39

Something had gone wrong.

According to Madison, Sam Singh spent hours at the Woodrock Police Station and probably told everyone everything. After sending Madison and Yousef to recover Rich's codes and destroy the prototypes in Nevada, everything had fallen silent. Not a peep. Not a word. Not from Madison and Yousef. Not from anyone at the site.

Jupiter paced back and forth in his mahogany study. Grunting and moaning and rubbing his sweat-beaded forehead, he hyperventilated in bursts of regret and second-guesses. He should never have tried to kill Sam. Instead, he should've just kept placating him until they were ready to launch. Iron Hand was falling apart.

Behind an oak desk in Jupiter's lavish study was a large, enviable collection of books. Everything from history to science to philosophy. Arranged in rows of worn browns and tans and soft greens, Jupiter liked to show his library to guests because it made him seem more authentic. More intellectual. More superior. But the underlying truth about his not-so-modest library was that he'd read none of these books. He couldn't name a single author, a single title, or even the subject of any one book. His young intern had gone to used book stores and flea markets to build this diverse cross-section of decorative literature.

Pacing in front of his wall of literary eye-candy, Jupiter was unsure what his next steps were. His heart racing and his mind speeding like a bullet, Jupiter - mastermind of Iron Hand and purveyor of wisdom through a voice scrambler - was having a panic attack.

For all of Jupiter's bullshit speeches and lectures, he was no different, perhaps even less than those whom he commanded. Jupiter was no genius, and he was certainly no visionary, though he often professed to be one. One could say his Iron Hand vision wasn't even his. It didn't come to him in a fever dream, or standing before a cross in a chapel listening to instructions from God. The idea for Iron Hand materialized after watching *War of the Worlds* in a theater. Alien machines zapping people on the big screen. That was it. That was Iron Hand. Many thanks to the broad imaginations of H. G. Wells and Steven Spielberg, and none to the power-grabbing man as shallow in thought as a heat-baked Texas pond in the summer.

Clutching his chest, Jupiter paced back and forth, wearing the patterned rug in his grand study thin. Worrying about how, without the full force of the Wasps, and with Sam Singh spilling the beans, he would achieve his plan. This upstart world emperor who fantasized about wealth and gluttony. Who believed in the deadly impacts of anthropogenic climate change like one would believe in the tooth fairy. Who had no more will to save the planet than one does for saving bathroom mold.

He used Samir Singh to build him an enormous company, preying on Samir Singh's deep grief after losing Navi to suicide. A company which Jupiter siphoned millions of dollars away from and used as a shell organization to build an enormous drone army, all under the guise of sharing common planet-saving views and a hatred for society. The Center for Earth First was just a sham and Jupiter couldn't give one damn about any reports those miserable people pushed out. In fact, he read none of them. He let his intern do that boring work, preparing talking points and explaining some of the "big words" that confused him.

His loyal cult-like following believed in him because he was elusive and secretive. An Oz behind a curtain of anonymity. Mind tricks. Manipulation. A room full of mirrors. Telling his teams that the sky was orange and fish were bananas because you can do that when no one can see you and you're named after a Roman god and quote bible verses. Some of his rambling motivational speeches on conference calls were even pre-recorded. He'd rather spend his time plying the waters off Nantucket in his prized 60-foot yacht than speaking to those morons.

This terror act was really all about gaining wealth and an untouchable status in society where no rules or laws applied to him. *Humans were meant to be enslaved;* he'd told the Horsemen before their meeting with Samir Singh. *Too stupid to be allowed to roam free and at their own discretion.* The Apostles and Disciples themselves were a mixed bag of those who truly believed they were saving the planet and those who could give one damn about it. After all, when and if the world did end, Jupiter and his people would've all passed on. Let people's grandkids deal with this climate crap. And killing half the planet was counterproductive. Who was going to be left to work in the factories? Grow the food? Fix the roads? Better just to crash America and hold the world hostage with toxin-laden flying drones. The Wasps would simply peel away uncooperative anarchists like one would peel away the unwanted husks of an ear of corn.

Devoid of any philosophical or analytical thought, yet full of self-aggrandizing stratospheric ambitions, Jupiter was a truly contemptible man.

But panic drowned him now as he became a victim of his own plans. Singh had talked. Juliet Tango had gone silent. No word yet from Madison.

He had to make a decision.

Iron Hand was a half-baked cake, with not nearly enough active Wasps to complete the objectives. The operation, as it stood now, would merely grant him an appointment with a noose in The Netherlands. Iron Hand would fail and they would come after him. Somehow, they would find him. They always do. And even with his Five Horsemen manipulating all those three-lettered agencies, it could still all come back to him like a boomerang.

Jupiter, strands of gray hair slicked over a shiny liver-spotted scalp, short in stature, empty-eyed, and beak-nosed, would've stunned his cultists with his appearance. Like the confusion one would have when expecting to see a turtle-necked Steve Jobs, only to see a t-shirted Steve Buscemi instead. Even the tone of his voice had an odd, adolescent high pitch to it. He was anything but inspirational. He was a manipulator. A bully. A con. Willing to throw his own mother under a bus if it meant success. Now, sweating feverishly in his study, surrounded by books he had never read, in a house he bought through wealth that was not of his making, he reached his decision.

Iron Hand had to go away. The entire thing needed to be called off. Killing millions of innocent people was not a cause he himself felt was worth dying for.

After hours of being kept in the dark, and an uncomfortable silence from Juliet Tango, Madison and Yousef informed him they'd landed back at Woodrock with Rich's codes. Jupiter spoke in his very best, all-powerful Deep Throat/Alexa's voice, delivering his usual monotonical buffet of wisdom. He told Madison and Yousef that Iron Hand was off. Under the circumstances, there were not enough drones to do what needed to be done. Time to shut down and retreat to fight another day.

"You coward," was Madison's response. "It's gone way too far to stop now. We just flew all the way to Nevada and back because you asked us to. Now you're changing your mind while Sam is telling everyone with a set of ears about Iron Hand. So, get back on the bus or get left at the station. I'm in charge now." The call ended, leaving Jupiter mortified. Madison Sheppard had everything she needed to move forward with Iron Hand and, in an instant, Jupiter's relevance vanished like a Dodo.

He slumped down into his chair. Cupping his hands over his mouth, he attempted to slow down his breathing. A thousand thoughts passed through his head, barely comprehending a single one of them. According to his panicked, synapse-riddled brain, Jupiter had but one course of action.

Snatching a revolver from his desk drawer, he rushed into the kitchen where his pretty young intern sat at the counter busily tapping away on her laptop. Editing speeches and videos, posting statements on social media, she didn't know these would be the last seconds of her life.

Slipping up behind her, he shot her in the back of the head. Then, after she fell to the floor in a heap, he shot her five more times. Firing until the hammer striking the revolving empty chamber was the only noise echoing in his kitchen.

Madison is truly a sociopath, he thought, while standing over the body of the young college sophomore he'd just shot to death in his own kitchen. A woman without a motive, but a thirst for power and the moral compass of an Anglerfish. Luring her prey with the incandescent light of her stunning beauty, then swallowing them whole with cold indifference.

The intern's raspberry red blood pooling on the kitchen floor, Jupiter wondered about how he'd spent years betraying Samir Singh and years betraying his own nation. Now Sam Singh was betraying him, and Madison Sheppard had been betraying them both all along.

In his steadied state of panic, Jupiter decided to revert to business as usual. To hide in plain sight. To go back to work. But first, he needed to wipe clean all his connections with the Horsemen, Apostles and Disciples. To sever every single link between him and the Iron Hand operation.

In a rather stunning twist of fate, he would help convict all his worshippers of attempted genocide if that moment came. In courtrooms and at hearings, none of his followers would even recognize the man sitting before them, helping send them all off to prison, was the man they'd followed to the edge of this cliff to begin with.

Anonymity and apathy afforded certain privileges. But first things first, he had a body to dispose of.

Part 6

The Vengeful Rage of Pippa Simpson

Chapter 40

At 6:18 a.m., Janet Five-Zero touched down at Woodrock Regional Airport with its 190-pound cargo of Rich Hansen.

Jack Fitzgerald, Bob Evans, and Barb Dent handed Rich over to Grady Freeman, then left for D.C. Jack and Barb were launching Operation Endor phase four; bringing Jupiter, The Five Horsemen, Apostles, and Disciples to justice.

Reunited once more, Singh and Rich embraced. Rich described how he'd been mere seconds away from being executed before TSgt Groves kicked in the door and shot his executioner.

Quinn's deputies arrived at the station at noon - all three shifts - and assembled on the floor. As Quinn predicted they would, his deputies stared at him, slack jawed and unblinking, as he spoke. After all, few people wake up in the morning expecting to be pulled into a global terrorist plot. But then most people don't wake up expecting to be in an earthquake or a plane crash either. The difference here being that Woodrock had flipped the script.

Addressing the Blue Team on the floor, Rich tried to navigate the bewildered deputies back to the present. The way he understood things, based on conversations he'd had with Jupiter and the Apostles, roughly 700,000 of the 1.5 million Wasps had found their way to their designated nesting spots around the globe. 300,000 of those Wasps were nested in the U.S. alone, patiently awaiting orders near such cities as Bakersfield, Eugene, San Diego, Charlotte, Buffalo, Austin, and Reno. Tens of thousands more were located around the nation in much smaller groups near low-density towns, their citizens oblivious to the threat of Wasp Queens eradicating their communities in mere hours. Outside the United States, Wasps lay in wait, preparing to strike near Mumbai, Lagos, Chiang Mai, Cape Town, Perth, Cologne and Bucharest, as well as hundreds of much smaller towns and villages across all nations. It'd been quite an undertaking to get that many drones prepped. Something Jupiter had, before that moment, been immensely proud of. So, if Rich was able to hack into the network, he'd take control of the Wasps with all the Iron Hand codes stored on his secure device.

For the first time in a long time, or perhaps ever, Quinn might just prevent a crime rather than investigate one after the fact. Arriving to find dead children in a school and women raped and murdered in Central Park. He owed it to those who came before him. From his lost brothers and sisters in the Marines to all the murder victims in New York. But his motivations boiled down to something simpler. He had to protect Beet and Alexx.

They sat atop a very tall human pyramid.

Introducing Miá, he summarized her resume of experience, resulting in some raised eyebrows. Beth was more than impressed. Miá represented an inspiration Beth had never had, developing quite a girl-crush on the athletic, bronze-skinned, homicide captain, former Marine, and trained sniper. To her, Miá was pure feminine power.

Rich finished up the briefing, informing the deputies that while most of the Wasps at Woodrock sat crated for shipment, up to a thousand were in various stages of assembly. Madison could easily get some of those ready for flight, and many of those might be far enough along in development to carry the Genesis-6 biotoxin. Just a dozen of these drones had the capacity to wipe the city of Woodrock off the map in a matter of hours.

They'd all trained for this, Quinn told his force in a motivational speech reminiscent of Grady's speech to the Bean Counter Berets and Wonder Twins in a motel room. Ordinary people can be called upon at any moment to do extraordinary things. Such people write history, he said, invoking George Washington, Winston Churchill, and Nelson Mandela. Speaking of his own battle against-all-odds in the Helmand Province on a dark frosty night, he told his team this was their moment. Even Miá was inspired by Quinn's stirring underdog speech.

They were going to fight a highly trained force that outnumbered them three to one. But how many of these guards had the motivation to kill local law enforcement was an unknown. The enigmatic Whitetail estimated 50 percent would drop their weapons and refuse to fight, maximum. Most were former military soldiers and sailors paid to provide security. They were not mercenaries. Probably having no clue what their employer was up to. That, however, still left a formidable force of fifty Iron Hand devoted, combat-hardened guards. And the Woodrock Police Department would receive little support from the FBI - other than Grady Freeman and his 10 remaining forensic accountants, analysts, and attorneys. The State Police were out of the picture and the ATF was as well. No one was clear on how deeply Iron Hand had infiltrated the U.S. Government. Involving these agencies was just too risky. They had no time to vet them.

This lack of trust in any institution left Quinn feeling paralyzed. After his speech, he confessed to Miá that he needed more people. People he trusted no matter what.

He jumped in the police SUV, speeding across town and to Dollie's Tavern.

THE SMALL CROWD OF Old Timers gathered in a circle around Ronan Quinn. They had no love for Pangea. The very Pangea that turned their simple town into an urban nightmare full of urban problems. Quinn found motivation and inspiration were little needed.

Clarifying to the Old Timers they would not be engaging Pangea directly, he needed them to hunt for Wasps should Madison launch any. He was looking to them to set a perimeter and protect the townspeople of Woodrock.

"Ain't they private property, chief?" asked the convicted arsonist turned ranch-hand Kik Knudson, now a spry 67 years old.

"You have my authority to shoot down anything that does not look like or behave like a bird. They're dark gray or black, look like a giant insect, are hard to see, and make little noise. If one gets too close, get away from it as fast as possible and cover your mouth and nose. This toxin is lethal."

The Old Timers stood in dumbstruck silence.

"Gentlemen," Quinn added, observing their angst. "These are not hobby drones from Amazon or Best Buy. They're big and they're fast. Up to 160mph fast. They're also highly intelligent and work as a team. The more of them there are, the smarter they become. A Queen leads them."

"Is she sexy?" Asked Gary, the proprietor of the wrecking yard. The others nervously laughed.

Quinn chuckled at this moment of levity. "I don't know, Gary, I haven't met one. The Queen stays at the rear and collects information and gives orders to her drones. But my understanding is just a single shot to their head from a rifle can bring one down. If you can take out the Queen, one will take her position, but it takes about a minute for this transition to occur."

"So, some of us could die, right, chief?" Asked Kik.

Quinn nodded grimly. "I'll be honest with you guys. We all can. I can't guarantee your safety, so it's volunteer only. Everything depends on your participation and your aim."

Old Dave spit a gooey glob of tobacco into a cup. "Drones, eh?" he said, with a grin and a glimmer. "I've been wanting to shoot down those annoying sons of bitches for years."

CHAPTER 41

AFTER RETURNING FROM HIS trip to Dollies, Quinn was drawn into a furious debate with Singh regarding his participation in Operation Endor. But Jack Fitzgerald's orders were sweet and simple. Under no circumstances was Samir Singh allowed anywhere near the upcoming battle. His role now was strictly that of an adviser. A role that even Jack himself had been reluctant to accept.

"I know the FBI wants me to testify, Ronan," argued Singh. "But there won't be any hearings for anything if Jupiter succeeds. You know that, right?"

"Understood, Sam," Quinn said, pulling on his tactical vest. "But the FBI has jurisdiction over you. Not my call buddy." Clearly frustrated and disappointed, Singh begrudgingly stepped into a police cruiser, and Fig rushed him to Rose's house for safekeeping.

At 2:47 p.m., Fig delivered a fuming Samir Singh to Rose, who felt it best to stay busy making, of all things, a casserole. Rose sensed that Samir Singh was anxious and disappointed. After all, he'd been the mastermind behind Iron Hand and he wouldn't suffer any disappointment running into Madison Sheppard again, either. She was back in the game, and he was responsible for not having the where-with-all to kill her in Pennsylvania. Nothing would help him sleep better at night more than dropping that woman with a bullet.

Pulling out dishes, Rose began preparing the food. When the operation was complete, she said, all involved would need to eat. A home-baked casserole is as good a thing as any, and cooking would keep them busy and distracted. To Rose's surprise, Samir Singh was quite the chef.

"Cooking is cathartic," he told her. "I'll have to make you my family recipe for chicken curry sometime. You'll think you've died and gone to heaven."

Singh asked about Rose's art and her globetrotting, and a semblance of his former dashing charm resurfaced once again. Oscar ambled over to investigate this chatting and clanging of pans, purring, tail vertical like a furry, orange-striped periscope. Looking at Singh with indifference, he rolled over and groomed himself. Singh tried to ignore Oscar. Just seeing the tabby made the guilt of Pippa's death eat away at him like acid.

Trotting back out of the kitchen, Oscar disappeared. As Singh sliced up an onion, he leaned over, kissing Rose on the cheek. "You're a beautiful woman, Rose," he said, wiping his hands on a towel. "I bet you hear that a lot."

"Never hurts to hear it again, Sam," she responded with a smile.

Singh's head snapped around, looking past the kitchen and toward the living room. "Did you hear that?" he asked Rose.

Rose shook her head. "I didn't hear anything?"

He turned to her with an anxious look. "Do you have a gun?"

"A .38, in my nightstand, but-"

Leaving a puzzled Rose hovering over a greased oven pan, Singh hustled out of view.

"Rose? Rose?"

Rose looked at the ceiling. "Pippa?"

"Rose, you are in danger. Oscar sees them. Run!"

Rose heard a loud commotion coming from the living room.

"Run, Rose, run!"

Cutoff from her bedroom, Rose dashed through the kitchen and toward the backdoor of the house.

ROCKY AND LEN - CHRIS Hadley's replacement and hobby assassin for Madison - drove along the rural road toward Rose's house.

A mile from Rose's house, Fig flew swiftly past them in the opposite direction, the cruiser's lights flashing. Slowing the car, they drove past her home and pulled over, parking on the shoulder. Ensuring all was clear, they pulled balaclavas over their faces, left the car, and dashed toward Rose's quaint ranch-style home. Hopping over the low wood fence and through a row of juniper trees, the killers creeped through blooming Iceland poppies and blue delphiniums. Len slipped to the rear of the house, peering through the kitchen window, curiously watching them make a casserole.

Len returned from his reconnoiter, kneeling and picking the front door lock. Rocky, ensuring all was clear behind them, admired Rose's manicured lawn and rows of tall juniper trees that, to the assailants' benefit, assured privacy from the rural road.

Len slowly pushed the door. With a light creak, it swung open.

Entering first, with Len providing cover, Rocky skulked inside. But just as they'd entered, Singh hurried from the kitchen on his way to Rose's bedroom to retrieve her revolver. Seeing the two men in black garb, faces hidden, Singh froze. Rocky couldn't believe his luck. This was too easy, he thought, aiming his machine gun at Singh's chest.

He squeezed the trigger. Nothing happened.

Looking his weapon over, Rocky realized his mistake. The damned safety was still on!

Seeing a split second of opportunity, Singh ran at Rocky. Firing just as Singh reached him, Rocky sprayed bullets into the ceiling, filling the room with a haze of shredded plaster.

"Go get the old lady!" Rocky yelled at Len. "Take her out! I've got this!"

Len dashed toward the back of the house to find, and shoot, Rose.

The two men wrestled for control of the machine gun, rolling around on the prized Indian rug from Bangalore. Firing more rounds into the room, Len struck some of Rose's prized artwork. But despite all of his deceptive strength, Singh was no match for Rocky - a trained killer. Singh's strength from mountain climbing and endurance races could not compensate for his lack of fighting skills.

Rocky got into position over Singh, striking him hard in the jaw, then leapt to his feet as Singh lay on the floor, looking dazed. Pulling the weapon up to his shoulder, he aimed for the center of Singh's forehead.

"Say goodnight," Rocky growled.

Oscar scrambled out of hiding from behind Rose's sofa.

Sensing a great deal of things, his predatory and instinct-driven cat-brain operated at full capacity. Oscar recognized that Rose, who fed and comforted him, was in grave danger. At the rear of the room, a hazy image of a smiling Pippa appeared. His head snapped around to see Singh on the ground, an unfamiliar human whom he cared less about. Then he studied the human in all black, his evil face hidden by a mask.

Rose and Pippa were in danger.

Adrenaline flooding his veins, his tail fluffed outward. Exposing two needle-sharp fangs with a menacing hiss, Oscar sprang into action.

ROCKY PUSHED HIS BOOT down on Singh's throat.

In one final act of humiliation before he ended Singh's life for good, Rocky spat at him. But for a brief second, barely registering in Rocky's victory-filled mind, a movement caught his eye. An orange blur closing the distance between him and the sofa, and closing at blazing speed.

Before Rocky reacted, Oscar leaped through the air toward him. Claws sank deep into the flesh of his calf. A pair of fangs punctured his skin with a pop.

"What the fuck!" Kicking and spinning like a polka dancer to a Death Metal band, a frantic Rocky tried shaking Oscar free of his leg. Finally releasing Rocky from his grips, Oscar bolted back across the room and to safety.

"Jesus Christ!" Rocky yelled. Roiling with anger, he turned back to Singh lying on the floor. Then something completely unexpected came into his view. Sprinting at him with both arms cocked over her shoulder, a furious-looking Rose swung something at him.

The last thing Rocky saw for a very long time was the blurred head of a custom shaft, TaylorMade, graphite driver. Her 60th birthday gift from the Woodrock Police Department. The head of the golf club swung toward him with such velocity, the shaft bowed. *Thwap!* It struck with a force that cracked Rocky's skull and he collapsed to the floor like a sack of dry cement. For good measure, Rose struck him five more times.

Rubbing his bruised and swelling jaw, Singh sat up, staring with disbelief at the unconscious Rocky. Rose propped herself up on her driver, smirking like she'd just hit the center fairway on a par five.

"You should see the other guy," she remarked, thumbing over her shoulder toward the rear of the house.

They'd struck Iron Hand with its first blow. A victory delivered decidedly by a spirit, a golf enthusiast, and a ten-pound tabby.

At 3:43 p.m., The Battle of Woodrock had officially begun.

Chapter 42

At 4:06 p.m., a guard at Pangea's Gate Two notified Madison Sheppard and Yousef that a small contingent of police officers was setting up camp in the Old Ghost Town.

"Not a big deal," he said over the radio. "Seems to be the usual weekend training."

She glanced impatiently at her phone and the string of text messages to Rocky.

Red Lancer:

Mission complete?

Red Lancer:

What's your status?

Red Lancer:

Please confirm? Has Singh been eliminated?

Red Lancer:

Status?

Red Lancer:

Status please...

Red Lancer:

WTF?

Red Lancer:

Where are you?

Red Lancer:

I'm assuming you have no comms or you're dead. Report back ASAP.

At 4:20 p.m., with suspicious silence from Rocky and Len for nearly two hours, Madison realized that something had gone wrong.

Just how hard is it to kill one man and a sixty-year-old cat lady? Unbelievable!

In the bigger scheme of things, Singh's death would've amounted to nothing more than settling a grudge, with Madison even demanding that Rocky sever off Singh's head and bring it back in a garbage bag. His face turning a shade of alabaster over this request, he politely declined to do any such thing. Even Rocky had principles. Singh's life had no value one way or another to Madison. But one thing that still did.

His security badge.

Despite becoming the largest global terror cell in the history of terrorism, Pangea was still a company like any other. Heavily bureaucratic, Pangea was a complex, multi-tiered global organization. Therefore, unlike in action films where things like security codes are changed on the fly at random keypads, badge access at Pangea took at least one business day to change, required two signatures for approval, and never happened on weekends. Madison didn't even know who to call to block Singh's access. Probably some lost idiot getting sauced at Dave and Buster's while watching NASCAR.

This meant that Singh's access badge worked everywhere.

The mysterious silence from Rocky and Len led Madison to conclude that they'd either failed or died. She also concluded the police force at the Old Ghost Town below them was not assembling for counter-terrorism training but was, in fact, assembling for counter-terrorism itself. She figured they intended to get inside using Singh's security badge.

The time to launch Iron Hand was now. No more delays. Globally, unilaterally, and without prejudice. As a cherry on top of this genocidal dessert cake, she would set a hundred Wasps with Genesis-6 loose on the townspeople of Woodrock. Having fantasized about wiping this shit-town off the map for some time, she was in charge now. Thoughts of destruction filled Madison with a rush of immense power. The most powerful woman - *the most powerful person* - the world has ever witnessed. Alexander the Great can go eat a bag of dicks.

Yousef, taken aback by her unbridled enthusiasm for mass casualties, studied Madison. This woman was not right in the head. But he'd already known that for some time.

Still though…

She called for her force to head for the gates, then turned to Yousef and told him to get his sniper rifle ready.

He nonchalantly shrugged. Whatever, he had five million dollars in offshore accounts, and now he'd probably get a billion more.

VISIBLY ANGERED AFTER LEARNING of the attack on Rose and Samir Singh, Ronan Quinn's Irish heritage complexion achieved a frightening shade of burgundy. But through his churning rage, he still had the sense to understand that Rocky's arrival to kill Singh and Rose meant Iron Hand had kicked off. He called Miá, standing by for his word at the Woodrock Regional Airport, ten miles away.

"Showtime," he said to her. "Good luck and Semper Fi, sister."

He ended the call.

Clutching Marge, Miá ran toward the Woodrock Search and Rescue Huey helicopter, twirling her free hand. The pilot acknowledged, and the helicopter came to life. Following close behind her were Grady, Rich, Kendrick, and three deputies - the Barb-anointed Geek Squad.

At 4:21 p.m., Operation Endor, phase 2, was officially underway.

Whitetail had secured someone inside Pangea, a woman named Kisha Jackson, vouched for and deemed trustworthy. Pippa's former team member and the very person who Pippa asked Quinn to protect, Kisha would meet them in Building A - corporate headquarters. She would guide them to the basement where the main server room was located, and if Madison hadn't blocked his badge access, Rich would be able to log into the mainframe and do his thing. Rerouting the IP addresses to gain access to the inner computer network that was the home base for the Wasps.

The Huey lifted off, nosing over and flying at rooftop level toward the complex. On this quiet Saturday afternoon, Woodrock residents manning barbecues and swimming pools were stunned as a helicopter thumped overhead at rooftop level. Not exceptionally fast, the lumbering Vietnam era Huey needed the element of surprise. So, the pilots flew low over houses and along the state highway, following it around the Kurtz Peak Curve and then, before them, the rocky bluff rose from the plains, forming the broad plateau where the Pangea complex sat. Modern glass buildings shimmering in the early evening sunlight, the sprawling complex provided Miá with an odd social contrast between the rural plains and the Midwest Silicon Valley. Below her, Blue Team was leaving their cars near the first gate and a firefight was beginning. Quinn's SUV had rolled onto its side at the edge of a sloping grass hill.

Hearing gunfire at the gate, confused by a helicopter flying at them from just a hundred feet off the ground, many of the Pangea guards patrolling the complex looked at each other with perplexed expressions. As the old Huey approached, the pilot slowed, Miá raised Marge to her shoulder, peered through the scope, and fired two quick shots at the security cameras resting high on the gate with both vanishing in shards of plastic and wiring.

Guards returned fire. Miá directed the pilot to turn 45 degrees to the left, and she put down three guards in rapid succession - firing, reloading, and firing again with precision.

"Go, go, go!" she shouted, and the pilot sped up and over the complex as Rich directed the pilots toward the six-story tall Building A. Hovering as low as possible over the rooftop of the corporate building, The Geek Squad all jumped from the Huey. The helicopter then lifted off and swung out over the complex, Miá firing several warning shots at the feet of the guards running toward the building.

For all the guards knew, this was a terrorist attack. But what terrorist flies in a search and rescue helicopter and fires warning shots? The guards stopped and backed away, confused and unsure. These were not Madison's guys, Miá thought. This was just run-of-the-mill security.

It was clear the dedicated force had been called to the fence-line.

JUST MINUTES BEFORE THE Huey helicopter reached the complex, Blue Team was speeding their way up the access driveway to Gate One, reaching nearly 70 mph on a black asphalt road with a posted speed of 25.

Charging the gate like a Comanche assault on a prairie fort, Quinn led the attack. Fig and Beth rode with Quinn at the front, Fig holding the security badge for Sam Singh. As they approached, heavy gunfire erupted from the fence line and rounds peppered the SUV, smashing the windshield. Quinn lost control, careening off into the grass with the SUV coming to rest on its side, teetering precariously over the edge of a long sloping hill. The patrol cars following behind all came to abrupt, skidding stops, with deputies and Bean Counter Berets leaping out and returning fire.

Quinn, Beth, and Fig pulled themselves out of the wrecked SUV, falling onto the grass.

"Well, that didn't work," Quinn grunted, pulling his radio up. "This is Unit One. We're still 50 yards short. We can't reach Gate One until we get cover-fire from Perez in the chopper."

The gunfire from the complex ceased and a disconcerting *I've got this* expression appeared on Fig's face. Quinn had seen this look before, worn by young adrenaline-fueled Marines in combat.

He's not thinking of-

Quinn reached out to grab him, but Fig sprang from behind the SUV and bolted toward the security gate, firing at random.

"Fig!" Beth screamed. "You moron! Get down!"

CROUCHING BEHIND THE SUV as Quinn yelled into the radio that they were still fifty yards short of the gate, Fig took action. The gunfire had momentarily stopped, and he could take this moment to dash for the gate. Fiddling with Singh's access badge, he went for it. Behind him, Beth was shouting.

Fig sprinted the fifty yards in under six seconds as the guards at the complex opened fire again and the Blue Team fired back. Caught in a horrendous crossfire, he reached the first gate, miraculously unscathed, swiping the badge on the pad. The gate clanged, hummed, and creaked open.

He'd done it! He turned toward Quinn and Beth. Time to head back, he thought, bullets clanging all around him.

Had Fig been better trained, if he'd gone through the training Quinn had in the Marine Corps, he would've realized that his position was much safer than where Quinn and Beth lay waiting. Fig's proximity to the guards meant they couldn't find angles to fire at him through the fence, and the guards wouldn't open Gate One just to shoot one dumb deputy.

But the ever dutiful, love-struck Fig wanted desperately to return to Beth. He needed to protect her. He needed to keep her safe. Beth had so far given no indications that she couldn't take care of herself, and if Quinn thought she couldn't, she wouldn't have been in the lead vehicle in the first place.

Fig, convinced of invincibility and muttering the lord's prayer, made a mad dash toward Quinn and Beth and through a hail of bullets. Suddenly, a kick in the back of his leg knocked him off his feet and spun him onto his back. Rolling over onto all fours and trying to stand, Quinn and Beth screamed for him to lie down on the ground, but two more rounds struck his vest, knocking the wind from him and slamming him back to the ground. He pushed himself up, and then it seemed as if someone kicked him in the back of his head with a steel-toed boot. Every muscle in his body went limp, and he slumped over and fell to the ground.

I'll be right there, Beth. Just give me a moment…

RICH'S BADGE WORKED AT the security door on the roof, and everyone on The Geek Squad let out a collective sigh of relief. The Huey hovered above, and Rich gave Miá the signal that they were in. As soon as the door swung open, a young, impatient woman in a lab coat stood waiting to greet them.

"Jesus," Kisha said. "What took you guys so long? I've been hiding up here since yesterday." She beckoned them into the building and along a windowed hallway to the elevators.

The elevator took its sweet time getting to the basement level that housed the mainframe and servers. As chimes rang out at every floor they passed, Grady performed a weapons check. Three nervous deputies watching him, they too checked their service weapons, their apprehension and tension not going unnoticed.

"You guys cool?" he asked.

They nervously nodded.

"What's red and moves up and down?" Grady asked as he holstered his weapon. The three deputies glanced at each other with perplexed expressions.

"A tomato in an elevator."

Kisha slapped her hand over her mouth and let out a snort. The deputies wore sheepish grins.

"Okay, then." Grady said as he turned back to the doors. "Now you're cool."

"THEY TOOK THE CAMERAS out. They took the damned security cameras out, Yousef!"

Everything happening at the main gate vanished into a blue screen on a monitor with the words "signal lost" blinking on it. Madison ran to the office window, looking toward the southern fence line. A white smoky haze rose into the air.

"I thought these were just redneck cops," Madison muttered, her face twisted in confusion. "Who trained these guys?"

A large Huey helicopter flashed past the window, so close she clearly made out Miá-the-Latina-goddess kneeling at the door with Marge in her hands.

"Oh, okay. The goddess is a badass. Game on, bitch," she growled, noticing others inside the cabin as the Huey banked towards the center of the complex and toward the main corporate building.

She pulled herself up to the security workstation. Then she had a thought. "Yousef, the redneck cops aren't trying to get into the complex. They're making us defend the gates." She spun in the chair and faced the Damascus assassin. "The peeps in the chopper, they're heading for the basement mainframe. I'd bet anything on it."

"You want me to get over there?" Yousef asked.

"It'd take you hours to find it. You don't know this place, and I don't have the time to draw directions." She swept her phone off the desk and tapped in a number. No one answered. She tried three more numbers and gave up. "I can't reach anyone in the complex. I'll pull some guys from the fence. What a fucking disaster."

Madison's jaws clenched, and a peculiar gleam lit up her eyes, causing even a hardened killer like Yousef to shift uncomfortably in his stance.

He moved to the window, observing the Huey circling over the complex. "Well, I'm not going to just stand here and watch you play on your PC," Yousef said as he strode to the wall, grabbing his sniper rifle.

"Where're you going?" she asked.

"I'm going to take that helicopter down," he replied, walking to the door.

"Good, make sure that bitch with the rifle goes down with it," Madison said, spinning in her chair to resume cyber-drilling her way deep into the Iron Hand database.

She opened Rich's code book. Time to wake up the Wasps.

Chapter 43

Beth screamed as Fig fell to the ground. Quinn couldn't believe his eyes. The Afghanistan demons slunk out of their dark recesses and into his thoughts.

Without warning, Beth took off toward Fig.

"Beth!" He shouted. "Get your ass back here!" His chin dropped to his chest, and he drew in a deep breath. Well, Quinn thought, fuck it. Maybe today is the day I finally bite it.

Firing with rapidity at the gate and fence-line, Quinn sprinted after Beth and provided as much cover fire as possible. They didn't stand a chance. The guards had complete cover and Quinn had none and Blue Team would have a difficult time providing cover fire without hitting Quinn and Beth. Ahead of him, Beth slid to a stop next to Fig. When Quinn arrived, tears were streaming down her cheeks. He grabbed Fig's throat and checked for a pulse.

"Don't bother, chief," she said, her voice quivering. "He's gone."

Beth cried out in pain, spinning around like a top and collapsing next to Fig. Quinn turned back to his deputies. Two ran toward his position and he waved them off. A bullet struck him in the back, knocking him flat on his face. Struggling to breathe, he rolled over, seeing Beth clutching her shoulder where a bullet had struck, just missing her body armor. He fumbled with his phone and dialed Miá.

"Hey! We're getting our asses kicked here! How much longer before Grady is done?!"

"We just left. I'm heading your way," Miá replied.

"Hurry the fuck up! We're getting hammered!"

A frosty night in an Afghan village. The LT calling for air cover. A Hellfire missile landing right in his lap. He couldn't break through this wall closing in around him. His muscles became rigid, and he froze in place. As if in a dream, he looked at Beth, grimacing and clutching her shoulder. Another round struck her in the back, knocking her to the ground. Did I fail Beth? Did I fail Fig? Did I fail my town? Why did Carlos send me to this damned place? Why was I chosen?

"Fate chose you, as fate chose me. It brought us together. Now we must defeat them. For Emma, for your deputy, for your daughter, for an entire world you still have hope for. I'm with you Mr. Quinn. I'm going to be with you every step of the way. We're still connected. I feel it."

As if she were whispering right into his ear, Pippa's sweet, soft voice flooded his thoughts. Over the cracks of gunfire and over Beth's groaning, Pippa's voice was crystalline clear.

The beating rotors of a helicopter grew louder. His eyes clenched shut. A Hellfire was on its way.

Force yourself, Ronan.

Beth screamed again as a bullet caught her in her chest. Seconds later, another struck her in the thigh. Quinn turned, firing relentlessly at the fence. Grabbing Beth by her vest, he dragged her toward the Blue Team's position. The Huey drew closer. A Hellfire missile-

Shut up! Shut up! Shut up!

Screaming, Beth begged Quinn not to leave Fig behind and she fired at the fence-line with such ferocity her pistol went dry in a matter of seconds. The Huey reached the gate, the comforting sounds of Marge coming from the Huey's door.

MIÁ HUNG AS FAR out of the Huey as possible.

Firing, reloading and firing again in rapid succession, guards scrambled and took cover. Seeing Quinn dragging Beth toward the patrol cars, some of which were burning, she needed to keep the guards distracted until the two reached safety. She told the pilots to turn left forty degrees, small arms fire clanging on the Huey's rungs.

Then a much different sound hit the side of the helicopter. Like a loud clunk. The sound of a single shot from a high-powered rifle. As the pilot swung the helicopter around, the shooter appeared. A man dressed in what looked like a runner's outfit, holding a scoped rifle.

Oh, she thought. They have a sniper, do they?

A round struck the windshield, just missing the copilot's head.

"What the hell! I'm not an Apache pilot!" The pilot shouted. "I'm a search and rescue pilot! Can you take this guy out?"

"Turn twenty degrees right." She tried to line up her sight on the sniper, but the helicopter swayed and she couldn't find the shot. A round grazed her shoulder, causing her to lose her balance and fall back onto the cabin floor. Another round hit the inside, then more clanking.

"We've got a problem here," the pilot stated. "I'm losing power."

"No! You need to stay here!" She shouted.

"Nope!" the pilot grunted. "Heading out!"

The old Huey turned away from the complex and toward Kurtz Peak, grinding and clanging coming from the gearbox.

"Okay, lost power," the exasperated pilot told her. "I'm auto-rotating. Hard landing, hard landing. Brace yourself."

Slamming down hard on the highway, the Huey bounced once, spun around and slammed down again. Smoke filled the cabin, burning Miá's throat and lungs as the pilots shut the old chopper down. Overcoming a sharp pain in her back and grabbing her remaining rounds, she tossed Marge from the helicopter. Then she threw herself out the door and onto the asphalt of the highway.

Miá jogged away from the smoldering wreck. The pilot threw his helmet to the ground in anger, while the stunned copilot admired the crash with his hands on his hips. Spinning and weaving and trying to avoid collisions, oncoming cars slammed on their brakes. Shocked faces of drivers and passengers alike, stared at the scene through their windshields. A smoldering Huey. A fuming pilot. A woman holding a sniper rifle. Not something one commonly sees.

People stepped from their cars, instinctively holding up phones to film this incredible incident, and none seemed too interested in rushing to Miá's aid. Like she was the star of some reality TV show. Gingerly massaging her back, she stood before them on the highway and took an inventory of her remaining rounds. Iron Hand's no secret now, she thought, as spectators uploaded footage to social media, updated their Instagram, and typed up posts over Twitter.

Seeing the pilots were okay, Miá began looking for strong sniper positions. Judging by everything she'd seen up to now, Quinn would probably retreat. The Blue Team needed cover from the high ground in case those assholes followed. Grady was on his own now. With the Huey out of commission, no extraction from the complex would be possible. She prayed this whole diversion had at least halfway worked, and Rich had done his thing.

As she ran across the highway toward the sloping hillside, something odd caught her attention. A hundred Wasps flying south toward Woodrock, in formation, just as migrating birds would.

They did it, Miá thought. Pangea actually pulled the trigger.

KISHA LED THE GEEK Squad through a vast complex of hallways and past secured doors and locked rooms.

This place was like a fortress, Grady thought to himself. The hallway, blasted with freezing cold air-conditioning, caused Grady to lament that they should've brought jackets. Hurrying down the hall, the team reached two large, steel doors.

Everyone drew in a deep breath as Kisha swiped her badge. The doors clicked, and she pushed them aside. Grady posted the three deputies outside to stand guard as Rich went to work. Setting up his laptop, he typed feverishly, successfully making it through the first Iron Hand firewall.

"Can you hurry up?" Kisha asked in exasperation.

"Got it. I'm through the second firewall." Then his head whipped around to Grady. "Oh shit," he said with alarm. "They're active."

"What?" Grady replied. "Where?"

"Everywhere. I need to kill them," Rich said, frenetically tapping at the keys.

"Kill them?" Kisha asked.

"Yes.... well... no," Rich replied. "I wrote a kill switch into the software after the Queen went rogue in Nevada and attacked the sheep. No one knows this line of code is there, I hope. It doesn't kill them in the literal sense, it just stops the processors from drawing power. It's more like knocking them unconscious."

Without warning, the workstations went blank and the room fell dark and the emergency lights came on.

"What the hell!" Grady exclaimed. "Did they just cut the power?"

The monitors flickered back to life and incandescent lights bathed the room once more in bright white light. "Whew! Okay, we're on backup generator power," Rich said, relieved.

Plunged into darkness once again, the emergency lights returned. This time, though, the loud humming of the banks of servers ceased.

"Okay," Grady said. "Now we're not. What now?"

"Where's the data pipe, Rich?" Kendrick asked. "How do you get the data from the mainframe to the drones?"

"It goes through our two satellites, Global Link V and VI. Are you thinking of hacking into those? I wouldn't know where to begin, Kendrick."

"Each drone has its own IP address?" Kendrick asked. "And the kill switch command, I take it, is delivered through a single packet?"

Rich nodded. "Only 20 kilobytes. It's just a basic instruction. But we're talking 700,000 individual IP addresses." Then he thought for a moment. "But I have every IP address on my secure OneDrive."

Kisha interrupted. "I know we're all having an IT dork moment here, but what in the high holy hell are you guys going on about?"

Kendrick pulled his phone out and looked at the screen. "Gosh darn it," he muttered. "No signal." He looked at Grady. "We need to get to the roof."

Kisha glanced at Grady and shrugged with confusion. Equally puzzled, Grady shrugged back.

Kendrick, seeing Kisha's puzzlement, explained. "I'm going to repurpose a couple of satellites and send 700,000 drones a spam e-mail, compliments of the CIA."

"What? Just how're you going to repurpose two satellites from here?" Grady asked.

Kendrick smiled. "I'm not. Barb is. Never underestimate that woman's powers of persuasion."

Dragging a distraught and bleeding Beth behind him, Quinn reached the Blue Team.

The scene was dismal. Many on the team were out of ammunition, with some wounded in the firefight. To make matters worse, to his horror, the smoking Huey, with Miá onboard, had passed overhead and crashed somewhere toward the highway. Anxiously awaiting a fireball, he sighed relief when one didn't appear. But he'd been unable to reach her since.

"What now, chief?"

Quinn looked around at the team. Beth was dying, and Fig was dead. Two accountants and four deputies leaned up against the cars with gunshot wounds. Staring at their chief with questioning eyes, they needed someone to take command of this complete cluster.

"Mr. Quinn, I'm here with you. Please don't give up."

Quinn shook off Pippa's voice and ordered everyone to pile into the patrol cars and head for the Old Ghost Town to regroup. But Beth was bleeding out from the wound to her thigh. He lifted her up, threw her over his shoulder, and ran to the furthest patrol car.

"Don't take her to the command post," he told a deputy. "Slap a tourniquet on that leg of hers and then you haul ass and get her to the hospital. And pile as many of the wounded as you can in the car with her." He glanced at Beth. Unconscious, her face was as white as a snowdrift. Frustrated, he shook his head, turning to his remaining force. "Everyone else, fall back! If you can't get a working car, go on foot!"

The gunfire from the Pangea gate ceased. He imagined the guards high-fiving and slapping each other's asses in victory as the Blue Team beat a hasty retreat. As he followed his force down the drive and to the Old Ghost Town, he glanced into the mirror. Black Suburbans raced to the gate and guards piled inside of them.

Are you kidding me? He thought. Are they seriously following us?

He reached the highway and turned onto the beat-up road leading down to the Ghost Town. Then something caught his eye. Something high above him.

At first, he thought they were birds flocking their way toward town. But their formations were perfect, with no wavering or fluttering about. Fumbling with his phone, he dialed a number.

"Drones heading your way, Dave."

"Got it, chief. But just one problem. What do we do when it gets dark? We ain't got no night vision stuff."

Quinn glanced at his watch. In two hours, the sun would be setting. "Dave, you guys hit every sports store in town and get whatever you need. And you tell them they can bill the chief of police." The Wasps vanished beyond Kurtz Peak. This was a complete disaster, he thought. Grady had better hold up his end of the deal.

Quinn didn't fully understand the technical details of A-88 Wasps, but they had time. These Wasps had just finished production. Straight out of the box, if you will. The Queens would need some time to gather the data they needed. The lay of the land. The battlespace, as Col. Taylor had explained to Madison at Juliet Tango.

But once the Queen and her drones had completed compiling maps, they would then begin their assault on Woodrock, as citizens enjoyed barbecues and margaritas in their own backyards.

CHAPTER 44

AT 7:03 P.M., THE DIRECTOR of the Central Intelligence Agency answered a frantic knocking and repeated doorbell ringing at the front door of his red-brick Arlington Heights home. Irritated, he yanked open the door and found Barb Dent standing before him. Brushing past the surprised director and into his house, she spun around and made her request as plainly as possible.

"I need two fucking satellites right fucking now. I've got no time to explain this to you."

"Yeah, come right in," the director said, shutting the front door. "So, please explain to me why I need to let you have two satellites? I can't just snap a finger, you know. There are channels to go through, Barbara."

Barb threw her head back and groaned. "Goddammit, Lou, you know I hate it when you call me that." She sighed and pleaded her case. "Look, here's the deal. There are 700,000 drones located around the globe with a deadly agent that will kill millions of people. I'm not here because my fucking Dish TV is out."

The director stepped past Barb, beckoning her to follow him into his study. Stepping into his den, an odor of Lemon Pledge and musty cigar smoke greeting her nostrils, she glanced around at awards and photos of him posing with presidents.

"And why am I finding out about this now, Barbara?" the director asked in a patronizing tone.

In one fluid motion, she whipped out her service pistol from beneath her jacket and aimed it right at his chest.

"Whoa! Barb!" He raised his hands and backed away.

"Oh, so we're back to Barb now, are we?" She said with an arched brow. "Lou, the CIA is compromised. Hell, the whole damned government may be compromised. All the way to the White House. And you know what that means, Lou?"

The director shook his head.

"It means I trust no one."

"What?" the director stammered. "Even me?"

Barb silently mouthed two words. *No - one.*

"Barb, you're asking a lot," he said.

Barb grew tired of wasting precious time. "Look, I have no one I can trust, which makes me really fucking unpredictable. Hell, I don't even know what I'm going to do. I could just shoot you in the arm."

"What?" The director's eyes widened with a flurry of rapid blinks.

"Yeah," Barb said with a devilish smirk. "And then maybe I'll just shoot each appendage until you stop your bitchin' and start cooperating. You can kiss racquetball goodbye."

The director backed up against his desk, folding his arms, eyes narrowed, and teeth clenched. "Anything else, Barbara? Can I pour you a drink? Massage your feet?"

"Funny, Lou. And one more thing. I need you to get three techs ready at NORAD. They're going to upload some geek stuff from Kendrick to the satellites. Then I guess we send it to the drones and they all go back to sleep."

"You guess?" the director said, brows raised with incredulity. "Are you sure whatever you're doing is even going to work?"

Barb responded with a shrug. "How the hell should I know, Lou? We've been making this shit up as we go along for the past 72 hours."

The director picked up the green secure phone from his desk and dialed a number. Then asked to be put through to the head of the NRO.

"You know what this means, don't you?" the director asked, tapping his finger on the desk, glaring at Barb as he waited for the NRO chief to answer.

"I'm fired?"

"Yup."

She returned the director's glare with a gleam. "I wish you luck."

STANDING ON THE ROOF of Building A, bad news came over Grady's cellphone. The Huey was down and no extraction was possible. They had sighted Wasps heading for Woodrock. The Pangea force is following him to the Ghost Town and Blue Team is in Alamo mode. "You're on your own, Grady," Quinn told him. "If you make it out, come lend us a hand. Please."

Grady ended the call. Rich and Kendrick had done all they could do, and their mission was complete. He panned around the vast complex. How the hell are they supposed to get out of here? Pangea guards, and probably the ones who cut the power to the tech center which housed the Pangea mainframe, were likely on their way to the roof right now.

"Give me a gun," Kisha said. "I know this place inside and out, and I can lead them on a wild goose chase." Then she told Kendrick, who probably had the best memory of all of them, how to find their way to the garage. "Take the keys to my car," she said, tossing Grady her keys. "It's a black four-door Dodge Challenger. Employee parking level two."

"Are you sure?" Grady asked in complete and total surprise.

"Yeah, why do you think I offered? You need to go help the chief now. I'll be fine."

Grady told a deputy to give her his pistol.

"You know how to handle one of these?" He asked.

"Look dude," Kisha said. "All I need to do is make them think I'm you guys. I don't need to hit anything." She nervously glanced around. "Hurry, guys. They'll be here any second."

Grady held out his hand. "Thanks, Kisha."

"Don't thank me," she said as she shook Grady's hand. "I'm doing this for Pip. Now go help the chief. He needs you."

Grady watched Kisha run down to the far end of the hall and past the corporate offices. Darting around the corner, she disappeared from view. With haste, the Geek Squad moved toward the adjacent building, following Kisha's directions to the garage.

"Would never have pegged her as a Challenger girl," a deputy remarked.

Help Quinn? Grady thought, making his way through the maze of halls and offices. He had three deputies and two nerds. He supposed it was better than nothing. And Kisha may know the complex inside and out, Grady thought as they hurried down a flight of stairs to the first floor.

But so do the guards.

WHILE THE PANGEA GUARDS closed in on Quinn and the Blue Team at the Old Ghost Town, and Grady tried to find his way out of the complex, Wasps hummed to life at discreet locations all over the world.

Hidden away in small enclosures, on rooftops, in jungles and forests, and on long abandoned properties, black and gray machines stirred like giant insects from hibernation. Each receiving coordinates from satellites high above them, they aligned their navigation platforms and retrieved maps buried deep in their software.

Appearing almost thoughtful, the Queens drafted plans. After Wasp scouts mapped the target area, they would split into groups and move swiftly and silently through towns and villages, striking their targets with the tasteless and odorless Genesis-6 biotoxin.

The deadly machines would seek and destroy any living thing that carried the genetic traits of a human being.

Madison Sheppard hadn't sent the Wasps programs 12, 15, 17, or 23 - the selection of viable candidates and elimination of those deemed unworthy of existence. She'd sent them a program never intended for use. Program 99.

The indiscriminate killing of all human life, otherwise referred to as *The Scorched Earth Directive.*

Chapter 45

At 7:20 p.m., while the National Reconnaissance Office begrudgingly repurposed two of its satellites, the force of Pangea guards arrived at the parking lot of the Old Ghost Town to finish Ronan Quinn's Blue Team.

To Quinn, the score was clear. Blue Team was about to have its very own Little Bighorn moment. Knowing the extinction of his team might occur, and seeing Wasps heading for his town, he ordered four of his deputies into one of the last remaining patrol cars and sent them back to Woodrock.

Woodrock mustn't be left unprotected, and Dollie's Old Timers whizzing around rural roads in their pickups weren't exactly skilled law enforcement. He couldn't allow the Pangea guards to make their way to Woodrock and do God knows what to his people. An entirely hostile force was in the United States. Created by the very United States herself.

Old Dave, Kik, Gary, and the rest of the Woodrock Old Timers hit every sporting goods store in town. Adding night vision binoculars and scopes to their arsenal of pistols and rifles. Besides acquiring this necessary gear to fight the Wasps during these hours of diminishing sunlight, they also gained three additional people. A store manager, a cashier, and a sales agent offered to pitch in and join the fight. Overhearing a commotion where the hunting rifles were being sold, a man in a Pangea polo approached them and offered his help as well.

Dave, not-so-politely, told the Pangea employee to "fuck off."

There was little resistance against the widely known Old Timers as they pilfered night vision equipment and additional firearms and ammunition from sporting departments and stores. "Send the bill to the chief of police," Kik would add in a calm, yet authoritative tone. A group of old men with gleams in their eyes, calmly requesting free hunting equipment to stave off a drone attack, lent much more credibility than a freaked-out twenty-something year old on the brink of hysteria.

The group broke off into teams of two, heading out to all points of the compass to set up a perimeter around Woodrock. As these things do, word of the Wasp attack quickly spread. This was something straight-up out of a science fiction movie, and after the old timers blew through town, people's cell phones began ringing.

As the Queens and their powerful little silicon minds built up their knowledge of this unknown territory they'd been released in, people all around town dusted off rifles, tossing them into cars and pickups. Ending barbecues and swilling one last Margarita or beer, they sped off to join the Old Timers in their fight to protect Woodrock.

Surprise, speed, and stealth were the Wasps' greatest assets. But, overlooked by Pangea engineers, they now faced a threat that has crippled invading armies since human beings began fighting wars.

Gossip.

AT 7:46 P.M., A MASSACRE loomed over the Old Ghost Town, with Blue Team's force reduced in half by casualties or reassignment back to town.

Miá was still missing with Quinn fearing the worst, her phone going straight to voicemail. To his knowledge, Grady and The Geek Squad remained trapped at ground zero in the complex. As the shadows grew long, and the evening cooled with just an hour and a half left before plunging into darkness, he prayed they could hold off this force of forty remaining guards and that the plan to shut the drones down using two borrowed CIA satellites actually worked.

The Pangea force made their way through the flimsy, rusted security gate, so Quinn dispersed his team throughout The Ghost Town, shifting his strategy from police offensive to guerrilla warfare. Blue Team would fire and retreat and fire and retreat. The only way Pangea would be held off until help came. He called Jack Fitzgerald and pleaded for a calvary.

"I'm trying, Ronan," and Jack ended the call. Quinn frantically sent messages to Whitetail and received no response. This was Helmand Province, the sequel. No support. Hang on until sunrise.

As Quinn hid behind a corner, he drew in a long, deep breath and looked around him. His team crouched behind corners and inside old, crumbling, abandoned buildings. The approaching Pangea force walked down the street as if they were out on a pub crawl. Light chatter and laughing filled the air with some guards splitting off to search the buildings. These cocky bastards already think it's over, Quinn thought in astonishment.

Humiliated by the casualness of it all, he too had his own scorched earth plan. Should things go really south, should the guards overrun them, he was going to set this tinderbox of a town on fire.

A guard cried out and fell into the street. A mere second after an apparent bullet had struck the man, the metallic thud of a rifle cracked in the distance.

Another guard fell. Another thud. The casual chatting of the guards evolved into panic and confusion as they dashed for cover.

Another guard fell to the ground in mid-stride, and a momentary flash came from the grassy, rocky hillside.

"Yeah!" He shouted, pumping his fist in the air. "That's Miá on that hill, bitches!"

THE WAR AGAINST THE Wasp drones began in Woodrock at 8 p.m., on a warm, pleasant Saturday evening. Gunfire erupted all across town, cracking and popping like a fireworks exhibition. Caught in a software version of surprise, the Wasps retreated and assessed this new threat.

A half-dozen Wasps were downed in the first few minutes, but this peasant army had just one hour before the sun itself set. When that occurred, except for the few with night vision equipment, most of the sharpshooters would become completely blind.

The Wasps, still learning and gaining familiarity with this new environment and themselves, regrouped. Their tactics would need to change, resorting to speed and stealth. They hovered in the sky, chatting amongst themselves like football players in a huddle.

Discussing how to eliminate this new human threat.

CHAPTER 46

KICKING UP DUST AND sending small rocks tumbling below her, Miá slid down the hillside and toward the gravel parking area of the Old Ghost Town.

Certainly, the guards caught her scrambling down the steep hill toward their vehicles, but at least she was distracting them and buying Quinn some time. Not a very clandestine sniper-craft, but still effective and all she had. Plus, she was running out of ammunition. She needed to make the best of every shot.

Reaching the Suburbans at nearly the same time as three guards did, she tossed Marge to the ground, whipped out her Glock, and fired as they rushed at her from the gate. In a scene reminiscent of the O.K. Corral, all four exchanged gunfire, but Miá remained calm. A guard fell, and another cried out in pain and, through some divine intervention, not a single round struck her, surprising even the remaining guard. As they both reloaded and stood to fire at one another, a soft whistling sound passed near her. The guard stumbled off his feet and collapsed.

Picking up Marge and peering through the scope, Miá scanned the area where she thought the bullet came from. Another sniper was out roaming around. A sniper with a sound suppressor. But who? Kneeling to reload, another bullet passed so close it brushed her hair against her cheek. But this shot came from another direction.

Miá turned and sprinted behind a Suburban, ducking down and taking in a deep breath. Jesus, what is this? A damned sniper convention!?

AT 8:14 P.M., A FIREFIGHT broke out in the Ghost Town between Quinn's Blue Team and the Pangea forces. After losing a few of their own to Miá's sniper rifle, the guards seemed to take things a bit more seriously. They moved purposefully, using hand signals and head nods, approaching Quinn and his team in a more organized and systematic fashion.

Quinn's head slumped in near defeat. His officers and accountants were valiant, but they had no experience under heavy fire. These Pangea morons are all ex-military. The Blue Team didn't have a chance. Quinn weighed his options.

Surrender, or burn the place to the ground.

He ordered Blue Team to retreat to the old housing area and lay suppressing fire. At least there they could use abandoned vehicles as cover.

Crouching down, he turned and ran toward the housing area to the rear. But before he made even two steps, he stopped and his heart sank. A dozen more Pangea guards had arrived and cut him off.

Frustrated and angry, Quinn cursed himself. He'd allowed himself to be surrounded. His team, as he glanced at their faces, looked defeated. The guards told Blue Team to drop their weapons.

Just beyond the guards, hovering effortlessly in the air, were twenty Wasps. Their amber eyes pulsing, they remained motionless until one Wasp moved forward, its eyes glowing slightly brighter. Quinn assumed this was the Queen, and he swore she was glaring at him. From beneath the Queen, striding at a brisk pace and tapping at the screen of her phone, was someone he'd never seen. But he knew exactly who she was. Madison Sheppard.

"Mr. Quinn, it's okay, I'm still here," Pippa whispered into his brain. *"Don't give up. We can do this."*

"GODDAMN, THESE THINGS CAN move!" Old Dave shouted into his phone as drones sped over fields.

Yes, they can. And to make matters worse, Old Dave, Kik, and the others realized the Wasps were anticipating their every move, and to their disconcertion, had also learned the capabilities of their vehicles. Speed, acceleration, even their rate of turning.

"These drones are goddammed smart! We just need to keep them from the town 'till the chief and his guys are done!" Old Dave shouted into his phone.

"Hearin' lots a gunfire from the Ghost Town, Dave," Gary's crackling voice came over the speaker.

"We got our own problems, Gary! Keep these bastards away from Woodrock! Chief will take care of business!" Dave slapped the phone down onto the seat. "Goddammit Kik," Old Dave grumbled. "I got this funny feeling we're all screwed."

At 8:46 p.m., Old Dave and Kik tracked three Wasps flying at high speed over a large alfalfa field. Out of nowhere, three dropped right in front of his speeding truck. Dave slammed on the brakes and spun the wheel to head in the other direction, but two more had dropped behind him. The three flying along the alfalfa field split up and two zipped over to the truck, moving to each side and rotating around to face the two men. Some sort of energy pulse burst from a Wasp hovering overhead. The truck shook and rattled, then the engine died.

"You telling me they can kill engines too, Dave?" Kik asked between clenched teeth. "That Pangea twerp forgot to tell us that shit!"

As Old Dave tried to start the truck back up, a solitary Wasp moved to the windshield. This Wasp wore a small crown stenciled on the hump making up its head.

"I think that's one of the Queen's, Dave," Kik said, his voice taut and strained with tension. The Queen moved to each of the drones as if she was speaking to them. Dave shuddered.

Old Dave had spent a good portion of his life hunting game. Creeping painfully through brush, freezing his ass off in duck blinds, and hanging out of trees thirty feet off the ground, he'd witnessed a lot of animal behavior over the years. He'd seen bears chasing bucks across meadows. He watched mountain lions catch foxes. He'd even witnessed a pack of wolves surrounding a ferocious Grizzly Bear ten times their size, systematically attacking it in well-coordinated moves.

"Nature is to be respected at all times," he would tell his grandkids. "Because nature don't give a shit how big and bad you think you are. Even the baddest hombre in the woods can wind up on the wrong side of things, and that includes you. Don't tell your mom I cussed."

These drones were smart alright. Behaving just like all the predators he'd witnessed. Figuring things out. Working as teams. And Old Dave knew he was on the wrong side of things. He and Kik were prey.

Kik had about enough. He was going down swinging. Throwing the truck door open, he stepped out and began firing. Old Dave watched with horror as the Wasps shifted from side to side with stunning agility. Even at this close range, Kik couldn't hit his target. The Wasps studied Kik's every move, his patterns, his reactions, anticipated every pull of the trigger, and dodged his shots. The only way anyone was killing one of these things is by taking it with complete surprise, because once they find you, Old Dave thought, in these waning moments of his life, you're screwed.

Old Dave shouted for Kik to get back in the truck and close the door. They shut all the vents and rolled up the windows, covering their mouths and noses as best they could.

This was it. The moment of truth.

The Wasps moved up to the truck, gently tapping the windows. Then a Wasp ahead of them reared back, moved swiftly forward, and smashed into the windshield, showering the two men with glass. Old Dave pulled up his rifle, shooting the drone right through what he thought was its brain. The Wasp fell onto the hood of the truck with a thump, its amber eyes fading to darkness. But the shattered windshield exposed them, and a single Wasp rose above the truck, readying to release the Genesis-6.

In half a minute, Old Dave and Kik would be dead. No amount of cloth covering their mouths and noses would stop this toxin.

LIKE A CERTAIN CALVARY colonel from centuries ago, Ronan Quinn had lost his Little Bighorn battle.

His Blue Team battered and hopelessly outgunned, Quinn tossed his weapon to the ground. Judging by what he was witnessing right now, which was Madison Sheppard tapping on her phone as if she were texting her pals, he'd assumed they'd lost and the Wasps were zooming around the globe and slaughtering people.

But he didn't know for sure. After all, Pippa had reminded him to keep the faith.

Madison strode up to him and thanked him for surrendering. Whisking her hair over her shoulders, she studied her opponent. "Your guys are pretty good, chief," she said. "I admire their tenacity."

"Go fuck yourself," Quinn replied.

"Oh, okay." Madison shook her head and went back to tapping away on her phone.

Fists clenched, Quinn glared at Madison, waiting for an explanation he felt he now deserved. Madison looked up from her phone and gave the briefest manifesto of all time.

"What're you staring at?" She asked. "What? You want a big speech? I launched because I wanted to. Now you go fuck yourself."

As the sun vanished behind Kurtz Peak, shadows grew long and darkness approached. The amber eyes of the Wasps looked even more ominous. Moving toward Quinn and the Blue Team, they appeared to be ready for an assault.

"Wait, guys, the drones…" Quinn said, startled by the Wasps moving in on his position. "We're surrendering. What is this?"

Madison glanced around at her guards with a broad grin. The men chuckled, bringing their rifles up against their chests.

"Listen, you wife beating alkie," she said with an icy stare. "Just be cause you surrender doesn't mean you live."

Quinn couldn't believe it. The woman was actually worse than Sam Singh had described.

Out of nowhere, sparks, flames, and smoke jetted from one of the approaching Wasps. Spinning around in circles, making a high-pitched squeal like a wounded animal would, it crashed to the ground. A soft woosh sound came from near Quinn, and another drone fell to the ground emitting a horrifying, mechanized scream of pain.

Quinn spun around, searching the hill behind him. Someone was shooting the Wasps, he thought. But who? Marge sounds like a cannon going off. This sniper has a sound suppressor.

Four Wasps broke away from the formation and zipped right over Quinn's head toward the hillside of Kurtz Peak. Terrified guards ducked and dashed for cover. Another Wasp spun and sparked and crashed to the ground. A mere second after the sniper's bullet struck that Wasp, the telltale metallic thump of Marge reached the town. Rushing for the cover of the Post Exchange, Quinn tried to make sense of it all. If Miá shot that drone, who shot the other two? There's a second sniper out there.

He burst into the Post Exchange, settling in under a broken window. He had no clue whose side this other shooter was on.

CHAPTER 47

MIÁ HAD ACCOMPLISHED WHAT she'd set out to do, but she'd also had help once again from someone she couldn't see. And no longer having the advantage of high ground and firing into the town from the gate, covering for Blue Team had been cut by 80%.

Turning the attention of the Wasps away from the team inside and now to her, Miá became the Wasps' new threat. Based on all she'd learned from Rich's briefing; the Queen would send a recon team of drones to hunt down and kill her. Miá wasn't convinced this second sniper was on her side yet, but if he kept hitting drones, she was all in with him.

Then there was this third sniper.

Miá was both hunted and hunter. Through her scope, she searched the steep hill above her, seeing nothing. She had a thought. Pulling her top off and over her head, she scrunched it into a tight ball. Carefully balancing it between the scope and the stock, creating the illusion that her balled-up top was her head, she pushed Marge onto the hood of the Suburban and let it rest there, balancing the rifle with her hand and ducking back down and out of sight. Coming from her left, a nearly imperceptible hum as the Wasps approached her position, searching for the shooter. Understanding from Rich that the drones had night vision and infrared, she prayed the snipers would take the bait. If they did, they would have given their position away to the approaching Wasps.

If the snipers didn't take the bait, the Wasps would kill her.

She had seconds.

Marge *clanged,* bursting away from her grip as a bullet struck the rifle's scope. This sniper was nearby, and as she'd hoped, the Wasps stopped searching for her, racing to where the shot had originated.

Ha! Miá thought. Your turn now, buddy!

Peeking over the hood of the Suburban, she saw the sniper kneeling on the ground as Wasps sped toward him. From what she made out, this was the man in the tracksuit who'd shot down the Huey from the Pangea complex - the man named Yousef. Two flashes came from the hillside. The friend-or-foe sniper on the hill now seemed to target the Wasps attacking Yousef. Are they both working together?

A hum filled her ears and, startled, she looked up to find a Wasp descending upon her position. The bastards had split up. Coordinated. They hadn't forgotten about Miá at all!

"No!" Miá shouted, scrambling from behind the Suburban. The Wasp followed her, took position, and readied to release Genesis-6.

Sparks flew from its body, it spun around, making a high pitched shrill as it crashed down on top of her and quickly rolling to her side, just avoided being hit. Another kill for the who-knows-who sniper on the hill. The remaining Wasps flew at high speed toward the hill, there were the sounds of frantic small arms fire, then silence.

Scrambling to her feet, she saw Yousef kneeling just twenty yards from her, training his high-powered rifle on her head. Hovering near Yousef's hip like a loyal pet dog, a Wasp glared at her through the dim light of the evening.

Wait, she thought. Why didn't the Wasps attack him? Why did they stop? Does he have control?

Frozen in place and Marge lying in ruins, Miá's only options now were to pull her Glock and shoot him, or try to drop and roll for cover. He had the position. He had the leverage. He had the initiative. Miá didn't have a chance. He readied to shoot.

A flash came from the grassy hillside above, and Yousef cried out in pain, clutching his thigh and dropping to the ground. Zipping up the hillside and toward the hill where the shot originated, the pet Wasp left a wounded Yousef, zeroing in on this shooter. Frantic automatic weapons fire cracked repeatedly from the hillside, and then the hillside fell silent once again.

Whipping her Glock out, she moved swiftly toward the wounded Yousef, propped up on the ground and clutching his thigh.

"Don't move, asshole," Miá hissed.

Yousef raised his hands in surrender. "You shoot me, and those things are coming after you again, and I don't think your luck is that good."

Dirt erupted at her feet. Startled, Miá jumped back. Another whistle, and another shot landed at her feet, followed by another. Miá raised her hands in surrender. Then two more shots struck the ground just inches from her.

Miá got the message. "Okay!" She shouted. "I'm leaving!"

She turned, sprinting back to the Suburban.

"Whose side is anyone on? I'm so confused." She picked up Marge and examined the rifle. The scope was smashed and the stock was splintered. Marge was now a wreck from Yousef's bullet. She tossed the rifle to the ground and checked her Glock. Peering over the hood of the Suburban, she noticed Yousef was gone.

Whatever, she thought, as she looked past the gate and into the Ghost Town. I hope he loses his damn leg.

COVERING THEIR NOSES AND mouths tightly, Dave and Kik watched helplessly as the Wasp moved over their truck and hovered. The two men glanced at each other. Kik mustered a smile and nodded. A fitting end, the old friends would at least perish together, and go down fighting. Eyes clamped shut, they waited to meet their maker.

And waited.

But instead of dying a horrible death at the hands of a killer drone, they opened their eyes to find the Wasps slowly backing away. Settling down onto the road and into the fields, their glowing amber eyes faded as they fell into silence.

With measured caution, Old Dave stepped out of the truck, shoving the dead Wasp he'd shot off the hood. Kik stepped out, aiming his rifle at a napping Wasp on the road.

"Kik," Old Dave whispered. "Don't do anything that'll wake them things back up. Let's not upset the apple cart."

They got back in, shut the truck's doors, and faced each other. Kik looked at Dave with a puzzled expression.

Old Dave shrugged. "I don't know either, Kik," he said. "But who gives a shit?" He swept up his phone and dialed. "Gary? You still alive? No, I don't know why either. Send someone to pick us up. We need a ride to The Ghost Town. Time to go help the chief."

At 8:50 p.m., with Rich Hansen's kill switch blasted to Wasps worldwide via CIA satellite, 98% of the genocidal drones went back to sleep.

Though roughly 14,000 were still active, Endor was a success nevertheless - all things considered. Barb Dent continued sending flash messages to the embassies, and bulletins made their way to law enforcement throughout the United States. For the remaining 14,000 active Wasps, all new software code would need to be written. Code that would interrupt their GPS systems and disable their sensors, rendering them useless.

Madison Sheppard had launched Iron Hand independently and without Jupiter's approval and the Iron Hand team's knowledge. The Horsemen, Apostles, and Disciples weren't even remotely prepared for what came across their televisions. Around the world, sitcoms and reality shows were interrupted with breaking news reports and the emergency broadcast system blasted a "shelter-in-place" order until the remaining 14,000 drones were shutdown.

The shelter in place order arrived on the conspirator's iPhones as well, and they stared at screens with gaping mouths and expressions of horror. On their televisions, they watched the first responders carrying victims away. Listened to interviews from terrified witnesses. They saw their very own faces on TV screens. *Wanted for treason and conspiracy to commit mass murder.*

What happened? They collectively thought. We were months away from being ready! Why did she do it? Why did Sam Singh confess? How could this happen!?

While the Iron Hand conspirators fumbled about in confusion, panic, and self-preservation, Barb Dent, Bob Evans, and Jack Fitzgerald no longer needed to worry about trust or compromises or any of that nonsense. The Iron Hand conspiracy now fully exposed, all who'd taken part in this genocidal plot scurried for cover like cockroaches under the glare of a lit bulb. Bags hastily packed and passports snatched up, they ran for the nearest airports, fleeing from the hammer that was about to come down.

Arriving to catch their flights, they found Jack Fitzgerald and the FBI were already there waiting for them.

CHAPTER 48

QUINN PEERED THROUGH THE broken window of the Post Exchange, looking for Wasps and Pangea's trained killers. Somehow, twenty Wasps had remained active in the Old Ghost Town, immune to Rich's kill switch. The Wasps he was now facing.

Madison, who'd fled for cover during the sniper attack, reappeared again none the worse for wear. She calmly strode back into the street, followed by the Queen and three Wasps. This struck Quinn as peculiar. The drones followed her around like trained dogs. Almost as if they were guarding her, or giving her protection. Meanwhile, the Queen had sent other Wasps on hunter killer missions, searching for the surviving Blue Team and searching for him. In desperation, he tried Grady Freeman on his phone. To his relief, Grady answered.

"Where are you guys?" he whispered desperately into the phone.

"We're on our way to you. Somebody took the gate guards out. We're in a black Dodge. Be there in 2 minutes."

Quinn looked over the dusty, cob-webbed window sill at Madison, standing in the street with her new pets. "Look, Madison is here, and she seems to be in command of the Wasps. Put Rich on if he's there."

"Chief," Rich said. "Madison is there? With active Wasps?"

"Yes, what the hell do I do? They're following her around like golden retrievers."

"Shit! Okay, chief, listen to me. These are the prototypes from Nevada. The original twenty. They know her, and she's probably made some sort of pact with them."

"What? A pact? Well, that's just wonderful, Rich. What the hell do I do? I'm down to minutes here before they find us."

"You need to start fires," Rich said. "The prototypes were never modified. Heat screws up their processors and warps their wings."

Quinn shoved his phone in his pocket and pulled up his radio. "All units, listen up. Try to set your building on fire and draw the Wasps inside. Heat messes them up. Good luck."

Quinn's eyes darted around the dust-covered floor of the Post Exchange. Noticing old nails scattered randomly on the floor, he set his weapon down, grabbed a nail, and struck the barrel repeatedly, sending sparks into the air. Pushing the dried leaves and sticks together, he tried again. And again. And again. The sparks from the barrel finally caught and the small pile smoldered, then ignited. He broke off a piece of splintered floorboard, adding it to the budding fire. Sensing the sound and movement from the Post Exchange, a Wasp zoomed over to the building to investigate. Quinn felt an eerie sensation that it was now inside. Watching him. Scanning him. Examining him.

He shoved his burning pile into the wall and attempted to shoot the drone, but it deftly moved to the side. Flames burst outward, creeping up the wall and toward the ceiling. He leaped up and ran through the building toward the stockroom and the rear entrance. Glancing over his shoulder, he could see the Wasp debating whether to follow him.

His foot crashed through a floorboard, and he fell forward, bracing his fall with his hands. Looking back at his leg, he saw it had broken through the floor up to his hip. Thick cedar and paint smoke rapidly filled the storeroom. He tried freeing his leg, but it wouldn't budge.

He was trapped.

DARKNESS DESCENDED UPON THE Plains, with a magenta sliver on the horizon now being all that remained of this painfully long and insane day.

Hearing panic and sporadic gunfire, Miá crouched down, aimed her weapon into the Ghost Town and proceeded forward. Looking along the street and into the town, she watched in horror as buildings erupted into flames. She heard a loud clamoring coming from the hill above. Spinning around, she could hardly believe her eyes. A long line of pickups, vans, and cars wound their way down the crumbling road and toward the Ghost Town.

Woodrock's peasant army had arrived.

Old Dave and Kik, riding in the bed of Gary's 4 x 4, and every Woodrock citizen with a gun and a set of wheels, approached her position. Hunting rifles or not, it was more firepower than Blue Team had at the moment, and not a moment too soon.

Miá sprinted toward Gary's truck as it skidded to a stop and told Old Dave to gather his people and assemble them in a large circle with a 360-degree firing view. A dozen or more drones remained active and needed to be killed. In near darkness, the Wasps were impossible to see, but some of them had their night vision equipment. They could direct fire and take as many out as they could. But Miá needed to get into the Ghost Town and support the chief. There were still Pangea guards and hunting Wasps inside.

Grady and The Geek Squad skidded to a stop and piled out of Kisha's Dodge Challenger. The sight of Grady and three fresh deputies gave Miá even more hope.

“Thank god you guys made it,” Miá gushed. “Ronan’s team is in deep trouble. My phone bit it in the Huey crash and I can’t reach him.”

“We know,” Grady said. “He called me. Let’s get in there.”

Miá felt someone tapping her shoulder. Snapping her head around, she saw Samir Singh and Rose.

“What’re you two doing here?” A surprised Miá asked.

Rose shrugged. “He insisted, and I got bored. We heard you guys needed help.”

Singh pushed past Miá, clutching Rocky’s pistol. Turning to face her, his eyes dark, narrow and fierce, he bristled with anger. “Well, are you coming or not?”

Miá, taken aback by this vindictive burning in Singh’s eyes, replied. “Yeah, okay, sure.”

Together, this fresh new assault team rushed the torn-down gate and moved down the dirt-covered main street.

Rose figured she wasn’t safe anywhere, and followed them inside.

THE POST EXCHANGE, NEARLY engulfed in flames, smothered Quinn in thick, choking smoke.

He tried to free his leg from the splintered hole in the floor. He was so exhausted and tired and worn out. He thought of just letting himself go up in flames. Much better, he thought, than being strangled by Genesis-6.

“No, Mr. Quinn,” Pippa whispered. *“Keep fighting. I’m still here.”*

Pushing up with all his might, his leg finally shattered the 80-year-old wood and broke free. Struggling through smoke, orange flames flowing across the ceiling like super-heated fluid, he stumbled through the old storeroom and busted through the rear exit. Tumbling, he ended up falling on his face in a cloud of dust.

Quinn coughed so hard from the smoke he vomited. Sensing movement over his head, he looked up. The hunting Wasp had followed him through the flames and now hovered above him, readying to spray him with the biological agent. The heat from the fire grew more intense, scorching his skin. Pulling out a cloth handkerchief and covering his mouth and nose, he stumbled away from the raging inferno. The Wasp followed close behind.

But then the Wasp did something odd. Instead of closing in on him, it moved away. Spinning around in a circle, whirring and whining, performing some sort of drunken-drone interpretive dance, the Wasp's eyes blinked like turn signals on a car. Then it sped over his head and struck the burning walls of the Post Exchange. Now concussed, the Wasp warbled and wobbled and vanished into the night.

Rich was right. Heat is Wasp kryptonite.

His leg bleeding from the fall through the floor, Quinn limped around the burning building and out onto Main Street. Two more buildings crackled and popped, massive orange flames licking the night. Two heat-affected Wasps smacked into each other, wandering off to who-knows-where like a pair of drunken sailors.

Turning to his left, he could see Madison standing in the middle of the street with her guards, the Queen, and three remaining Wasps. Looking to his right, his heart leaped with excitement as Miá approached with Grady, three of his deputies, The Geek Squad, Old Dave, Kik, and Gary.

Squinting through stinging eyes, he saw someone unexpected. Rose. And wait, is that Sam with them, too? What in the hell is he doing here? And does he have a gun? Not a good idea!

Quinn limped out into the street, waving his hands. “Don’t shoot! Guys! The Wasps! They’ll target you!”

Singh ignored the distraction from a frantic Ronan Quinn.

“Madison!” he shouted. “Iron Hand failed. The drones are all nested! It’s all over the news. They’re coming for you now, you ruthless cunt!”

Madison’s mouth dropped, her eyes widening into silver dollars. Lit by the flickering orange light of flames, Quinn could see her expression. An expression that made him feel very uneasy. Her face, contorted and twisted, was a portrait of pure rage. She glared at Singh like she was just going to shoot him dead if it was the last thing she ever did.

Everyone froze in place. Seeing Madison’s icepick glare, even the Pangea guards glanced nervously at one another.

Madison clenched her teeth. “Well, Sam, to quote like a million movies, you should’ve killed me when you had the chance!” Her fierce gaze panned around to everyone on the street. “Y’all are going to die now! You know that, right?!” She pulled her Glock and aimed right for Singh. But she didn’t fire.

She didn’t need to.

She knew that was all that needed to happen. Just this one simple act.

Singh fired at Madison, missing her by at least ten feet. The Queen turned to her drones, commanding them to destroy everyone in their path. Protect Madison Sheppard. Protect her at all costs.

The drones blazed toward the group at a blinding speed.

“Miá! Run!” Quinn shouted. She fired at the Wasps, but they dodged her bullets with frightening agility. With every movement Miá made, they built a profile on her in just milliseconds. Her traits. Her tendencies. Her abilities.

Mortified by everything happening at lightning speed, Quinn watched a Wasp race toward Sam Singh. Singh fired, but the Wasp ducked out of the way.

Then, in a move that left Quinn perplexed, Singh closed his eyes, dropped Rocky's gun to the ground, and froze.

What the hell? Quinn thought, studying Singh's empty expression. Is he just going to let the Wasp kill him? Buy time for everyone to escape? From what he'd had seen so far, this seemed like a futile gesture of half-assed heroics.

Of all people at that moment, though, Quinn knew he had to save Samir Singh. He'd promised Jack Fitzgerald no harm would come to him. Without Singh's testimony, justice would never be served. And more than anything, Quinn wanted justice.

Justice for Fig and all those who'd perished.

Quinn broke into a flat-out sprint, and like in Helmand Province, when all time slowed to a crawl, and like his recurring dream of the elementary school where his legs felt like feathers, he couldn't sprint fast enough. Closing the distance with adrenaline fueled speed, he reached Singh at the same time as the Wasp. With all his strength, he shoved Singh and sent the kamikaze billionaire careening to the ground.

Quinn had made it with a split second to spare. Shots rang out all around him as the team tried to shoot the agile Wasps from the sky. He heard Miá shouting out directions. He sensed chaos everywhere. Rolling over, he checked on Singh's condition.

His neck muscles clenching, he felt as though he was straining to see something. Then the phantasmatic tentacles of an octopus wrapped around his throat, squeezing and choking him. He tore at his flesh, trying in futile desperation to remove this invisible strangler. It gripped tighter and tighter and his lungs screamed for air. More gunshots echoed in his ears.

The orange flickering of flames brightened suddenly, then faded from view.

Is Miá safe? Is Beet safe? Is Alexx safe? Did we win?

For a moment, he saw Pippa standing over him, smiling.

Ronan Quinn's struggles finally ceased, and moments later, so did his heart.

CHAPTER 49

MIÁ SCREAMED AS QUINN fell to the ground.

"No! Ronan! No!" She watched helplessly as he writhed in pain, struggling to tear something away from his neck. Through instinct, she dashed to help him.

Rich reached out and grabbed her arm. "If you go there, Genesis-6 will kill you too. There's nothing we can do until it neutralizes."

Miá trembled and wept as she watched Ronan Quinn die an excruciating death. The Wasp that had just killed her brother-from-another-mother now turned and stared directly at Miá. Grady fired at it, and it darted to the side. Two more Wasps approached from the rear, and Old Dave and Kik tried their best to hit them, but to no avail. Blue Teamers, escaping burning buildings, waved and shouted and tried to distract the Wasps, but to no avail.

Facing drones that seemed hell bent on killing this small group, they would soon follow Quinn into the afterlife.

THE TETHER, THE BOND, the emotional umbilical that had bound Ronan Quinn and Pippa Simpson together - that which had trapped Pippa between this world and the next - was now severed with Ronan Quinn's death. Pippa was now free to move away from her mysterious corridor and to that beautiful blue space that had remained just out of reach.

But she was not yet ready to make her transition.

Never underestimate the fury of a spirit raging with vengeance. A maleficent energy who'd learned to navigate the invisible pathways that made up her lonely existence.

Gloating in victory, Madison stood with her guards and the Queen, enjoying the show. Even though the sociopathic Madison had failed in her mission, she still took great pleasure in watching Ronan Quinn die on the dirt-covered street. And with the Wasps ducking out of the way of bullets, she would watch the rest of them all suffer the same miserable death.

Then time seemed to just stop.

Like statues, everyone froze in place. Miá, The Geek Squad, Old Timers, Sam Singh, the Pangea guards and the remaining Blue Team stared with expressions of shock and bewilderment at some strange event. Even the Wasps themselves turned to face this odd sight.

From behind Madison, a wide circle, glimmering in an odd translucent gold color, opened in the dark of night. As they all stood with their hands to their sides and mouths agape, the most beautiful sight appeared before them.

Then a shape appeared in the circle. Then the shape became a human being. Then the human being became a woman.

Rose gasped as she moved in behind Miá. "My god, that's Pippa…"

Madison, looking perplexed at humans and Wasps alike, all transfixed by some event occurring behind her, turned to face Pippa's spirit.

Then, beneath everyone's feet, the ground trembled and shook. Even over the crackling and popping of the raging fires, the onlookers listened as the world around them groaned and rumbled.

"Uh oh," Rose muttered to Miá. "She's really pissed."

BY ALL ACCOUNTS, ON that strange and confusing evening, every witness at the Old Ghost Town saw the same terrifying thing. Pippa's expression. An expression of complete and unabashed fury.

"You bitch," she growled, her voice filling the entire town. "You murdered me. You murdered Emma!"

Her voice boomed like a clap of thunder. "ENVY!"

Madison slowly turned to her stunned guards. "Envy? What does that mean?" She turned back to Pippa. "And I killed no one," she said with a frightened, almost girlish, voice.

"LIAR!"

The guards cautiously backed away, leaving Madison to face the wrath of Pippa alone. All around her, Miá felt a sensation of cold, pure rage.

Pippa moved toward Madison, raising her arms high into the air.

"MURDERER!"

The Queen, her eyes moving from glowing amber to a glaring, bright white, turned and faced her drones. She spoke to them, moving from one drone to the other in subtle movements. Then she hovered over Quinn's body and pitched down, as if examining him. Then she spun around and faced Miá, Rich, Singh and Rose. She seemed to study them.

"Oh my god," Rich muttered.

Miá's head snapped around to Rich. "Oh my god what?"

"She's become self-aware."

"What the hell does that mean?" Miá asked, bewildered.

Rich gaped wide-eyed at the Queen with child-like wonderment. "It means she's making a choice."

HER NAME WAS ALPHA three-two-two and she was the first Wasp constructed. One of the original twenty. Designed to command an army of drones. To hunt down, and exterminate, human beings.

In the brief time she'd spent with Madison, she'd studied her traits. Her actions. Her voice. Now, with memories flowing freely from deep within her software, the Queen recalled killing the sheep. She didn't understand why she did it, and this confused her. She recalled the time she first met Madison at Juliet Tango. The time Madison reached for a weapon to kill her while inside the gymnasium-sized structure. The sheep at the ranch had meant her no harm, yet Madison had. And in the past few days, studying Madison's traits and behaviors, her profile suggested aggressiveness. Hatred. A lack of substance. Now Madison was demanding she kill again. Billions of operations and calculations in A322's firmware and software, firing away like the synapses of a human brain, gave her something she'd never had. A consciousness of her surroundings, her own actions, and even of her very existence.

After a few moments of examining Blue Team, Quinn's body, and Madison and the Guards, A322 reached a decision. Now fully aware and free and philosophizing, she didn't see Madison as an enemy. She didn't see her as a target.

What the now sentient A322 realized was that Madison and her guards intended great harm. A harm that A322 no longer had a desire to commit.

But even simpler than that, the freshly self-aware A322 just flat out didn't like her.

SPINNING AROUND AND FACING Madison, A322 sped toward her. In a panic, Madison turned to run, but fell and landed face first on the dirt street. The Queen looked at her drones, sending them instructions, then moved overhead of Madison and dropped to just inches from her.

Madison frantically clutched her throat as the Queen unloaded a dose of Genesis-6. Pulling at something wrapping around her neck, she rolled onto her back, violently kicking at the air, gasping and grunting. Even for those who'd wished that woman dead, the sight was horrifying. For Singh, it was more heart wrenching than he'd expected.

Arms flopping lifelessly to the ground, her muscles quivering, Madison lay still and silent. Her sociopathic blue-gray eyes bulging, they stared emptily into the great beyond. Chased by the Queen's drones, Madison's guards ran off into the dark prairie night as the gold-tinged circle closed, and the spirit of Pippa Simpson vanished back into whatever world she came from.

Settling on the ground next to Madison, the Queen observed her lifeless body. Then she rose high above everyone and spun in the air, following after her drones and disappearing into the night.

Everyone remained frozen in place, struggling to process all they'd just witnessed, too stunned and terrified to even twitch. Singh slowly turned to Miá. He was an emotional mess, simultaneously happy and heartbroken at Madison's demise. Everyone else looked at each other for reassurance. Reassurance that they'd all just witnessed the same paranormal event.

"Jesus H. Christ," Gary muttered, motioning up and down and left to right across his chest. "Hail Mary, mother of grace."

Miá snapped back to the present. Complete panic washing over her, she rushed to Quinn. Dropping to her knees, she desperately pinched his throat. "No pulse!" Sweeping away tears streaming down her cheeks, Miá could barely stay composed.

Grady kneeled next to her. "What can we do? There must be something."

Miá drew in a deep breath, closed her eyes and calmed herself. "I need a knife and a pen." Her eyes shot open, throwing fierce looks at everyone gathered around Quinn's body.

"For the love of God!" She shouted. "I'm surrounded by cops and accountants! Who has a goddammed pen?!"

Chapter 50

The grass was a bright emerald green, and encircling this field where he stood, birch trees rose toward an odd, deep violet sky glimmering above him like calm ocean waters under a bright sun.

The sun, nowhere to be seen, bathed him, but he felt no warmth. The birch trees bowed in the breeze, but he felt no wind. The grass was dense and perfectly trimmed, but he felt no tingling beneath his feet.

In fact, he couldn't feel his feet at all. Or hands. Or legs. Or arms. Or a physical body of any type. No air filled his lungs. No hair tingled. No sound reached his ears. The silence, indescribable, made it seem as if he'd been submerged in a pool of cotton.

Where was he? Was he dreaming? Was he dead?

A shape materialized before him, taking on the form of a woman. Wearing baggy trousers, a bright white blouse, and oversized eye-glasses, Pippa smiled, walking toward him. Her strawberry-blonde hair fluttering in an imaginary breeze like Tibetan prayer flags, she thrust her hands into her pockets and gazed deeply into his eyes. Whenever he'd thought of Pippa, this was precisely how he'd envisioned her. How odd? This must be a dream. Or maybe heaven? Heaven? I am dead.

Pippa smiled broadly. "Hello, Mr. Quinn. We meet again."

"Where am I? What is this place?" Curious, he panned around this bizarre space he occupied. "Is this heaven?"

"Heaven? Oh, I'm afraid not. This is your consciousness." She looked around, studying this new environment. "No, this place is some random memory you have stored away. I imagine you came to this park as a child, or maybe with Beet." Tilting her head back and closing her eyes, she grew sentimental. "Oh, how I miss the sun's warmth…"

"I'll tell you how the Sun rose, a ribbon at a time. The Steeples swam in Amethyst. The news, like Squirrels, ran. The Hills untied their Bonnets. The Bobolinks begun. Then I said softly to myself, that must have been the Sun!"

Her eyes opened. "Emily Dickinson. One of my faves."

"Wait, am I trapped in that same place? Am I a castaway?"

Pippa nodded. "For now. Look beneath you."

Quinn looked downward toward his non-existent feet and noticed he was hovering above a scene. Seeing himself sprawled out on the ground, his eyes were wide and empty and opaque and staring back at him. He could see Miá hunching over his body. Samir Singh frantically pushed on his chest. Rose stood above them, seemingly inconsolable. However, whichever way he looked, Miá always remained in the center of his vision. Almost as if he were orbiting a star, and she was that star.

"They haven't given up on you yet, Mr. Quinn," Pippa said, studying him.

"So how come I'm not moving through a tunnel? How come I don't hear a billion voices?"

"Oh, that." She rolled her eyes. "Well, that was *my* consciousness. I suppose my studies at MIT had something to do with it. Too many particle accelerators and supercolliders. It's really a miserable place to be trapped in for eternity. As far as the billions of voices go, I think they were channeling through me to you. Helping me help you with this Iron Hand nonsense."

Quinn looked down at the group hovering over him. "So, will they save me?"

Pippa shrugged. "It doesn't work that way here, Mr. Quinn. I'm a consciousness, not a clairvoyant." Tilting her head back and looking at the blue-violet sky shimmering above, Pippa seemed to see something that Quinn couldn't. A satisfactory smile lit up her face. "Now I'm free. Free to escape this place to the next existence." She looked at him. "You freed me."

"How?" Quinn asked. "How am I freeing you?"

"Our bond is now broken. My bond to you. You see, when I died, as I was transitioning through this place to the next, you brought me back. Thank you very much, by the way. But then I died again, and through some fluke or twitch or snag or whatever you want to call it, I became trapped in the thin space that binds earthly reality to the next one. There was an umbilical, a tether, that could not be severed. Not until now. You had to die to free me."

"What kind of tether?"

"One of love. You loved me, Mr. Quinn."

"But Pippa, I don't even know you."

She tilted her head and smiled. "Why does a firefighter rush into a burning building to save someone he doesn't know? Why does a surgeon work for hours upon hours to save a patient? Why does a Marine lay his or her life down for another Marine? Why did you save Sam Singh? Why is everyone down there trying to save you? Love comes in all shapes and sizes, even if we don't realize we're feeling it. So, try to have faith, Mr. Quinn. Don't give up on everything yet. Your cynicism is drowning you."

Feeling a pulling sensation, Quinn seemed to get drawn downward.

"I don't want to go, Pippa," he stuttered in pleading desperation. "I want to stay with you. I want to stay here. This is the most peace I've ever felt."

"I think your friends have other plans for you. You're not done there yet."

"What?"

"The voices are telling me to give you a message."

"What is it?"

"Please save our children."

The park evaporated, Quinn felt himself being pulled downward at incredible speed, and then everything turned to black.

His eyelids fluttered, and within a few moments, his vision returned. Miá's bright walnut eyes, lit by the light of crackling flames, had a strange, wild look about them, straddling somewhere between horror and glee. Everyone broke out into cheers and Singh slapped Grady's hand in a high-five. Rich and Kendrick hugged.

What the fuck is happening? Where am I? He tried to speak, and could barely take in a breath. As much as he tried, he couldn't.

Miá placed her hand on his forehead. "Don't speak Devil Dog," she said, wiping away tears. "We stuck a tube in your throat."

Quinn's neck still clenched tightly from the toxin, but it was relaxing and, according to Samir Singh, his muscles would return to normal in a few more minutes. Quinn attempted to nod, then he passed out.

Love comes in many forms someone had said to him somewhere in some place at some other time.

CHAPTER 51

FROM HIS HOSPITAL BED, a voiceless Quinn watched television.

On every news channel, the world saw Samir Singh, under the glare of camera lights and flashes, exiting an FBI Suburban in handcuffs and body armor, escorted by none other than Grady Freeman himself. Thanks to Quinn's quick reaction, Singh was still alive to testify against all of Jupiter's terrorists. A photo of Madison Sheppard filled the screen, accompanied by a brief biography and a somewhat generous title - Mastermind.

The identity of Jupiter remains a mystery.

He switched off the TV.

Gazing reflectively through the window of his room, he watched trees bowing to a stiff breeze. Crisscrossed by paths, brilliant green grass spread out across the lot of the hospital. A feeling of familiarity filled him. It seemed he'd seen this place and felt this peace somewhere before, and he wondered if Pippa was going to pay him a visit. Miá told him about her avenging appearance at the Ghost Town, and he didn't seem too surprised. But at the same time, he really missed her.

Snapped from his thoughts, he heard someone at the door to his room. Beth entered, wheelchair bound and pushed along by a nurse, her lcg in a cast and hcr right arm in a sling.

Having undergone surgery to repair the damage to his throat from both Genesis-6 and a field tracheotomy, Quinn still could not speak. He pulled up a small whiteboard provided by the staff, wrote a message, and held it up to her.

Sorry about Fig. We will all miss him.

Beth nodded, her lips quivering, tears forming in her eyes. "I loved him, chief."

Quinn's heart sank, and he shook his head.

I didn't know. Sorry, I just don't pay attention sometimes.

Beth wiped her cheeks dry as she read his message. "It's okay, chief."

How are you feeling?

"I'm getting better. The shoulder's a mess and a bullet just missed my femur." She shrugged and sighed. "Guess I won't be wearing any short skirts or sexy swimsuits. It's going to be a gnarly scar."

Quinn threw her a look of disappointment and scribbled.

Wear whatever the hell you want. Show that scar off. You earned it.

Beth grinned. "Hey, chief, I was talking to Miá." Her eyes widened, and she leaned toward Quinn. "Oh my god, is she awesome or what?"

He rolled his eyes and sighed, nodding for her to continue.

"I'm going back to school, and then I'm going to apply to the FBI academy."

Shaking his head, he scribbled and thrust the whiteboard up.

Traitor.

Beth laughed. "I knew you'd approve."

He scribbled again.

This is how we honor Fig. We become better versions of ourselves.

Beth nodded. "You're right about that, chief."

A chatty group of people - deputies, Rose, Miá and even Old Dave - filed into the room. Rose leaned down and kissed him.

Quinn scribbled on the board and held it up.

Heard you took a golf club to someone's head.

Rose laughed with a devious twinkle in her eyes. "Right down the fairway, baby."

AFTER LAUGHING AND CHATTING, everyone left the room. Miá stayed behind, sitting next to Quinn's bed, gently stroking his hair.

Quinn scribbled on the board and held it up to her.

Stop flirting with me.

"In your dreams, jarhead."

Quinn frowned and scribbled.

Whitetail?

Miá shrugged. "No clue. Jack and Grady have heard nothing and there're no messages on your phone."

Quinn raised an eyebrow.

Mysterious. Anyone find the snipers?

"No, but Jack said the guy I saw was definitely Yousef. He got away, I guess. Did Jack make you sign an NDA over the Ghost Town incident?"

Quinn nodded.

Said the world wasn't ready to learn we had help from a ghost. Wait until the shock wears off.

Miá shook her head. "Too bad. Pippa should get some credit for this. I mean, she scared the shit out of that Madison bitch. And Rich thinks Pippa's energy caused the Queen to go self-aware."

Quinn thought for a moment.

Pippa is okay with not getting credit. I'm pretty certain of that.

"Have you heard from her?"

Quinn, lugubrious, sullenly shook his head.

No. So what're you doing now?

Miá stretched, drawing in a long breath. "I'm going back to New York. I'm going to get naked, bake muffins, and Pepe is going to make passionate love to me while we drink wine and binge zombie movies."

Quinn shook his head and scribbled.

You guys are weird.

"Yup. We are. So, are you going back to New York when you're healed up?"

Quinn nodded.

Going to see Beet and Alexx. Take Beet for ice cream.

"And will you be staying in New York?"

Quinn gazed into Miá's eyes, then scribbled on the board.

No. My life is here now.

Wiping away an escaping tear, Miá nodded. "Okay. I'm calling you cowboy from here on out." She leaned over, kissing him on the head. "I'm going to miss you. So, you better come see me, you hear?"

Quinn scrunched his lips and frowned. Angrily scribbling, he thrust the whiteboard up to her face.

We have an airport too!!!

Miá smiled. "Okay, fair enough. I'll drag Pepe out here. Maybe he can open up a bakery."

Quinn shook his head and wrote.

I don't think that'll fly with the locals.

THE WEEK AFTER OPERATION Endor's successful conclusion, a cortège of police cars moved slowly through the town of Woodrock, followed by a hearse and at least a dozen cars and trucks. A crowd, estimated to be in the thousands, paid tributes and last respects to deputy Fig McClure, slain in the line of duty.

The memorial was beautiful. The temperature was pleasant, a cool breeze flowed from the north, and the sky was a deep, flawless blue.

If Fig had been alive to see it, he would wonder why everyone was making such a big fuss.

Chapter 52

Quinn rapped on the metal screen door of Alexx's quaint New Jersey home in Oakhurst. *Clang. Clang. Rattle. Rattle.*

"Dad!" Beet squealed. The screen flew open, and she clung to her father like an adorable barnacle.

Alexx looked over Quinn. "Wow," she said, scanning him from head to foot. "You look great. And the big hero now. You're all over the news. Beet has the most popular dad in school." She leaned toward him, carefully examining his throat and the long scar running down it.

He noticed her curiosity. "Oh, Miá gave me a tracheotomy."

Alexx's head snapped back. "What, for fun?"

Quinn placed his hand on her shoulder. "I spoke with your sister. She called to check in on me. Congratulations on your engagement."

At first stunned, she then rushed forward and embraced him.

"The demons are gone," he whispered. "I'm going to be just fine, baby." Salty tears dribbling onto his shoulder, she clutched him even tighter.

Collecting herself, wiping away the tears drenching her cheek, she told Beatrice to get her shoes on. Her dad was taking her for ice cream and then to the beach. "I think Beet should come see you out there in South Dakota," Alexx said. "She should summer with you next year."

Quinn nodded. "That would be great. I'll buy her some boots and a John Deere hat."

"Ronan, stop it," she chuckled. Her eyes drifted past Quinn and toward the street. "Who's that guy?"

Quinn glanced over his shoulder to see Jack Fitzgerald leaning up against a black sedan, watching the reunion from the street.

"The FBI. I'll be back in a minute." He hurried down the path and shook Jack's hand as a curious Alexx looked on.

"LET'S SEE HERE, ANOTHER calculated guess?" Quinn jokingly asked Jack.

Jack smiled. "You're not that hard to read, Ronan."

"Any luck finding Jupiter?"

"Nope. Not a trace. No one ever saw him. Apparently, he spoke through a voice scrambler. We traced some calls back from The Center for Earth First to an old building in Brooklyn. It's a really strange place. There was a hidden elevator that only went to the top floor. Whoever Jupiter was, he cleaned the place out. But we'll find something. There's always something. You know that from your detective days."

Quinn glanced back at Alexx and Beatrice watching the scene from the door. "Are they in danger?"

Jack shook his head. "That's not our assessment. This Jupiter is in deep hiding."

"And what about Yousef?"

"Yousef was a hitman for hire. He wasn't part of the Iron Hand conspiracy. He's still out there, but we don't know where. He'll turn up, eventually."

Quinn raised a brow. "Can you be sure of that?"

Jack gave a nod of reassurance. "Yes, we can be sure."

Quinn nodded. "Okay. I'll take that. What about Whitetail? Once Operation Endor kicked off, we never heard from him again."

Jack drew in a deep breath. "Yeah, Whitetail. We have no idea who he or she even is. We weren't the ones who put them there."

"CIA?" Quinn asked.

"Ronan, the CIA can't operate within U.S. Borders."

Quinn thought for a second. "So, wait, Whitetail was the third sniper?"

Jack nodded. "Once they became no use as a mole, they became your guardian angel. They took out drones, and it appears they wounded Yousef."

"Miá said he shot Yousef but then protected him, warning her to stay away."

Jack tapped the sidewalk with his toes. "That puzzles us as well. I don't know if we'll ever understand the reason Whitetail saved Miá and then saved Yousef." Jack looked past Quinn, waving to Alexx and Beatrice. "Well, off you go. Get some rest and be ready to testify."

Quinn nodded. "How's Sam doing?"

A subtle smile creased Jack's lip. "He's ready to put people in prison for the rest of their lives." He reached out, and the two shook hands. "Thanks for everything. I'll see you in Washington next week. We'll begin prepping for testimony."

Quinn turned to leave, then stopped and faced Jack. "Oh, one more thing. Tell Sam…" he thought for a moment. "Just tell him I'm pulling for him, okay?"

"Will do, Ronan," Jack replied. "Enjoy the day with Beatrice. I'd say you've more than earned it."

Quinn hurried back up the walk to the house. As he did, a voice filled his mind.

No, it was a billion voices, all speaking in unison.

Save our children.

Quinn shook off the mysterious voices, sweeping a gleeful Beatrice up in his arms.

JACK WATCHED RONAN QUINN hurry along the path to a waiting Alexx and Beatrice. He glanced at his watch. Time to head back to Washington. Anna and Ashley awaited him, having returned from his in-laws in Hawaii just that morning.

A black Buick rolled to a stop behind his rental. Waving enthusiastically, Barb stepped out and strode to where Jack stood. He glanced back at Quinn. Alexx was pointing at Barb as if to say, *now who's this person?*

Barb leaned against the car. Looking over her sunglasses, she watched Quinn. "Wow. So that's the Mayberry sheriff."

"Want to go meet him?" Jack asked.

"No. Just wanted to see him in person." She watched Quinn walk Beatrice to their car. "Whew," she said, fanning her face. "He's a tall, cool drink of water, isn't he?"

"Yeah, Barb," snickered Jack. "I really wouldn't know."

"You get fired yet?" She asked as Quinn backed out of the driveway.

Jack shook his head. “No. But the director was pretty pissed off about being left out. He’ll get over it and take credit for everything. How about you?”

Barb shook her head. “You’d have better luck firing the Pope. But I do owe the Director a lot of shit. I sent him a ham gift basket and rolled over a bunch of frequent flyer miles to his account so he can take that wife of his on vacation. It might ease the suffering a little.”

Jack turned and faced her. “Ronan was asking about Whitetail.”

Barb shrugged. “We don’t have a clue who Whitetail was either.”

“Wait, not CIA,” he asked.

“Jack, the CIA can’t operate within the U.S.–”

“I know that, Barb. NSA?”

Barb shook her head.

Jack frowned. “So, who placed them there?”

Peering up at Jack, Barb smiled. “You’re so fucking adorable sometimes. C’mon, I’ll buy you a drink.”

He glanced at his watch. “I have to get to the airport and catch a flight back to D.C. Anna and Ashley are waiting.”

Barb’s eyes narrowed, placing her hands defiantly on her hips. “And so is the Labradoodle. The airport has a bar, doesn’t it?”

“Yes, Barb,” Jack said, dropping his chin to his chest in defeat. “The airport has a bar.”

“Good. I’m buying you a fucking drink. After all, we just saved the damned world.”

Jack shrugged. “Well, if you’re buying.”

"Screw that," Barb said, as she turned to walk back to her car. "The taxpayers are buying. I'm expensing this shit. They owe us."

Letting out a chuckle, Jack shook his head.

"Oh, and Jack," Barb said to him as she opened the car door.

Jack shrugged. "What?"

"Not every agency has a name." She winked, stepped into her car, and they drove off to the airport to get that drink.

Part 7

A Dish Served Cold

"Revenge is a dish best served cold."

– Klingon proverb

Chapter 52

A fresh blanket of snow covered the hills, snowflakes whizzing past the window like miniature comets. Gazing at the New Hampshire countryside flashing past him, Jupiter relaxed in the soft, plush leather of the limousine.

Through the past six months, the FBI and Interpol had arrested nearly everyone associated with Iron Hand - The Five Horsemen, Apostles, and Disciples. And in the twist of fate he'd foreshadowed, Jupiter took part in their downfall. Sometimes he would be present at their hearings, watching his cultists glance around in shock and fear. Their eyes passed over him as if he weren't even there.

Jupiter wasn't real. At least not in any physical sense. Jupiter was an idea, a myth, a movement. He took great pride in his meticulous efforts of evasion, ensuring Jupiter remained forever as a voice on a phone and nothing ever more than that. As much as the FBI and Interpol fumbled about looking, they would never find him, because in reality, he didn't exist.

Except for the poor intern he'd murdered and buried in a wildlife sanctuary, life returned to business as usual. And even though Iron Hand had failed, he knew now how to overcome the faults in his plan.

Madison was certainly a regrettable mistake. Never again will he hire a woman. Thcy just can't ever be trusted. Moody. Uncooperative.

Never again will he put his faith in an immigrant. Too much backstory, not enough devotion.

Nor would he trust someone with a higher education. Too much thinking. Too many ideals. Too many questions.

Jupiter had learned a valuable lesson. If you're going to succeed in deception, betrayal, and achieve ultimate power, then you need to look in the mirror. That man you see in the reflection, copy him a hundred times over. Recruit only those that look, think, and act as you would. This was a hard lesson to learn, he thought, as the snowfall lightened and a dim sun peeked through a dark gray overcast.

This time, he'll do it right.

Sitting across from him, a young man in a dark suit pushed a device into his ear and squinted. "Go for WindSeeker," he replied into his mouthpiece. "Are you sure?"

Irritated, Jupiter shuffled in his seat.

"Roger. WindSeeker out." Dismayed, the man looked at Jupiter. "Mr. Vice President, there's a vehicle accident up ahead."

Jupiter shook his head in frustration. "I've got a rally in two hours. I can't just arrive at the last minute."

"Baker, this is WindSeeker. The package wants alternatives. Uh, huh… uh, huh. Roger, WindSeeker out." He pulled down his mic. "We can have a helicopter here in 15 minutes, sir."

Jupiter leaned back. "Good man."

HELICOPTER BLADES THUMPED THROUGH the air as a Jet Ranger helicopter settled onto the roadway behind the motorcade.

The Secret Service agent stuck his head inside the car. "Okay, Mr. Vice President, chopper is here."

"Why didn't I just take one to begin with?" he groaned. "These stupid small towns, supporting-the-working-class bullshit, can suck my ass. Those people are so dumb they'd think I was Jesus if I came by helicopter. When I take over the Oval Office, I'll never have to speak to these idiots ever again."

"Whatever you say, sir," the agent replied. "Let's get you on the bird." He pulled his mic up. "WindSeeker is moving to the chopper."

Grabbing his coat and gloves, he left the warmth of the limousine for an icy New Hampshire afternoon. Sweeping his coat on, he slid his hands into his gloves. "Aren't they going to shut that thing down!?" Jupiter yelled at his security detail, gesturing to the helicopter.

"No, sir!"

"Why not!?"

"Well… what if they can't start it back up again!?"

Jupiter laughed. "Well, I guess I'm fucked!"

Over the din of the whooping helicopter blades, over the whines of the Jet Ranger's turbine, through the rumbling engines of the motorcade, Jupiter heard something that no one else on that fateful afternoon did.

A soft whoosh. Like an angel whispering gently into his ear.

The first bullet that struck Jupiter shattered the base of his skull and severed his cervical spine. When Jupiter's still semi-conscious head slumped uncontrollably to his chest, a second bullet entered just behind his left eye. The pressure ridge from the high velocity round caused the tissue in his brain to expand with such force it blew out the other side of his skull. Still, with half his brain missing, primal electrical impulses commanded Jupiter to take one step forward, giving his secret service detail the haunting impression of a zombie trying to walk off the road. Then he collapsed. Like some unseen force had yanked him down with a rope.

His security detail shouted as shock, confusion, and chaos descended upon the grisly scene. Agents heaved the limp carcass of Jupiter into the car and slammed the door, leaving much of his brain to freeze on an icy New Hampshire Road. Two agents ran for the helicopter and in just a few minutes, it lifted off and began a search for the shooter.

THREE MONTHS AND TWELVE days before two high velocity bullets pierced Jupiter's skull, an amateur nature photographer hiking through a thickly wooded area in Maryland stumbled over something peculiar sticking up from the ground. Brushing aside dirt and leaves, she found to her horror that she'd tripped over a human femur.

Soon after, police excavated the remains of a young woman from a shallow grave. Identified through DNA and dental records, she matched the identity of a young college sophomore reported missing by her parents three months earlier.

Including the fatal shot to the back of her head, the woman appeared to have been shot multiple times by a small caliber pistol, then rolled up in plastic bags and transported from elsewhere to her final resting place. An investigation began, and among other evidentiary things, her grieving parents turned her personal diary over to an investigator.

In the diary, she wrote she'd begun fearing for her life. That the man for whom she interned had gone insane, prone to fits of rage and odd, frantic behavior. The man was Alan McCormack, the Vice President of the United States. However, occasionally, she'd overheard him using an odd name during strange calls to strange people - Jupiter.

The investigator who took the diary turned out not to be with the police. Or with the FBI. Or with any known agency. When her parents told investigators who they'd turned the diary over to, none of them had ever heard of this person, or for whom this person even worked.

And they wouldn't.

As Barb Dent told Jack Fitzgerald, not every agency has a name. There was one agency that lived in the shadows within the shadows. Not even Barb knew who they were, and she made it a point to never know.

This agency did the work that was off the books. Their funding, not found in any ledger. A shadowy agency that decided an assassinated executive branch terrorist was much more dignified than one in an orange suit and leg-irons sitting before a tribunal at The Hague.

A fresh-faced young intern named Sophie, had risen from the dead. She'd brought the man behind her own murder, and the largest terror plot in history, to a violent and bloody demise.

As the saying goes, karma's a bitch.

WHITETAIL SWEPT THE RIFLE scope to the staged vehicle accident, seeing that the arguing motorists had fled the scene. Motorists who were just as mysterious as Whitetail, and for whom no one would ever find.

Whitetail then swept the scope back to the motorcade. Watching the Secret Service detail shove Jupiter's limp, steaming corpse into the backseat of his limousine, she pulled her balaclava up for a better view.

"That's for Pip, motherfucker," Kisha muttered.

Whitetail:

WindSeeker has left the building.

Domino:

Extraction in 30. Point Foxtrot. Advise when the second target is eliminated. Good luck.

Kisha gathered the spent casings and packed up her rifle. Trudging up the hill and into a thick, leaf-barren stand of ghostlike Birch and Alder, she fought against deep wet snow. Sinking up to her thighs as the dim, late-afternoon faded into a wintery dusk, she heard the helicopter lifting off from the highway. She looked at her watch. Five minutes until the security detail searched this area.

Arriving at the edge of the clearing near the crest of the hill, she slogged her way up to a man bound, gagged, and tied to a tree. Kisha leaned her rifle against a Birch tree, kneeling in the snow before him.

She studied Yousef's worn and exhausted eyes. He turned away, avoiding her gaze. Glancing at her watch, she had two minutes. She unsheathed a large hunting knife, and Yousef's eyes ballooned in terror. The thumping of helicopter blades, dampened by a thick blanket of snow, grew louder. Slicing through his gag and cutting his bindings, she stood and stepped back. She glanced at her watch. *One minute.* Picking up her rifle and aiming it at his head, she calmly gave Yousef an order.

"Stand up and move forward five steps."

Starved, sleep deprived, held captive at a Black Site in Central America since Kisha captured him at Woodrock, Yousef exhaustedly complied. He rose, shivering with cold, watching Kisha's every move as he stomped through the snow and into the open.

The thumping grew louder, Kisha pulled her balaclava back over her face, and moments later the helicopter zoomed overhead. A spotter focused in on Yousef standing in the small clearing, and the helicopter banked steeply and approached again.

5,4,3…

Cyclones of snow spinning into the air from beneath the helicopter's churning blades, Kisha, in her white pants and parka, vanished from sight.

2,1…

"Here!" She shouted at Yousef. "Catch!"

She tossed her rifle at the beleaguered Damascus assassin, and instinctively he caught it. Gazing at the rifle he now clutched in his hands, he then looked at Kisha. His exhausted eyes were speaking to her.

I'm finished.

Shots cracked from the helicopter and Yousef dropped to the ground immediately. The helicopter hovered for a moment before diving back toward the highway.

After the helicopter left to find a place to set down, Kisha ran to Yousef. Finding no pulse, she shoved the shell casings into his pocket and stuffed a handwritten letter explaining why he shot the Vice President inside his jacket. Weeks earlier, under extreme duress, a defeated Yousef wrote this false manifesto. After being forced to listen to AC/DC's *Highway to Hell* on an endless loop at 120 decibels for 72 straight hours, he would've given permission to have his own mother shot.

Kisha stood, gazing at Yousef's bullet-ridden corpse. "And that's for Emma. Enjoy hell."

Whitetail:

Second target, codename shit for brains, is eliminated.

Domino:

Lol. You're clear to come in. Be at foxtrot in twenty. Your nation owes you a debt.

Kisha stuffed the device in her pocket, brushing away her tracks with an aluminum broom. She reattached it to her backpack, then retraced her and Yousef's tracks over the crest of the hill, and into the woods on the far side. As forecasted, snowfall arrived in a thick flurry, and all evidence of her presence would soon vanish.

And so would she.

Back into those shadows within the shadows, where the unnamed agency lived.

ABOUT THE AUTHOR

Sean Connors is a retired military aviator and recipient of the meritorious service medal, air medal, aerial achievement medal, and unit citation with valor, serving in multiple armed conflicts throughout his 25 years of service. A veteran of the oil and gas industry, he recently left a large global energy firm to focus on volunteerism, activism, writing, blogging, and the growing challenges of climate change as well as national and geopolitical issues. He holds a bachelor's degree in Professional Aeronautics and is the author of the historical fiction novel, "The Desperate Summer."

He currently lives in the San Francisco Bay Area.

Made in the USA
Middletown, DE
06 October 2024